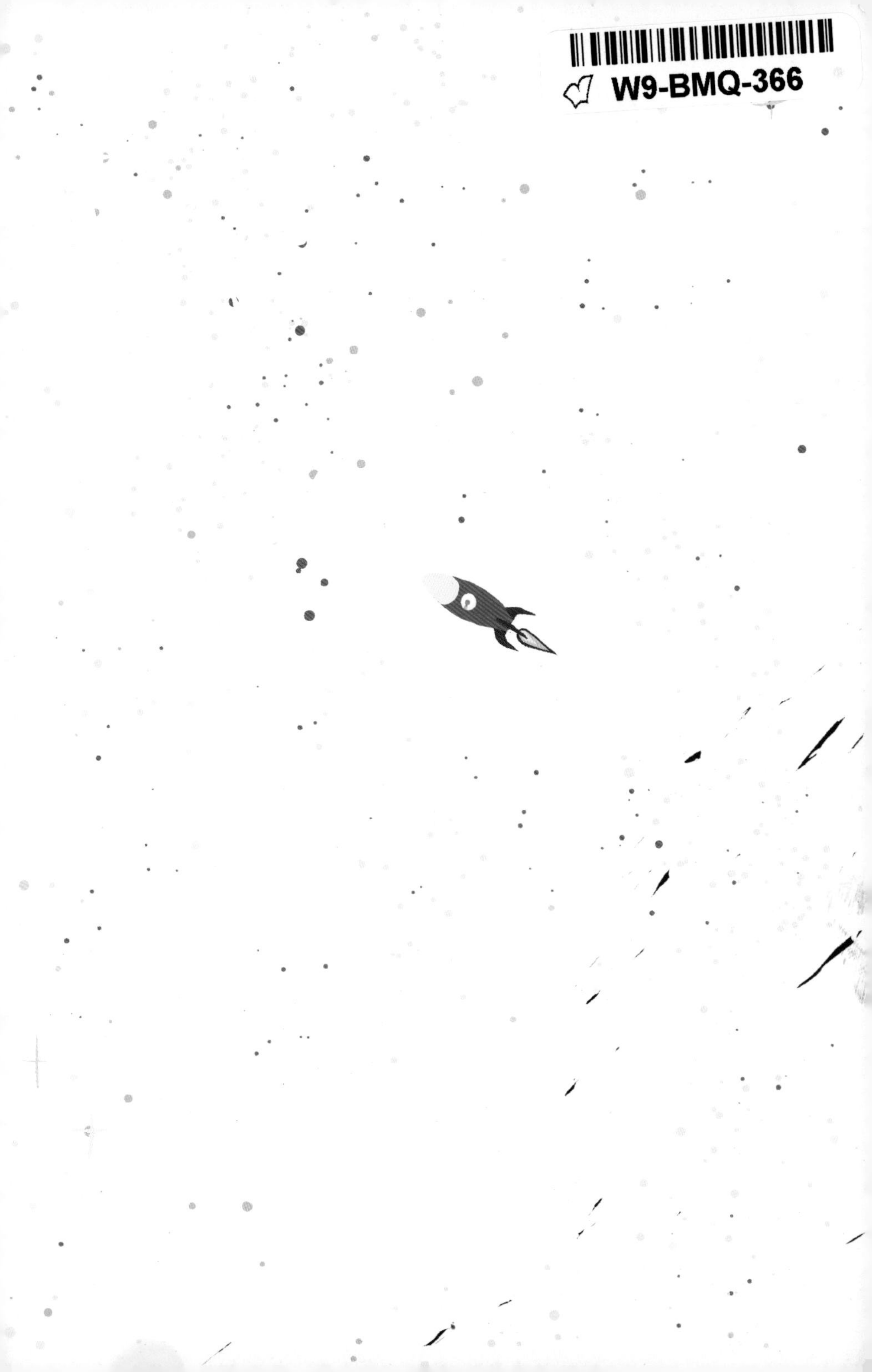

Stephen McCranie's

S P A C E

B O Y

VOLUME 2

Written and illustrated by
STEPHEN McCRANIE

DARK HORSE BOOKS

President and Publisher **Mike Richardson**
Editor **Shantel LaRocque**
Assistant Editor **Brett Israel**
Designer **Anita Magaña**
Digital Art Technician **Allyson Haller**

STEPHEN McCRANIE'S SPACE BOY VOLUME 2
Space Boy™ © 2018 Stephen McCranie. All rights reserved. Dark Horse Books® and the
Dark Horse logo are registered trademarks of Dark Horse Comics, Inc. All rights reserved.
No portion of this publication may be reproduced or transmitted, in any form or by any
means, without the express written permission of Dark Horse Comics, Inc. Names,
characters, places, and incidents featured in this publication either are the product of the
author's imagination or are used fictitiously. Any resemblance to actual persons (living or
dead), events, institutions, or locales, without satiric intent, is coincidental.

This book collects Space Boy episodes 17–32 previously published
online at WebToons.com.

Library of Congress Cataloging-in-Publication Data
Names: McCranie, Stephen, 1987- author, illustrator.
Title: Space Boy / written and illustrated by Stephen McCranie.
Other titles: At head of title: Stephen McCranie's
Description: First edition. | Milwaukie, OR : Dark Horse Books, 2018- | "This
  book collects Space Boy episodes 1-16 previously published online at
  WebToons.com." | Summary: Amy lives on a colony in deep space, but when
  her father loses his job the family moves back to Earth, where she has to
  adapt to heavier gravity, a new school, and a strange boy with no flavor.
Identifiers: LCCN 2017053602| ISBN 9781506706481 (v. 1) | ISBN 9781506706801
  (v. 2)
Subjects: LCSH: Graphic novels. | CYAC: Graphic novels. | Science fiction. |
  Moving, Household--Fiction. | Self-perception--Fiction. |
  Friendship--Fiction.
Classification: LCC PZ7.7.M42 Sp 2018 | DDC 741.5/973--dc23
LC record available at https://lccn.loc.gov/2017053602

Published by Dark Horse Books
A division of Dark Horse Comics, Inc.
10956 SE Main Street | Milwaukie, OR 97222
StephenMcCranie.com | DarkHorse.com

To find a comics shop in your area, visit comicshoplocator.com

First edition: October 2018
ISBN 978-1-50670-680-1
10 9 8 7 6 5 4 3 2 1
Printed in China

Neil Hankerson Executive Vice President • **Tom Weddle** Chief Financial Officer • **Randy
Stradley** Vice President of Publishing • **Nick McWhorter** Chief Business Development
Officer • **Matt Parkinson** Vice President of Marketing • **Dale LaFountain** Vice President
of Information Technology • **Cara Niece** Vice President of Production and Scheduling •
Mark Bernardi Vice President of Book Trade and Digital Sales • **Ken Lizzi** General
Counsel • **Dave Marshall** Editor in Chief • **Davey Estrada** Editorial Director • **Chris
Warner** Senior Books Editor • **Cary Grazzini** Director of Specialty Projects • **Lia Ribacchi**
Art Director • **Vanessa Todd-Holmes** Director of Print Purchasing • **Matt Dryer** Director
of Digital Art and Prepress • **Michael Gombos** Director of International Publishing and
Licensing • **Kari Yadro** Director of Custom Programs

[redacted]

[redacted]

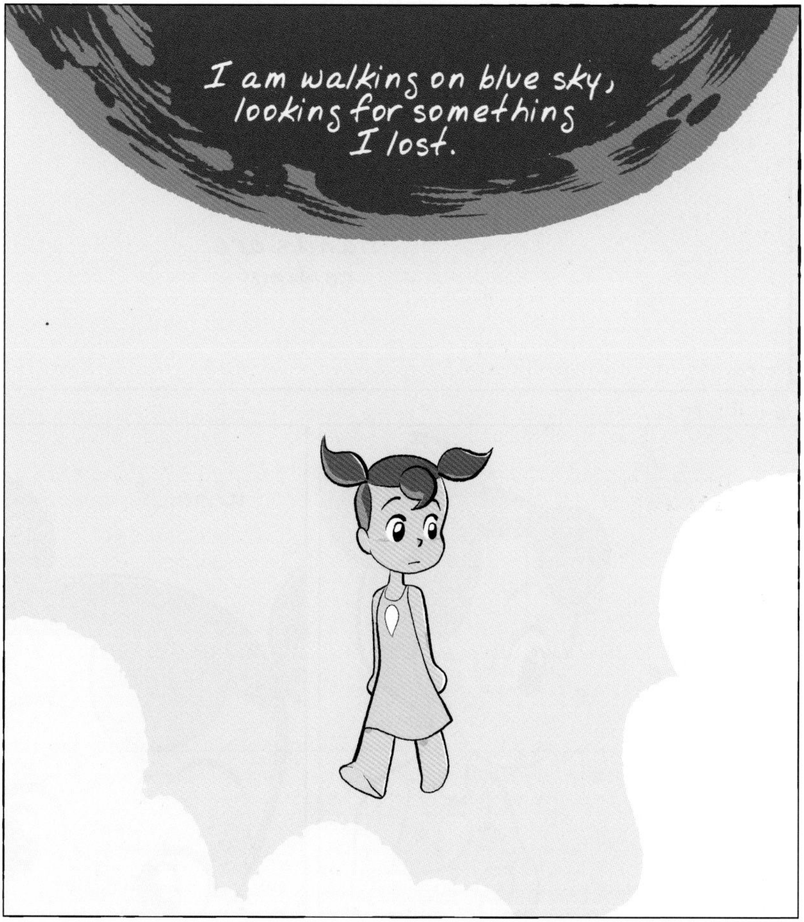
I am walking on blue sky, looking for something I lost.

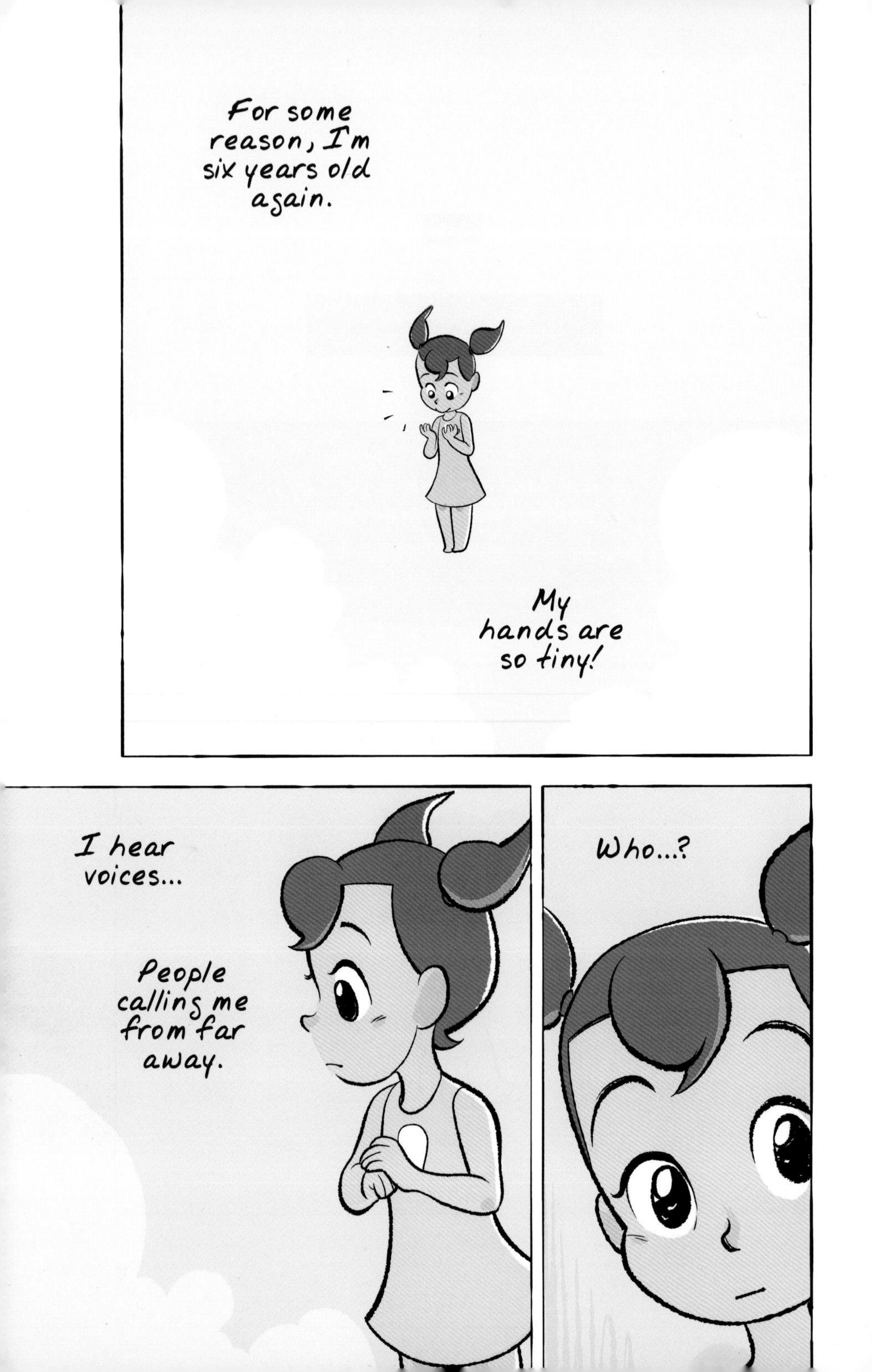
For some reason, I'm six years old again.
My hands are so tiny!
I hear voices...
People calling me from far away.
Who...?

There in
the distance,
Pammy and Eli
wave goodbye.

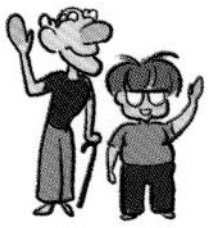

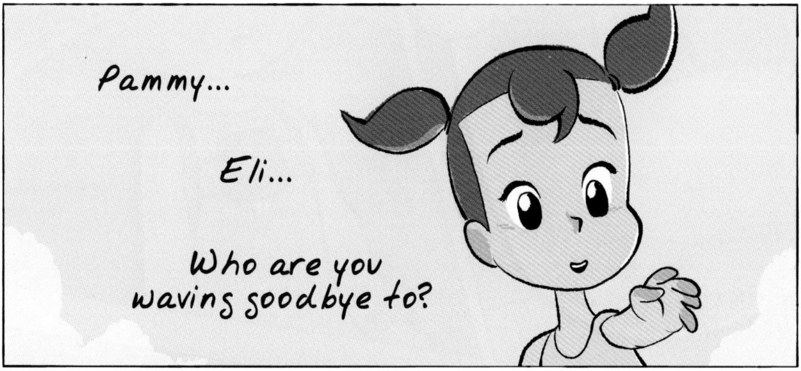
Pammy...
Eli...
Who are you
waving goodbye to?

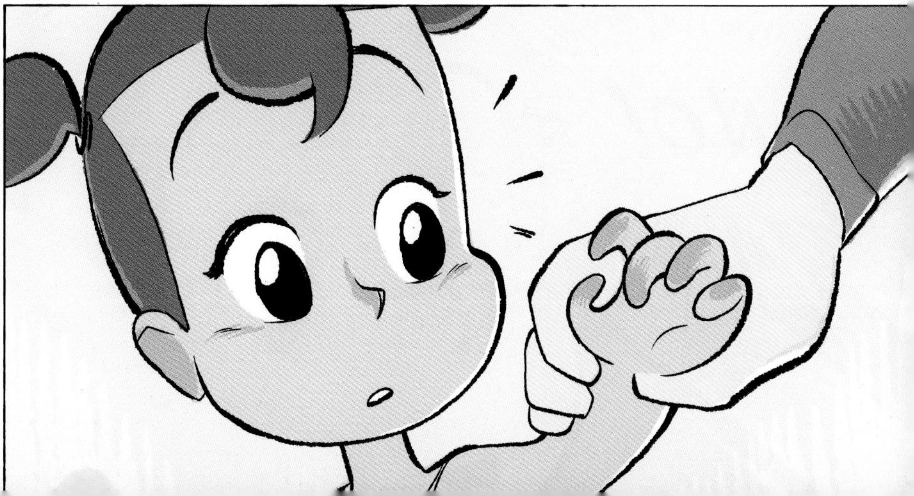

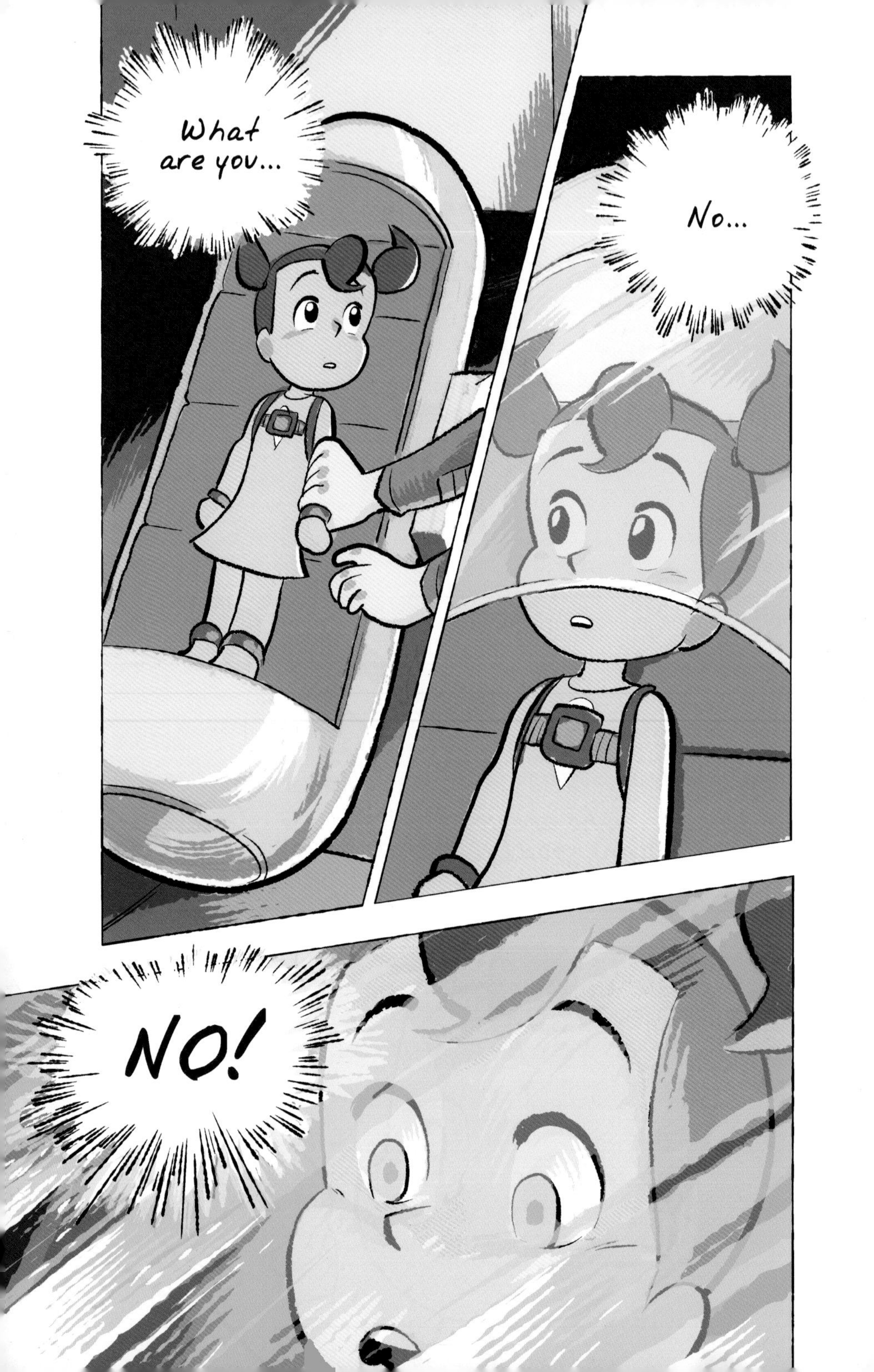
What are you...
No...
NO!

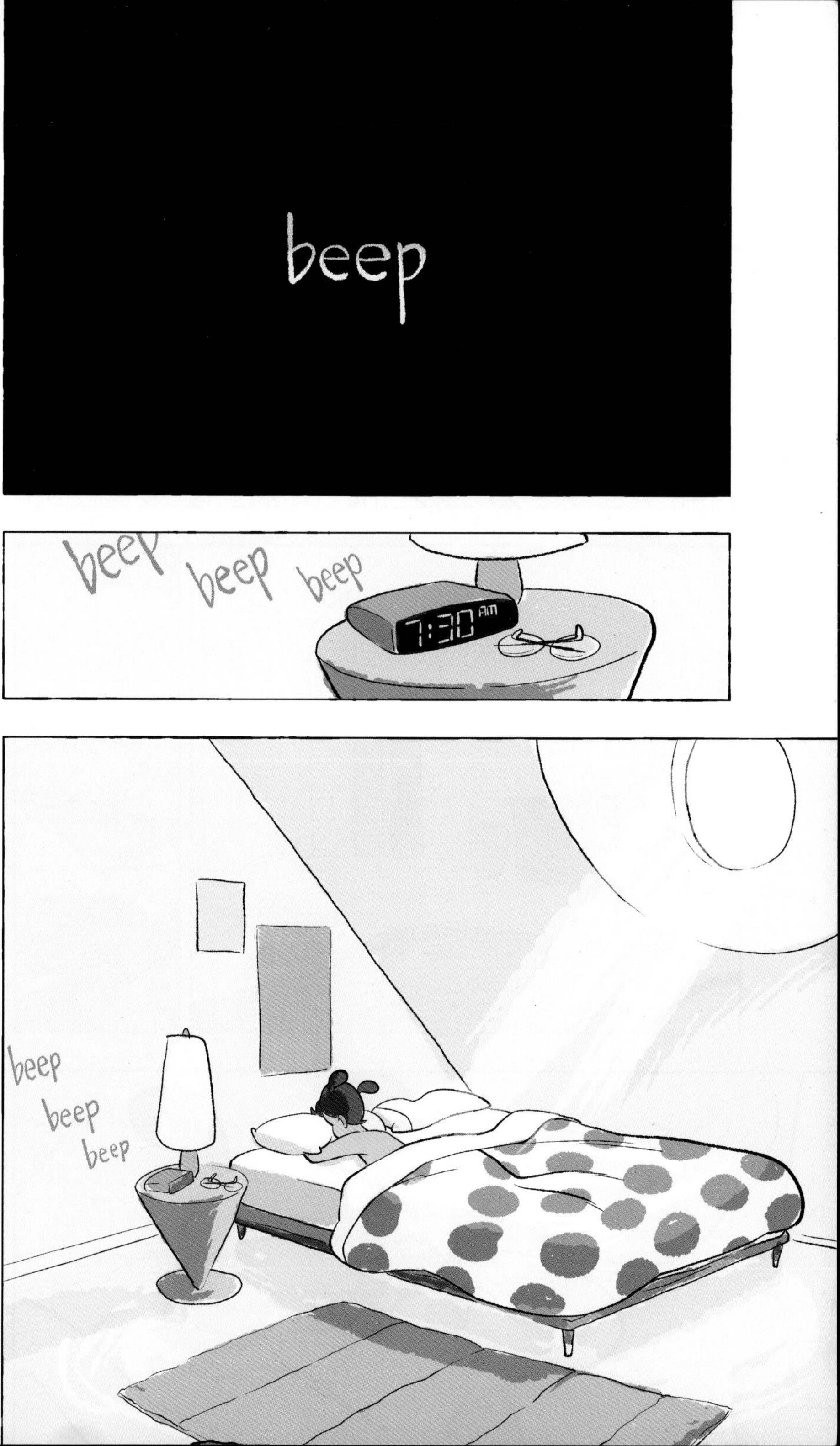
beep
beep beep beep
7:30 AM
beep
beep
beep

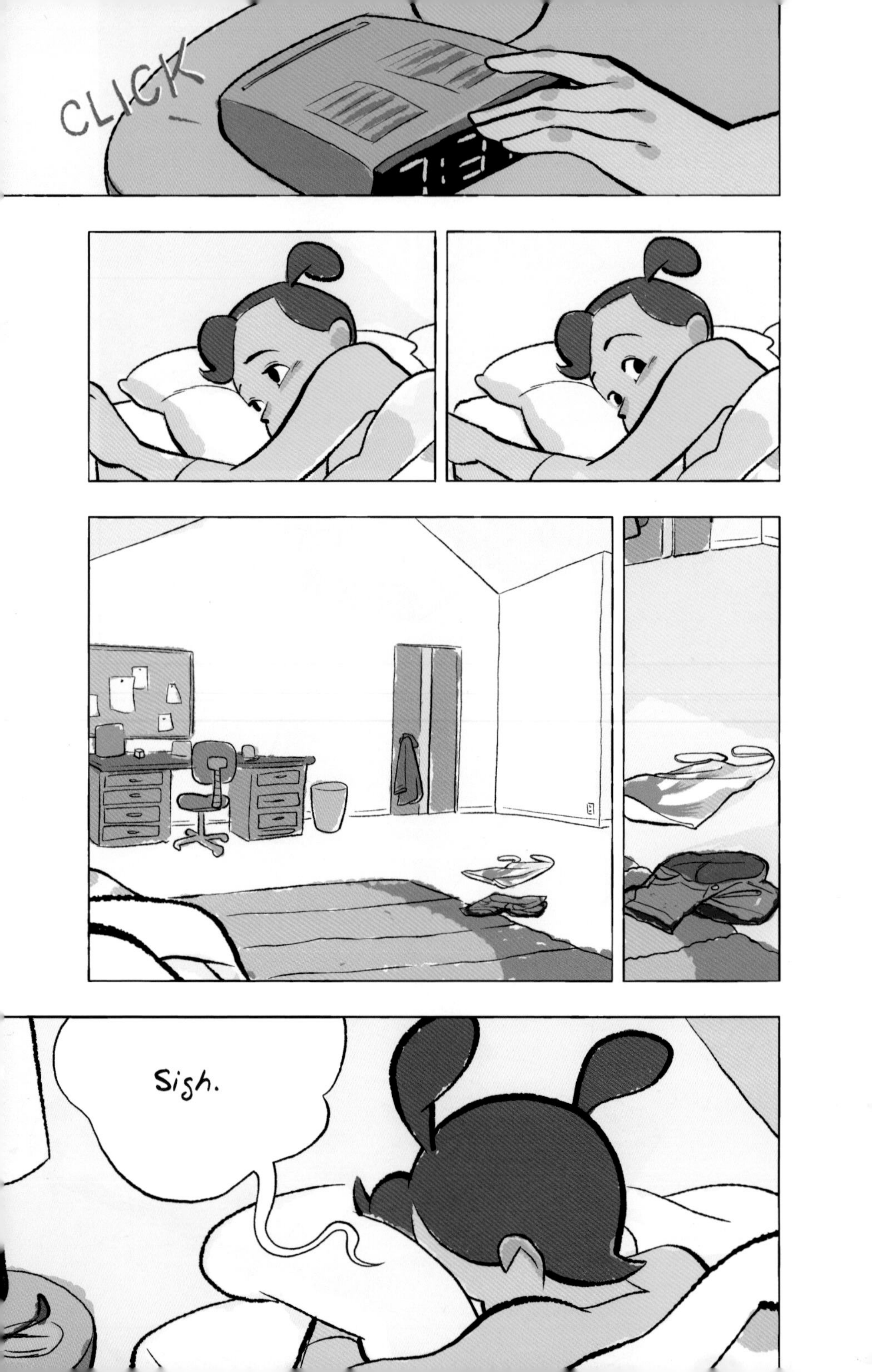
CLICK
Sigh.

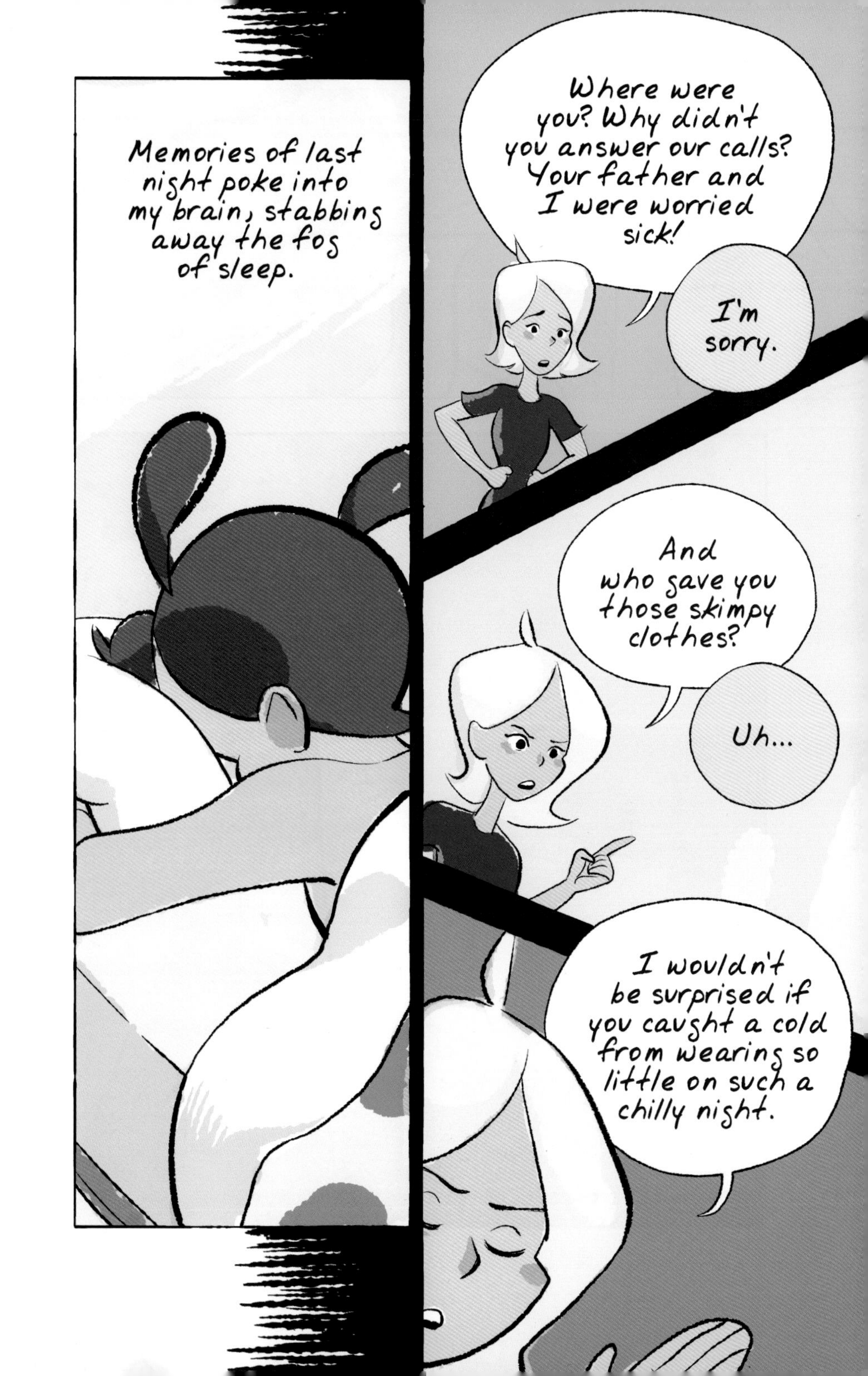
Memories of last night poke into my brain, stabbing away the fog of sleep.
Where were you? Why didn't you answer our calls? Your father and I were worried sick!
I'm sorry.
And who gave you those skimpy clothes?
Uh...
I wouldn't be surprised if you caught a cold from wearing so little on such a chilly night.

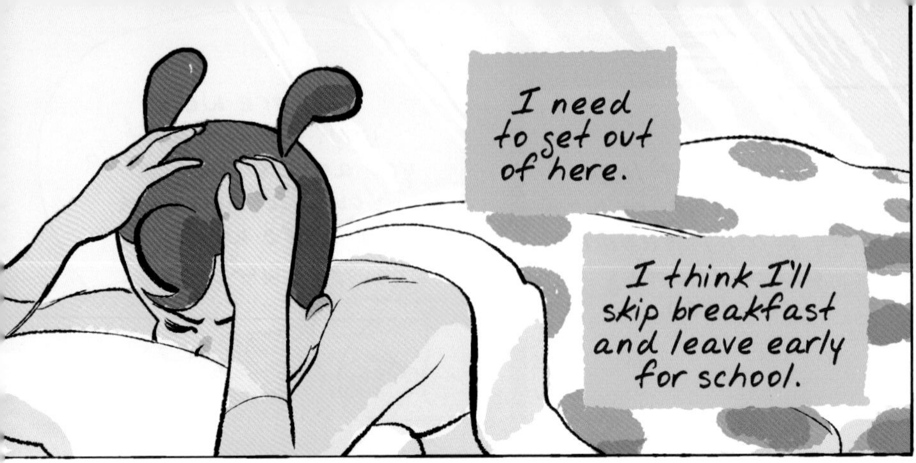
I need
to get out
of here.
I think I'll
skip breakfast
and leave early
for school.

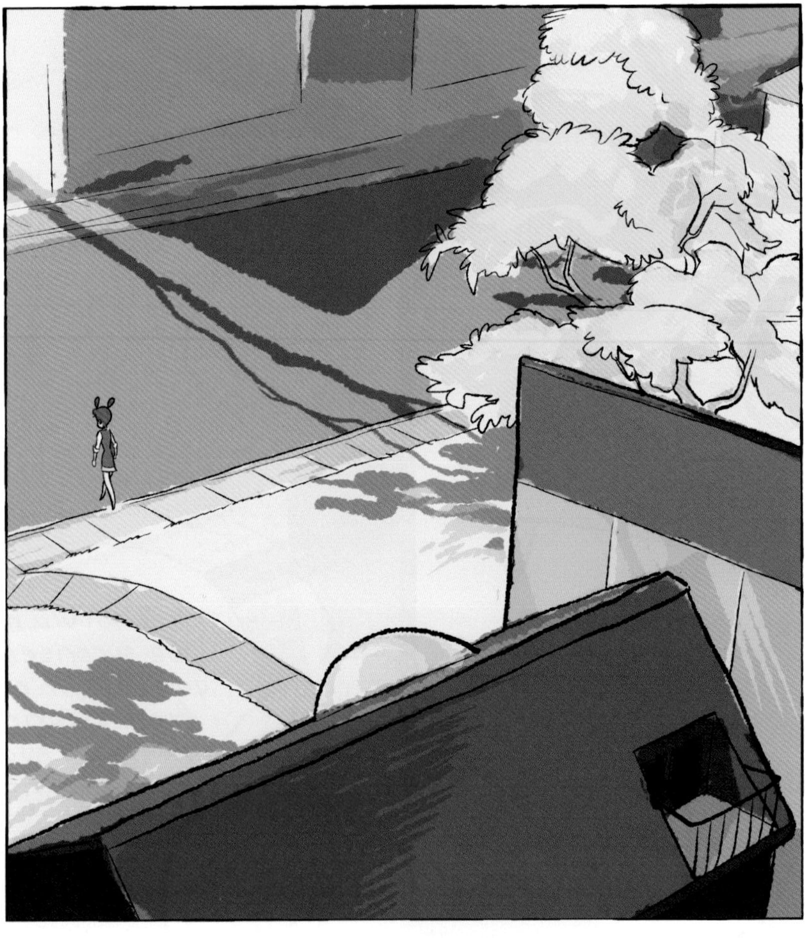

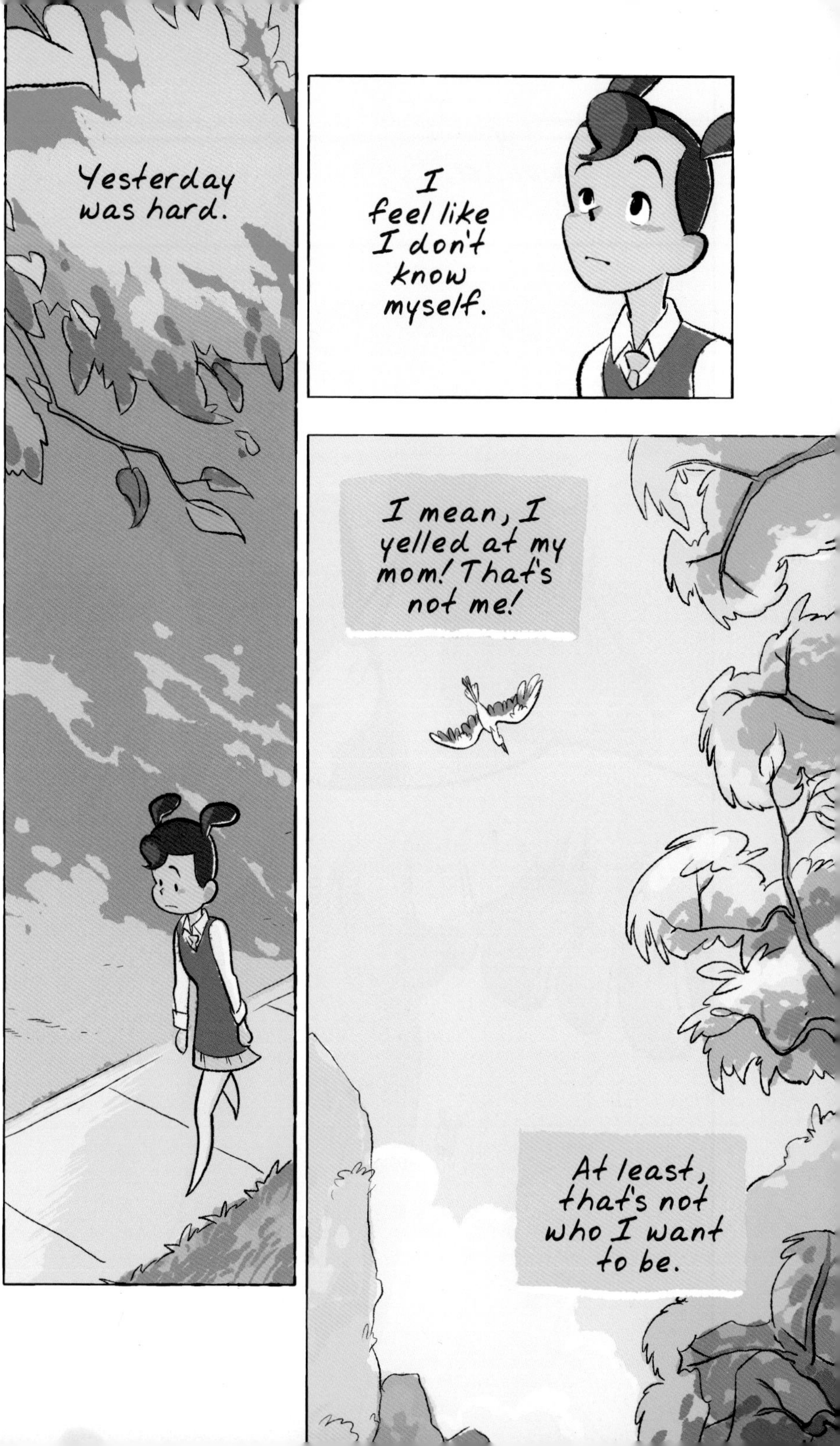
Yesterday was hard.
I feel like I don't know myself.
I mean, I yelled at my mom! That's not me!
At least, that's not who I want to be.

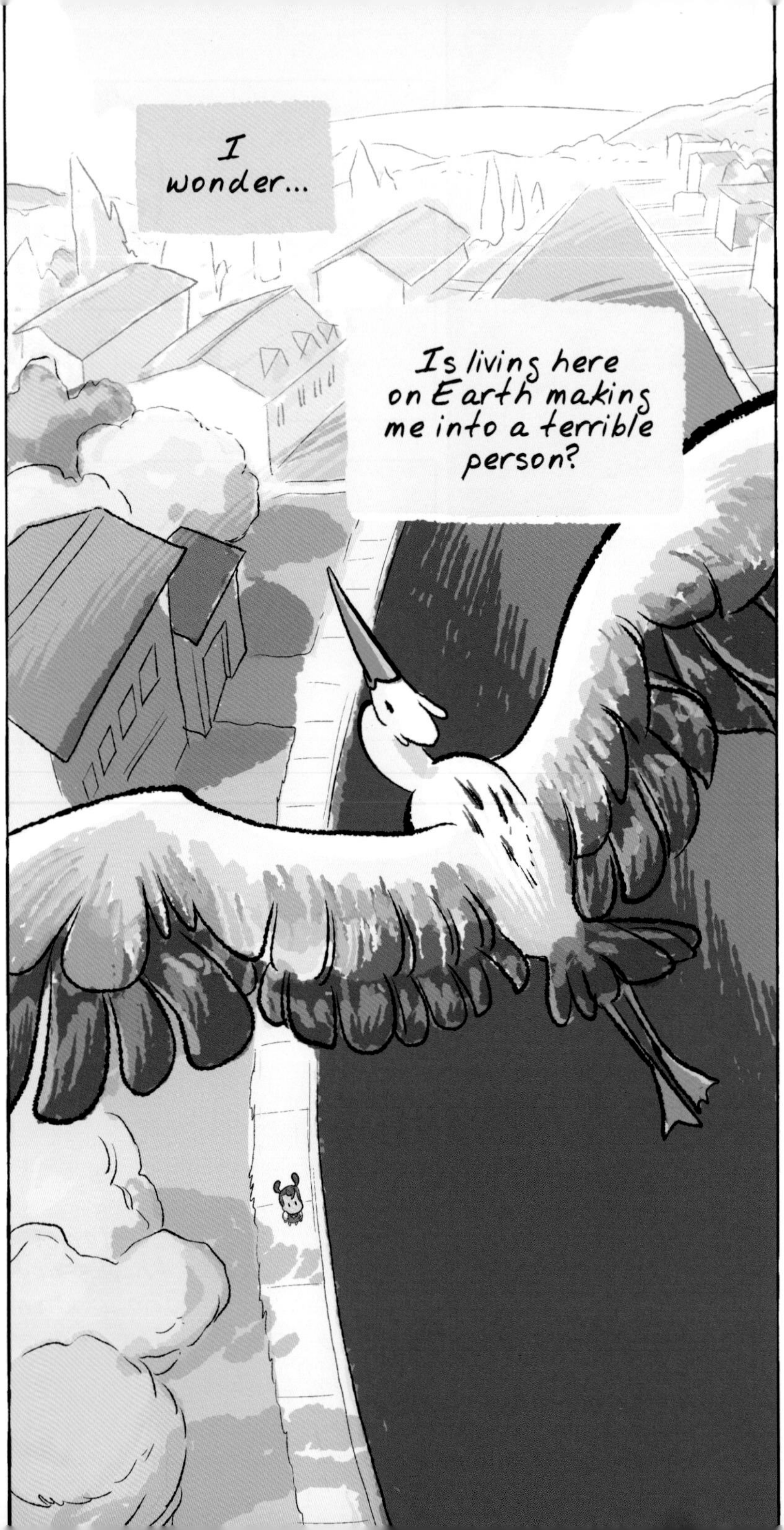
I wonder...
Is living here on Earth making me into a terrible person?

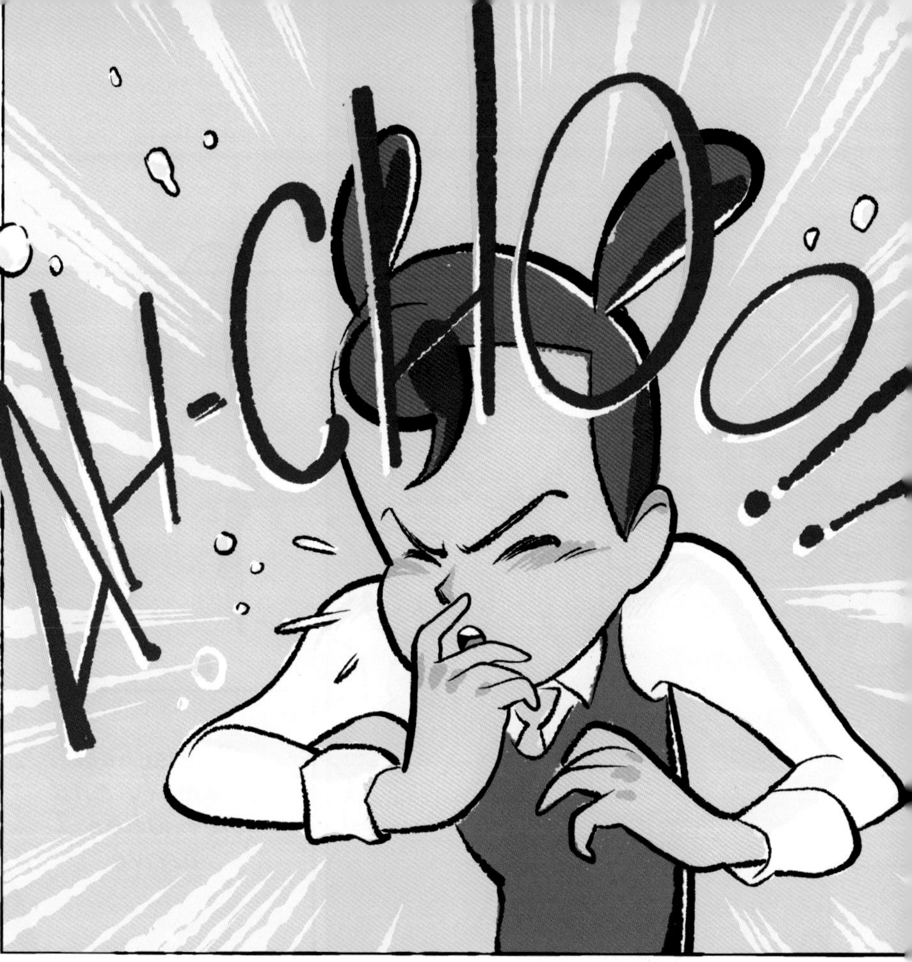
AH-CHOO!!
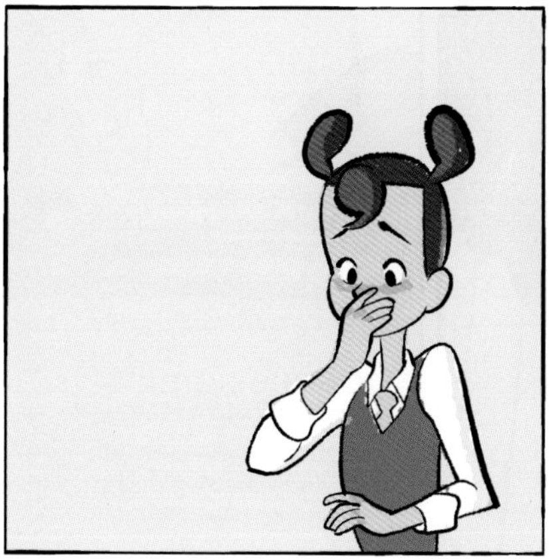
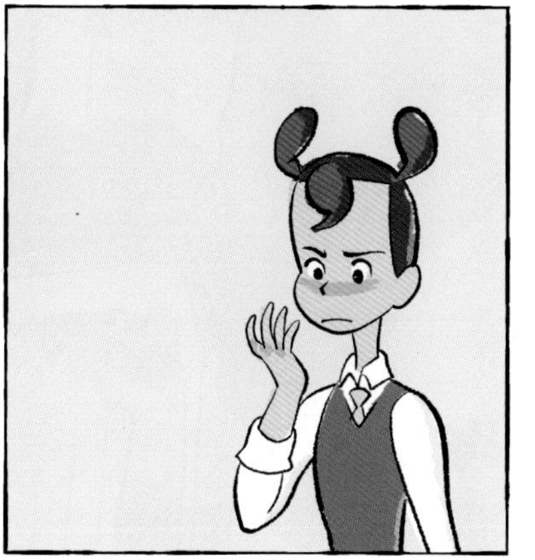

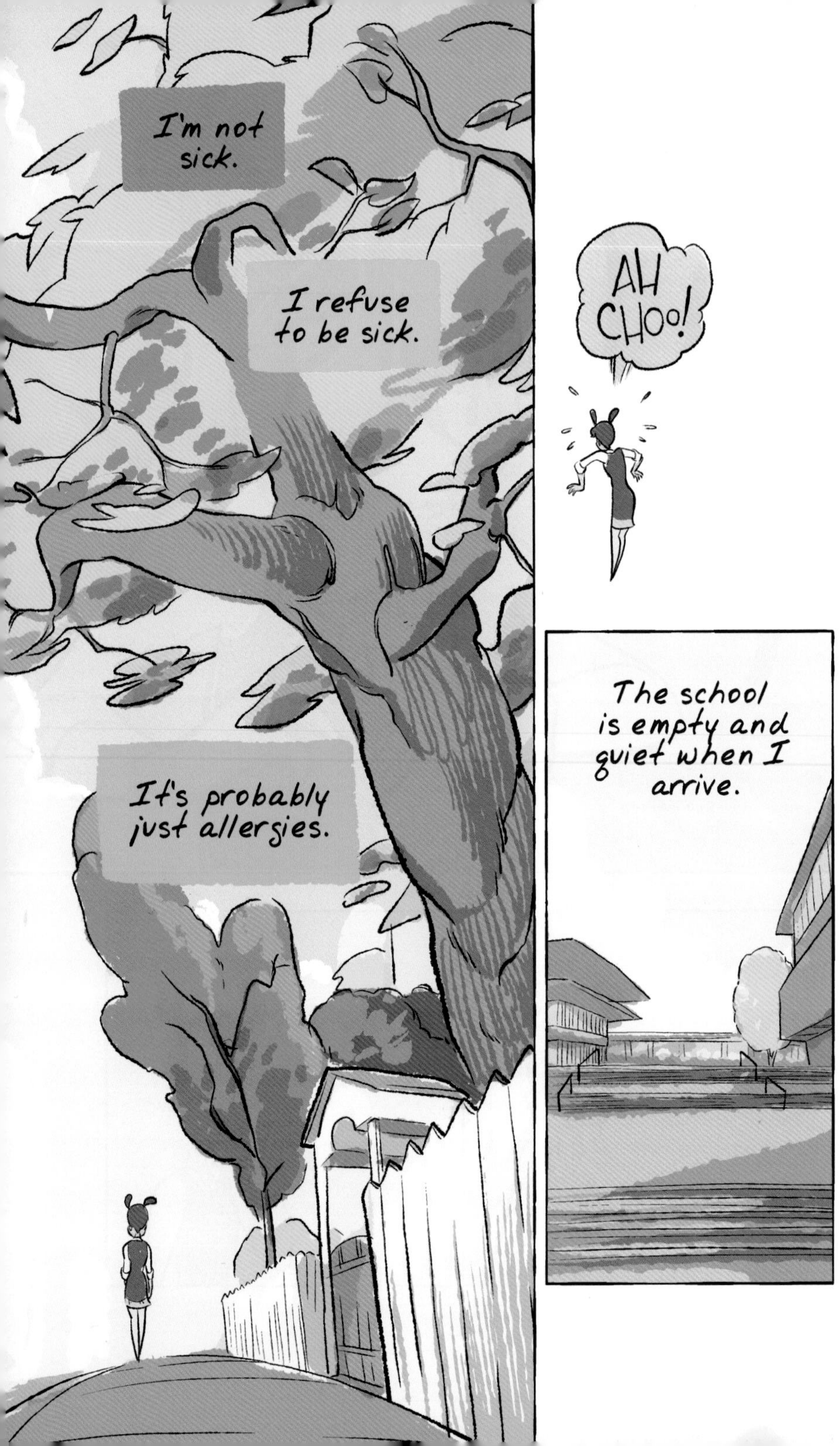
I'm not sick.
I refuse to be sick.
It's probably just allergies.
AH CHOO!
The school is empty and quiet when I arrive.

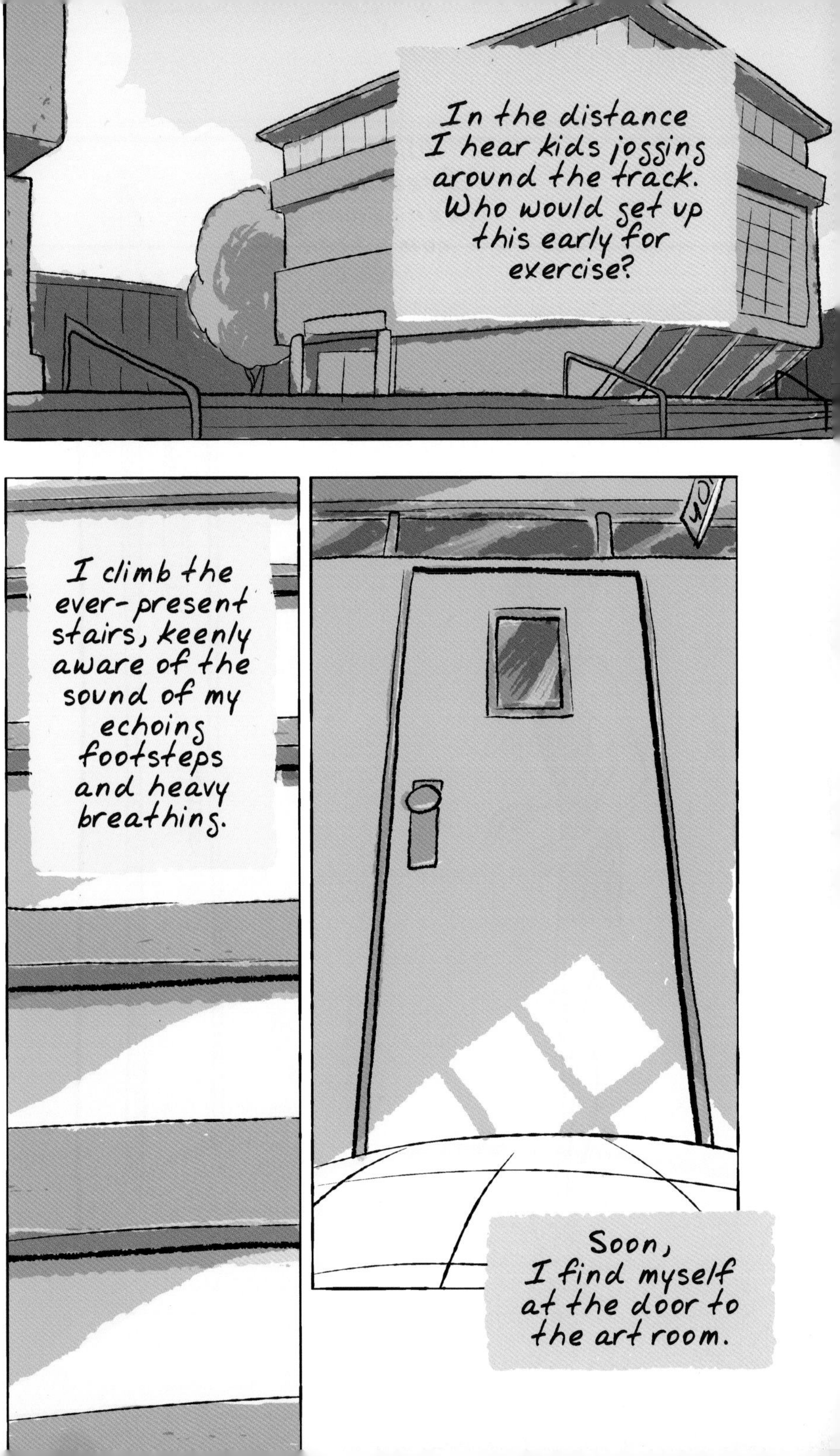
In the distance I hear kids jogging around the track. Who would get up this early for exercise?
I climb the ever-present stairs, keenly aware of the sound of my echoing footsteps and heavy breathing.
Soon, I find myself at the door to the art room.

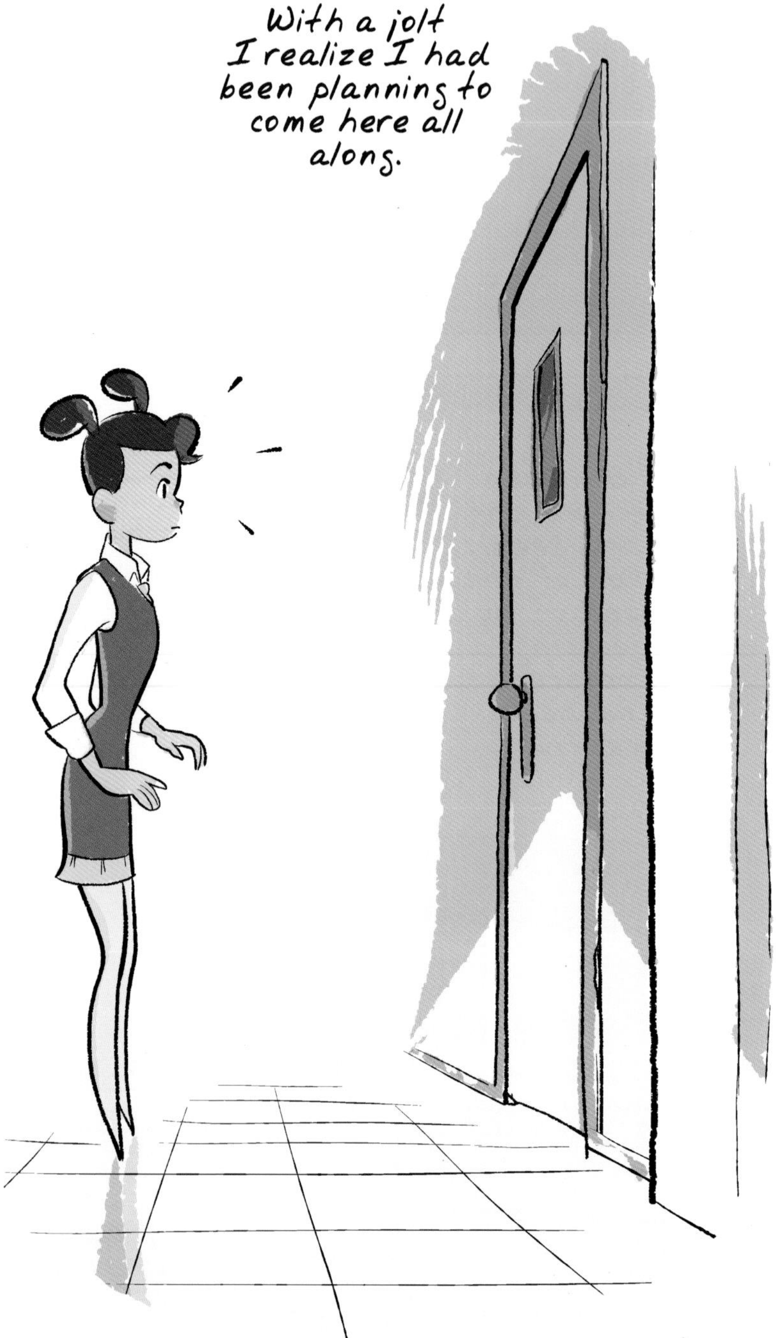
With a jolt I realize I had been planning to come here all along.

I never got a chance to see what the boy with the empty smile had been painting yesterday.
I never got a chance to discover what had allowed fragments of his flavor to bleed out like that.
Now, before anyone gets here, I should have just enough time to take a peek.

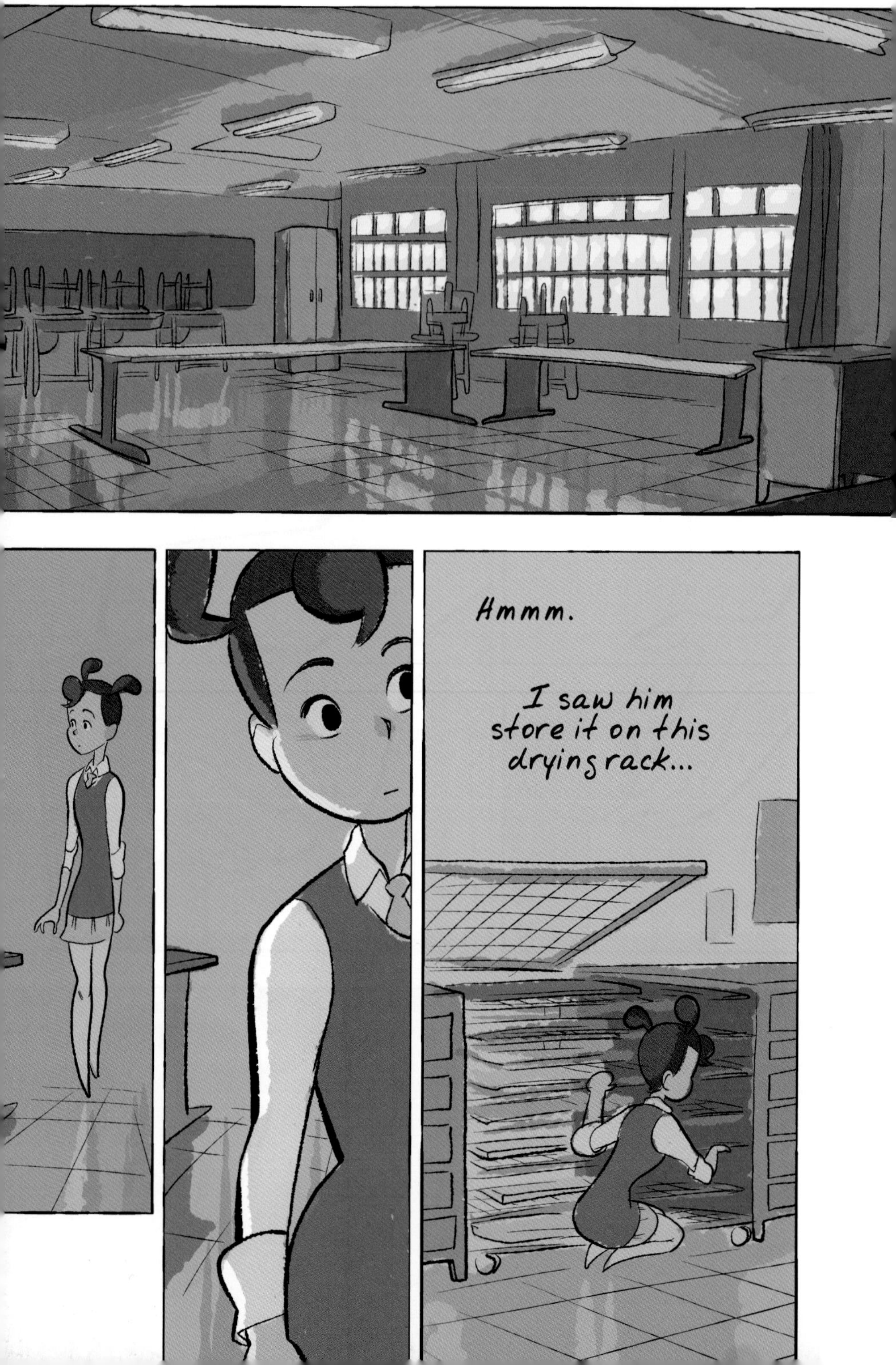
Hmmm.
I saw him store it on this drying rack...

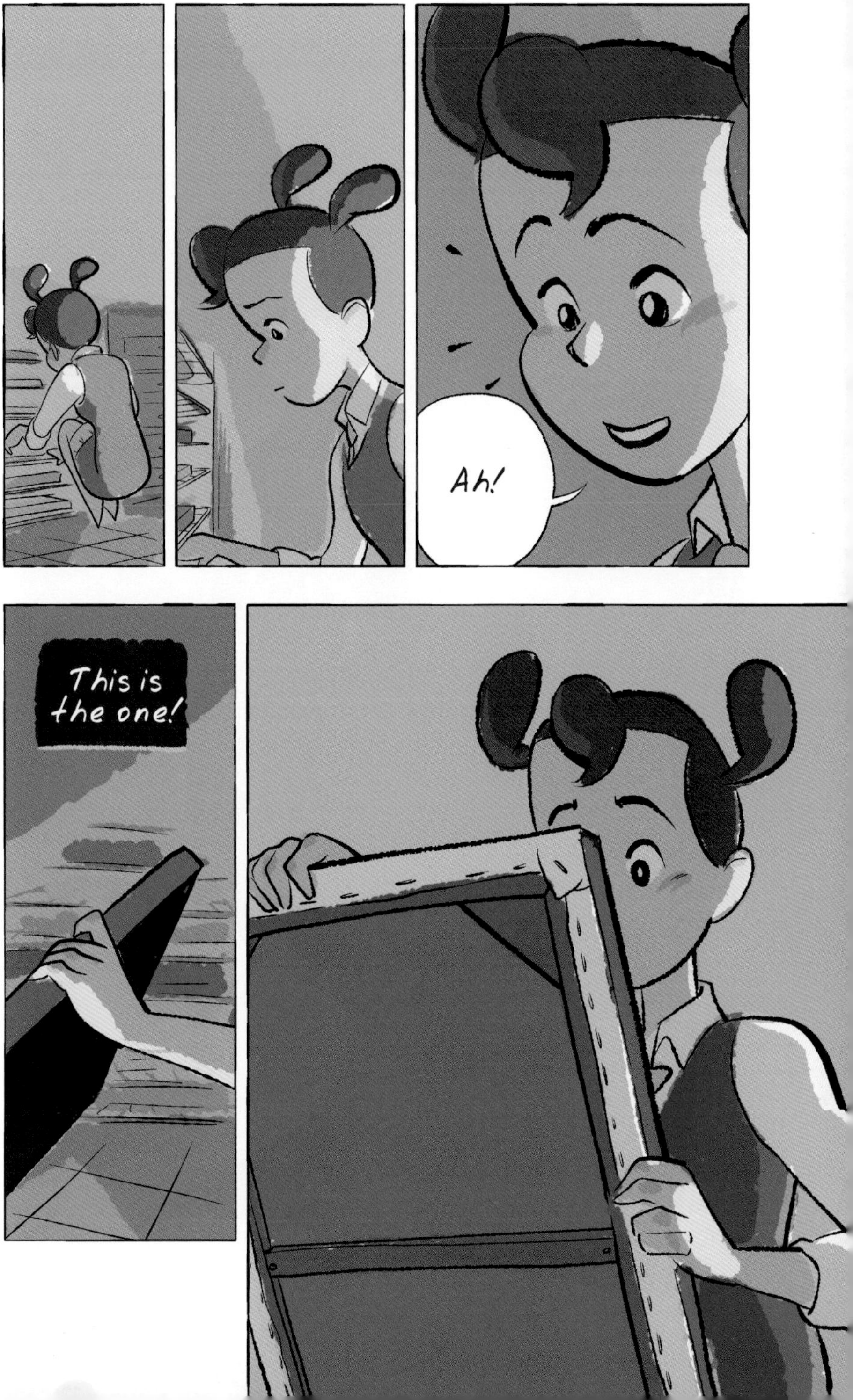
Ah!
This is the one!

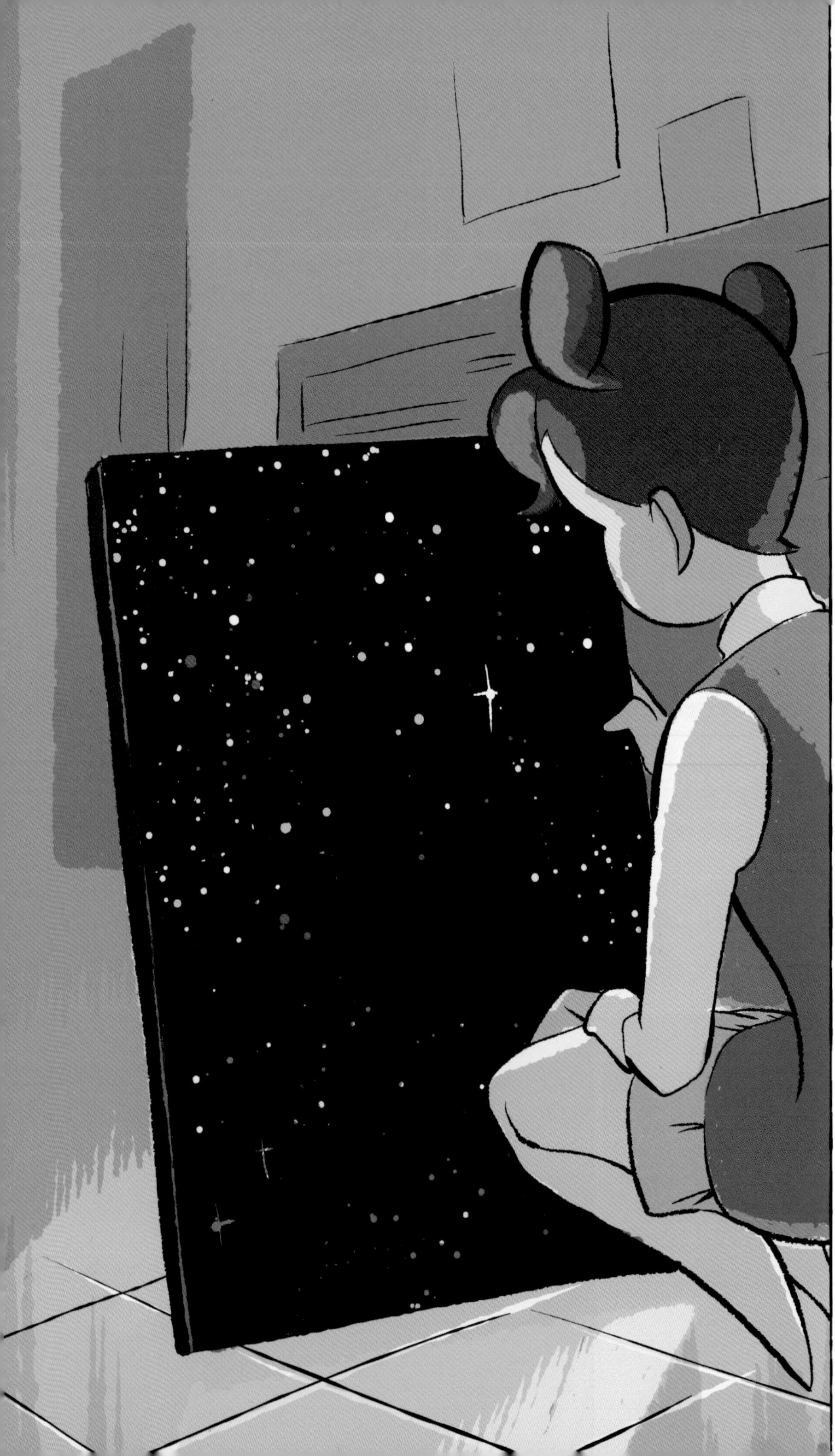

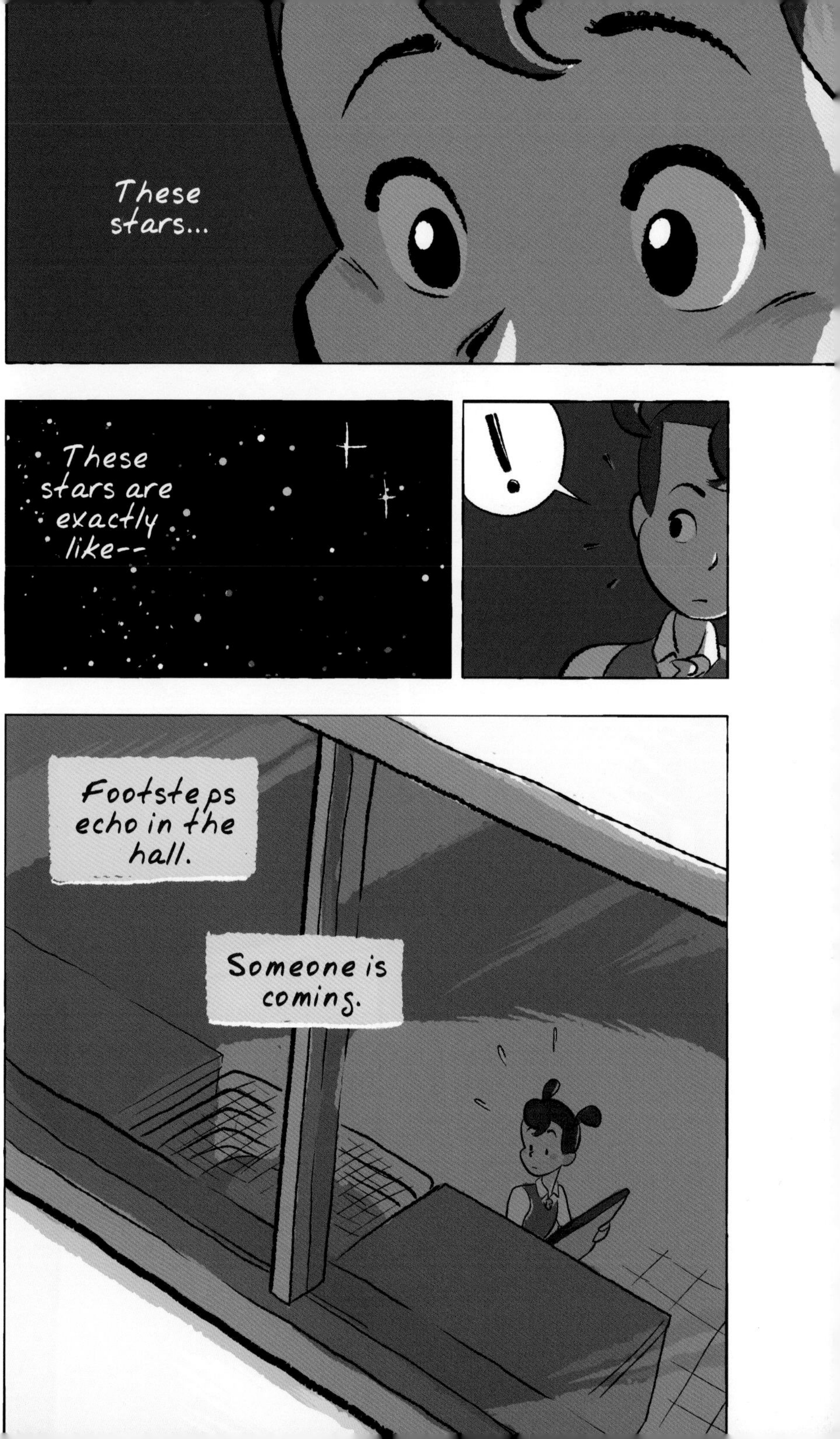
These stars...
These stars are exactly like--
!
Footsteps echo in the hall.
Someone is coming.

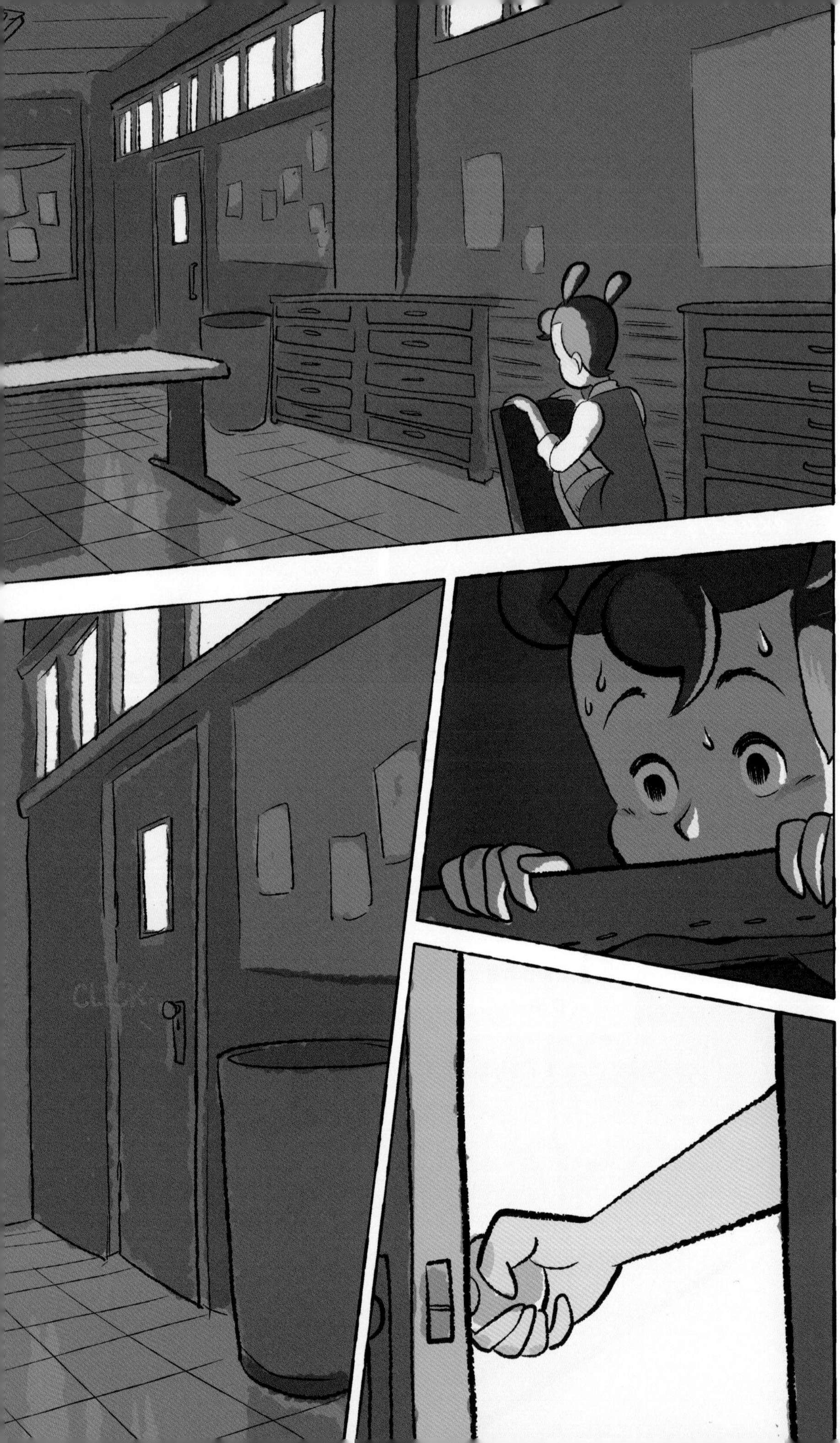
CLICK

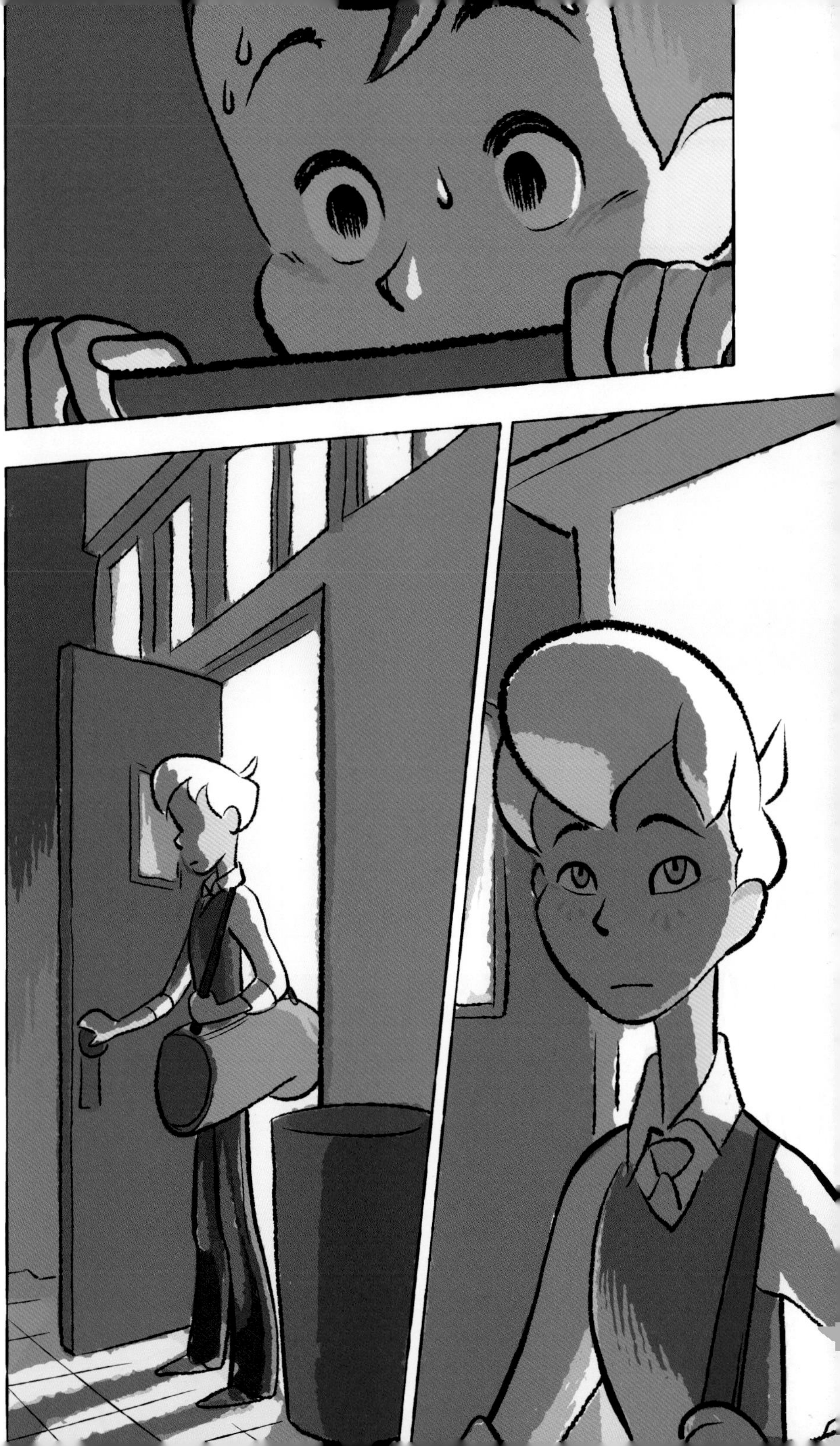

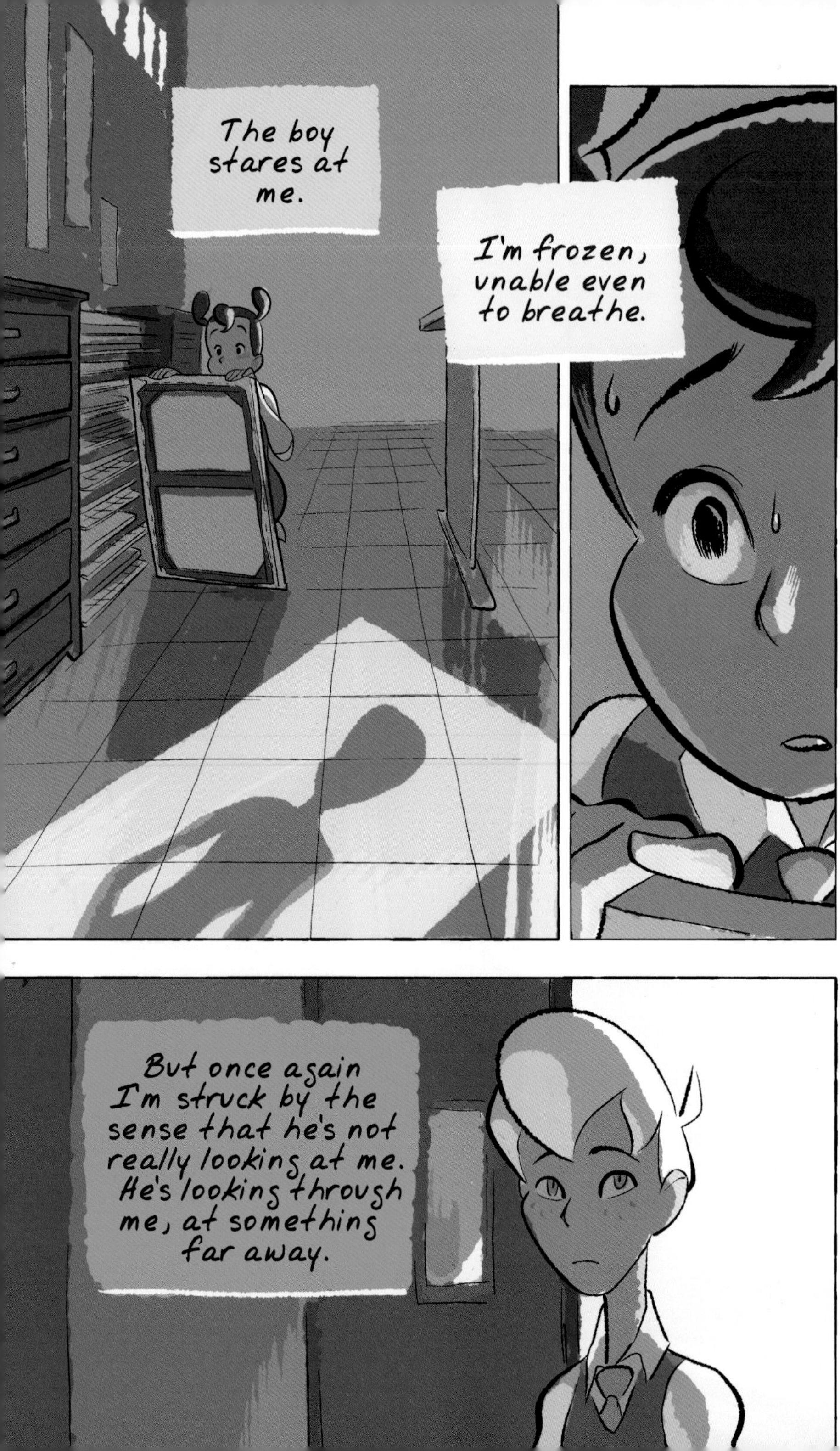
The boy stares at me.
I'm frozen, unable even to breathe.
But once again I'm struck by the sense that he's not really looking at me. He's looking through me, at something far away.

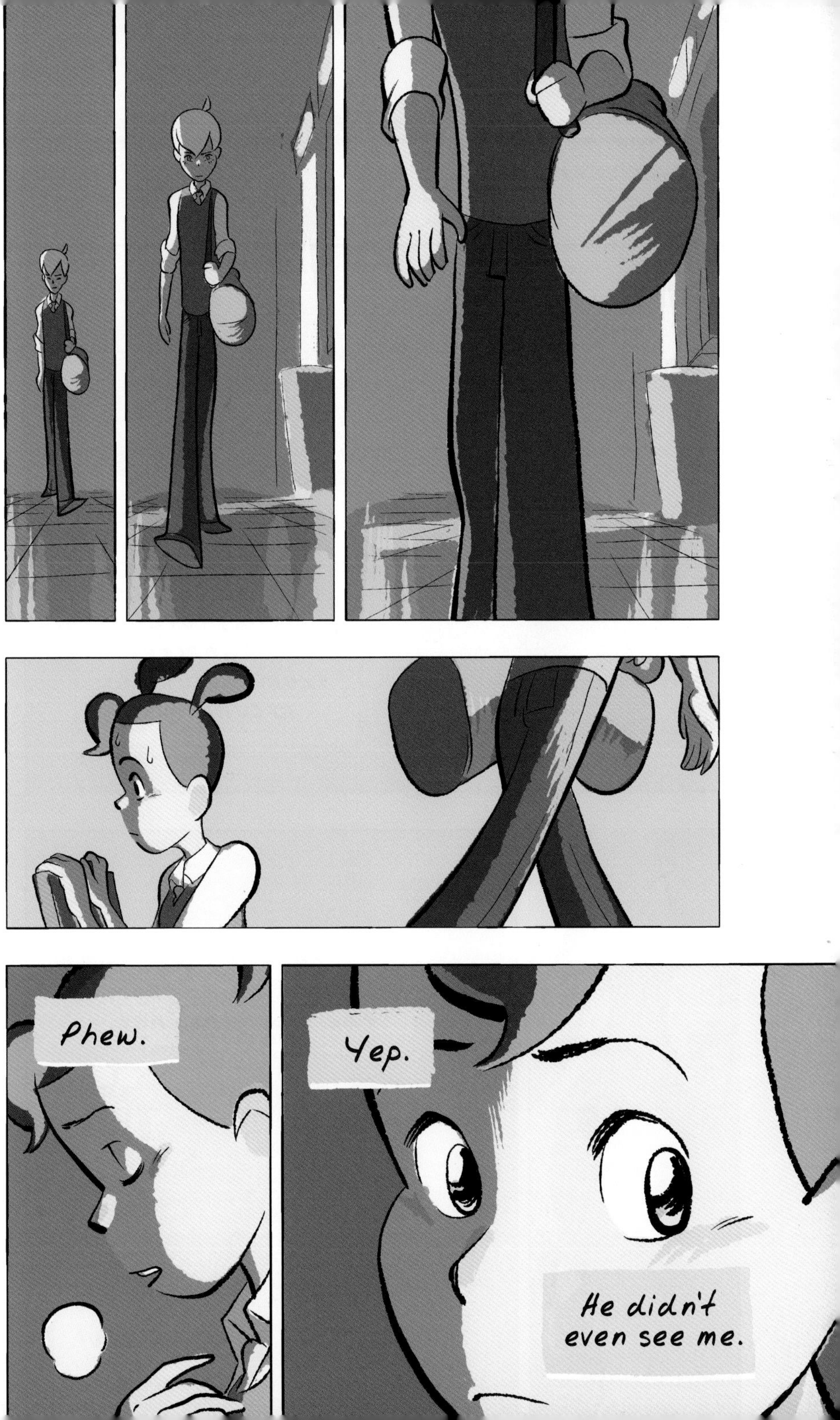
Phew.
Yep.
He didn't even see me.

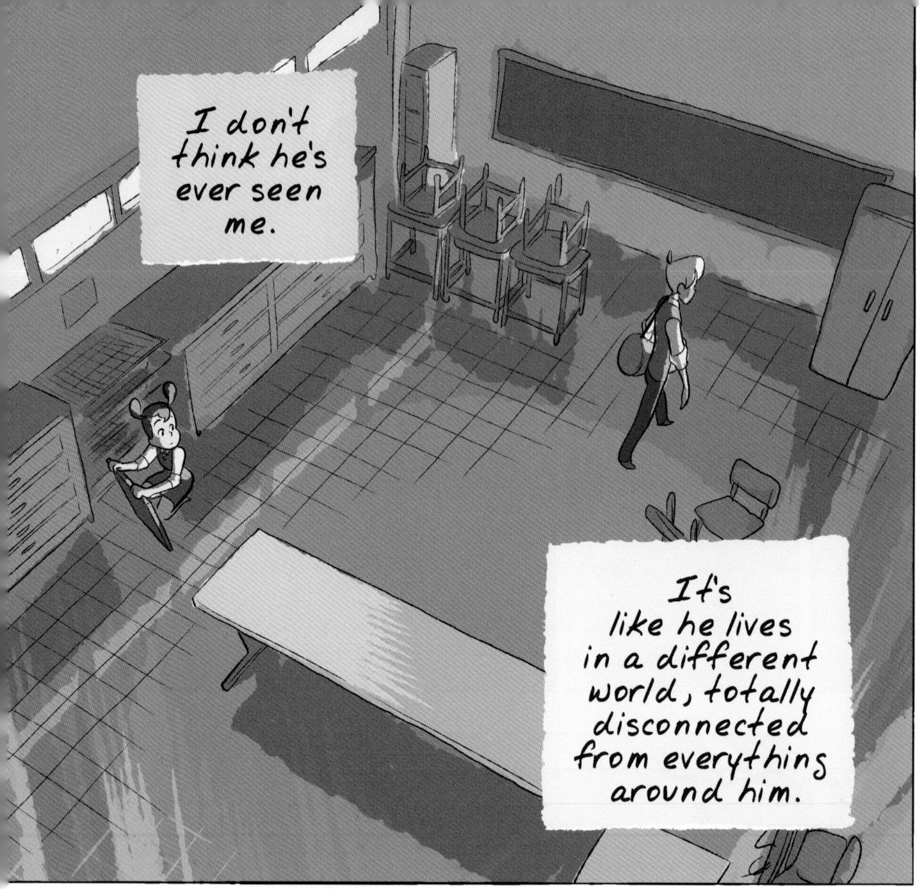
I don't think he's ever seen me.
It's like he lives in a different world, totally disconnected from everything around him.

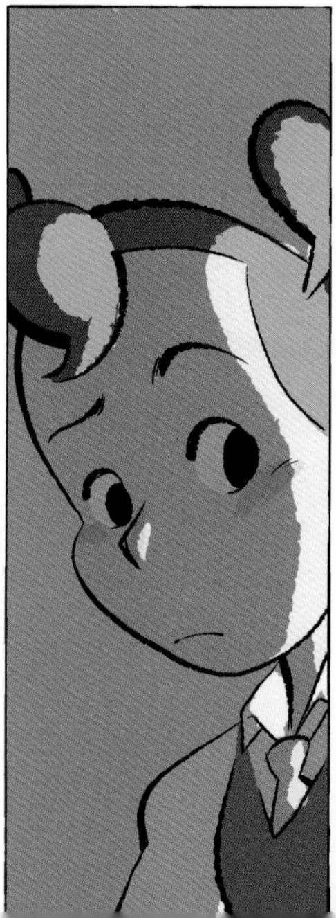

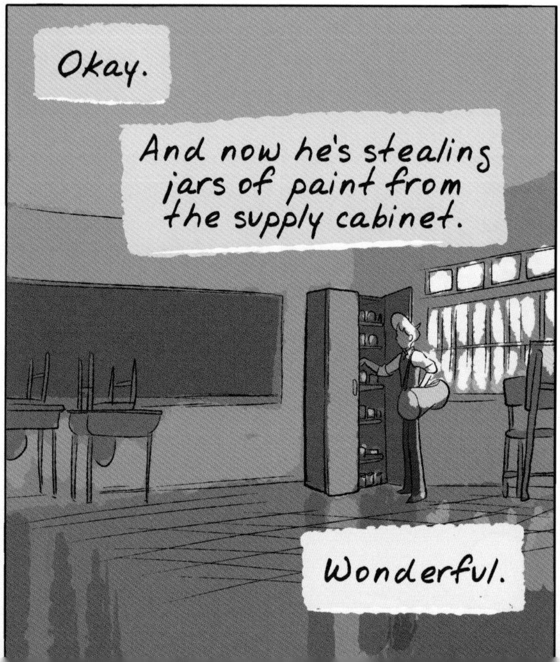
Okay.
And now he's stealing jars of paint from the supply cabinet.
Wonderful.

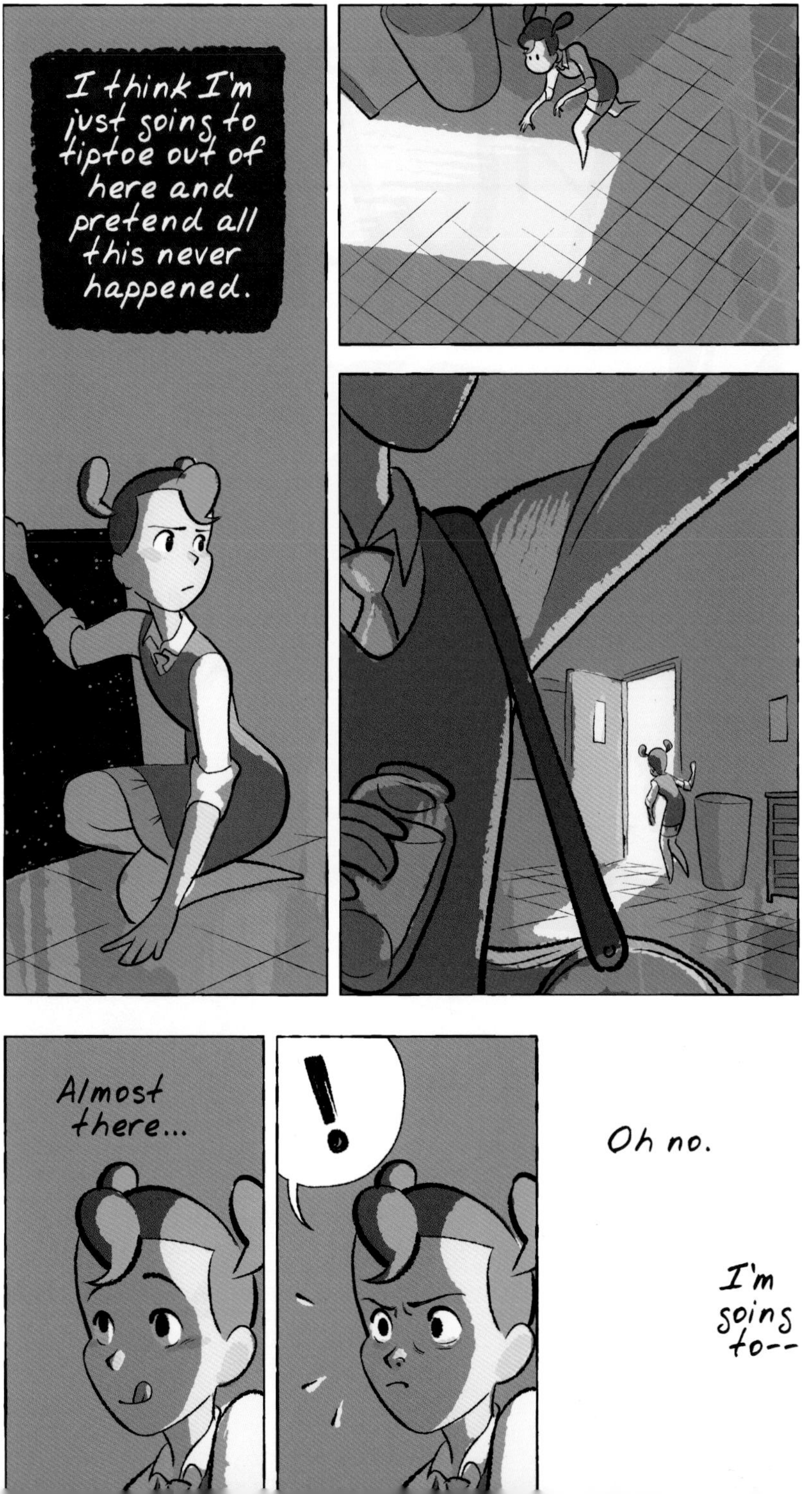

I think I'm just going to tiptoe out of here and pretend all this never happened.
Almost there...
!
Oh no.
I'm going to--

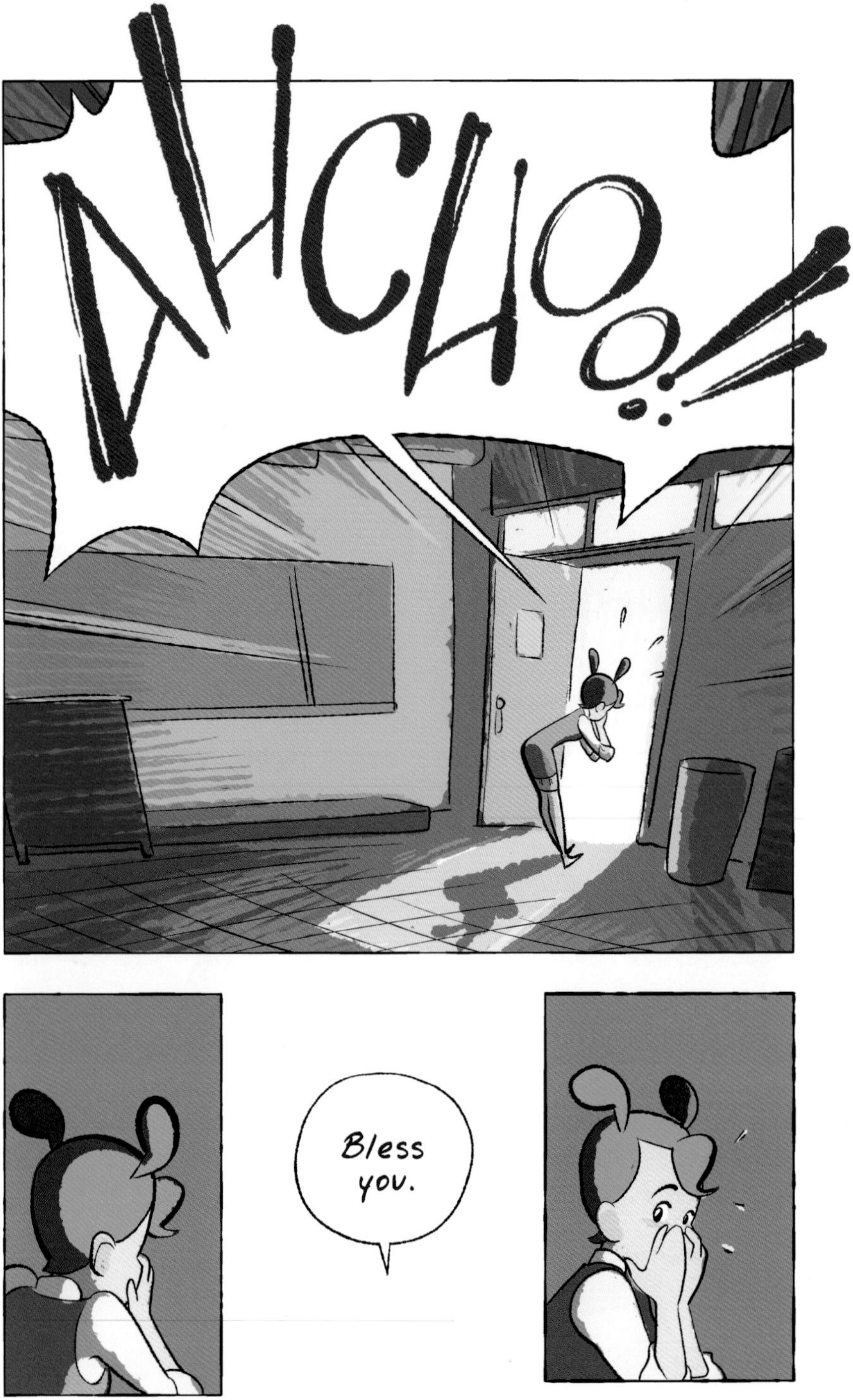
AHCHOO!!
Bless you.

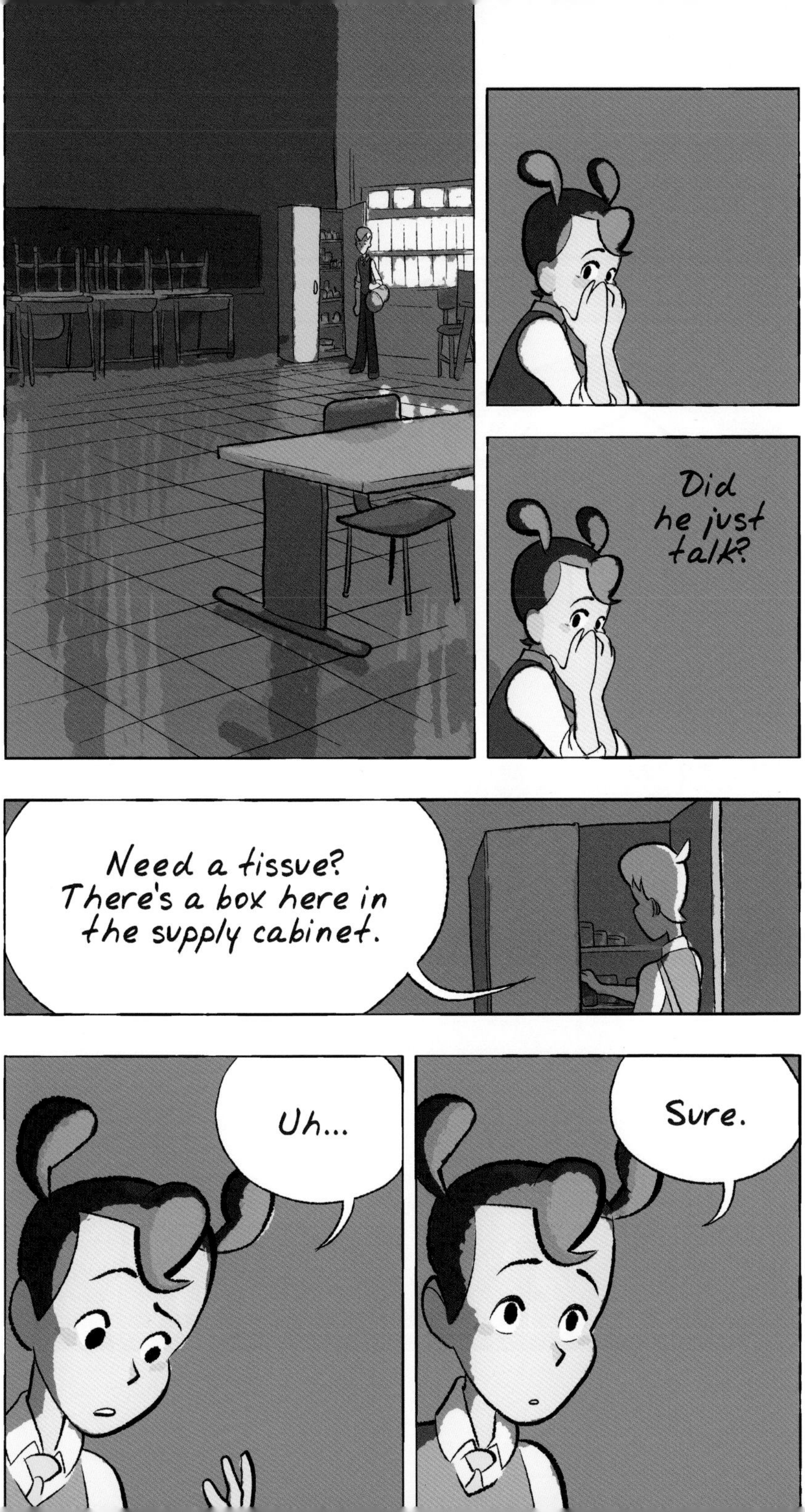
Did he just talk?
Need a tissue? There's a box here in the supply cabinet.
Uh...
Sure.

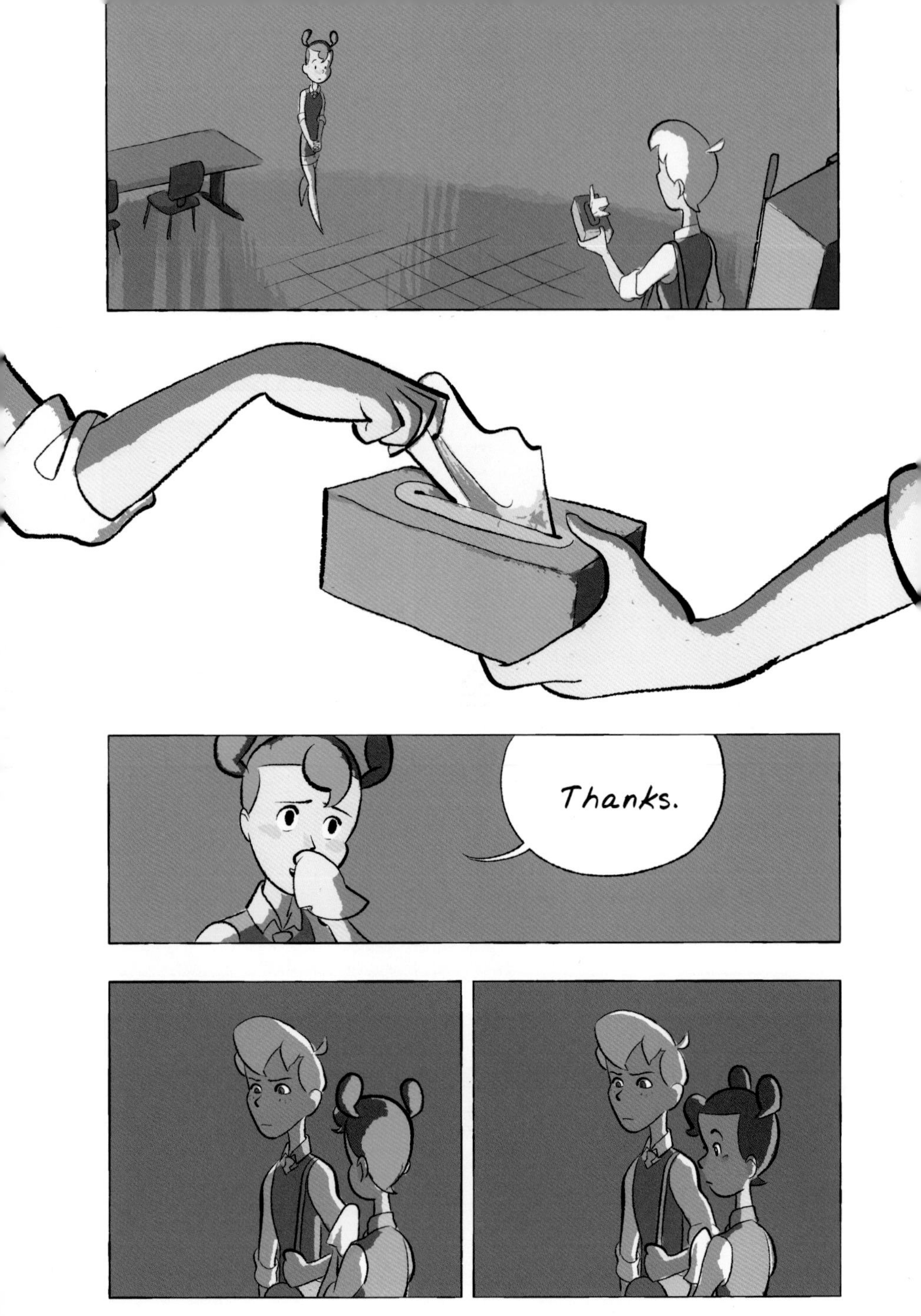
Thanks.

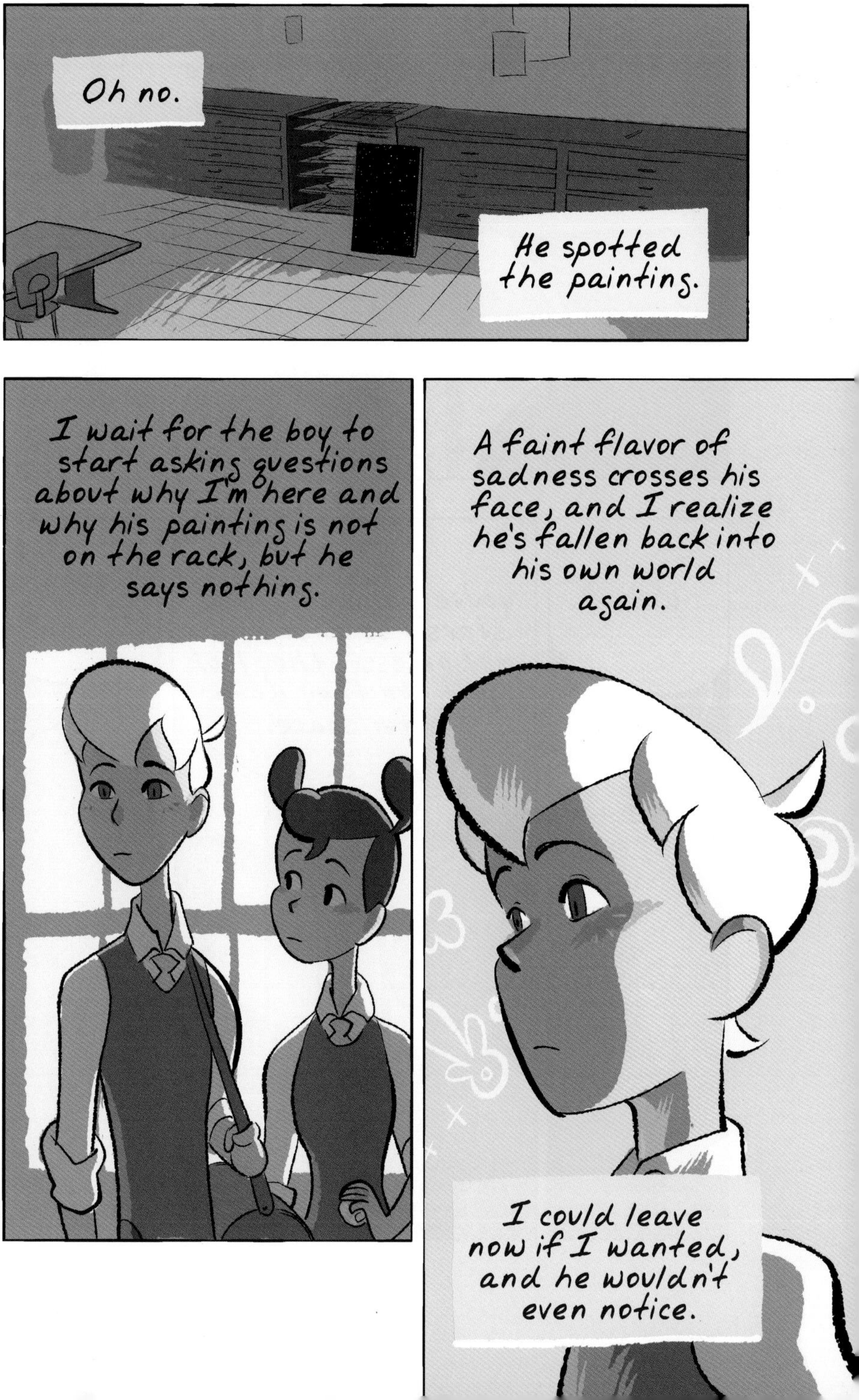
Oh no.
He spotted the paintings.
I wait for the boy to start asking questions about why I'm here and why his painting is not on the rack, but he says nothing.
A faint flavor of sadness crosses his face, and I realize he's fallen back into his own world again.
I could leave now if I wanted, and he wouldn't even notice.

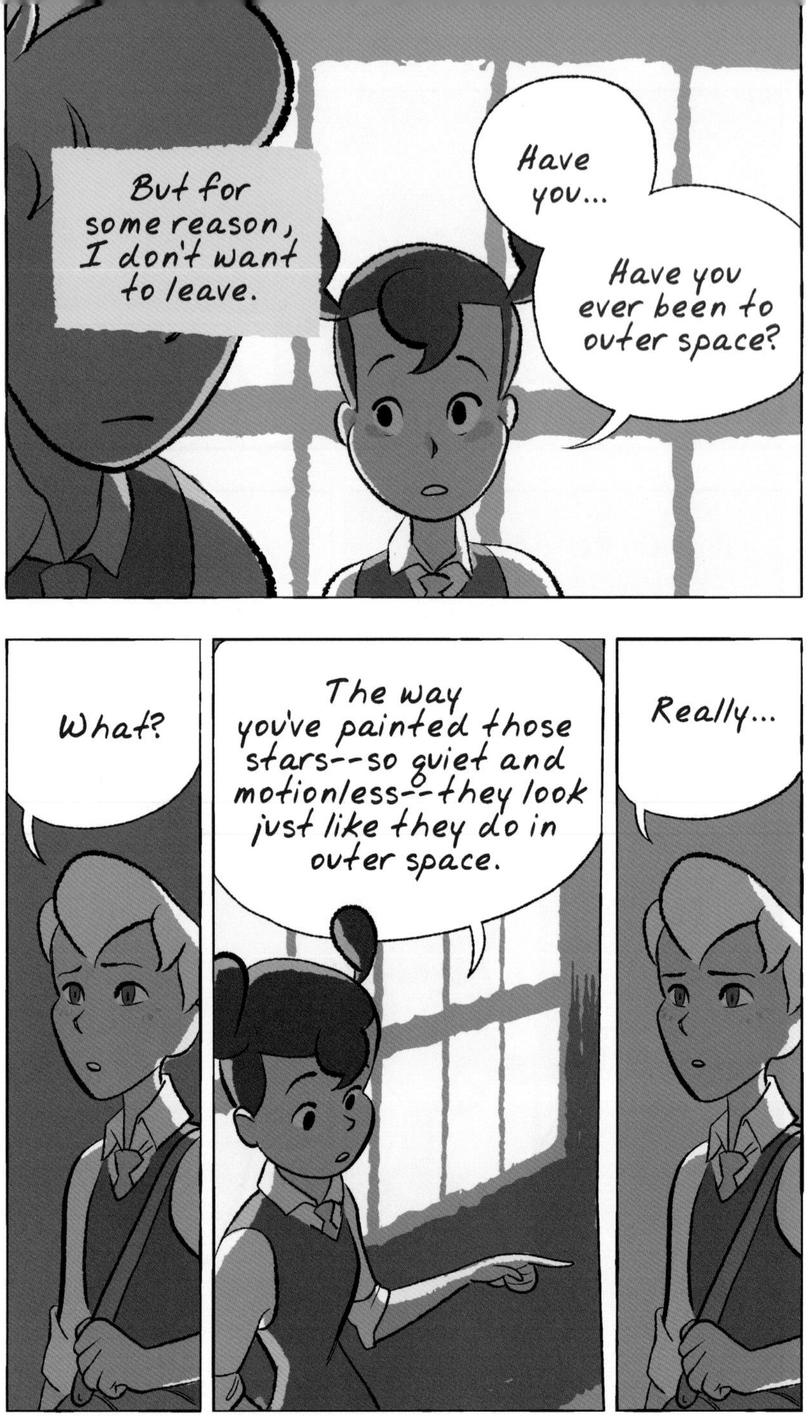
But for some reason, I don't want to leave.
Have you...
Have you ever been to outer space?
What?
The way you've painted those stars--so quiet and motionless--they look just like they do in outer space.
Really...

Yeah. In space, the stars don't twinkle, you know.
That only happens when you look at the stars through the atmosphere of a planet.
Huh.
I didn't know that.

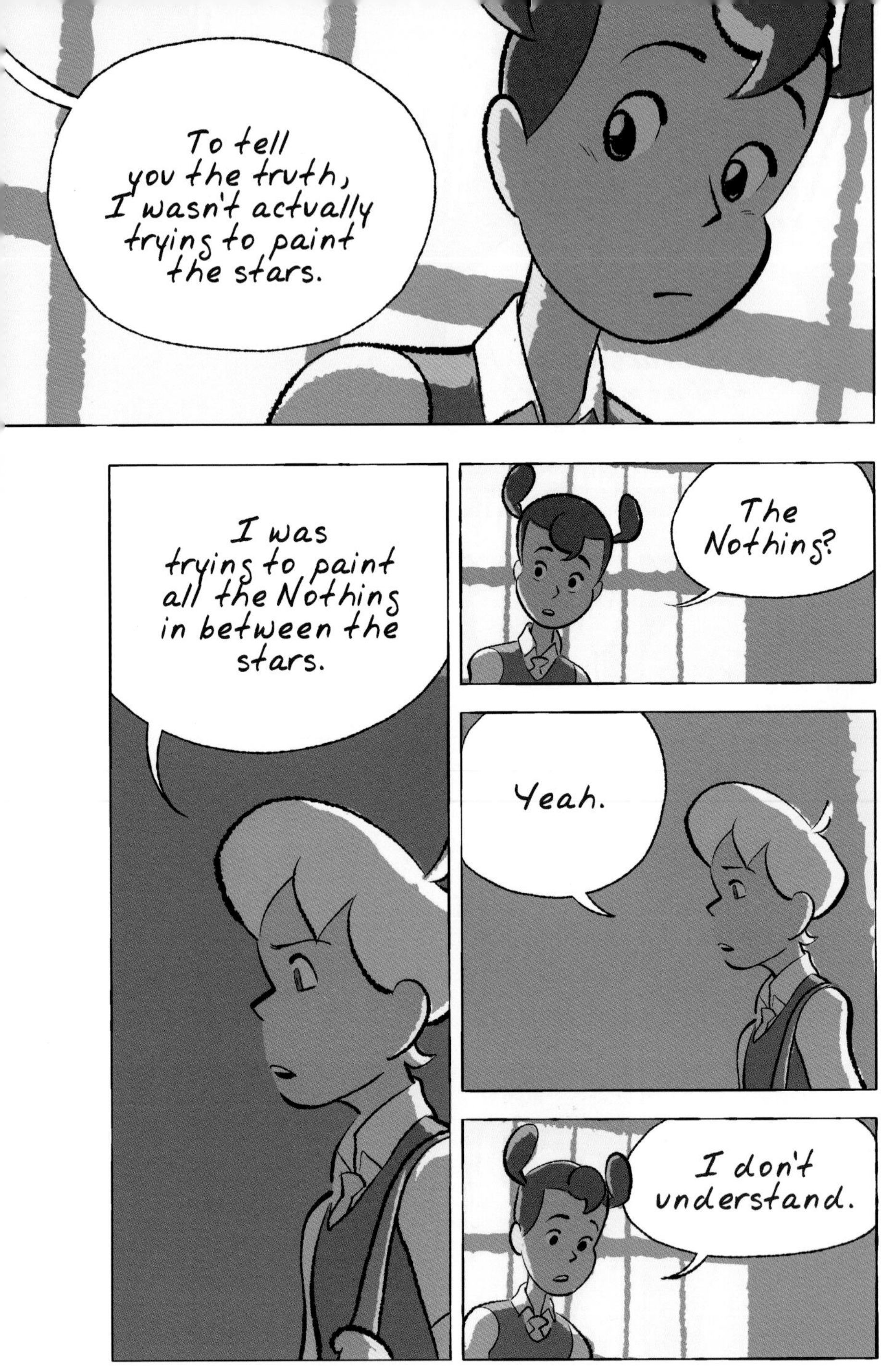
To tell you the truth, I wasn't actually trying to paint the stars.
I was trying to paint all the Nothing in between the stars.
The Nothing?
Yeah.
I don't understand.

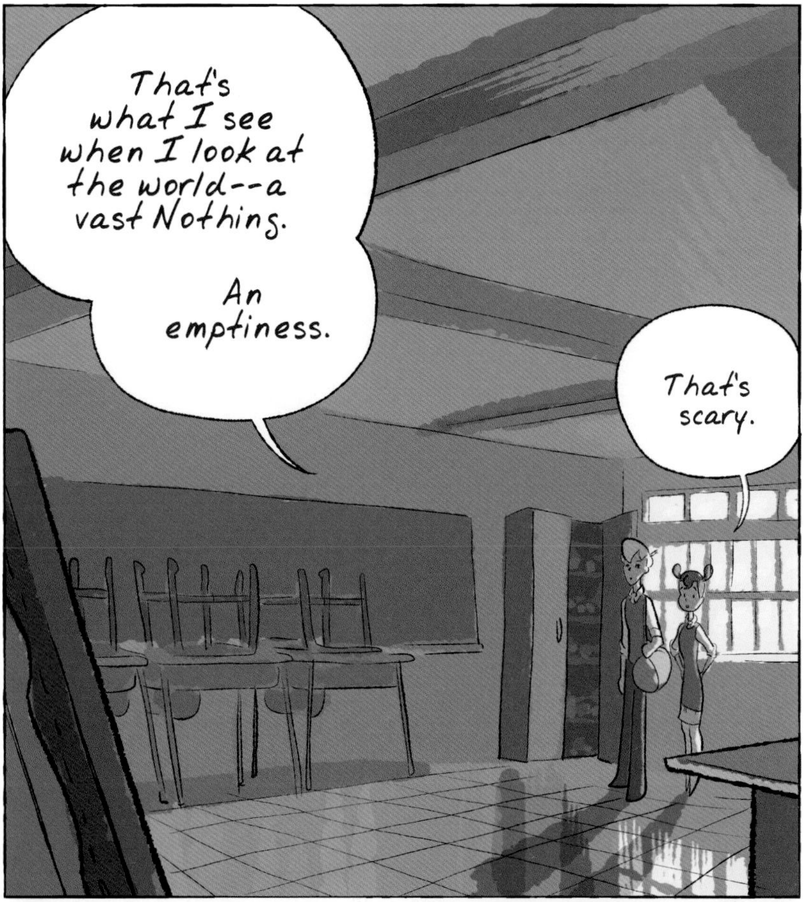
That's what I see when I look at the world--a vast Nothing.
An emptiness.
That's scary.

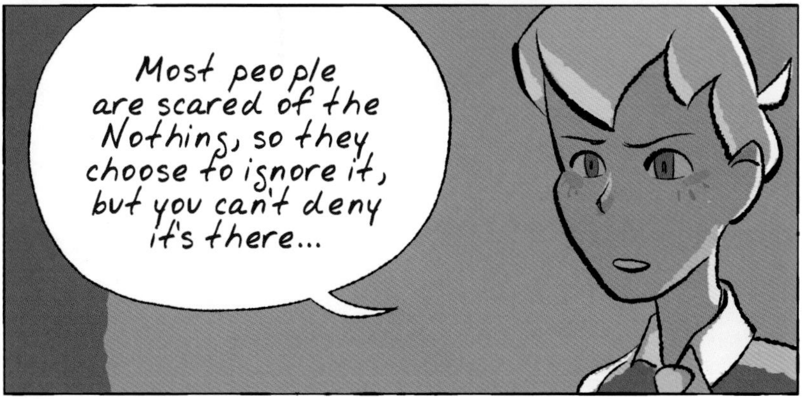
Most people are scared of the Nothing, so they choose to ignore it, but you can't deny it's there...

The universe is almost entirely made up of Nothing.
Even the atoms in our bodies consist primarily of empty space.
We are all just bits of matter, floating in the void.

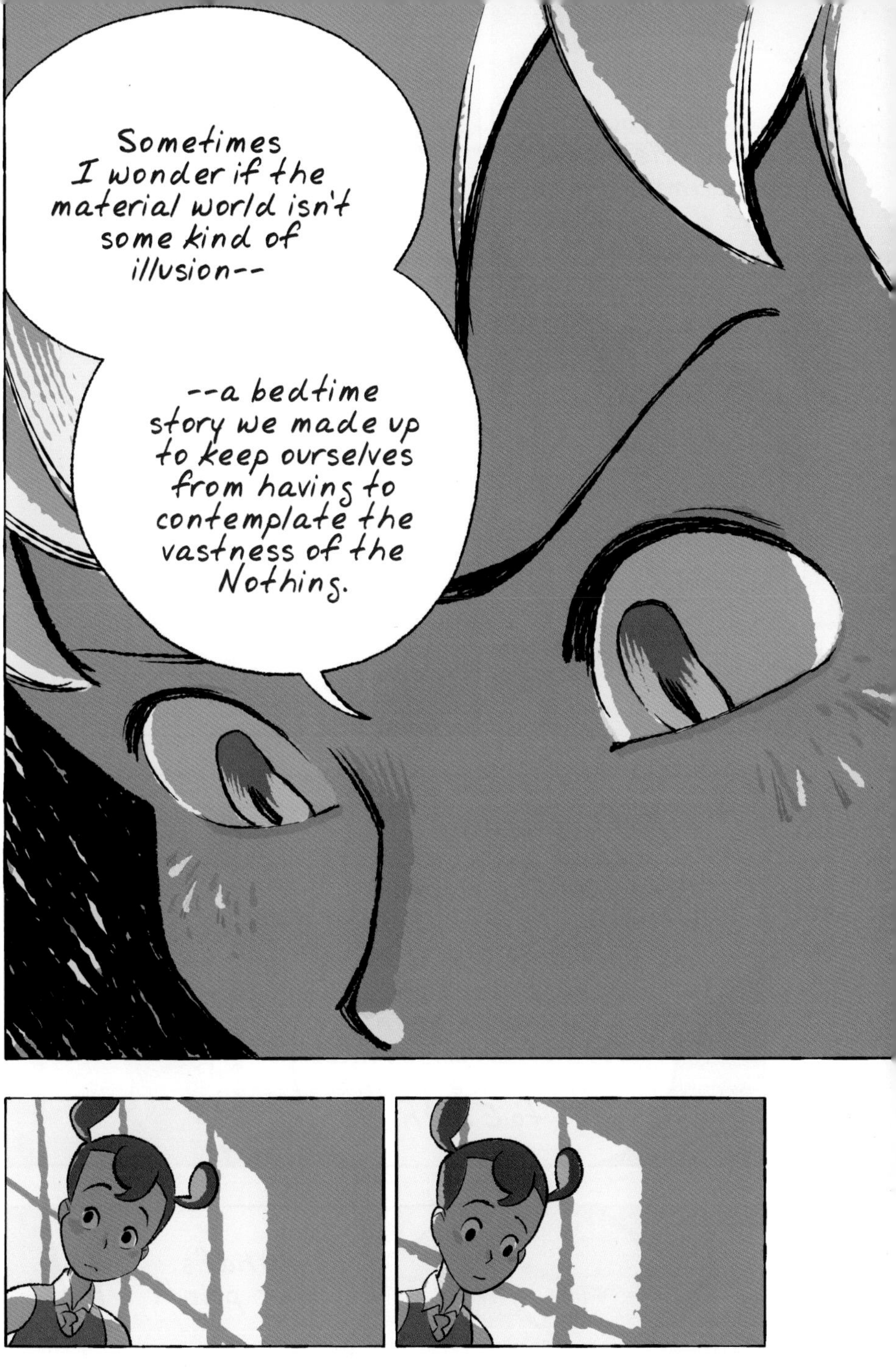
Sometimes I wonder if the material world isn't some kind of illusion--
--a bedtime story we made up to keep ourselves from having to contemplate the vastness of the Nothing.

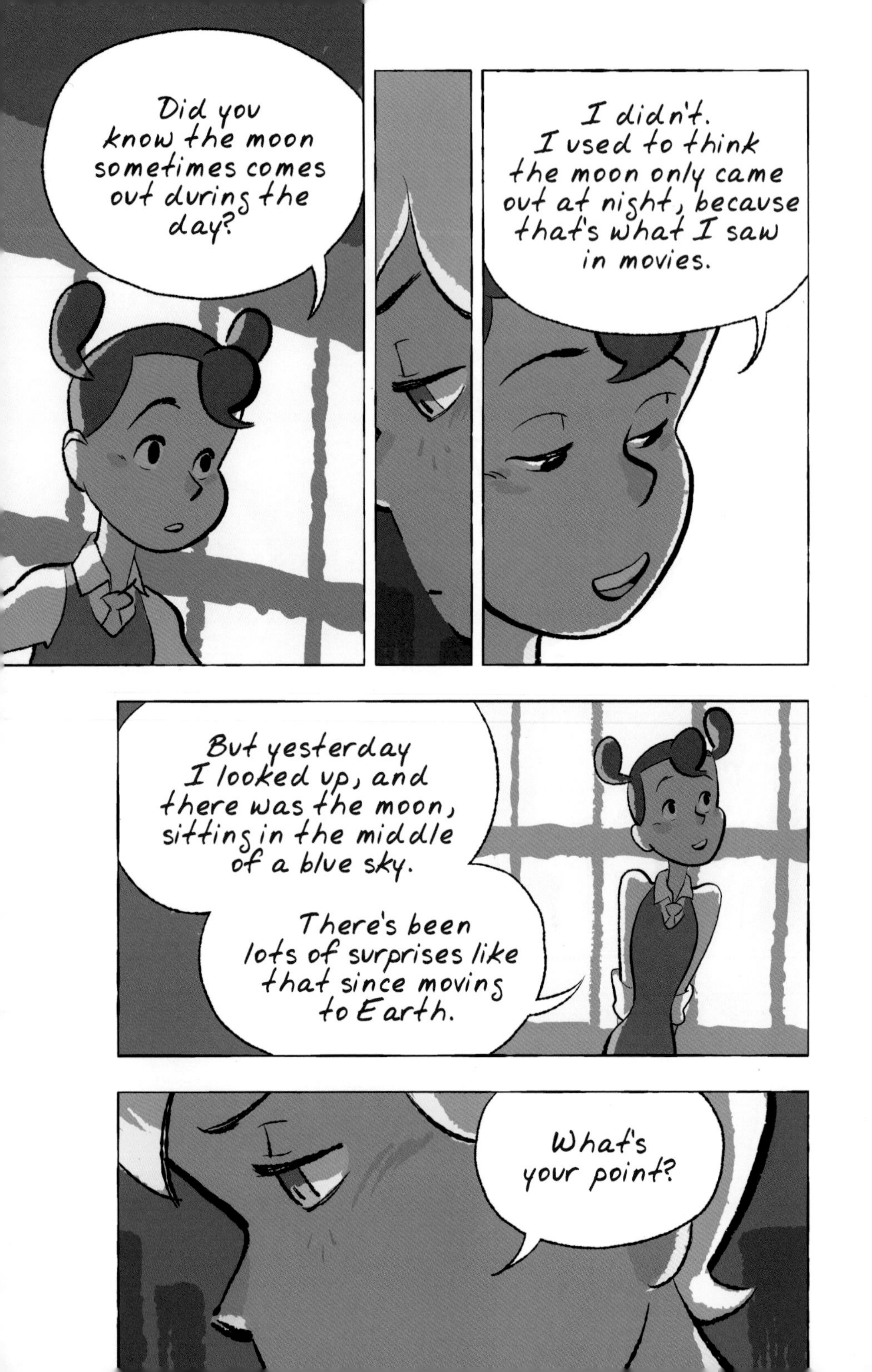
Did you know the moon sometimes comes out during the day?
I didn't. I used to think the moon only came out at night, because that's what I saw in movies.
But yesterday I looked up, and there was the moon, sitting in the middle of a blue sky.
There's been lots of surprises like that since moving to Earth.
What's your point?

My point is, the world is stranger than any story I could ever make up, and more beautiful than any illusion I could ever cast.
Hmmm.
You say that, but how can I believe you? You might be part of the illusion.
Ha!
Come on. I'm just as real as you!

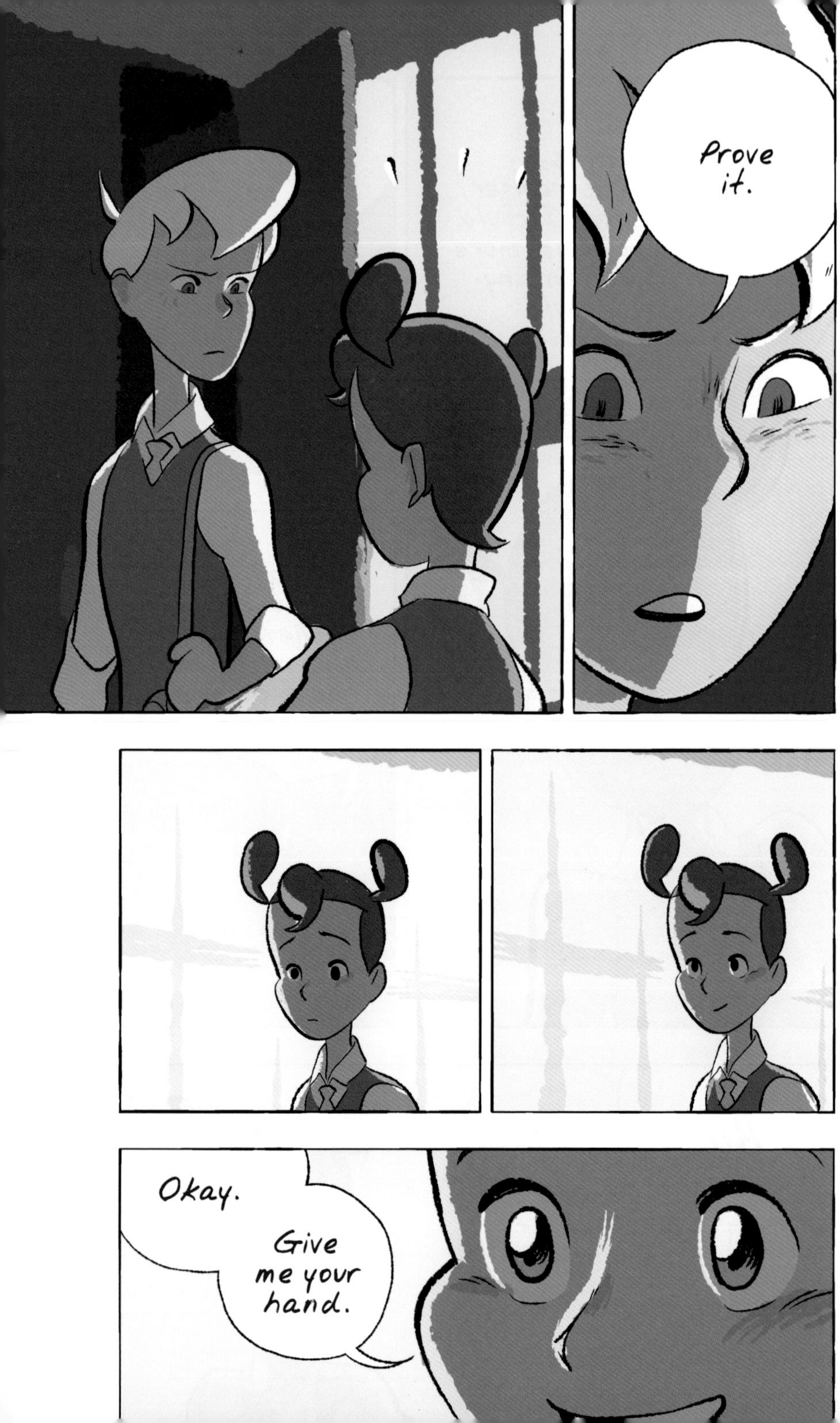
Prove it.
Okay.
Give me your hand.

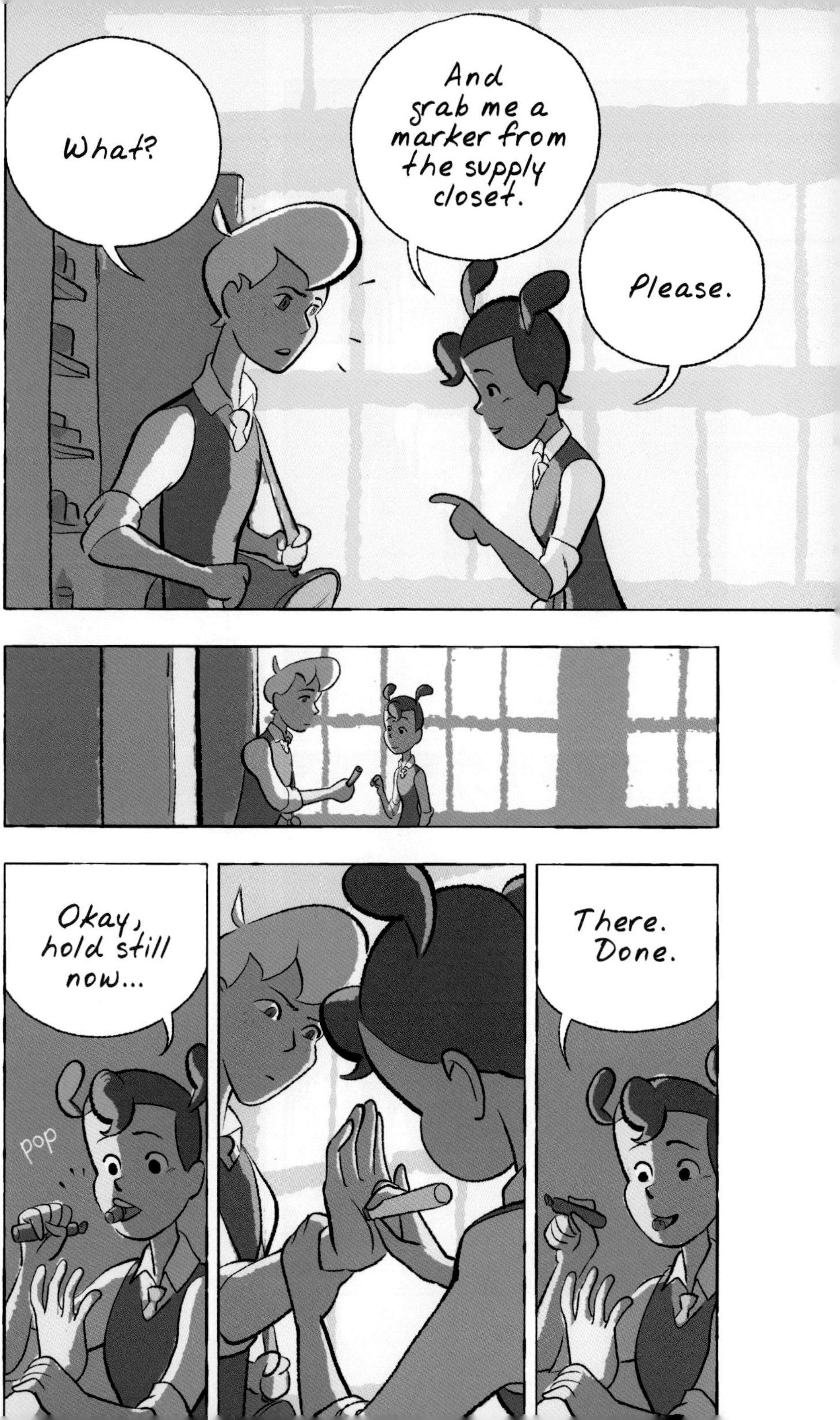
What?
And grab me a marker from the supply closet.
Please.
Okay, hold still now...
pop
There. Done.

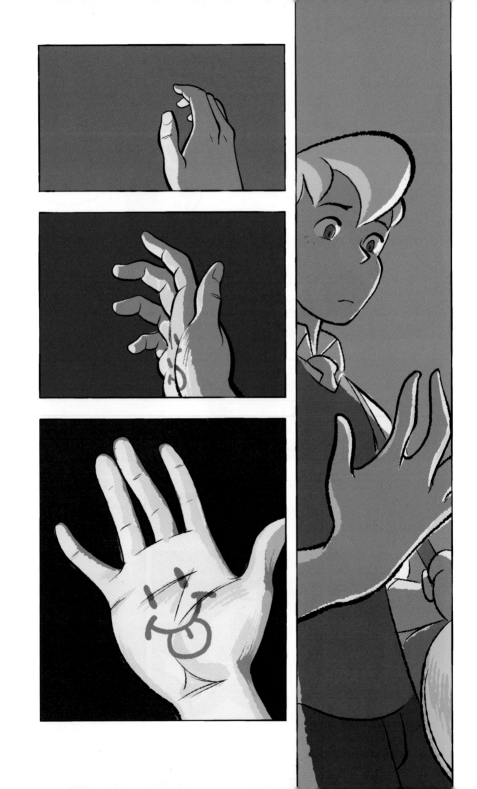

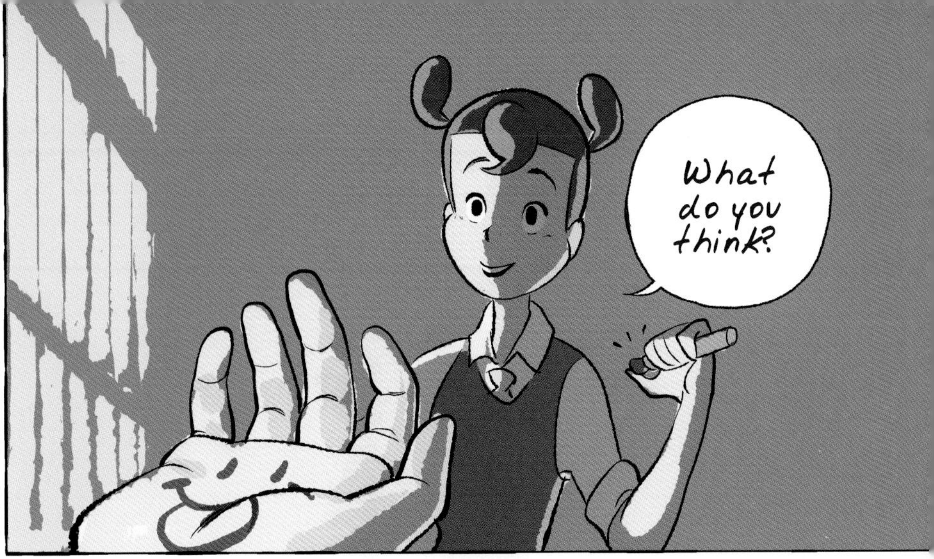
What do you think?

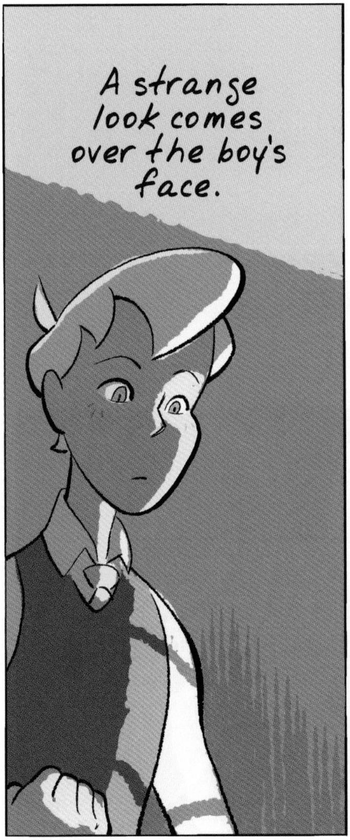
A strange look comes over the boy's face.

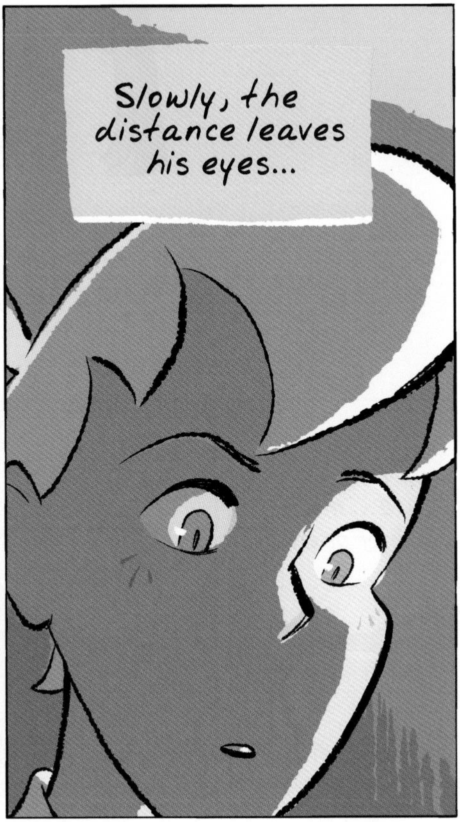
Slowly, the distance leaves his eyes...

And then,
he sees me.

For the very first
time, he sees
me.

Have
we...met
before?

No.
I don't
think we
have.

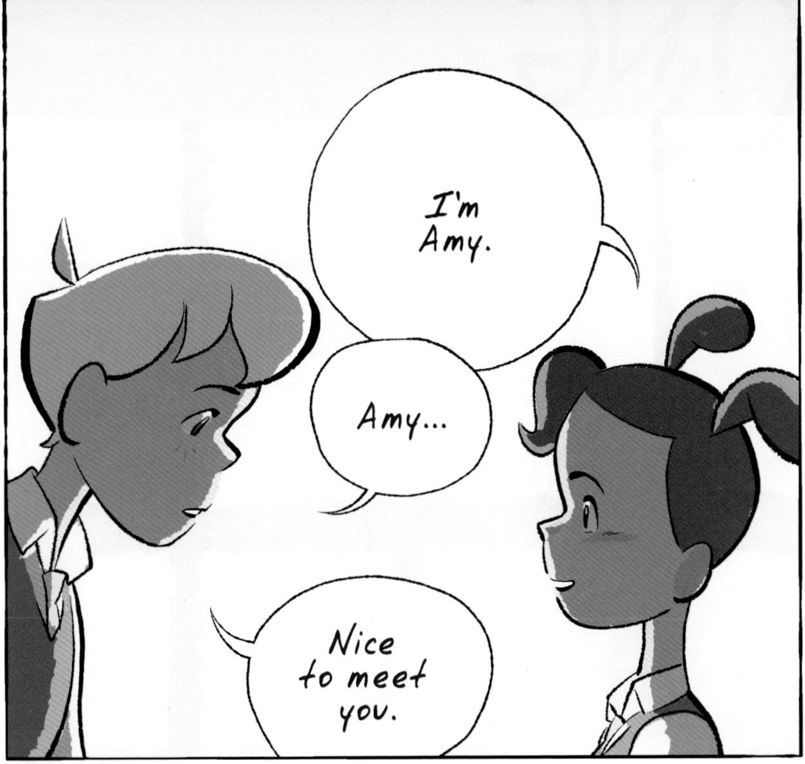
I'm Amy.
Amy...
Nice to meet you.
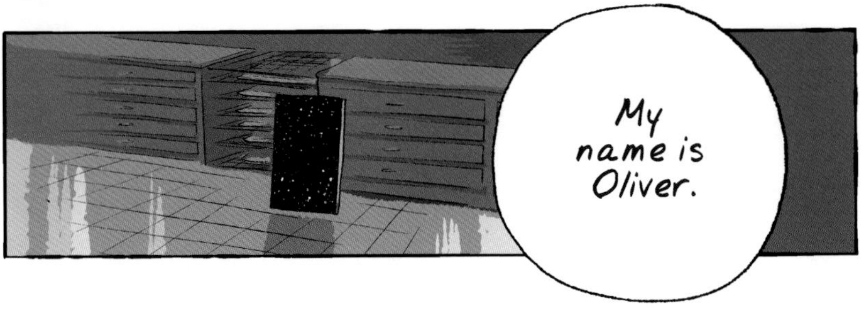
My name is Oliver.

And then the bell rings.

And it's time for school.

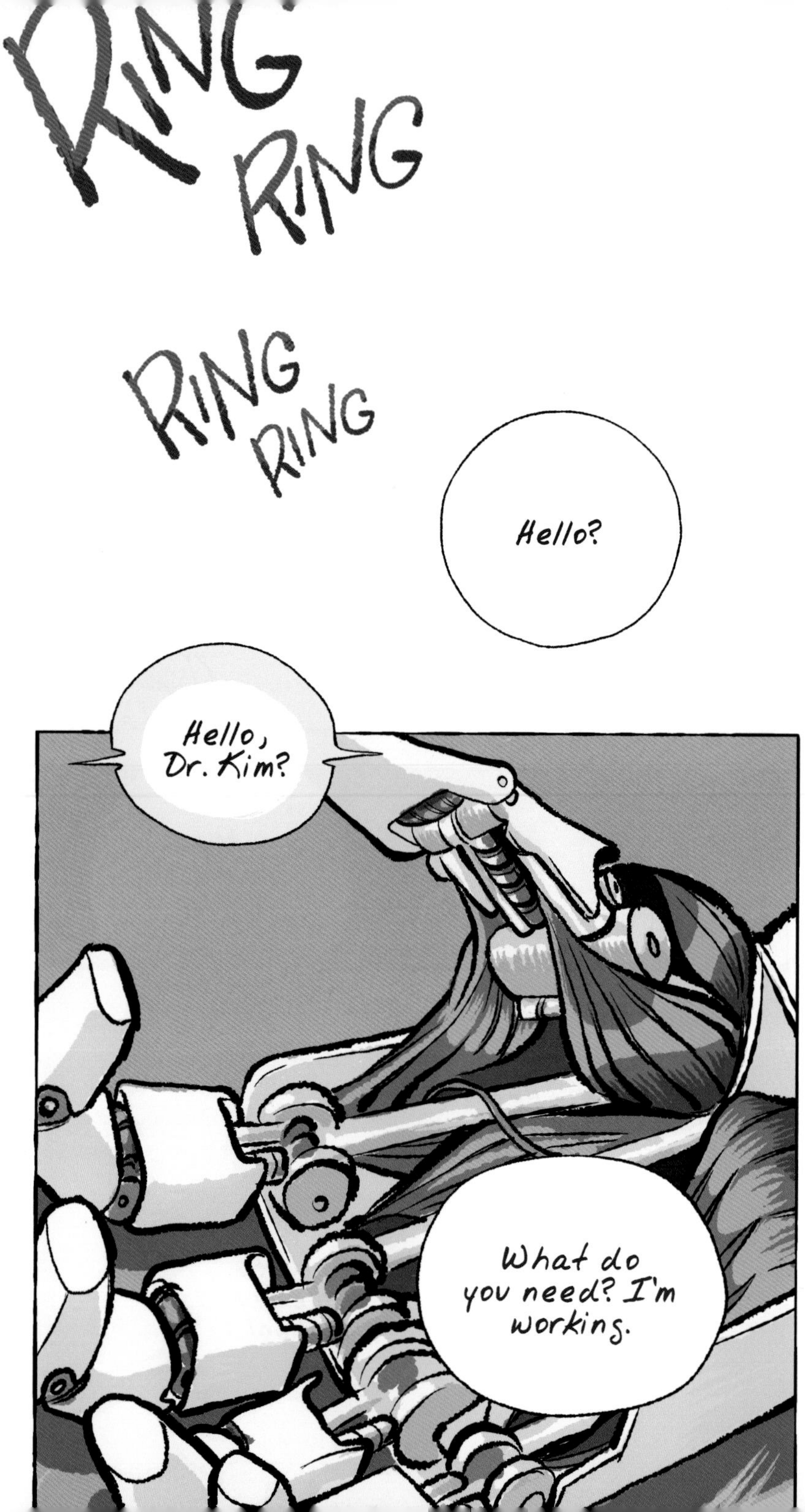
RING RING
RING RING
Hello?
Hello, Dr. Kim?
What do you need? I'm working.

Oliver is exhibiting behavior beyond his normal parameters.
We're concerned.
That's not exactly my department. Why don't you talk to someone on the psychology team?

Given your relationship with Oliver, we believe your opinion will be more helpful.

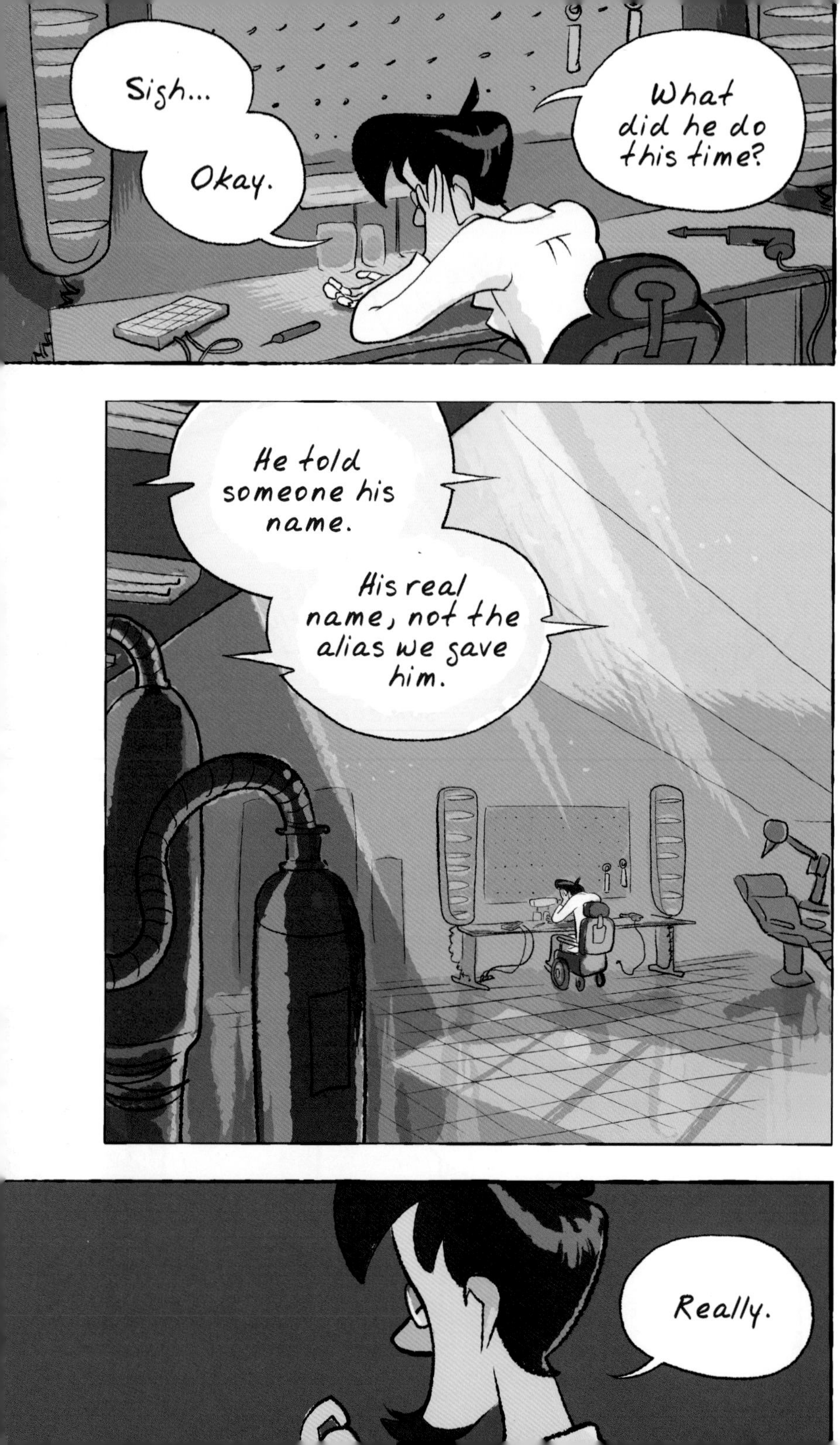
Sigh...
Okay.
What did he do this time?
He told someone his name.
His real name, not the alias we gave him.
Really.

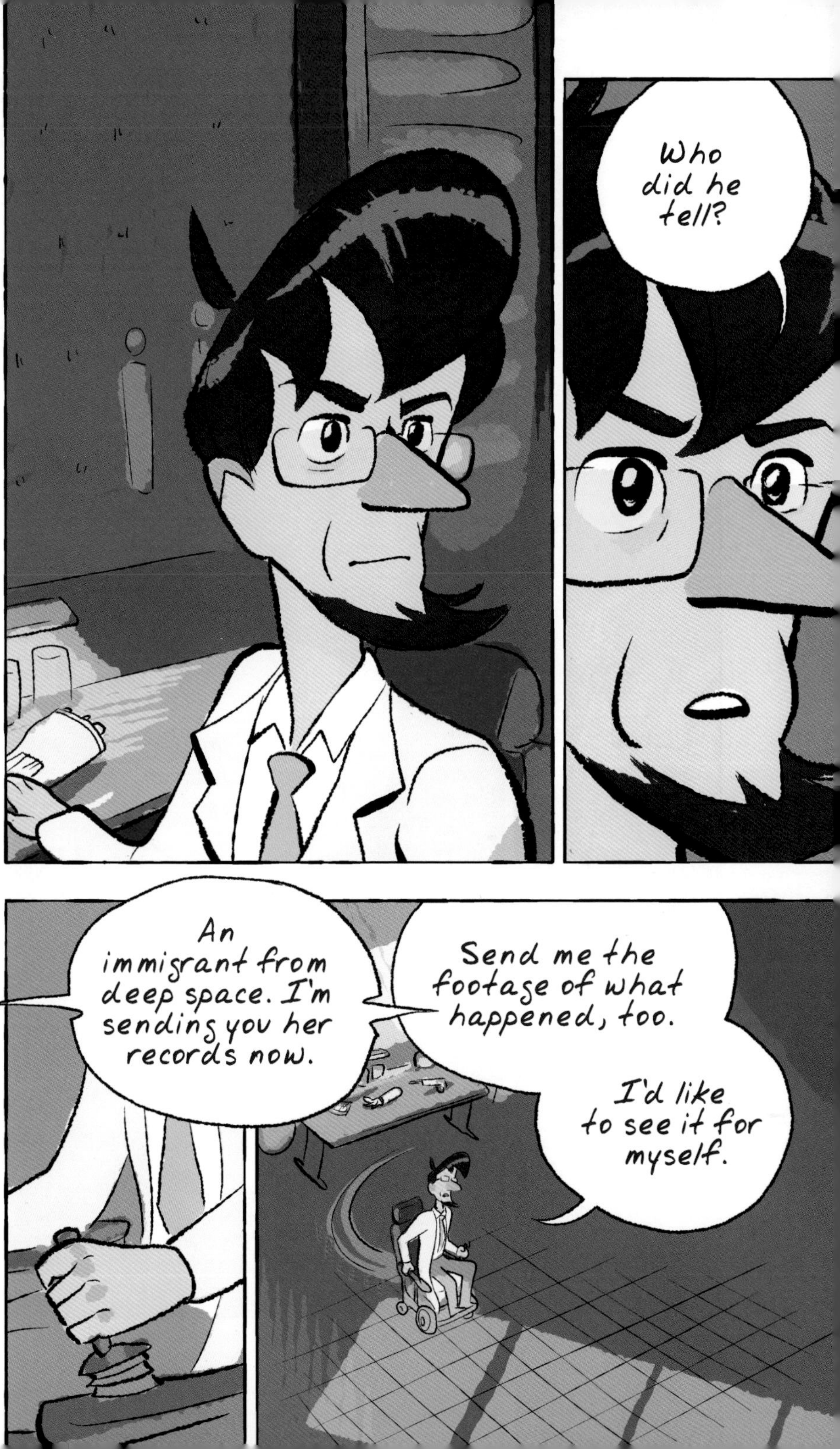
Who did he tell?
An immigrant from deep space. I'm sending you her records now.
Send me the footage of what happened, too.
I'd like to see it for myself.

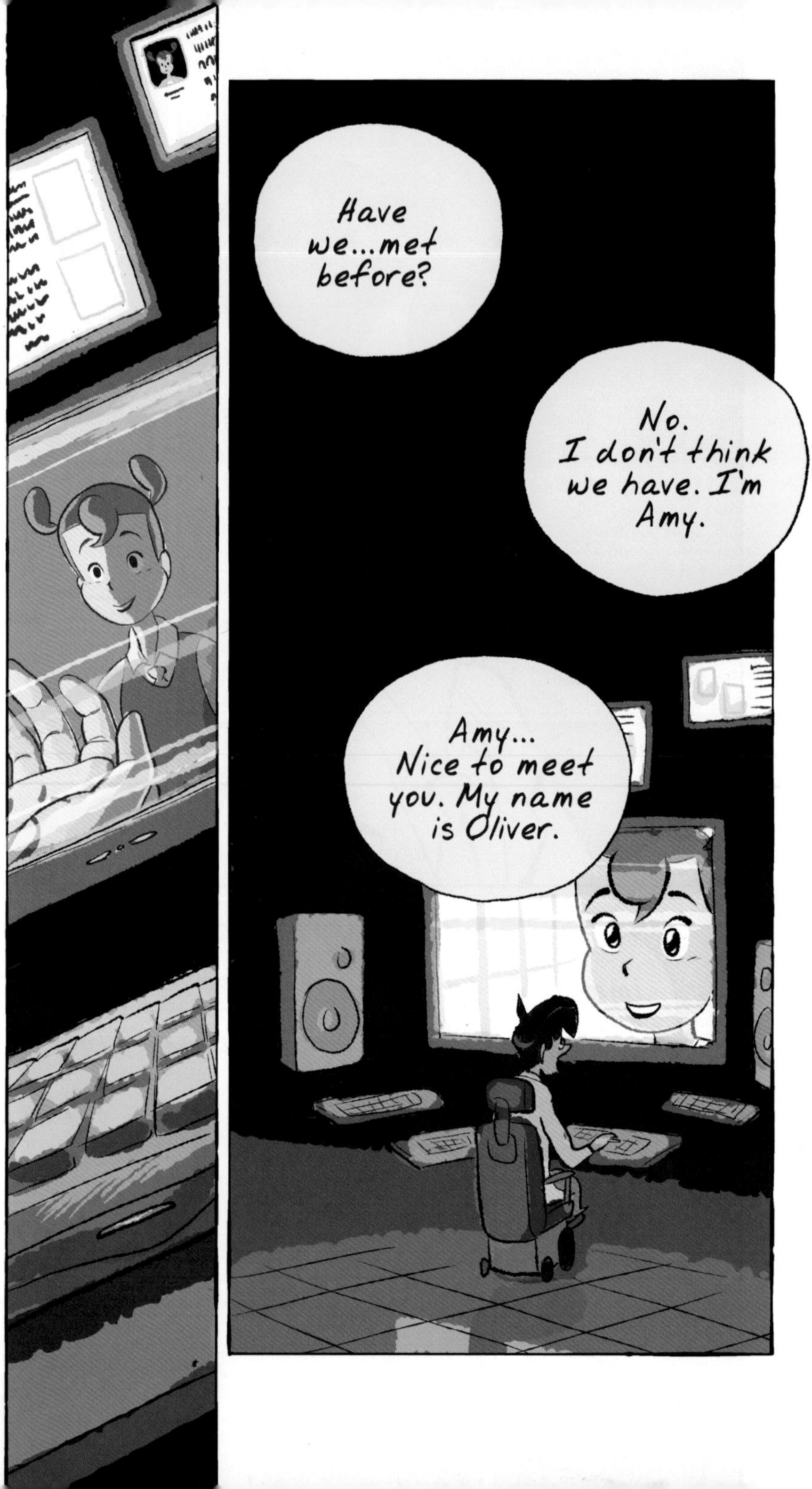
Have we...met before?
No. I don't think we have. I'm Amy.
Amy... Nice to meet you. My name is Oliver.

Wow...
What do you think? We're concerned he's going to continue leaking classified information to this girl.
Classified information?
What-- you mean his own name?
It could compromise the mission. We're considering relocating you and Oliver again.
!

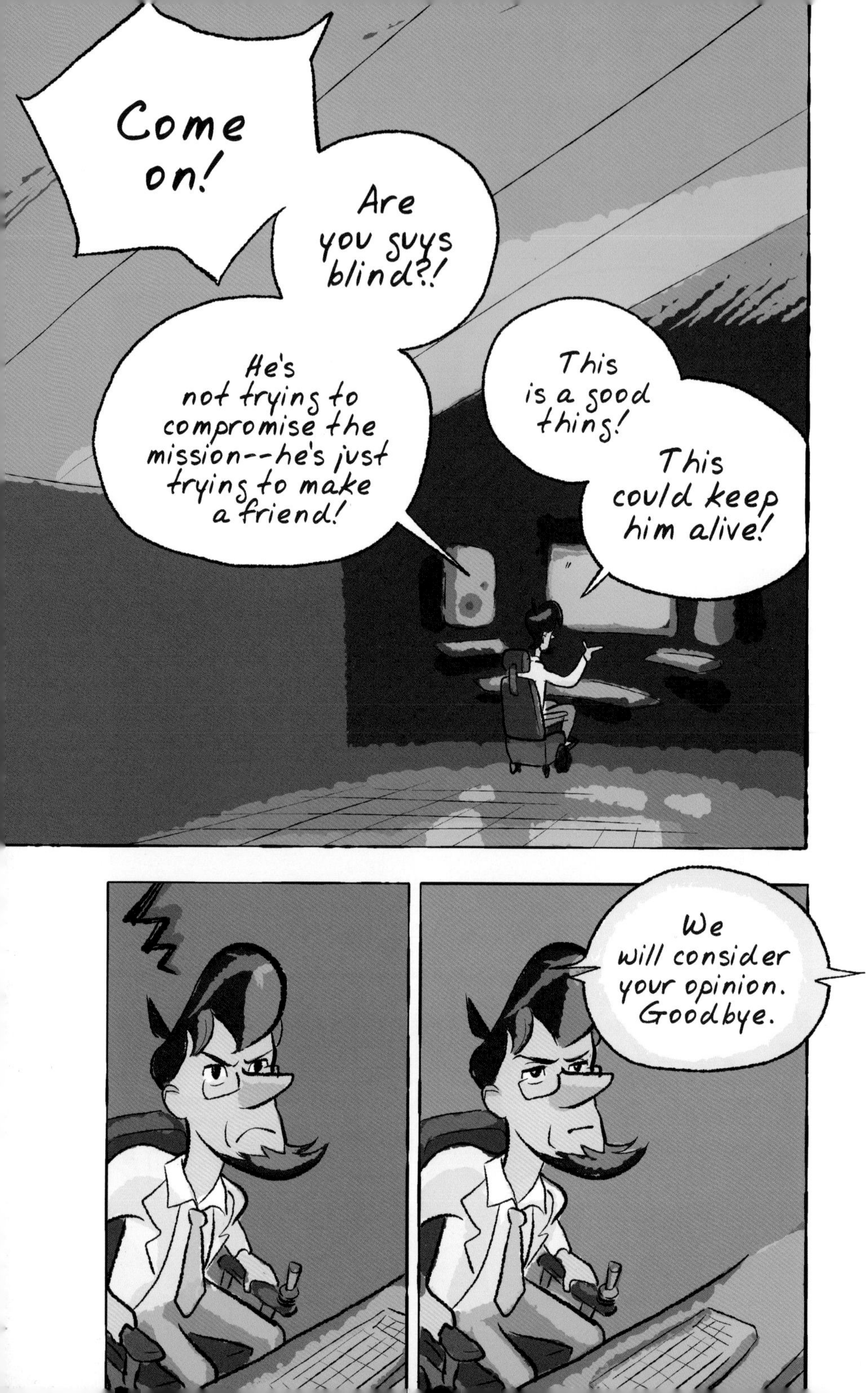
Come on!
Are you guys blind?!
He's not trying to compromise the mission--he's just trying to make a friend!
This is a good thing!
This could keep him alive!
We will consider your opinion. Goodbye.

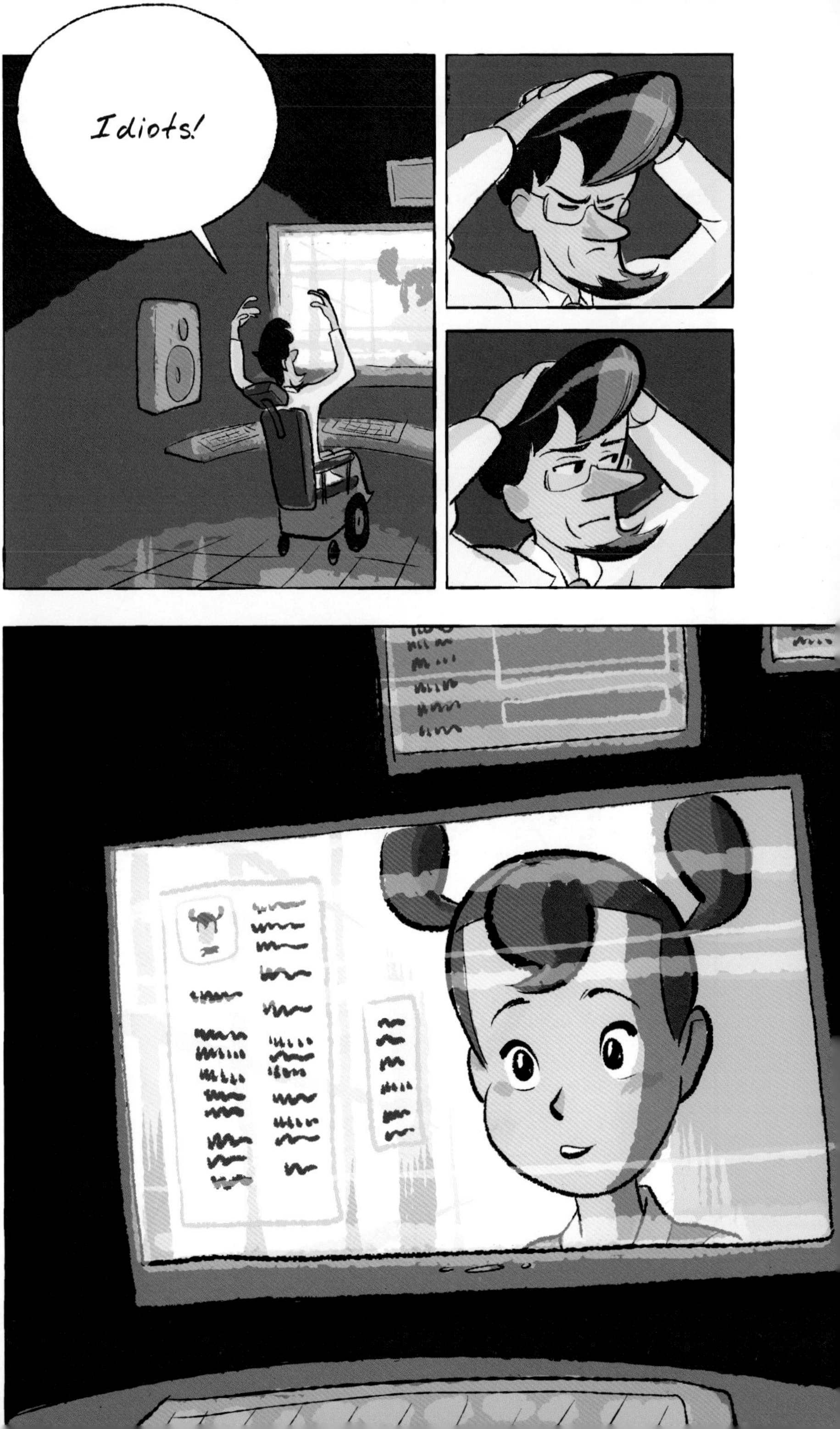
Idiots!

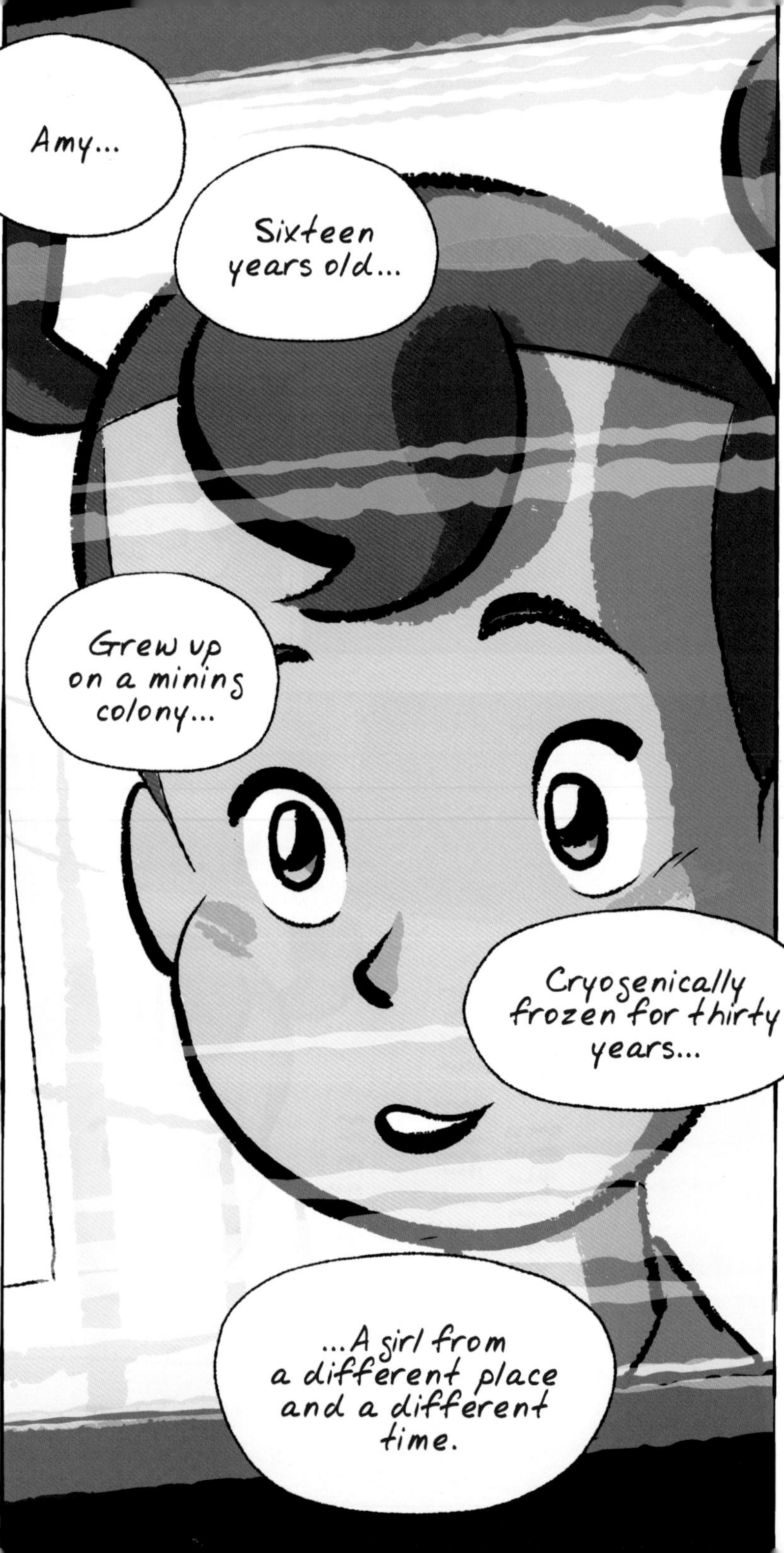
Amy...
Sixteen years old...
Grew up on a minins colony...
Cryogenically frozen for thirty years...
...A girl from a different place and a different time.

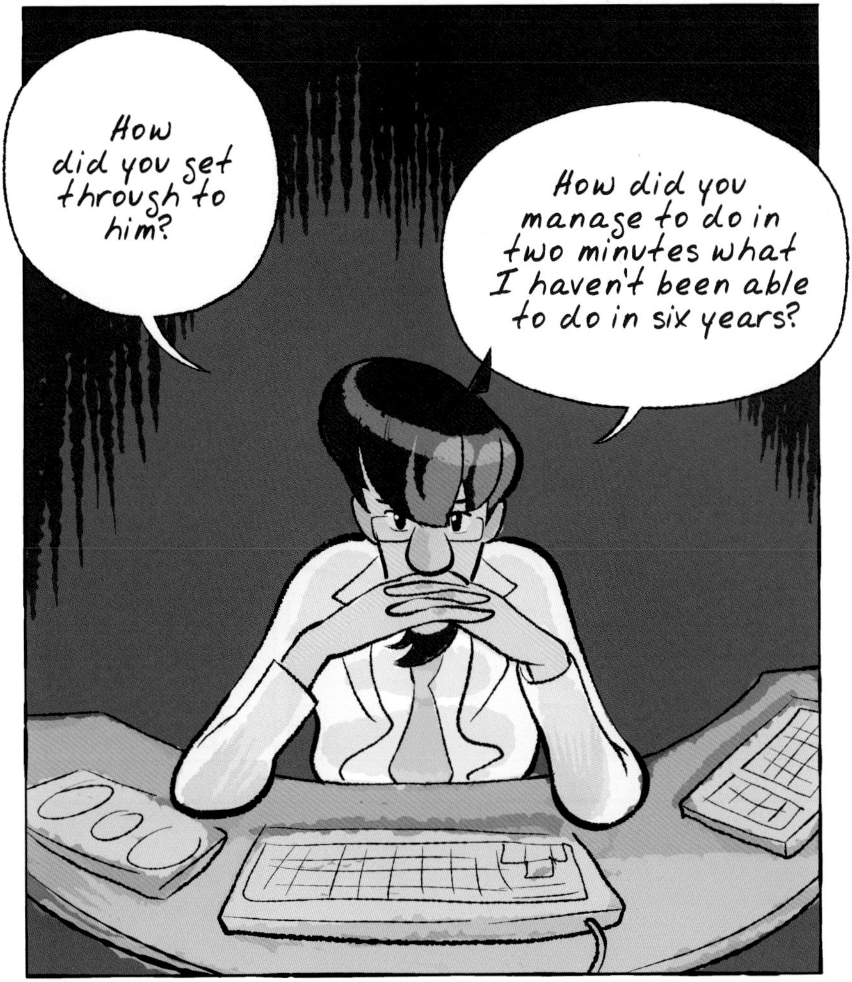
How did you get through to him?
How did you manage to do in two minutes what I haven't been able to do in six years?

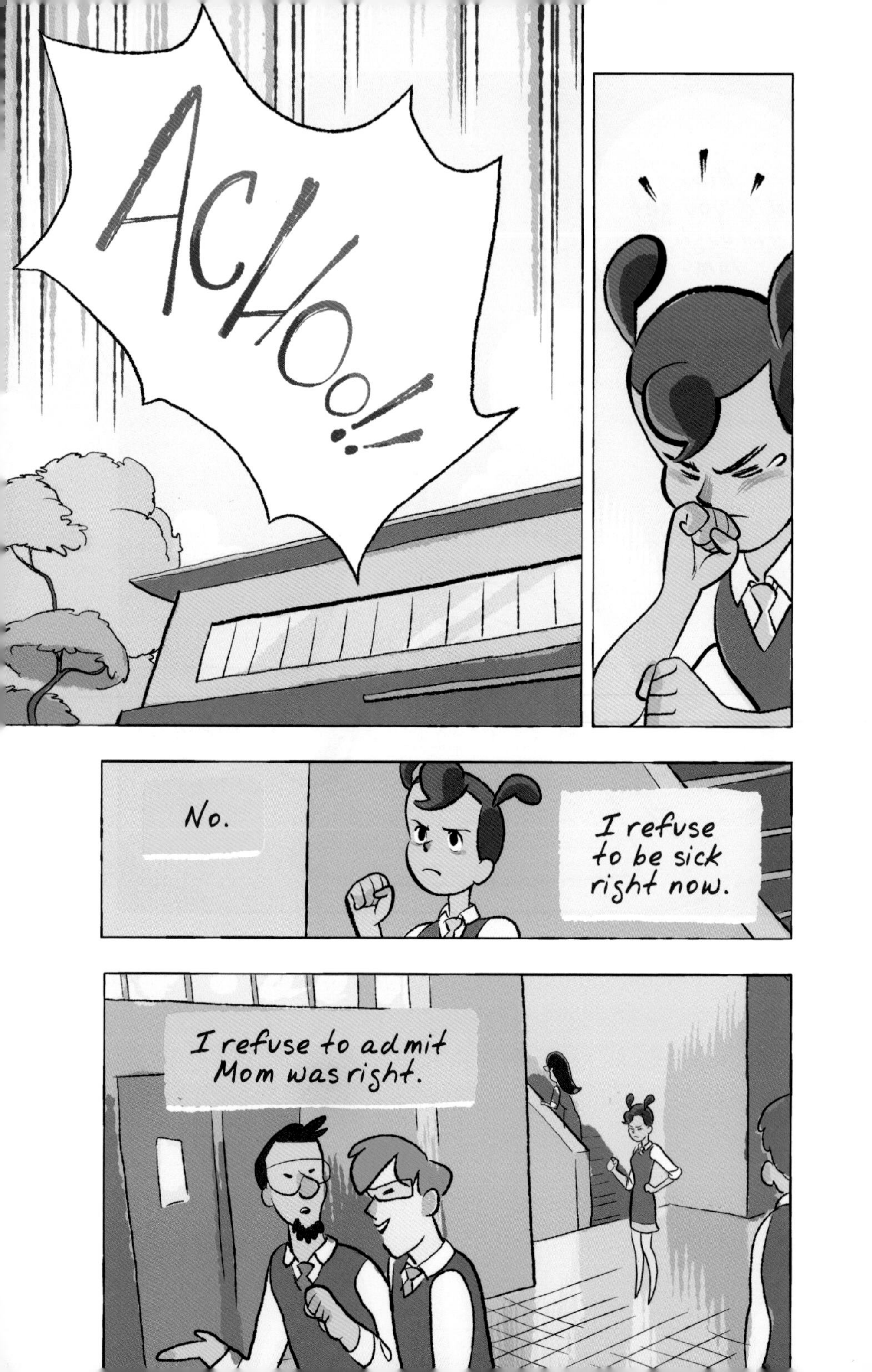
ACHOO!!!
No.
I refuse to be sick right now.
I refuse to admit Mom was right.

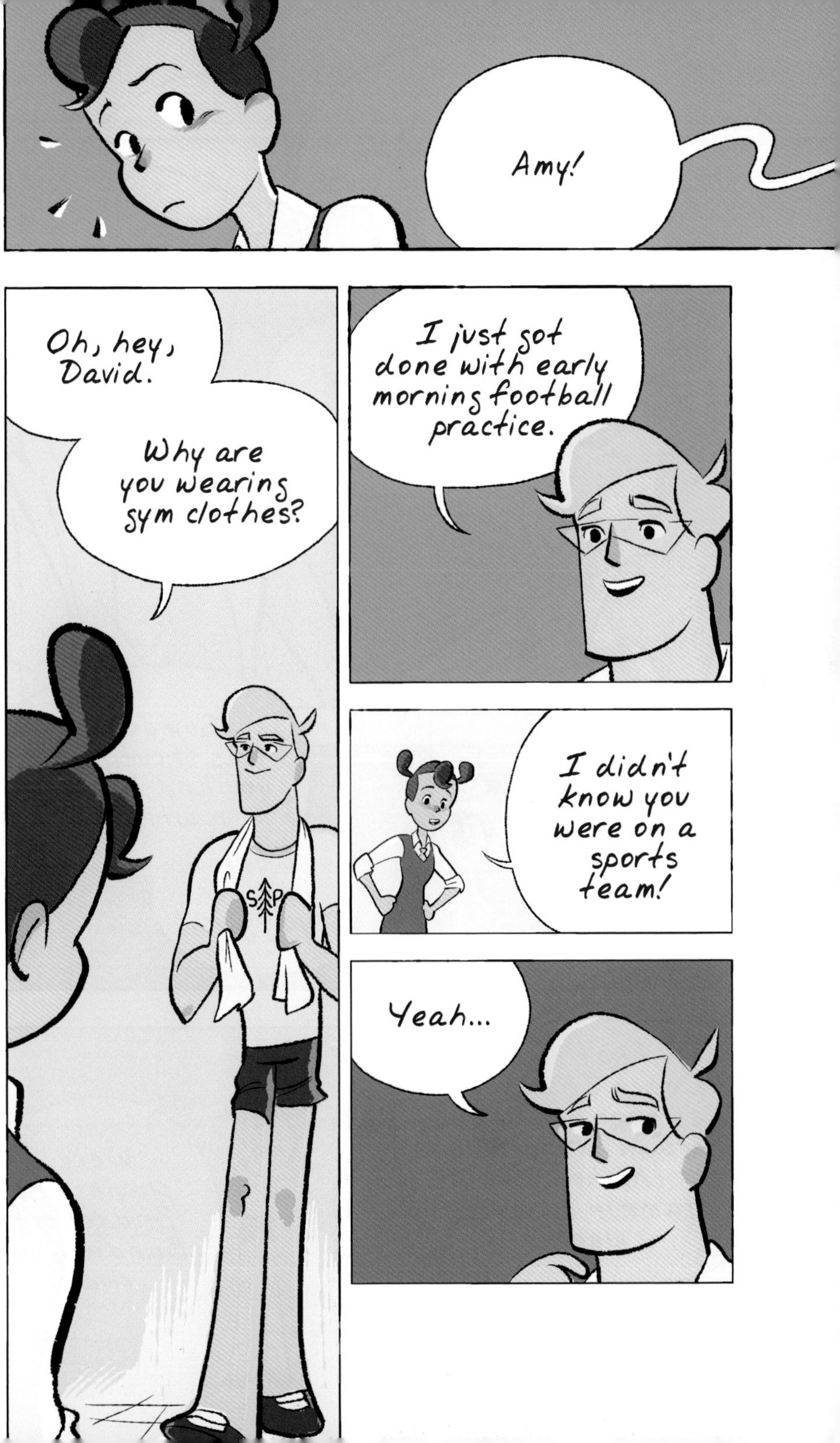
Amy!
Oh, hey, David.
Why are you wearing gym clothes?
I just got done with early morning football practice.
I didn't know you were on a sports team!
Yeah...

Wait, I think I might have heard you guys jogging around the track this morning.
Yep. We were doing sprints.
Someone was shouting at you and blowing a whistle.
I felt bad for you guys.
That was Coach Chamblin. He's been working us hard in preparation for the homecoming game in a couple weeks.
We're playing the Bridgeport Bandits, our rivals.

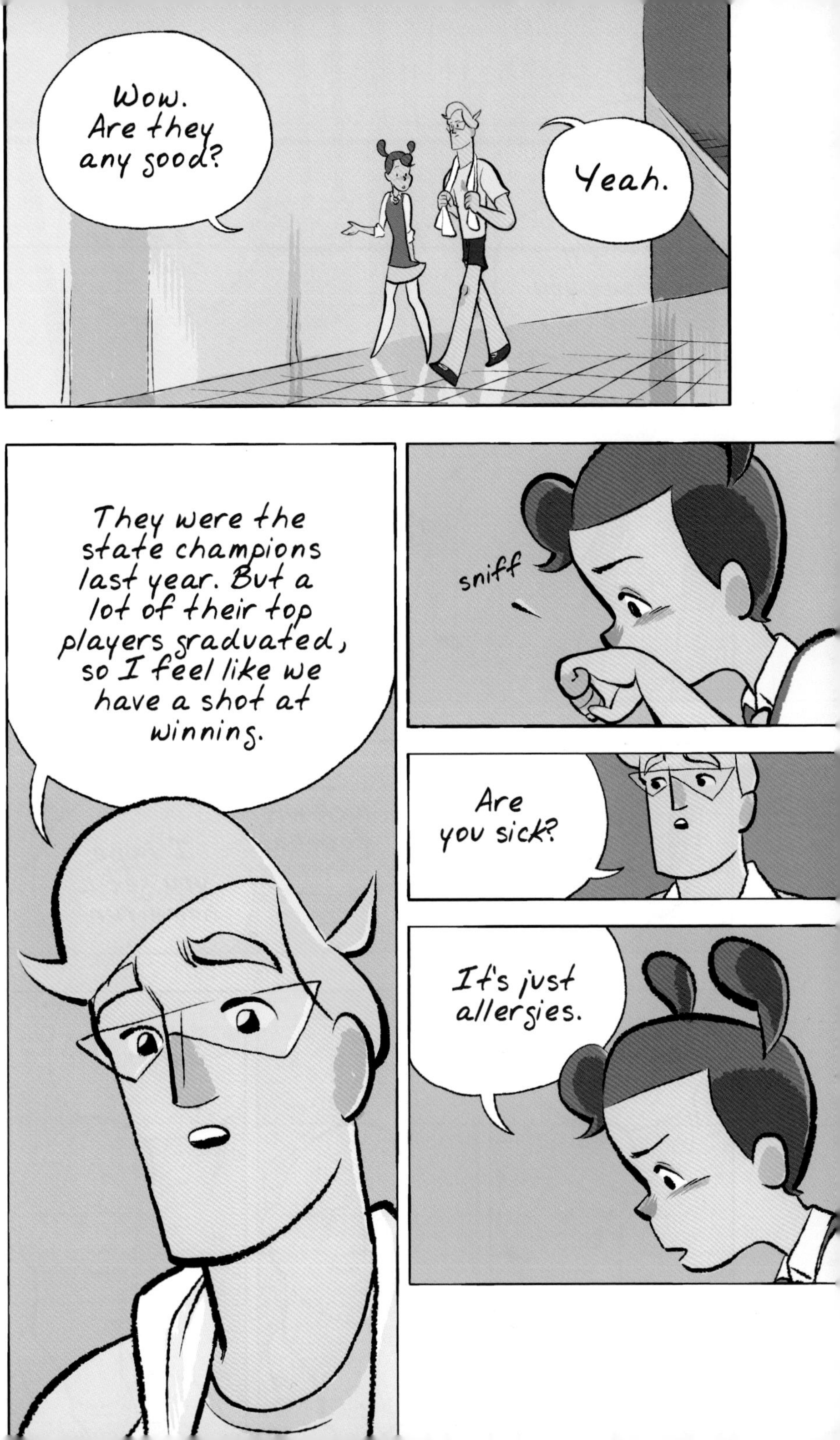
Wow.
Are they
any good?
Yeah.
They were the state champions last year. But a lot of their top players graduated, so I feel like we have a shot at winning.
sniff
Are you sick?
It's just allergies.

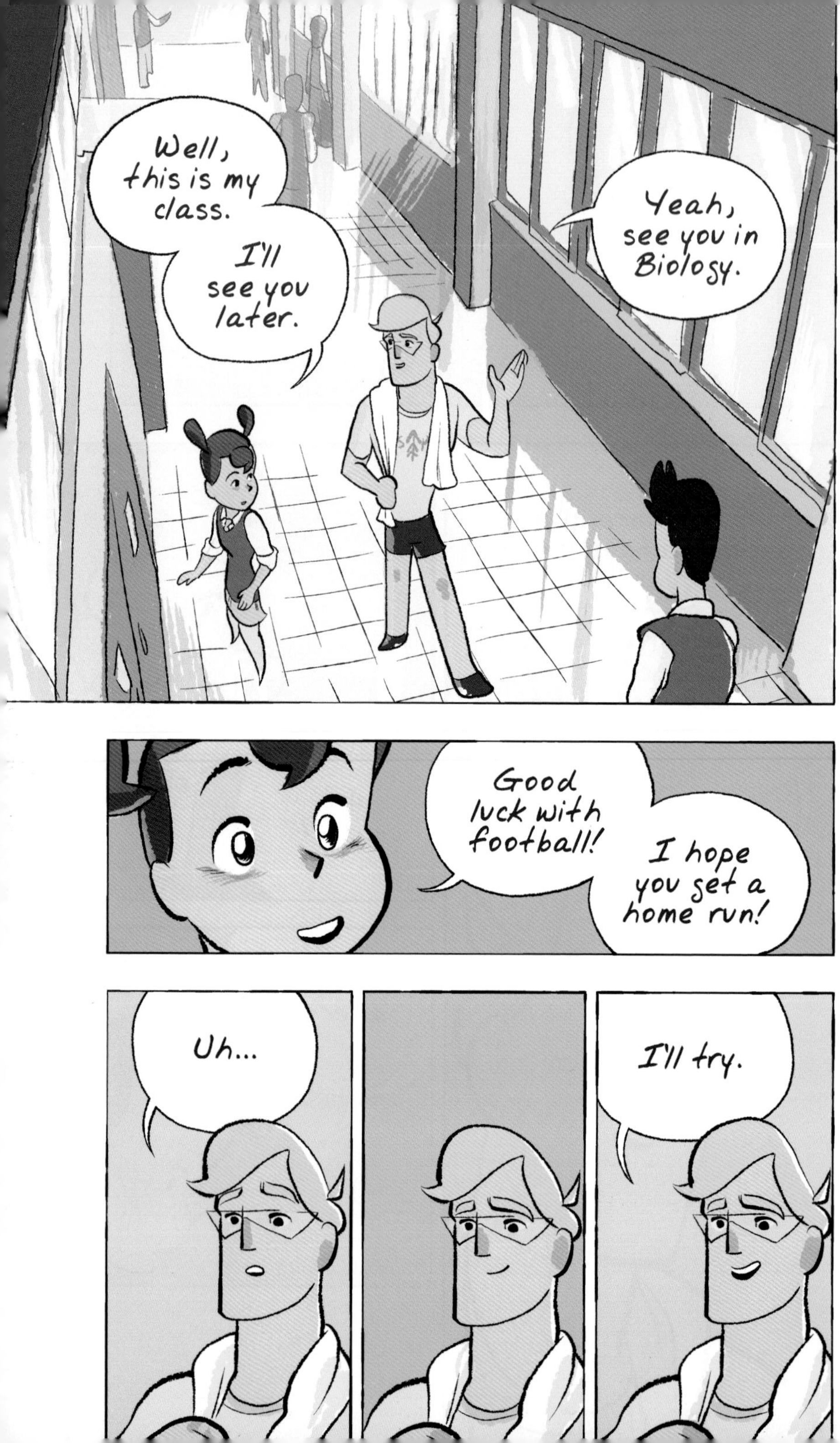
Well, this is my class.
I'll see you later.
Yeah, see you in Biology.
Good luck with football!
I hope you get a home run!
Uh...
I'll try.

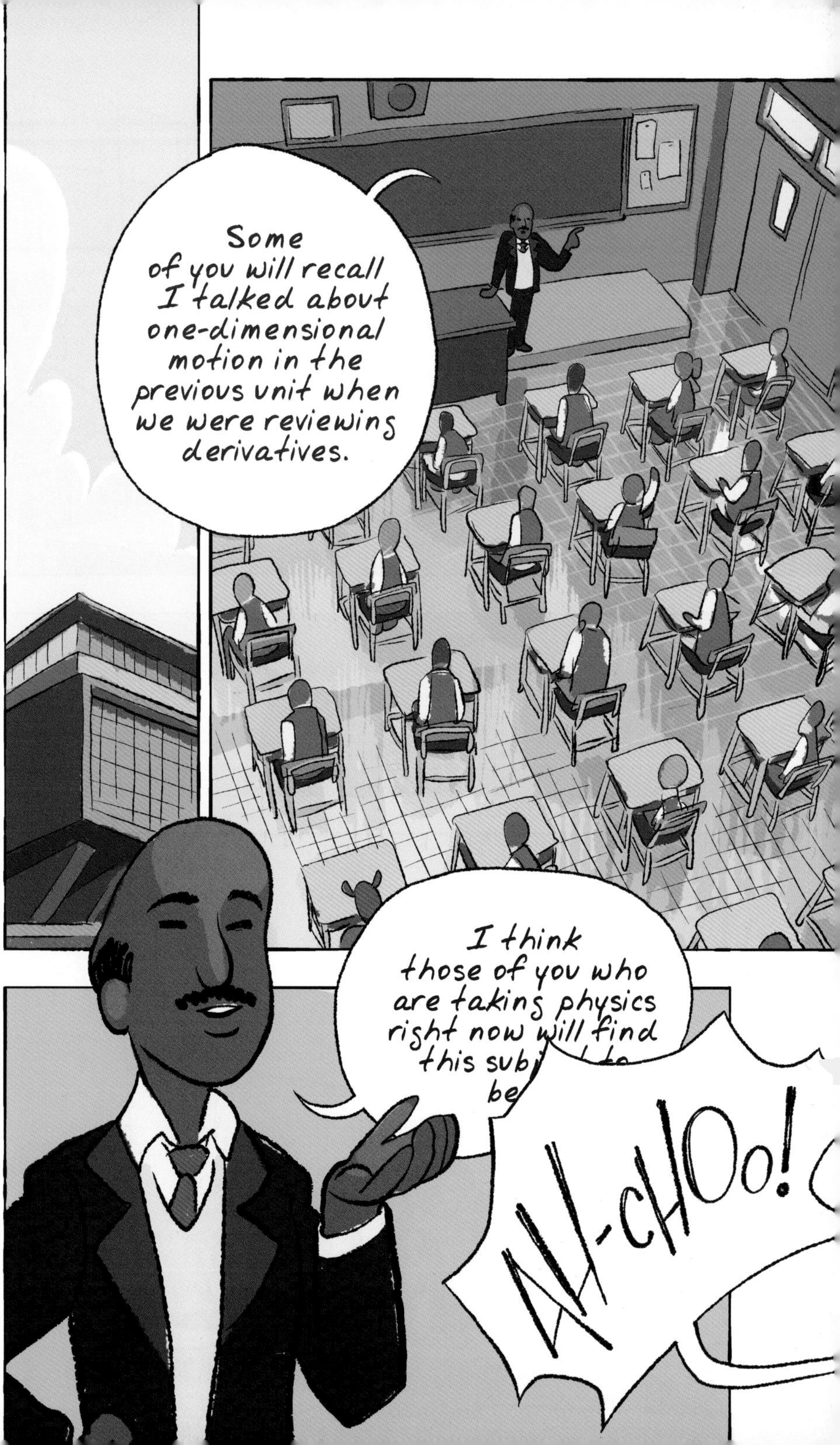
Some of you will recall I talked about one-dimensional motion in the previous unit when we were reviewing derivatives.
I think those of you who are taking physics right now will find this sub
AH-CHOo!

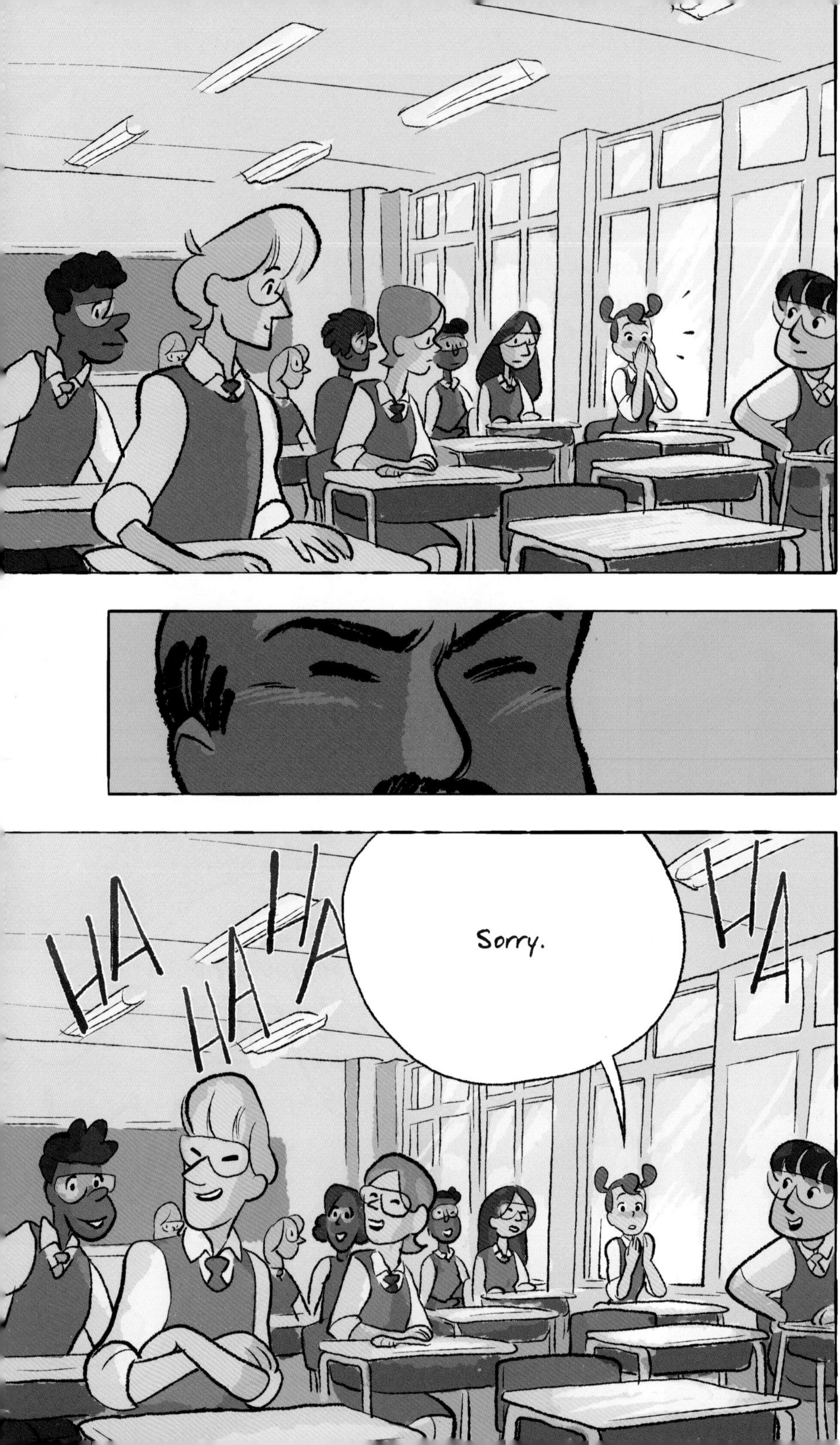
HA
HA
HA
HA
Sorry.
HA
HA

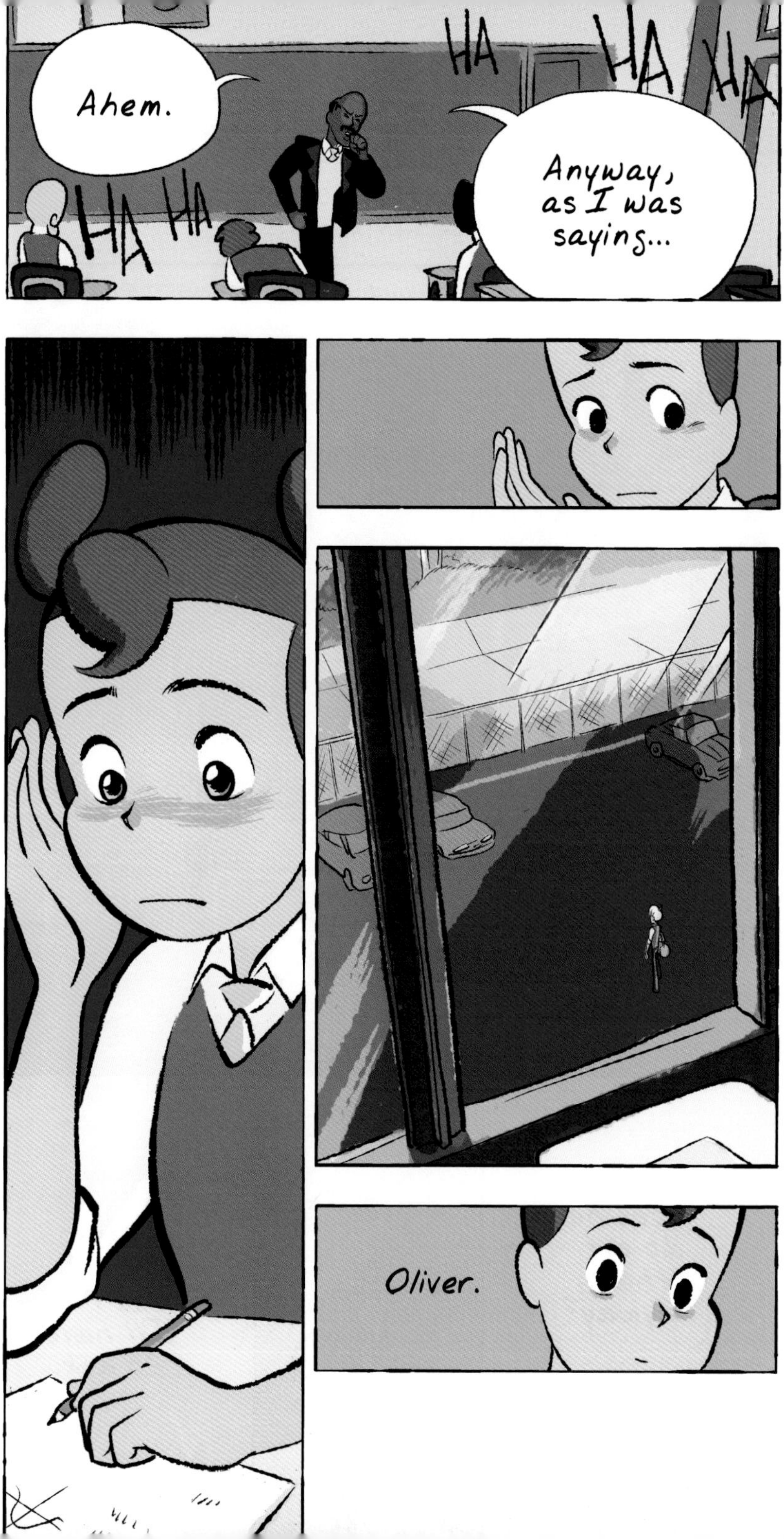
HA
HA
HA
Ahem.
HA
HA
Anyway, as I was saying...
Oliver.

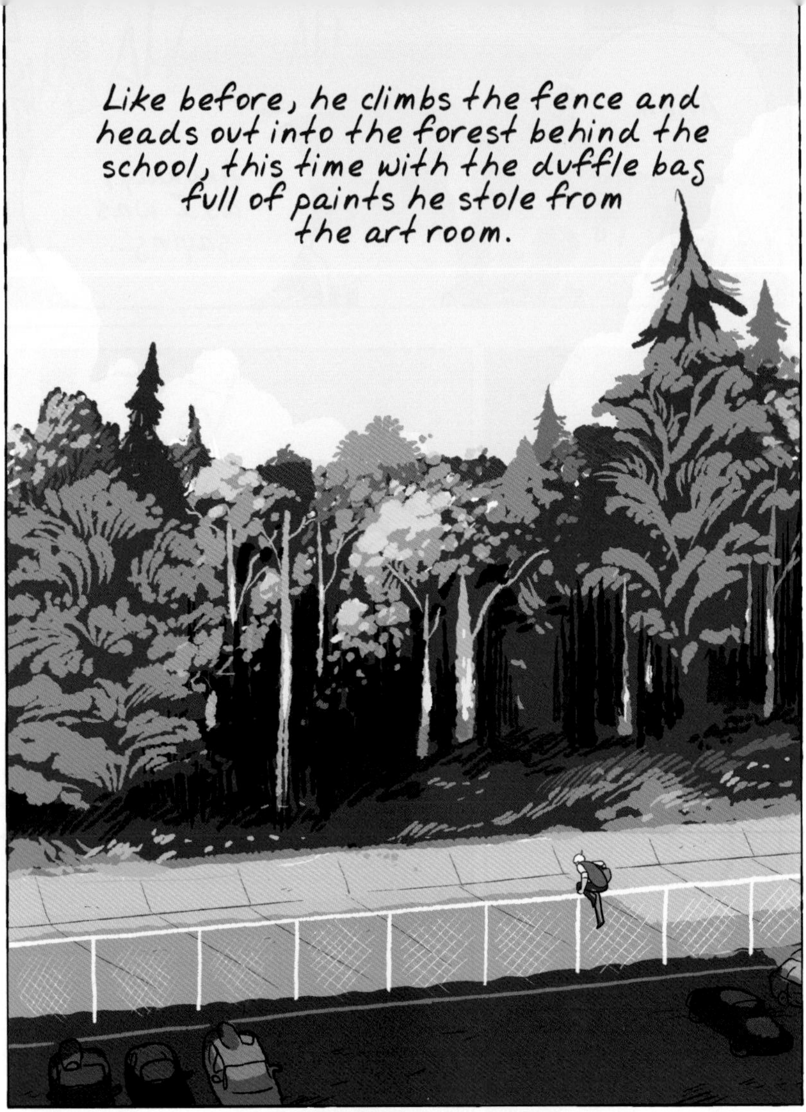
Like before, he climbs the fence and heads out into the forest behind the school, this time with the duffle bag full of paints he stole from the art room.

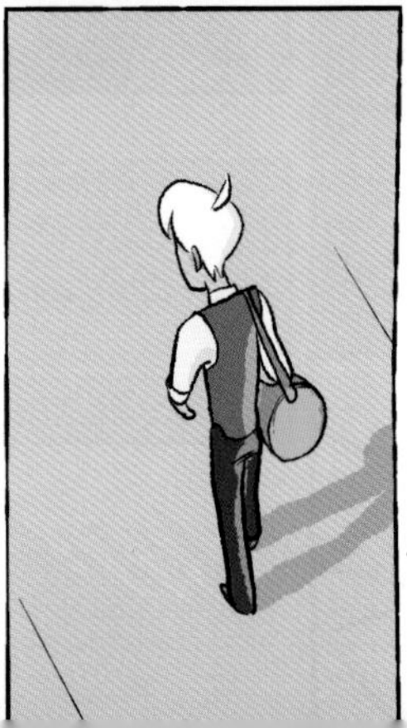
What does he do out there, anyway?
Next time I see him I'll have to ask.

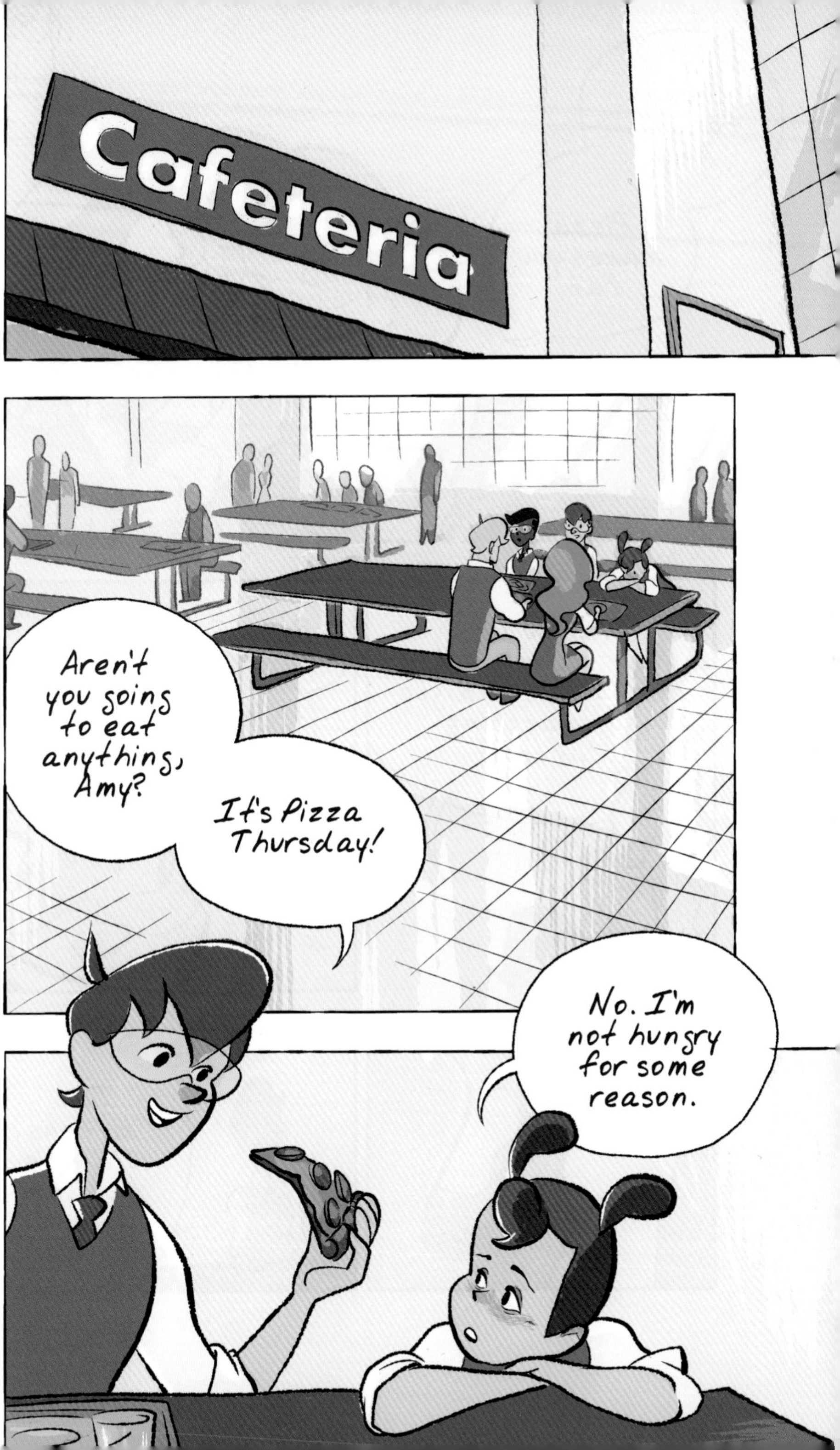
Cafeteria
Aren't you going to eat anything, Amy?
It's Pizza Thursday!
No. I'm not hungry for some reason.

Good for you, Amy.
Pizza makes you fat.
Did you guys hear Haley Becker and Zola Okadigbo got matching tattoos?
Really?
What'd they get?
Two kittens riding a tandem bike.

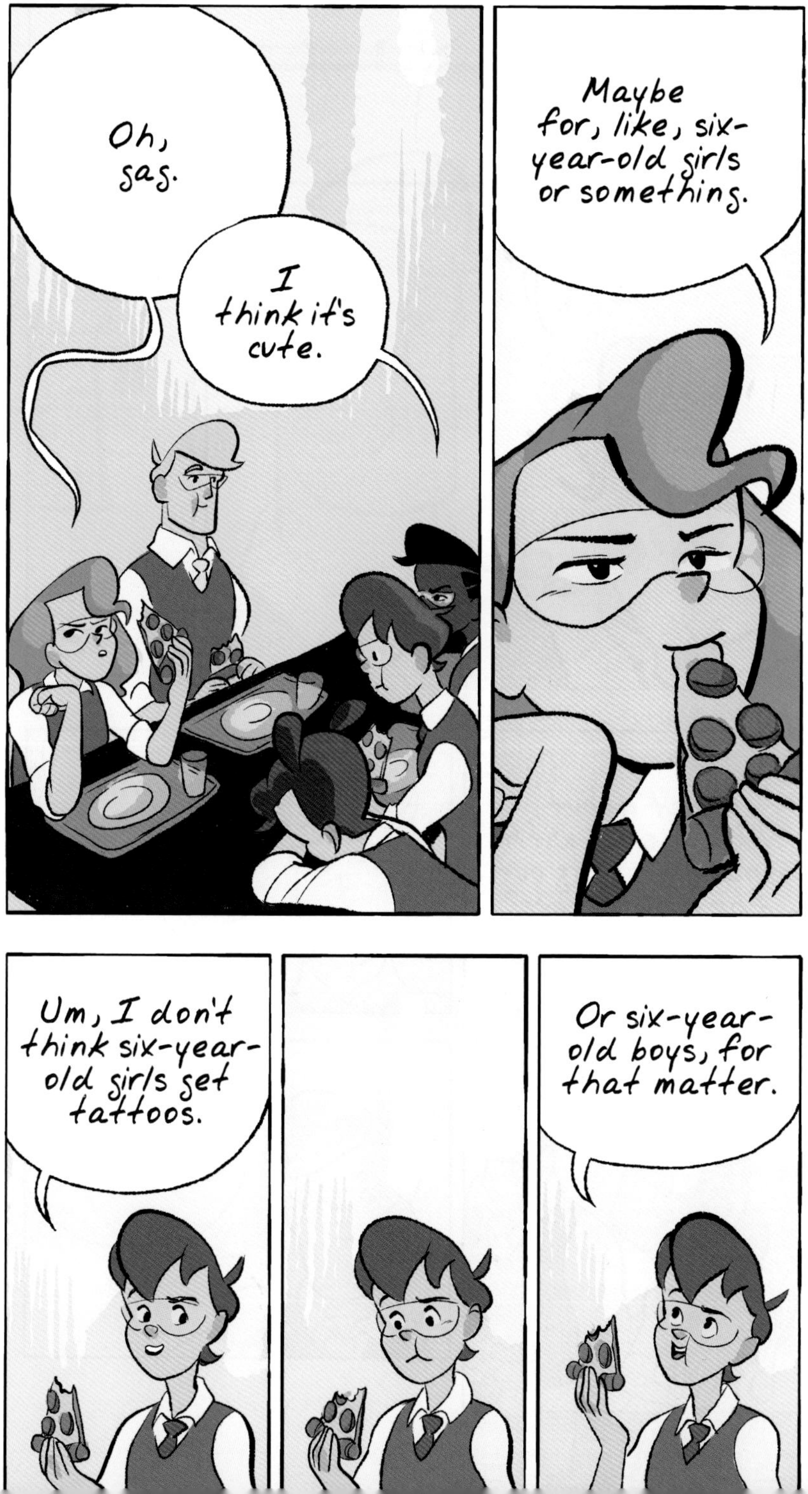
Oh, gag.
I think it's cute.
Maybe for, like, six-year-old girls or something.
Um, I don't think six-year-old girls get tattoos.
Or six-year-old boys, for that matter.

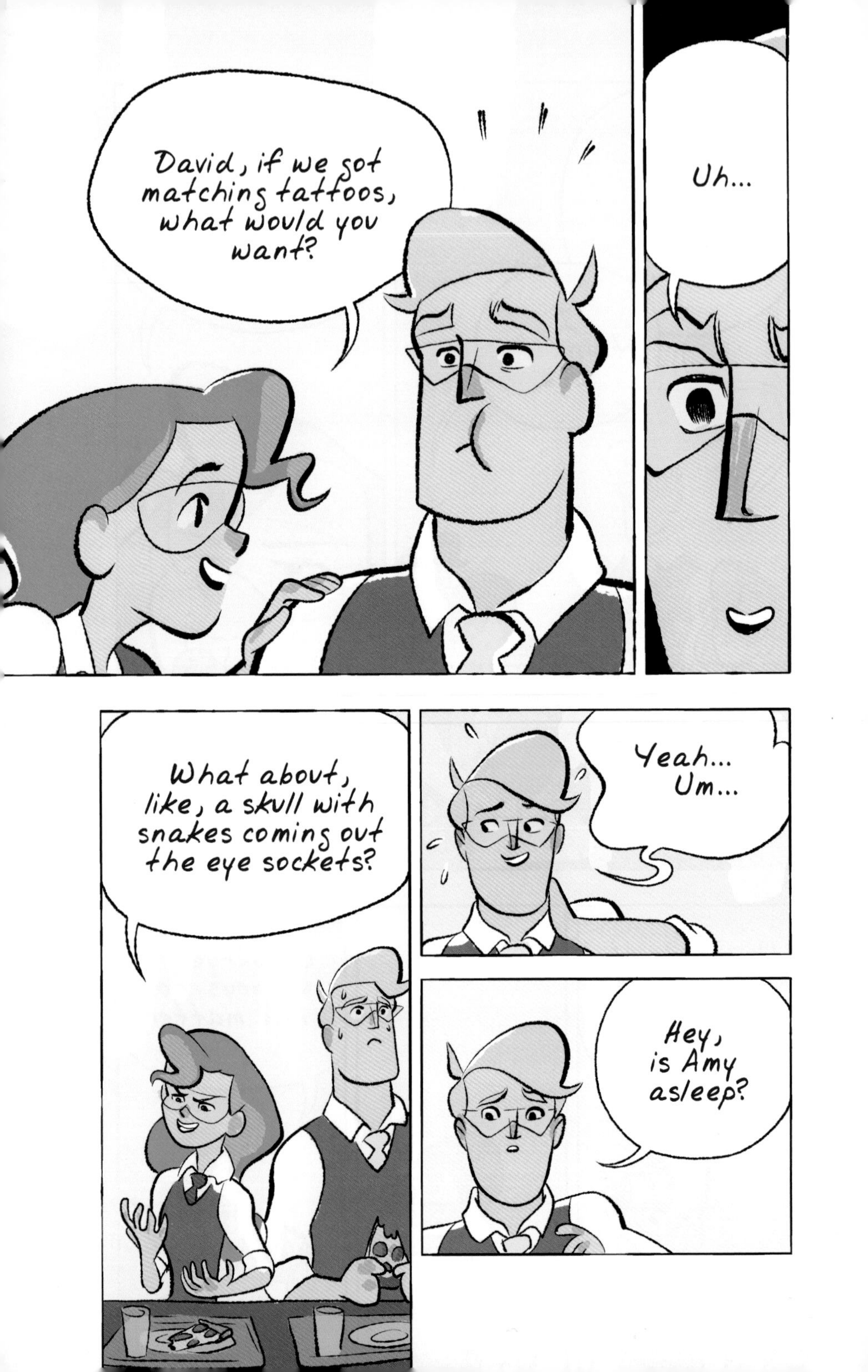
David, if we got matching tattoos, what would you want?
Uh...
What about, like, a skull with snakes coming out the eye sockets?
Yeah... Um...
Hey, is Amy asleep?

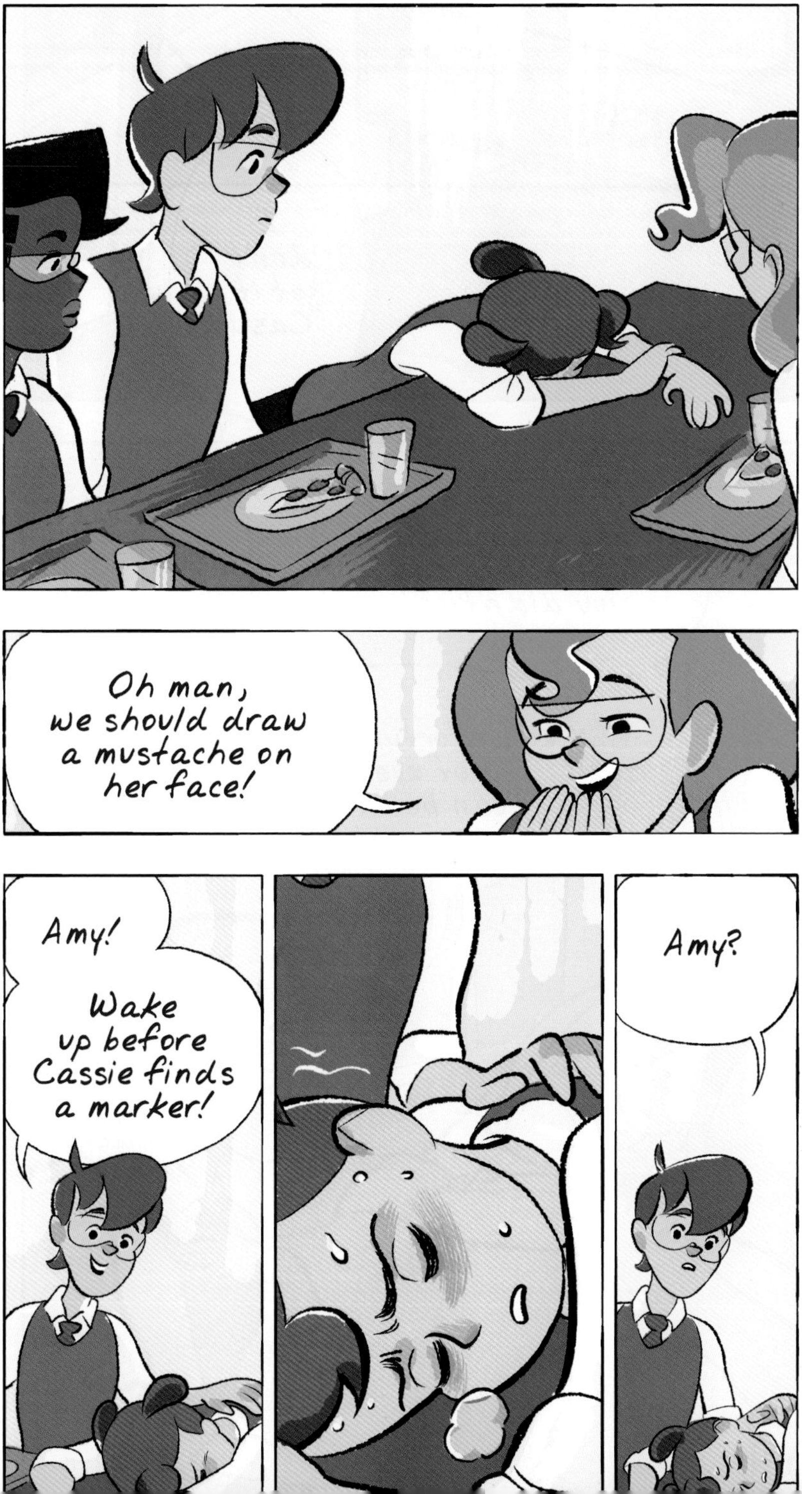
Oh man, we should draw a mustache on her face!
Amy!
Wake up before Cassie finds a marker!
Amy?

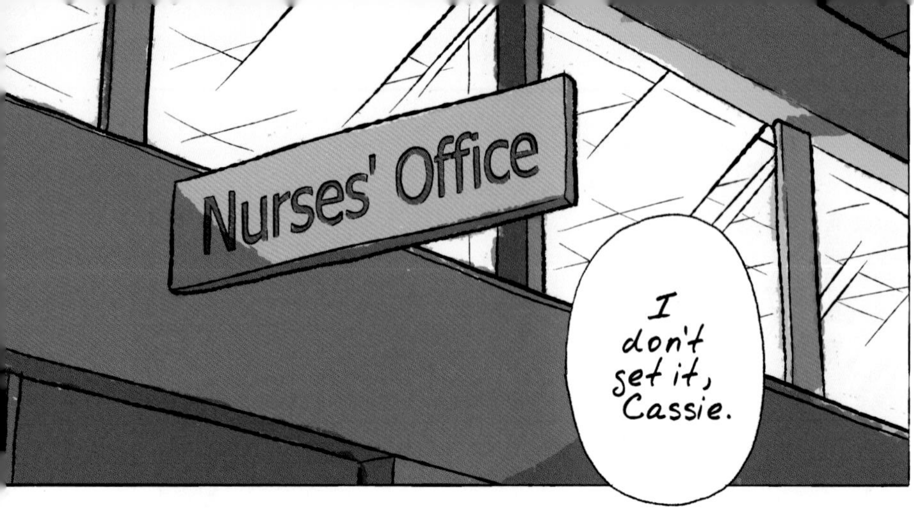
Nurses' Office
I don't get it, Cassie.

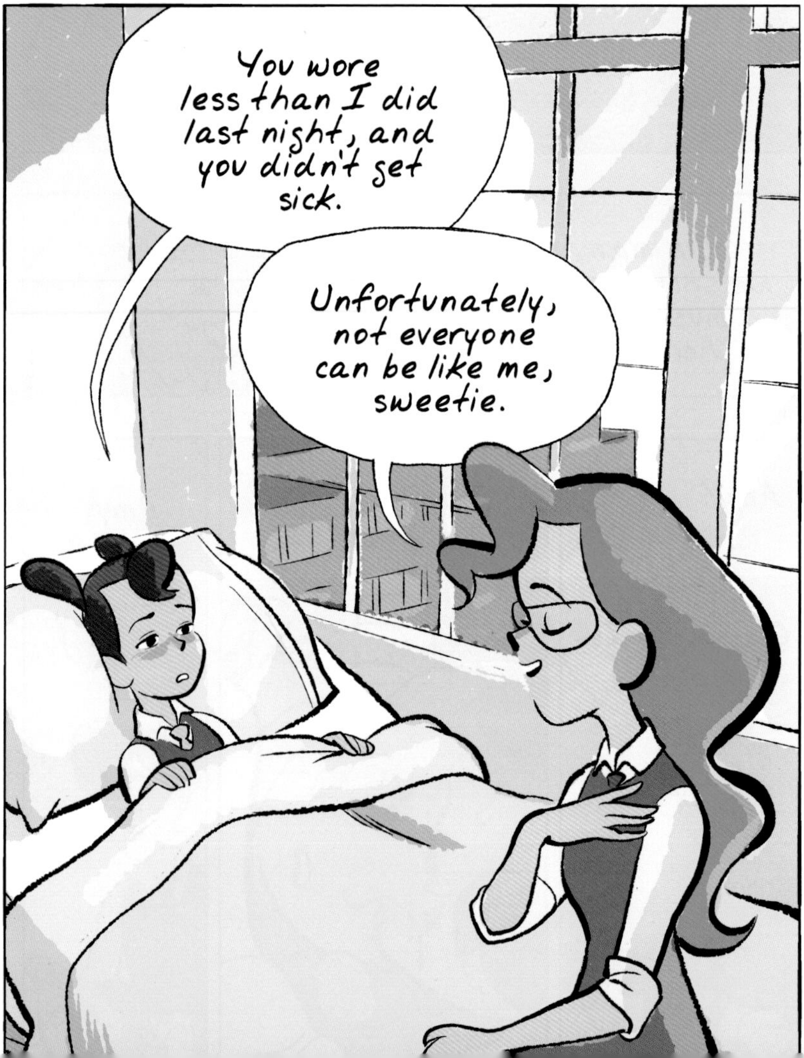
You wore less than I did last night, and you didn't get sick.
Unfortunately, not everyone can be like me, sweetie.

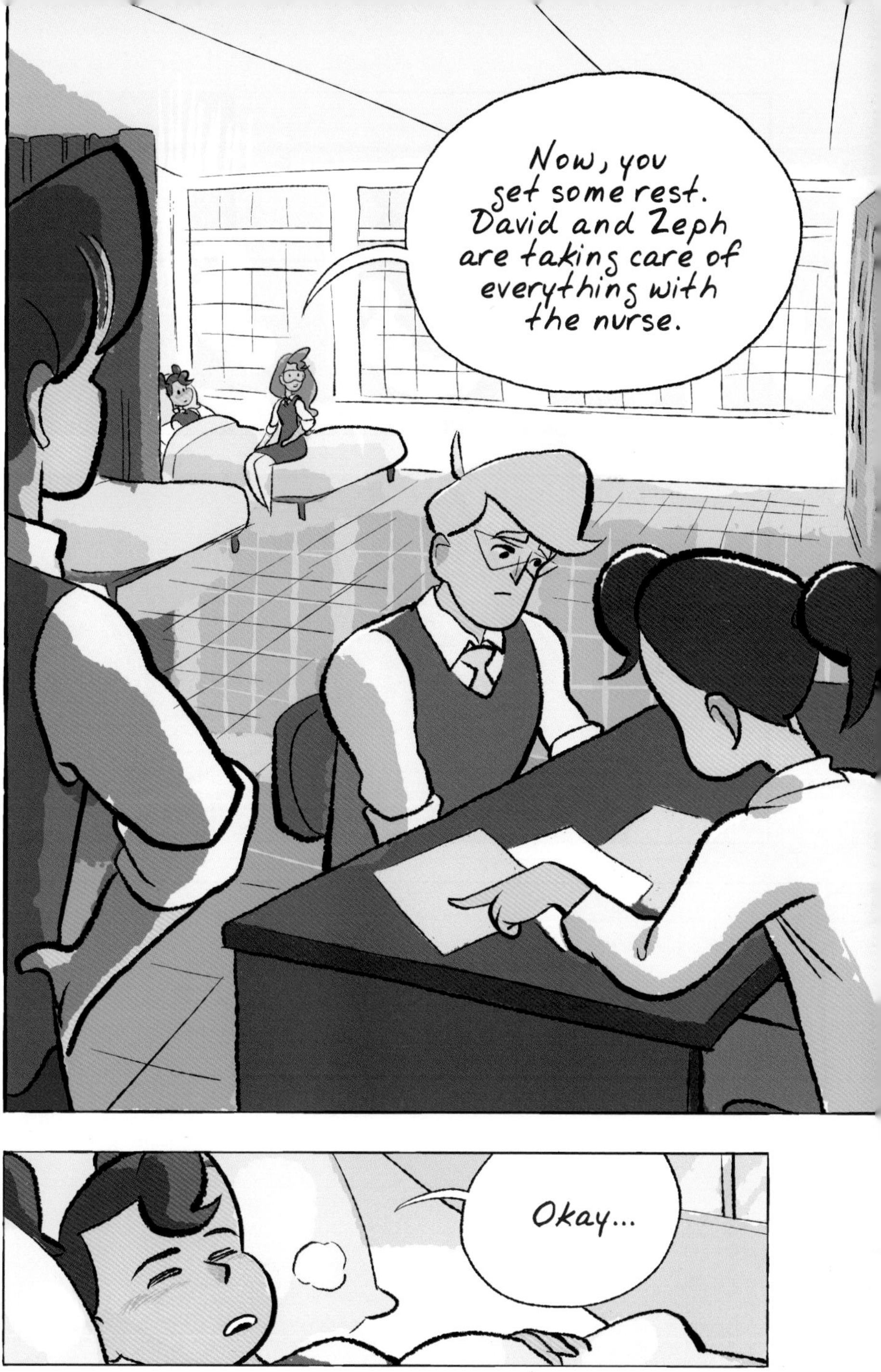
Now, you get some rest. David and Zeph are taking care of everything with the nurse.
Okay...

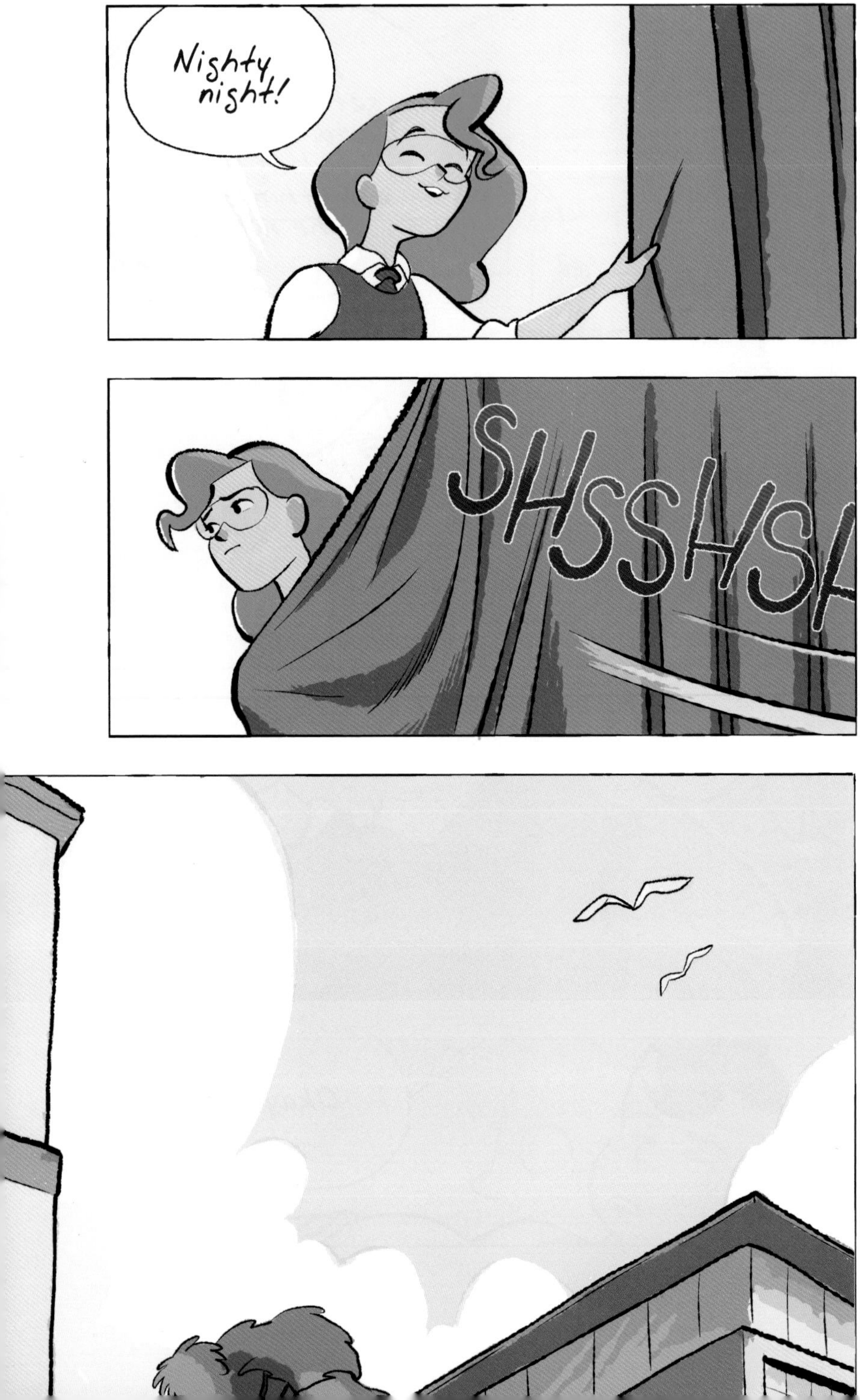
Nighty night!
SHSSHS

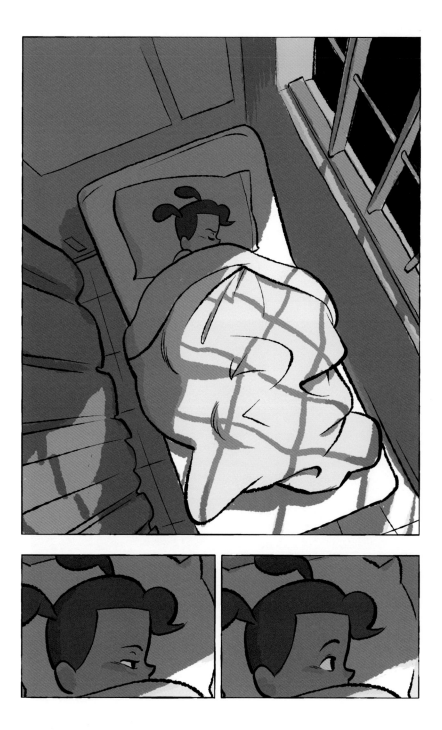

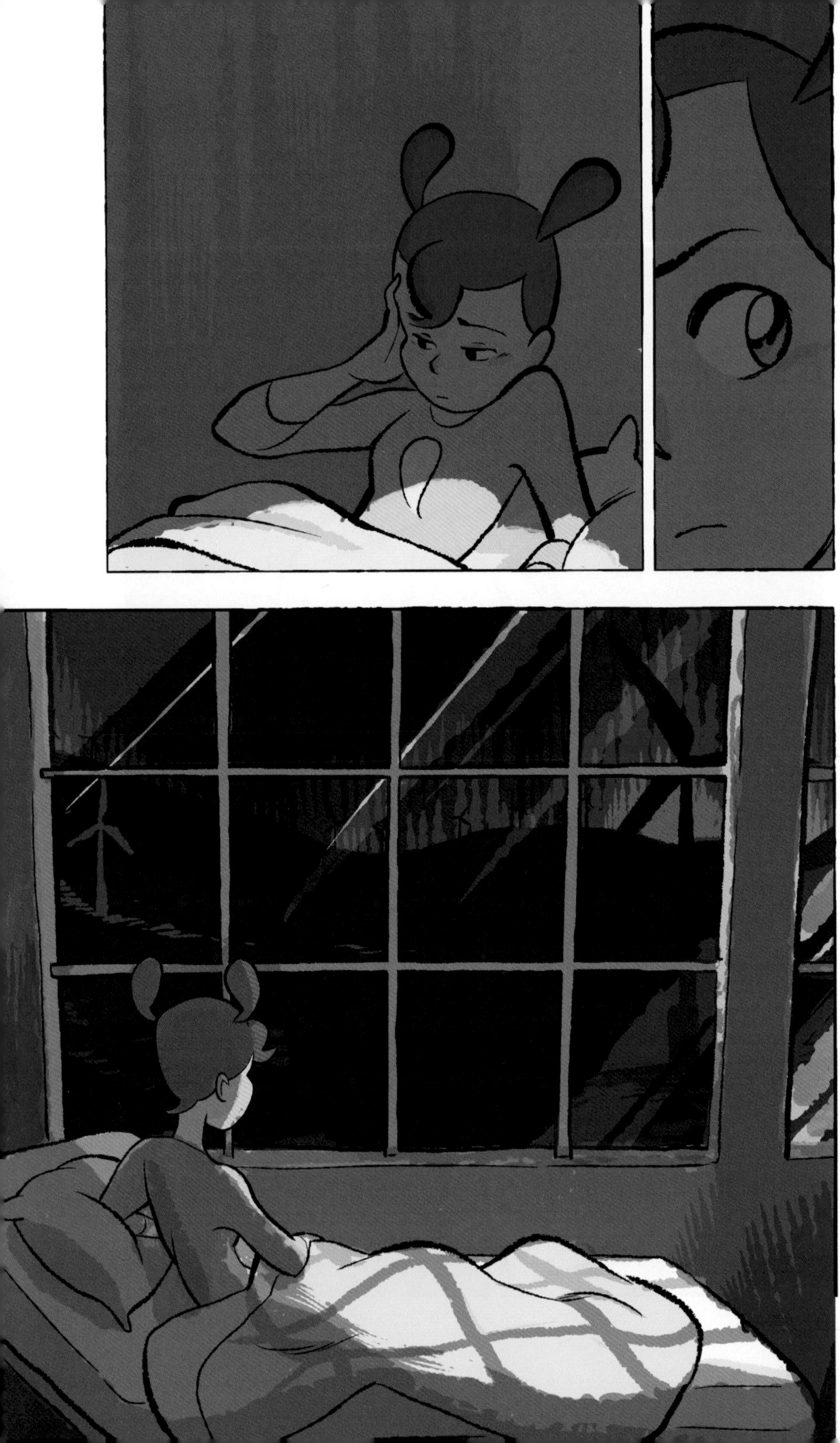

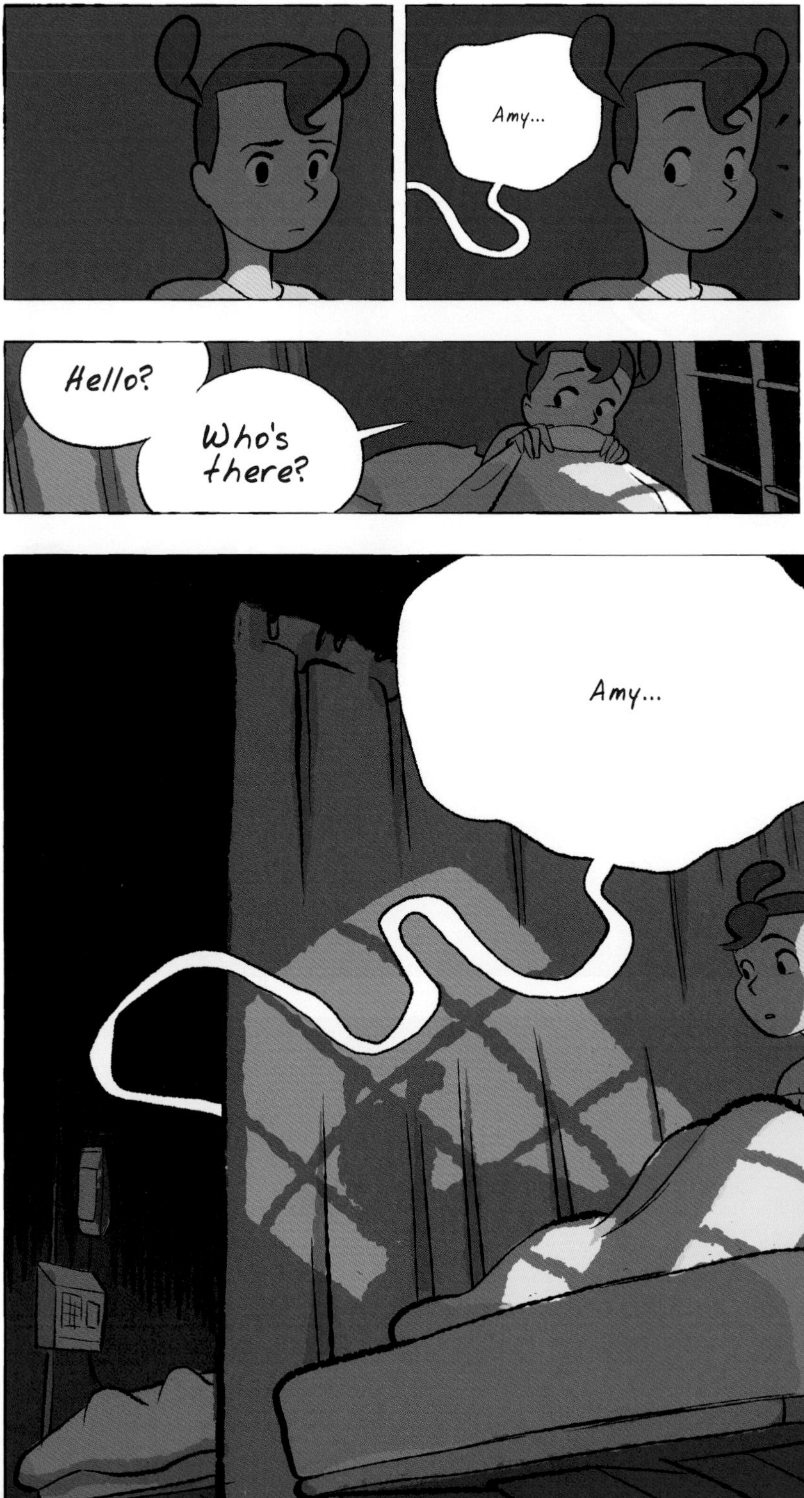
Amy...
Hello?
Who's there?
Amy...

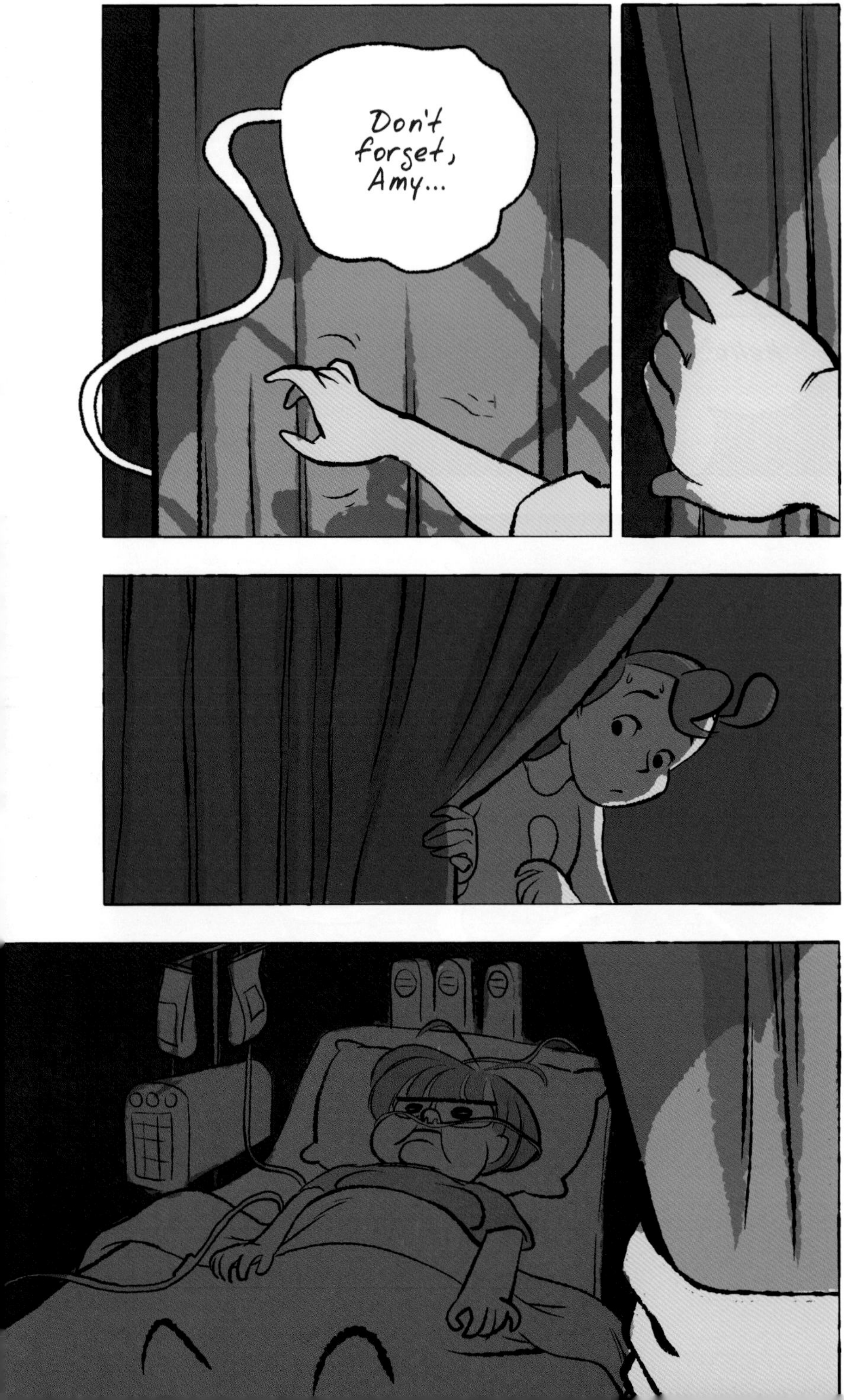
Don't forget, Amy...

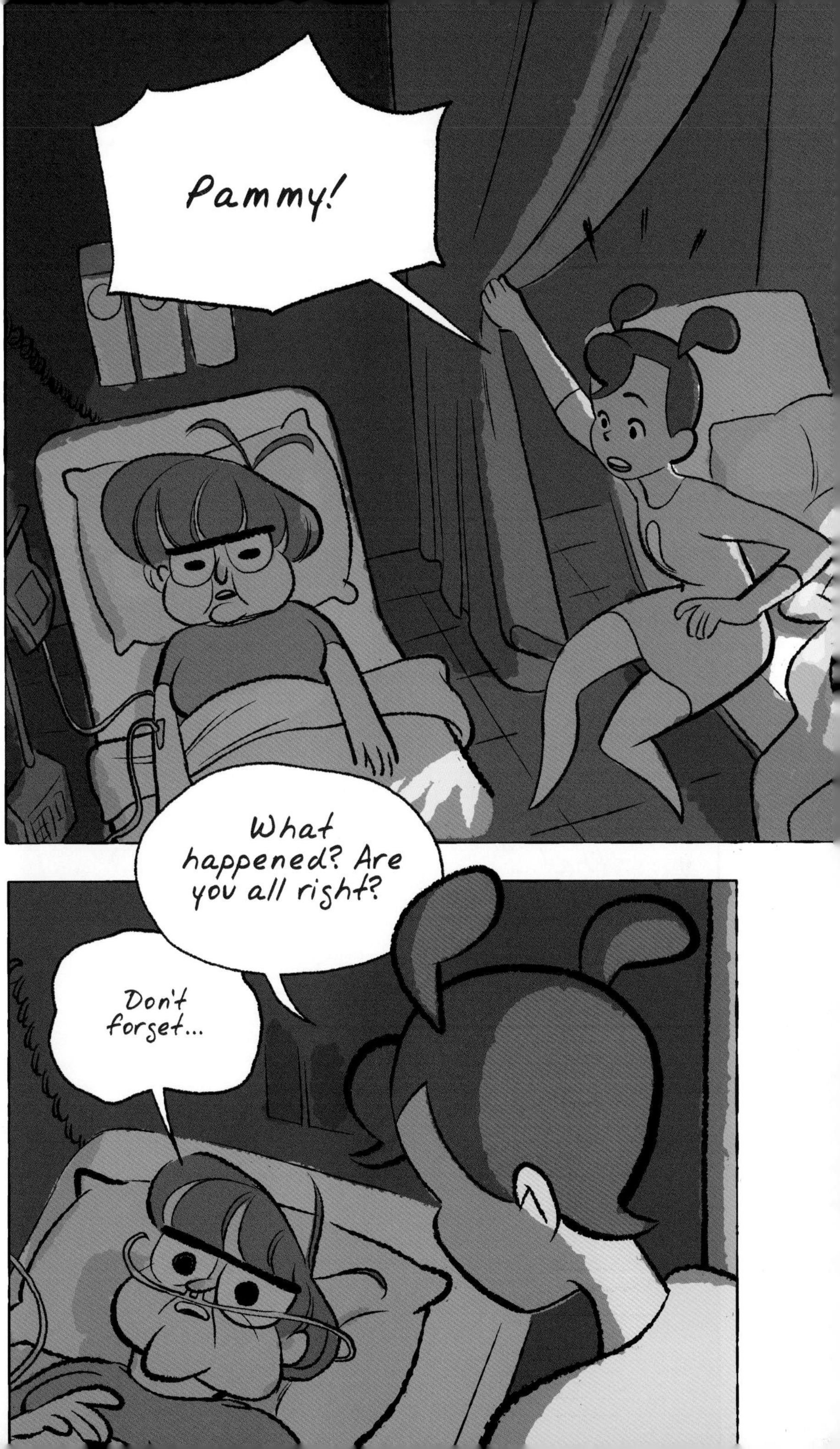
Pammy!
What happened? Are you all right?
Don't forget...

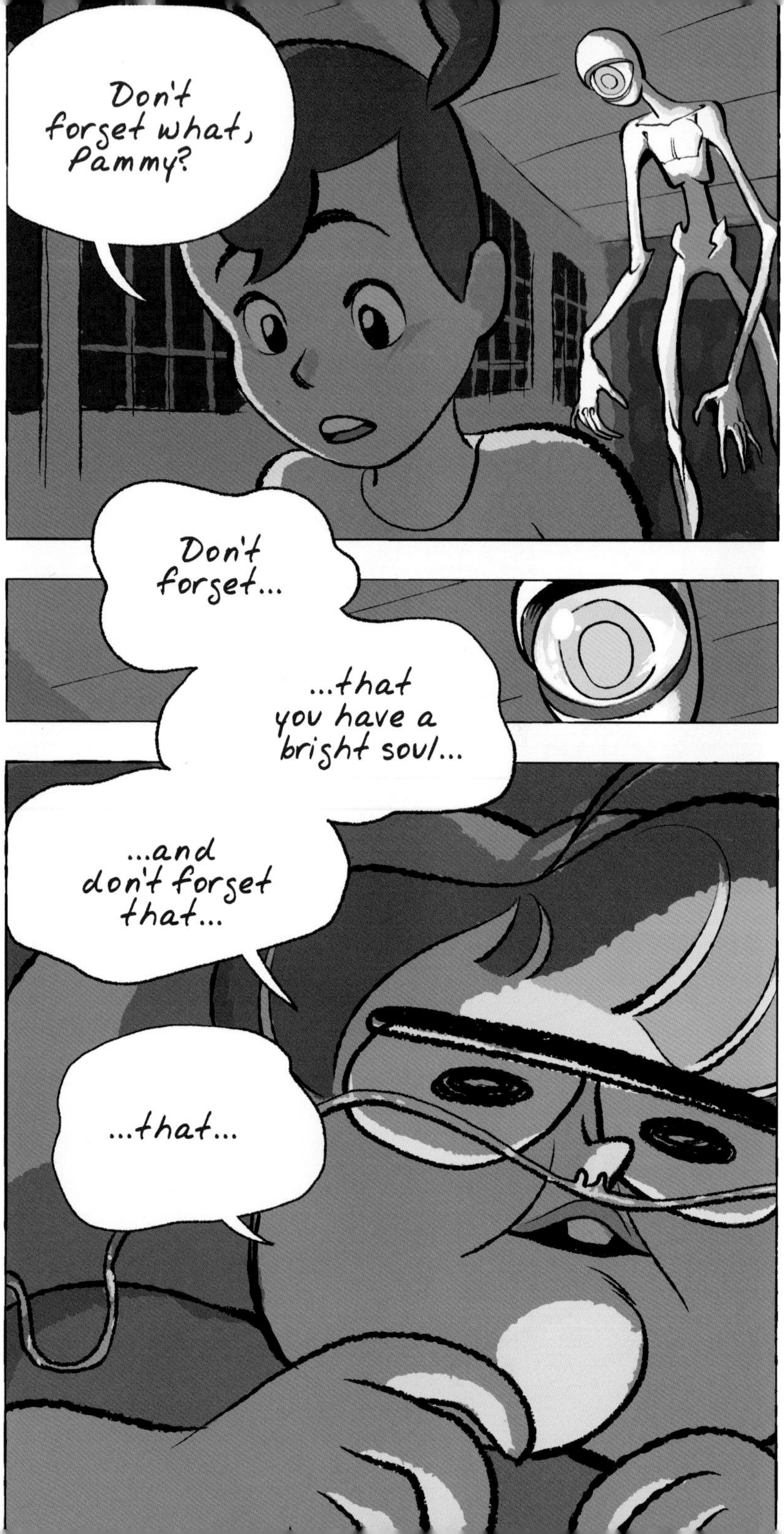
Don't forget what, Pammy?
Don't forget...
...that you have a bright soul...
...and don't forget that...
...that...

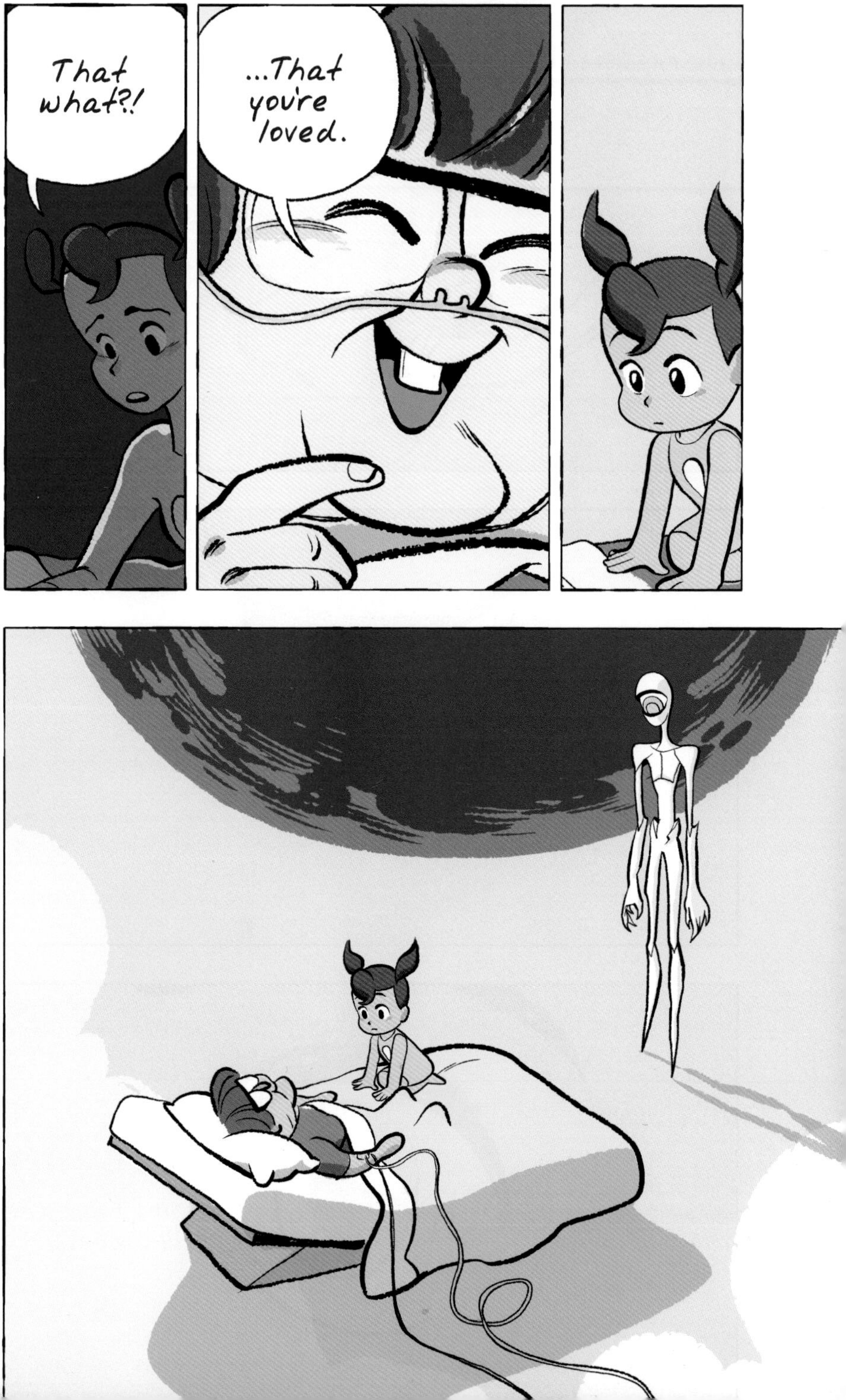
That what?!
...That you're loved.

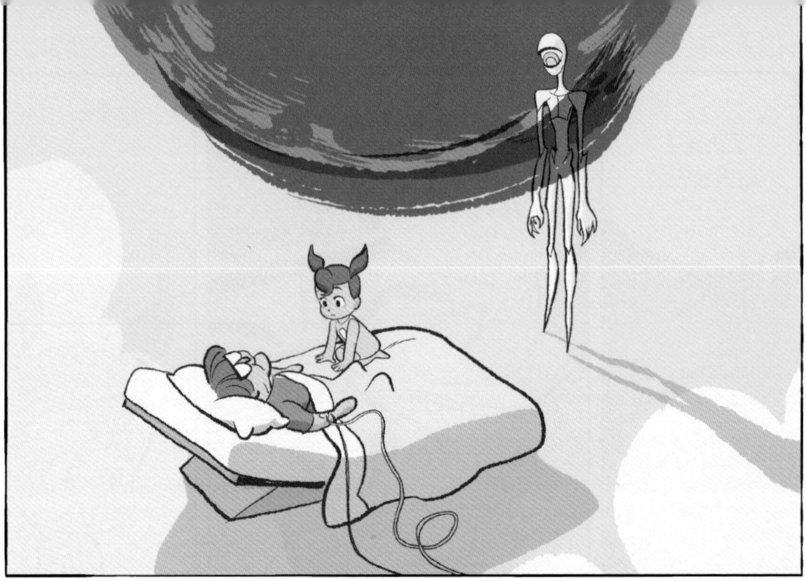
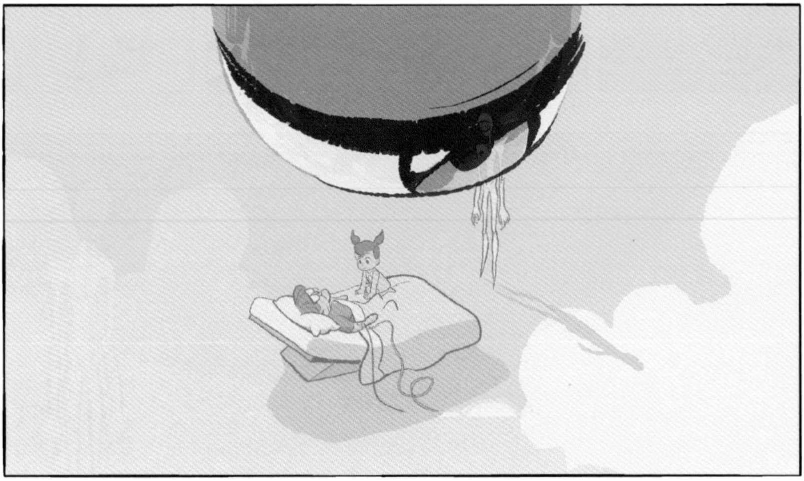
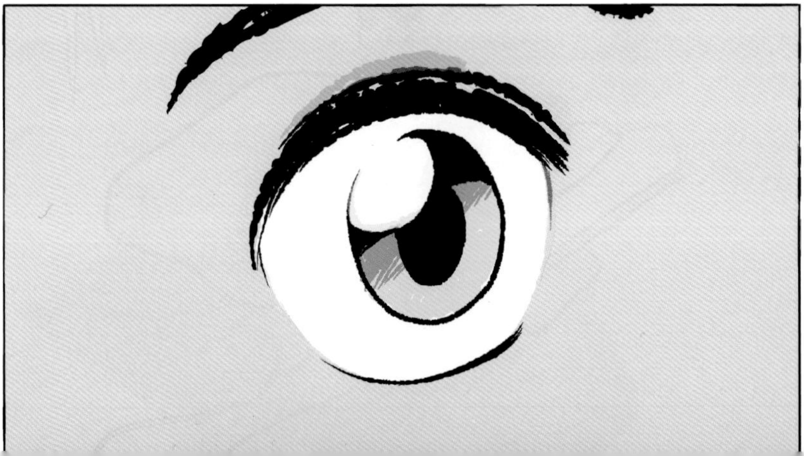

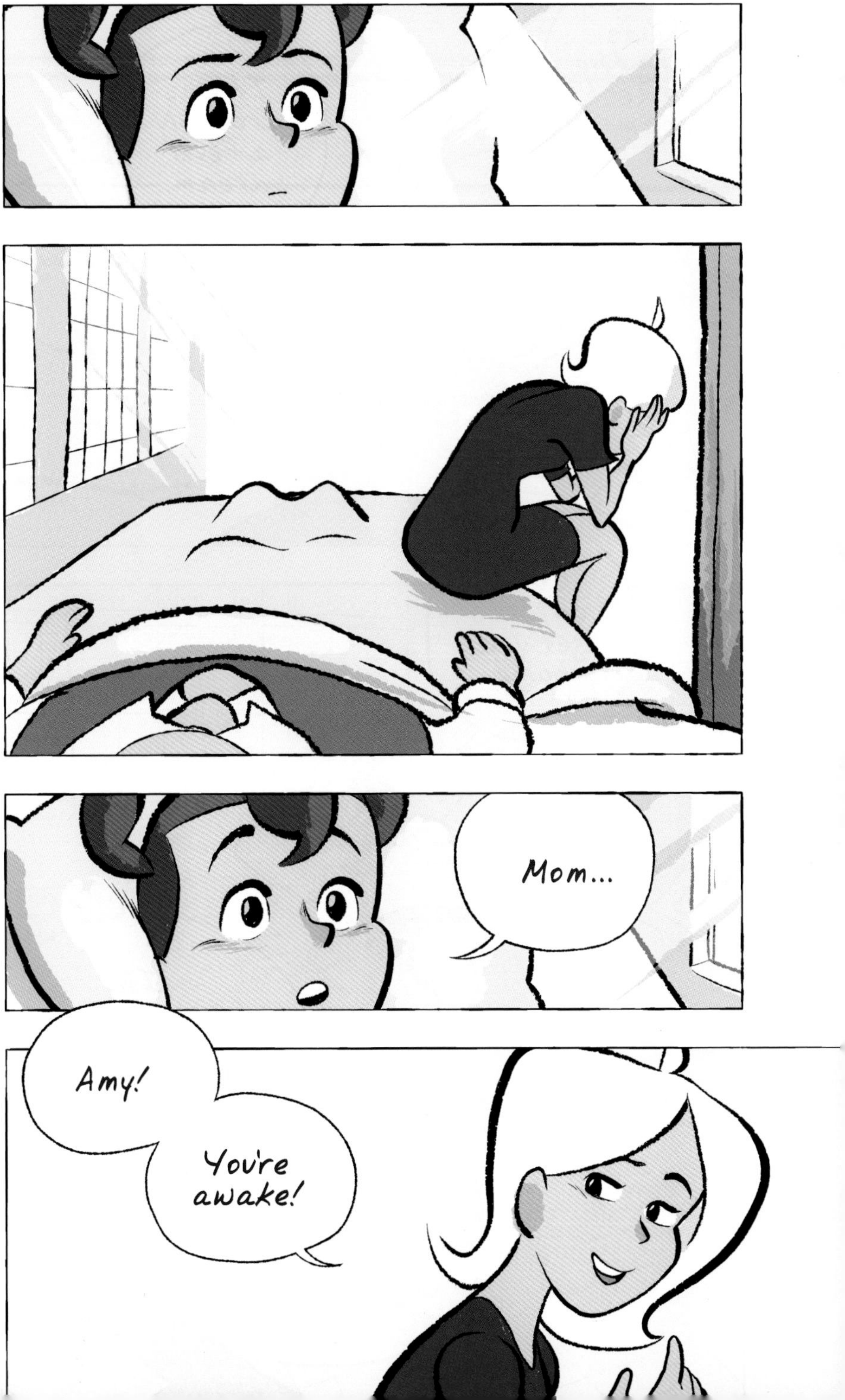
Mom...
Amy!
You're awake!

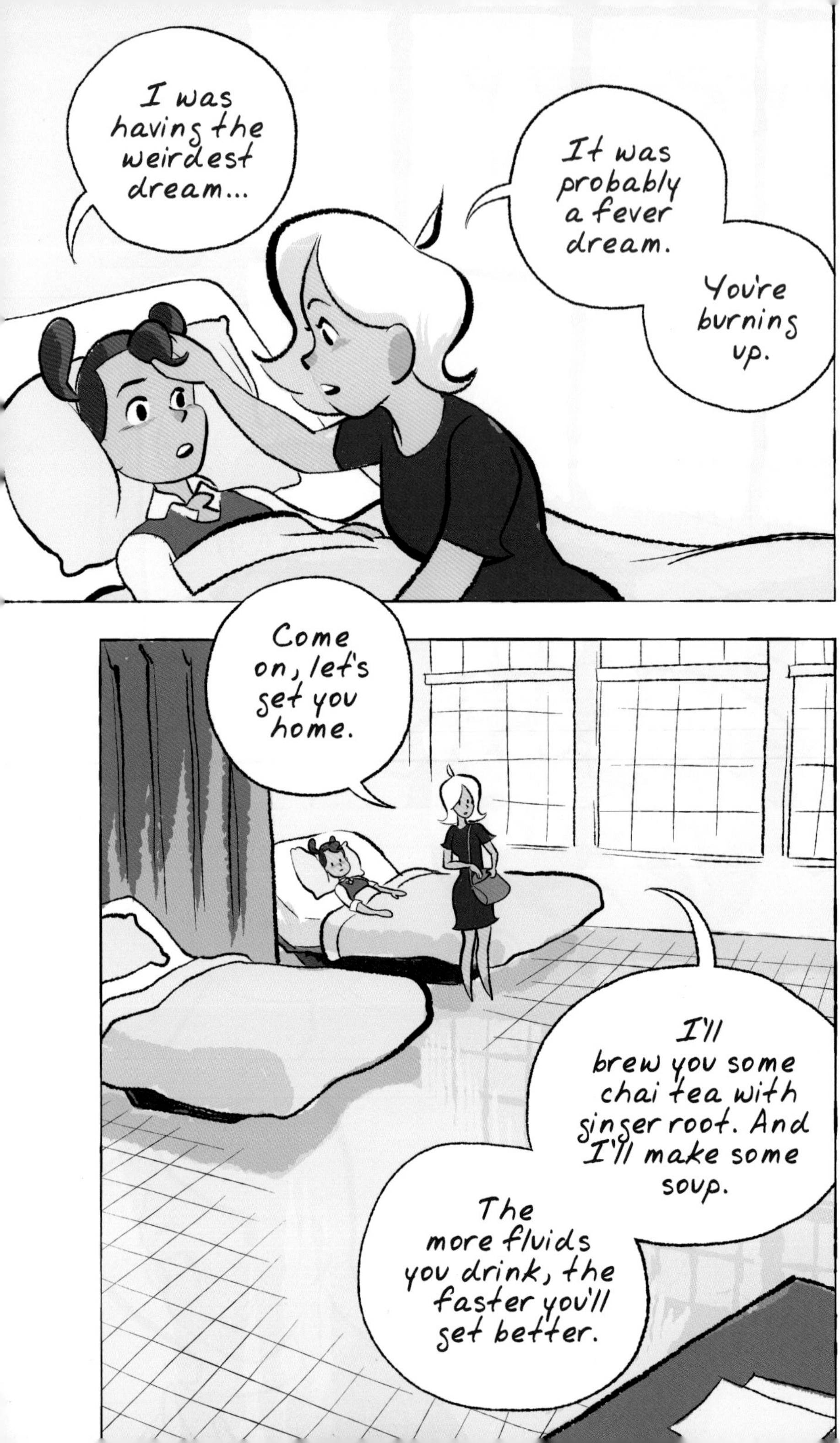
I was having the weirdest dream...
It was probably a fever dream.
You're burning up.
Come on, let's get you home.
I'll brew you some chai tea with ginger root. And I'll make some soup.
The more fluids you drink, the faster you'll get better.

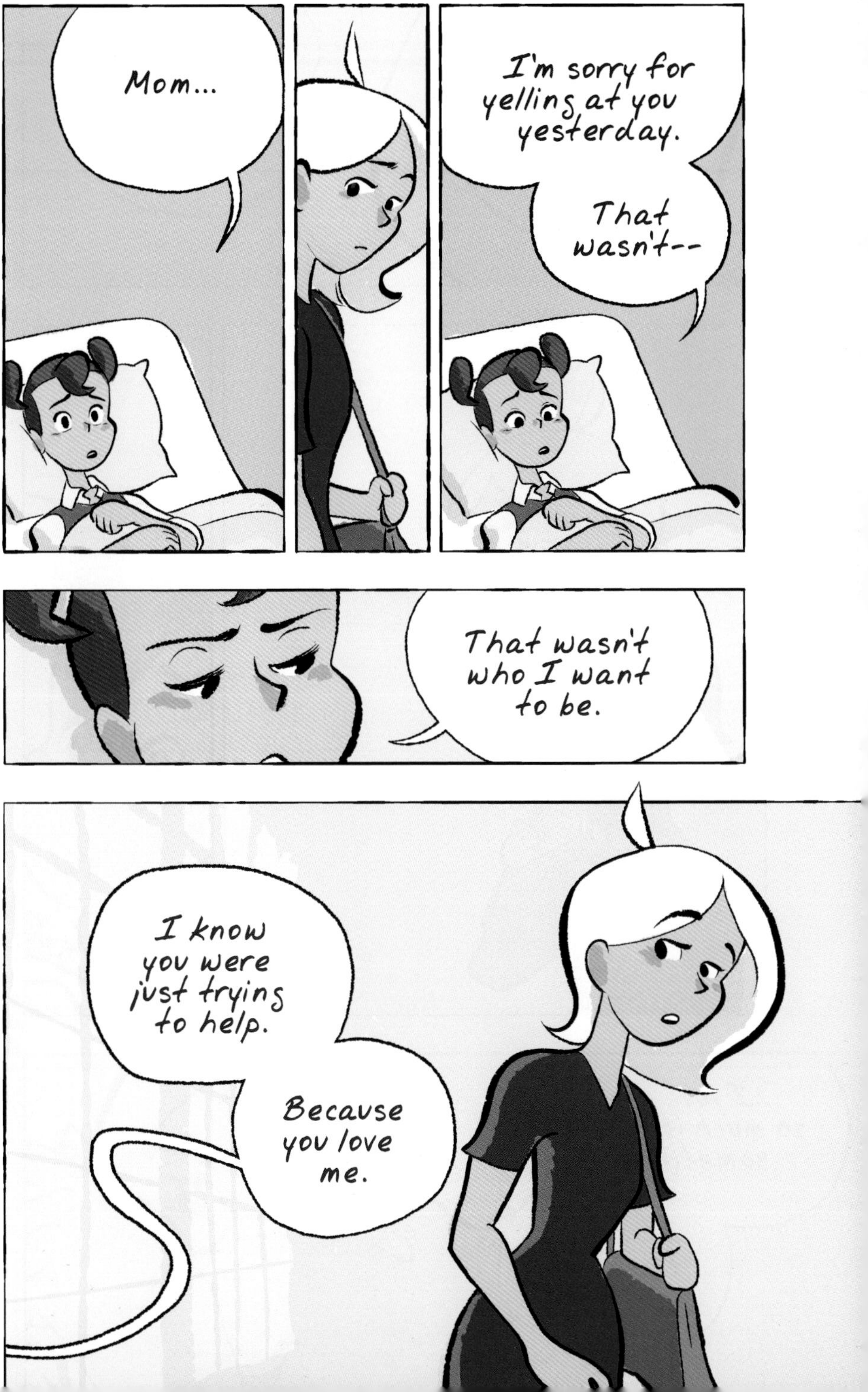
Mom...
I'm sorry for yelling at you yesterday.
That wasn't--
That wasn't who I want to be.
I know you were just trying to help.
Because you love me.

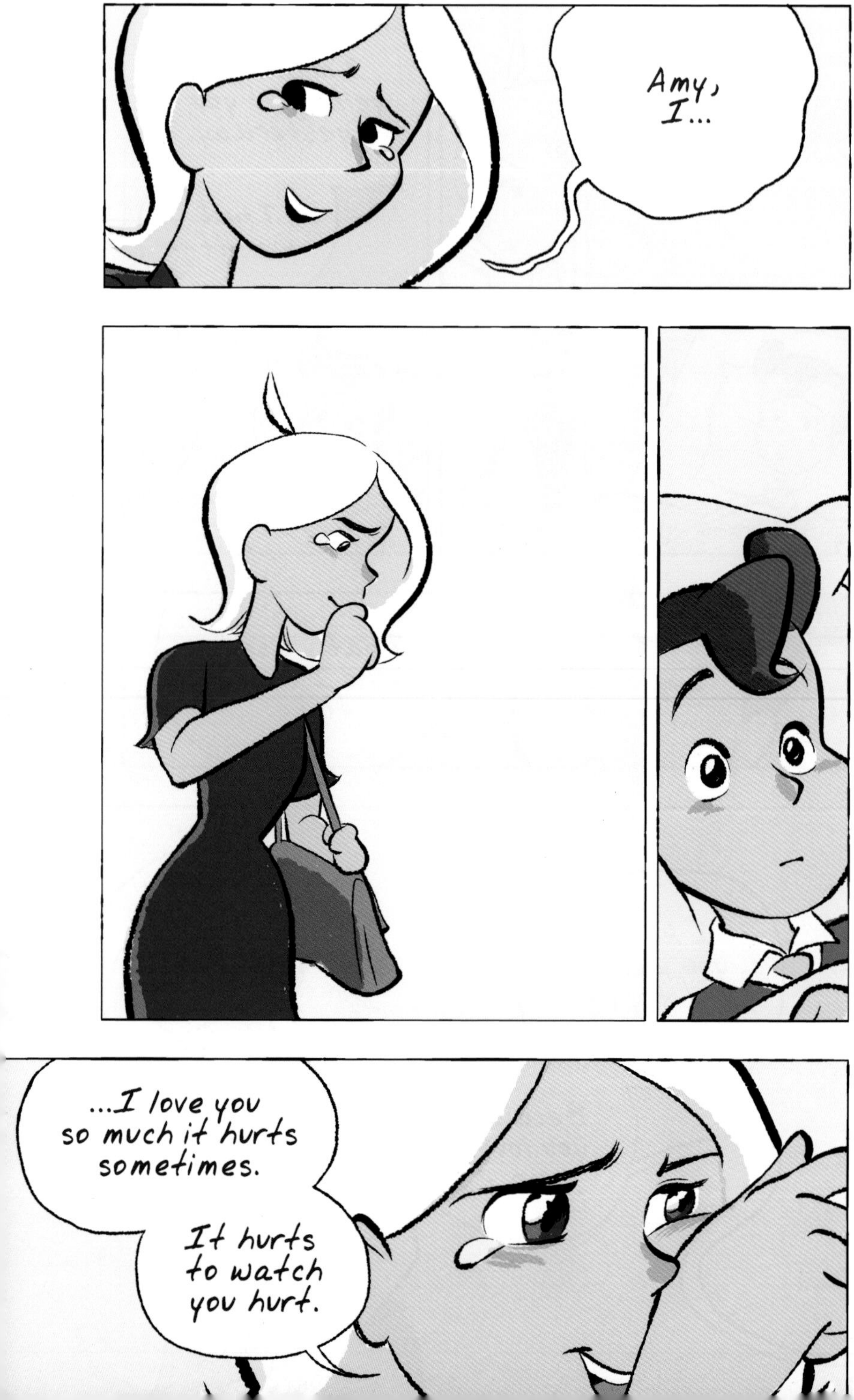
Amy, I...
...I love you so much it hurts sometimes.
It hurts to watch you hurt.

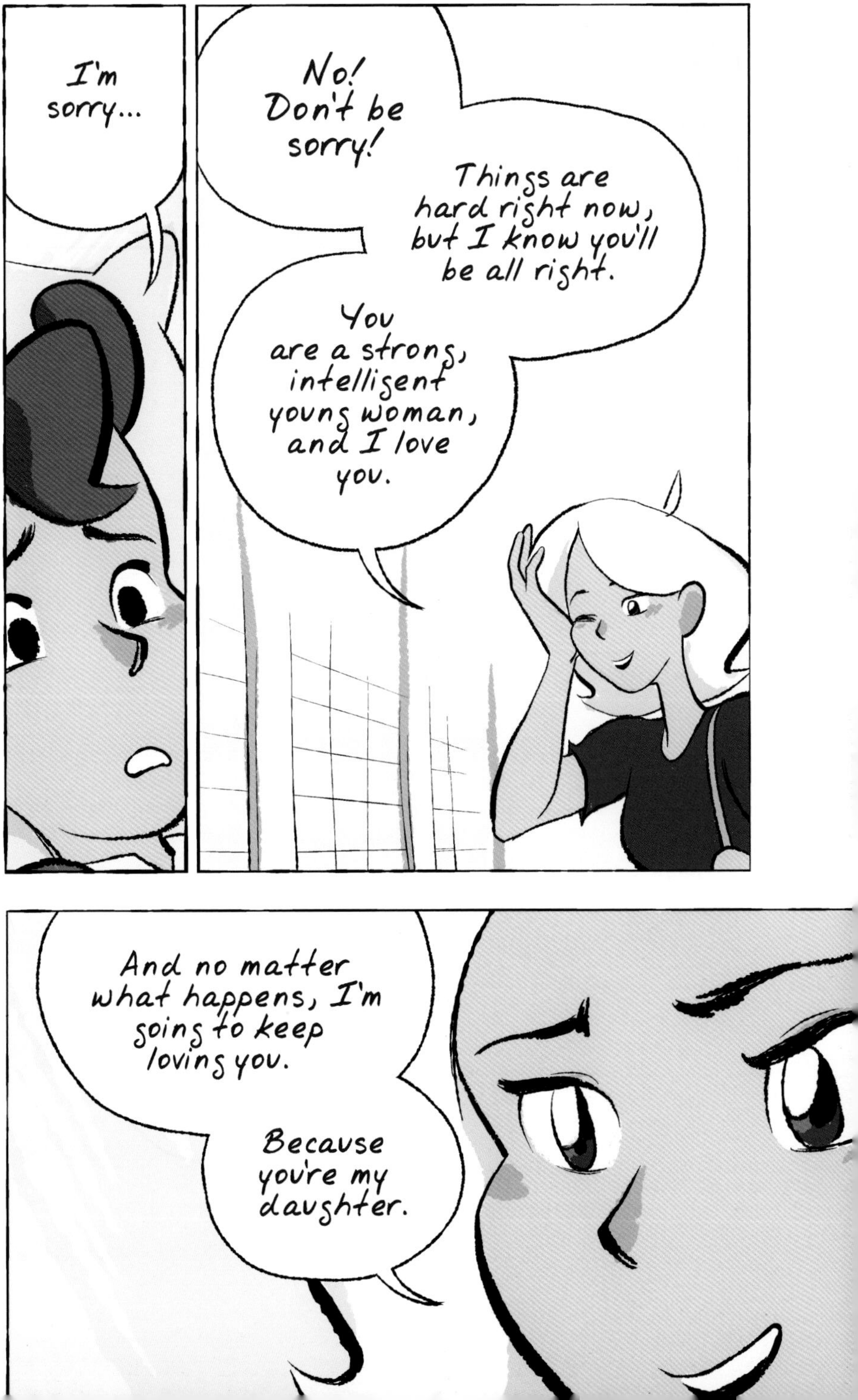
I'm sorry...
No! Don't be sorry!
Things are hard right now, but I know you'll be all right.
You are a strong, intelligent young woman, and I love you.
And no matter what happens, I'm going to keep loving you.
Because you're my daughter.

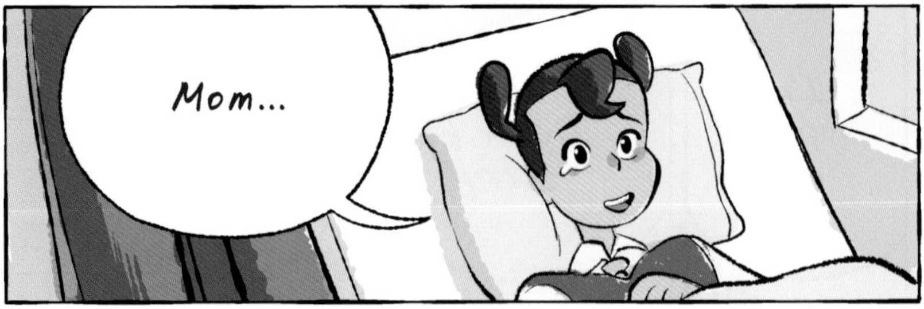

Now then, let's get you home.

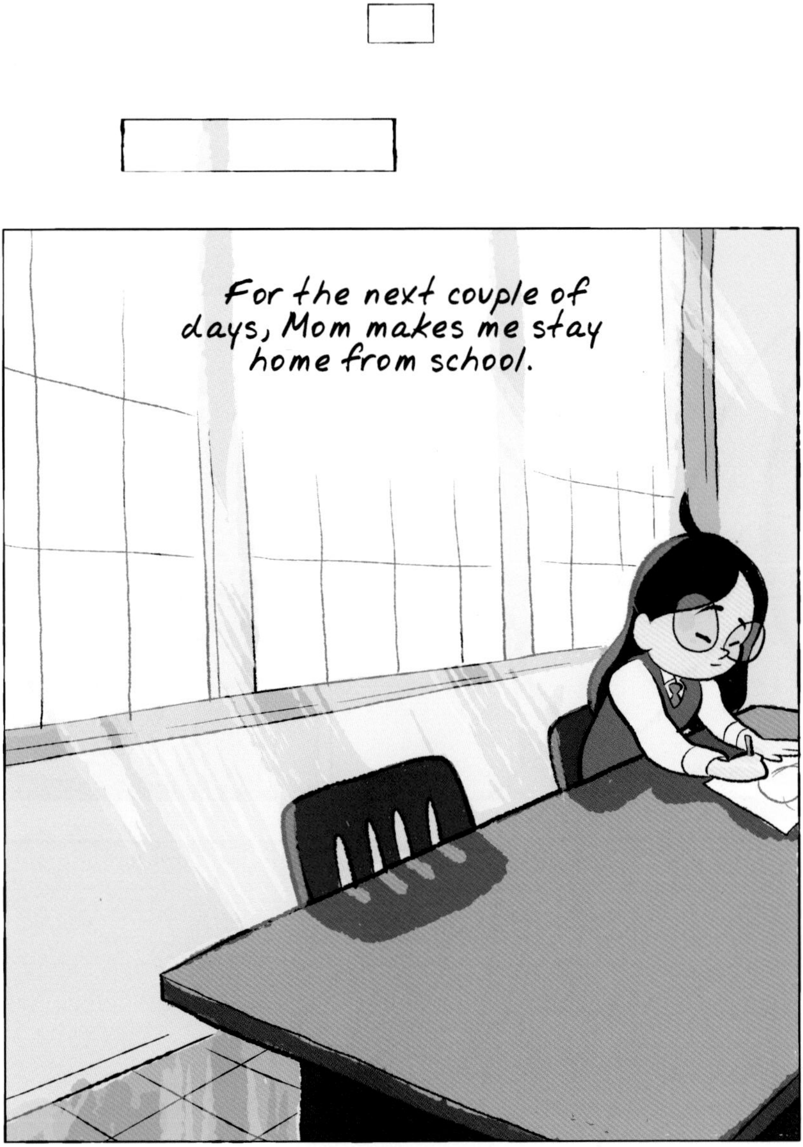
For the next couple of days, Mom makes me stay home from school.

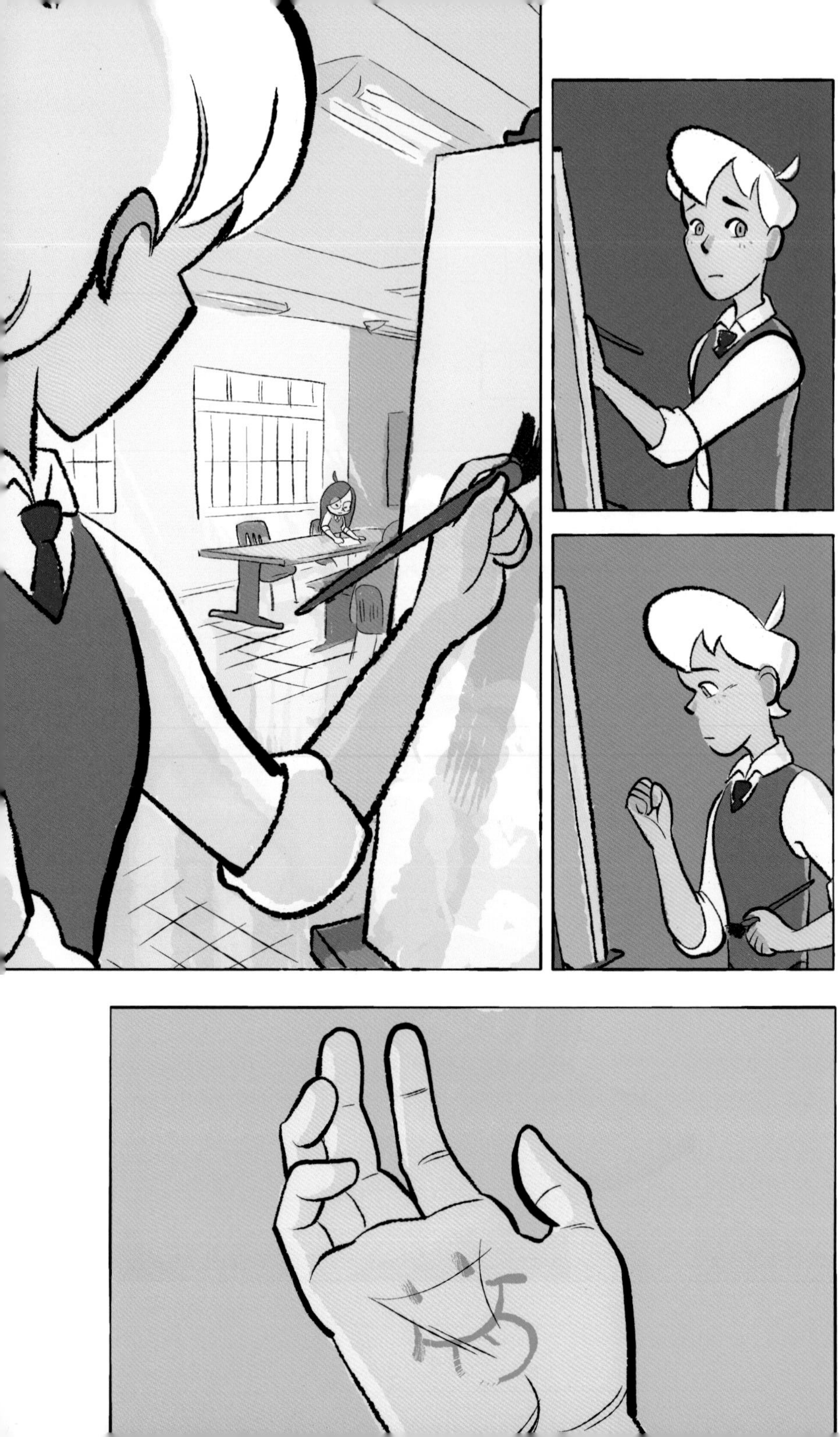

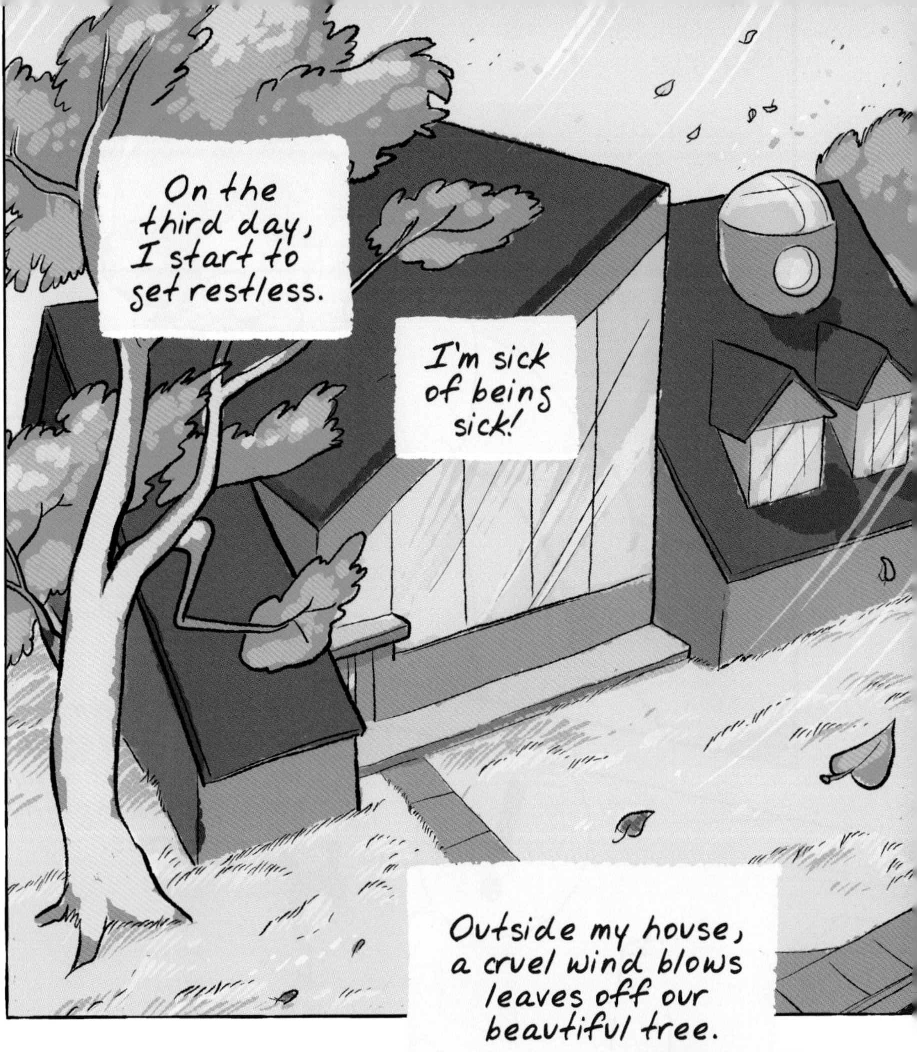
On the third day, I start to get restless.
I'm sick of being sick!
Outside my house, a cruel wind blows leaves off our beautiful tree.
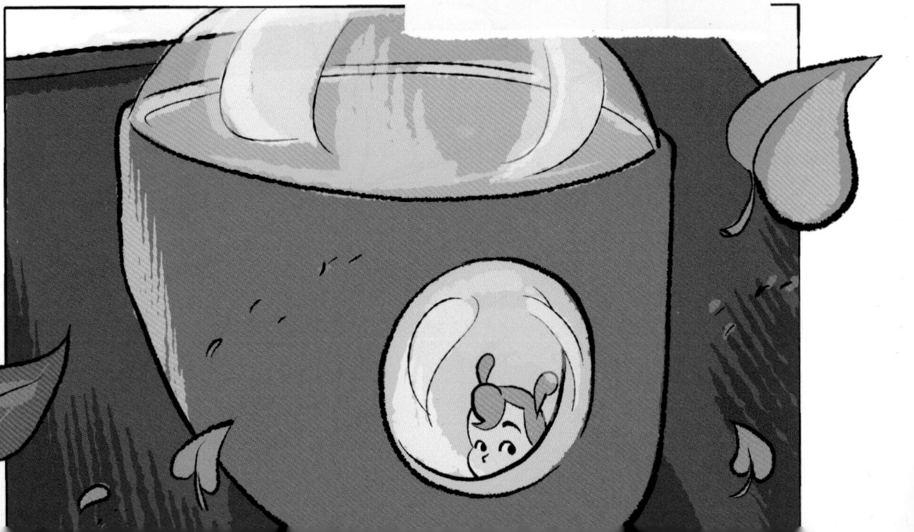

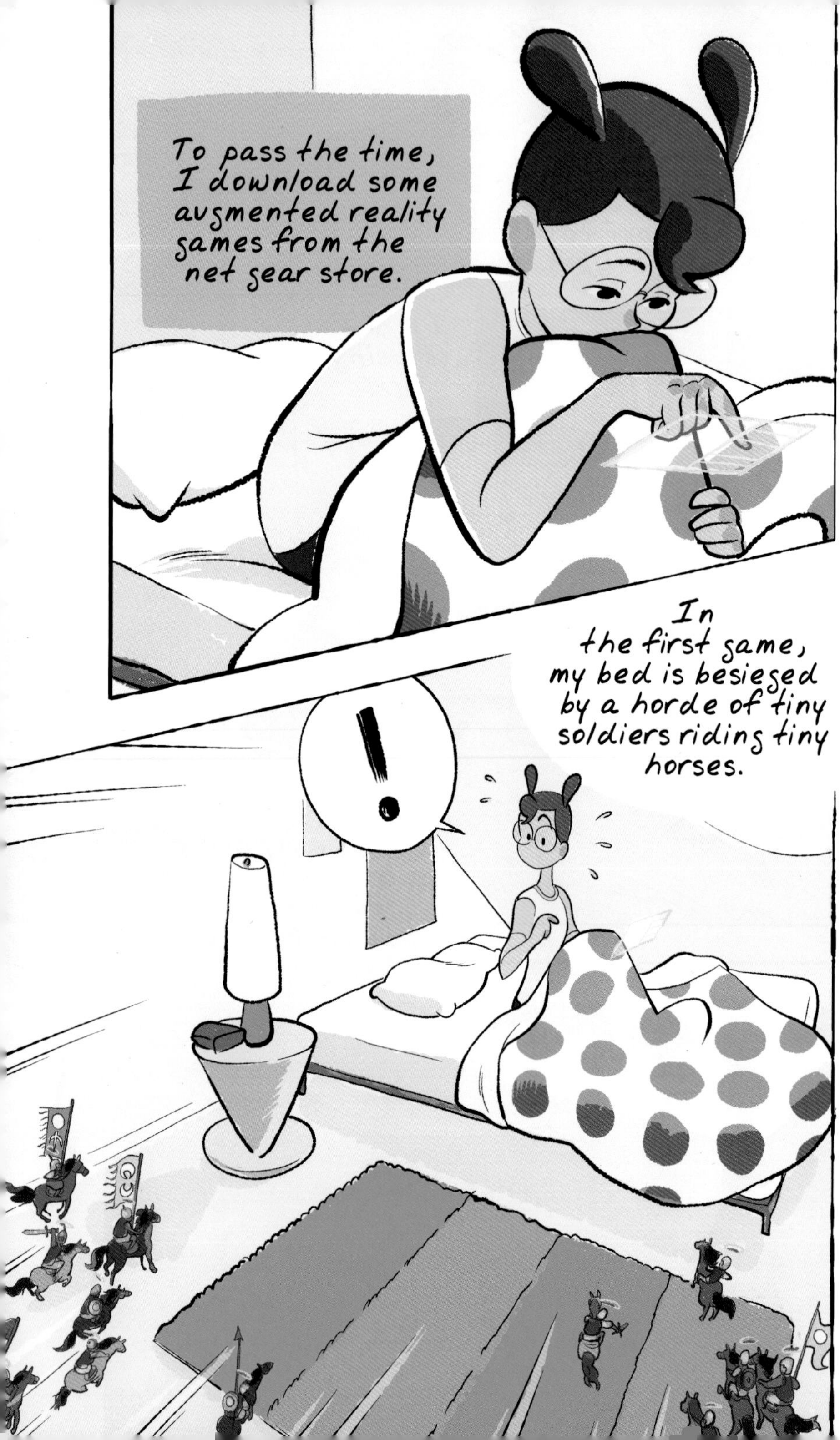
To pass the time, I download some augmented reality games from the net gear store.
In the first game, my bed is besieged by a horde of tiny soldiers riding tiny horses.
!

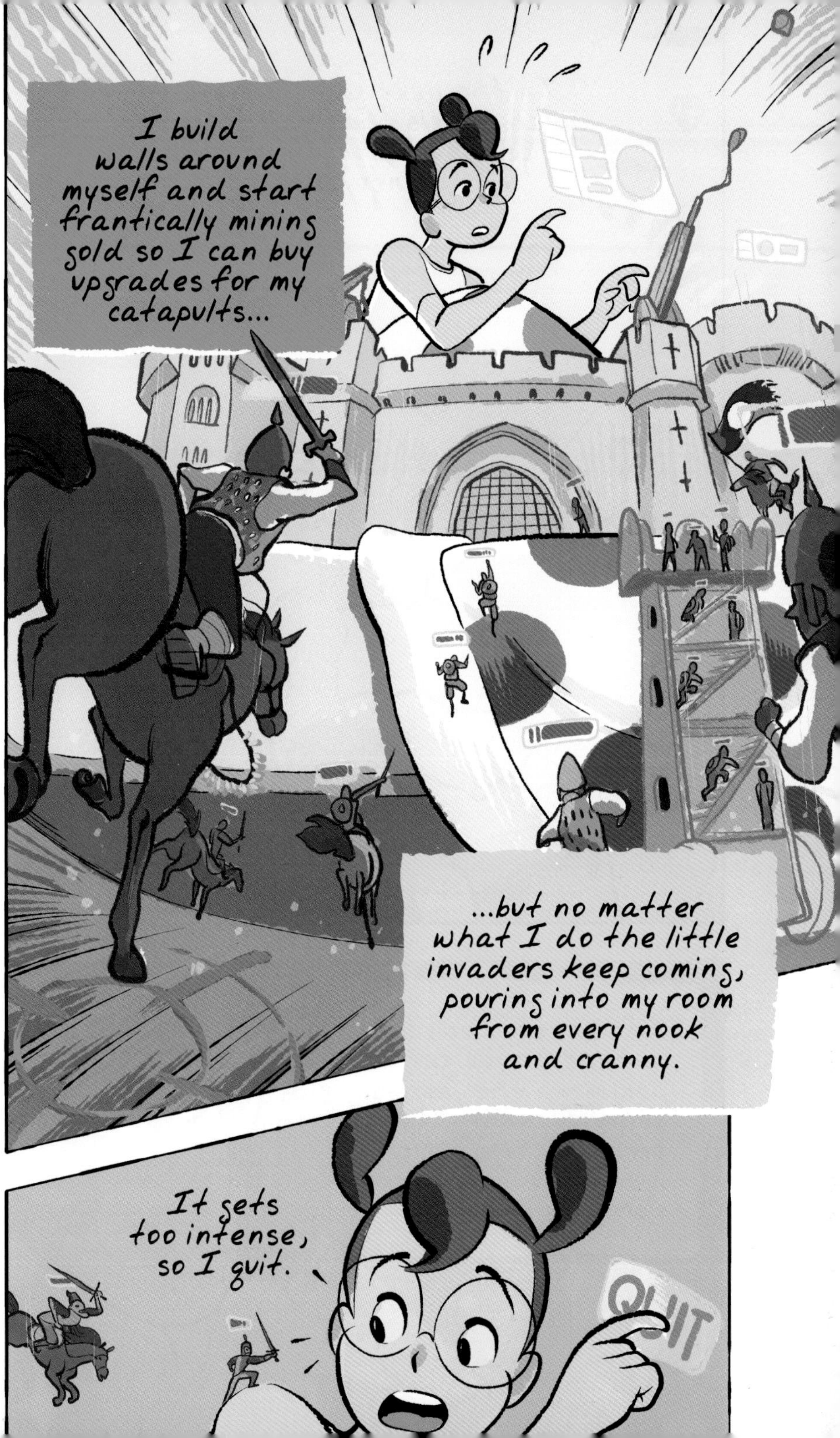
I build walls around myself and start frantically mining gold so I can buy upgrades for my catapults...
...but no matter what I do the little invaders keep coming, pouring into my room from every nook and cranny.
It gets too intense, so I quit.
QUIT

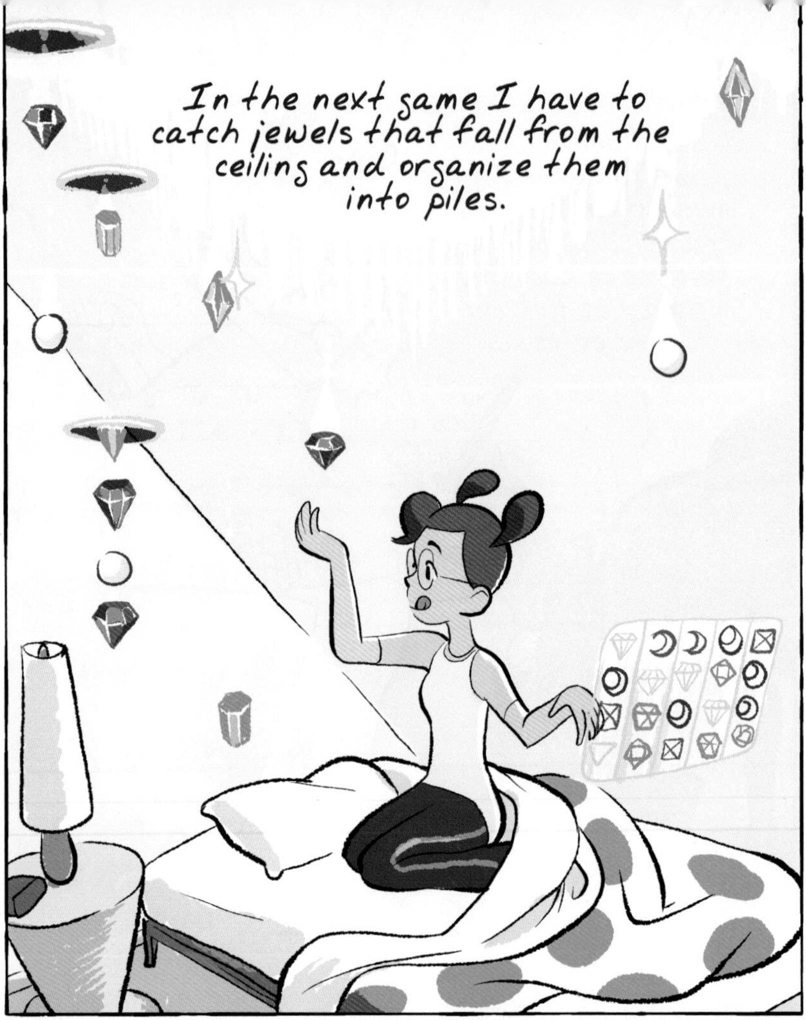
In the next game I have to catch jewels that fall from the ceiling and organize them into piles.

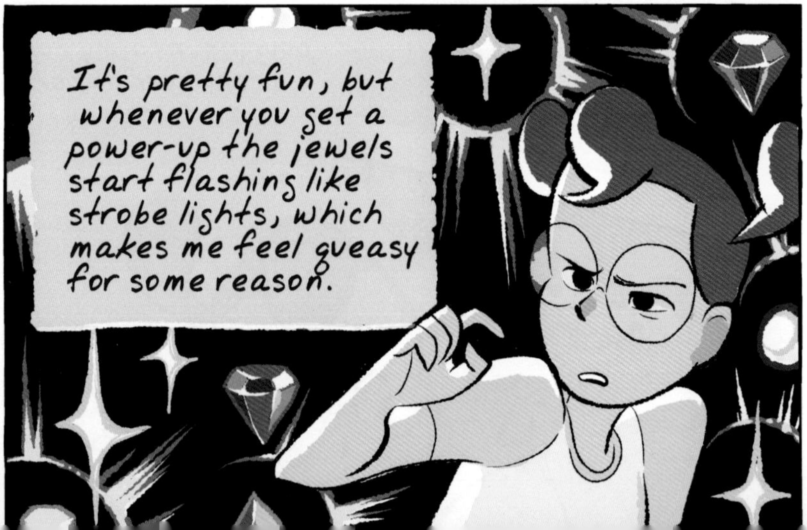
It's pretty fun, but whenever you get a power-up the jewels start flashing like strobe lights, which makes me feel queasy for some reason.

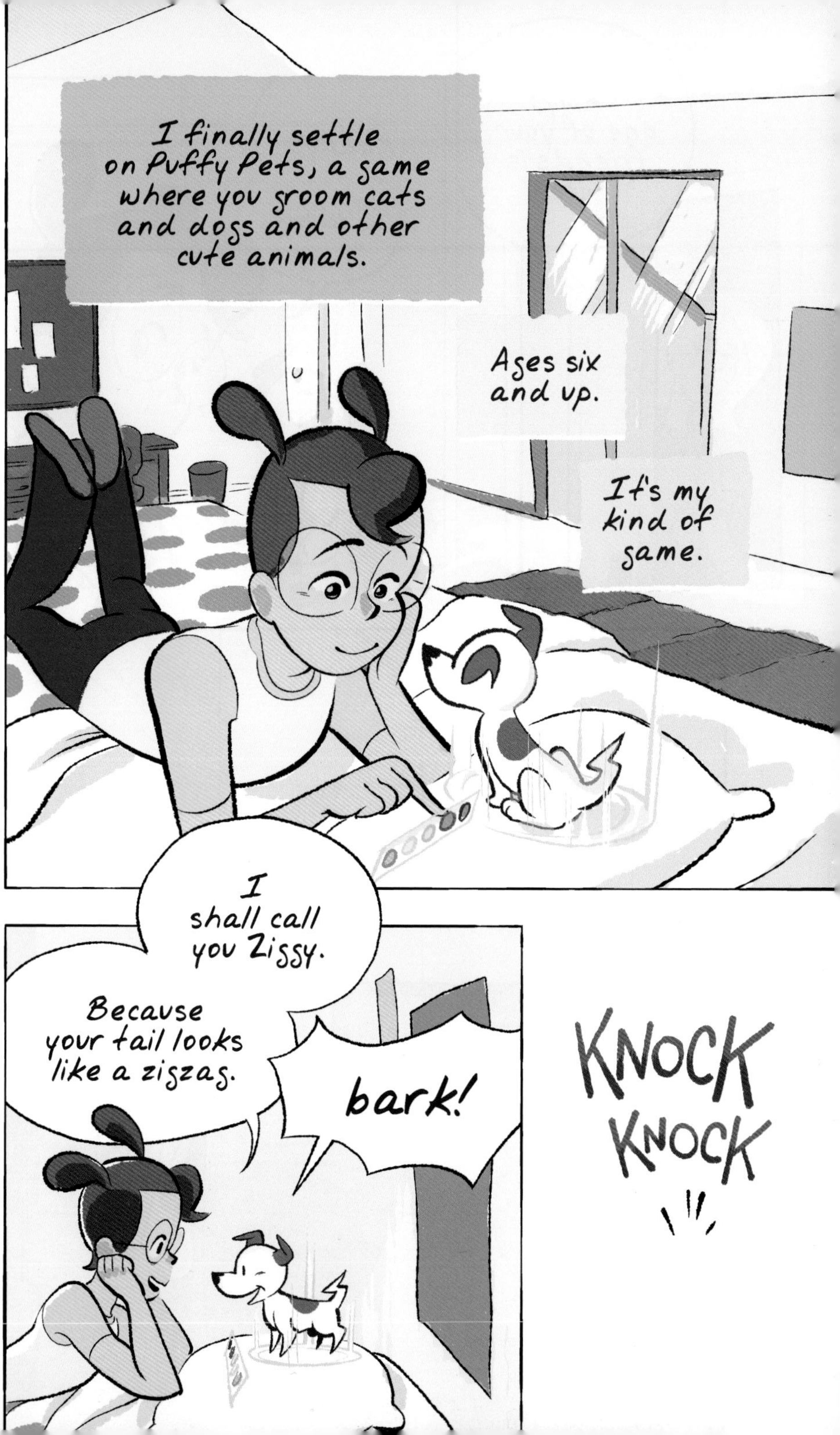
I finally settle on Puffy Pets, a game where you groom cats and dogs and other cute animals.
Ages six and up.
It's my kind of game.
I shall call you Ziggy.
Because your tail looks like a zigzag.
bark!
KNOCK KNOCK

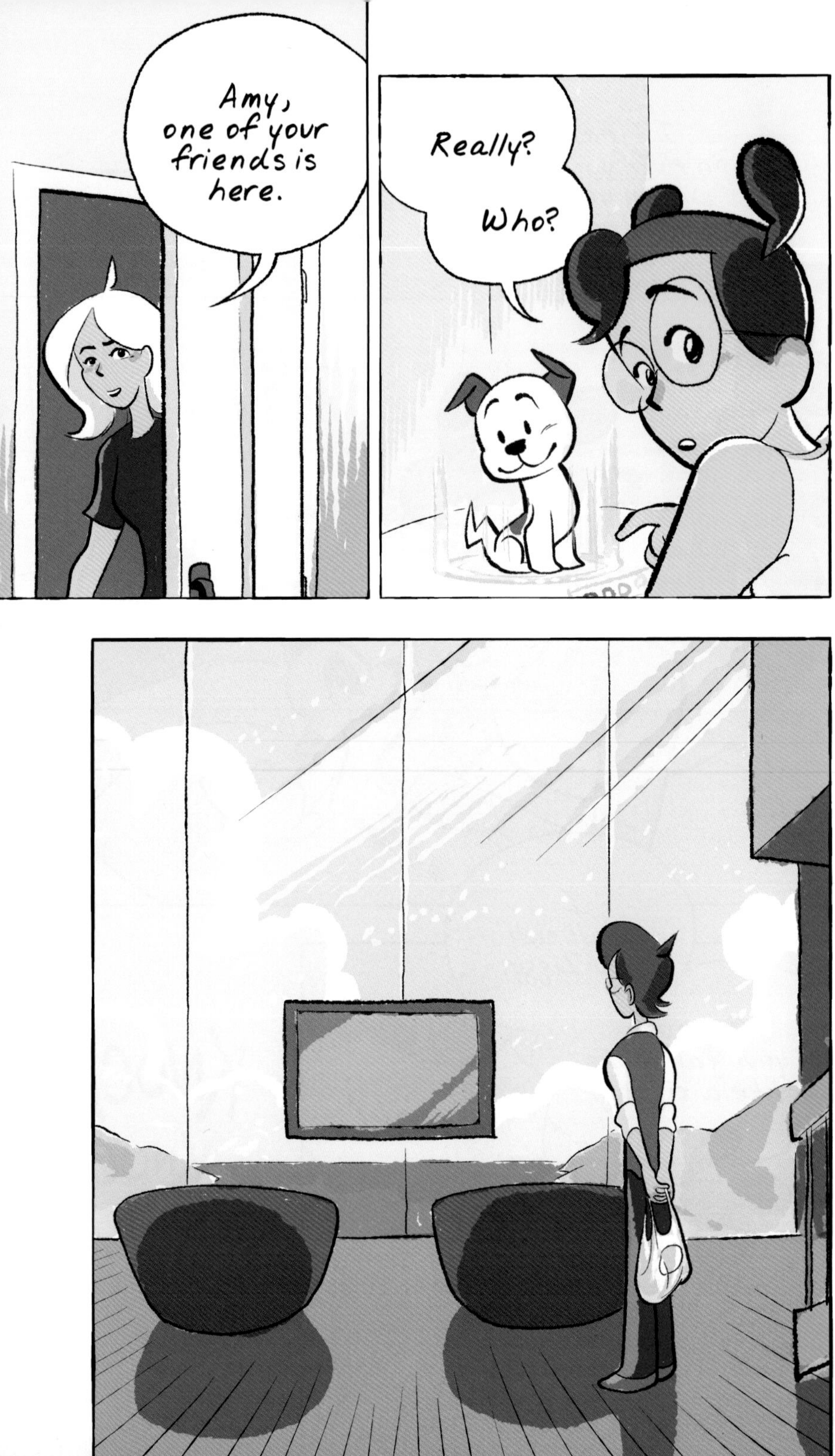
Amy, one of your friends is here.
Really?
Who?

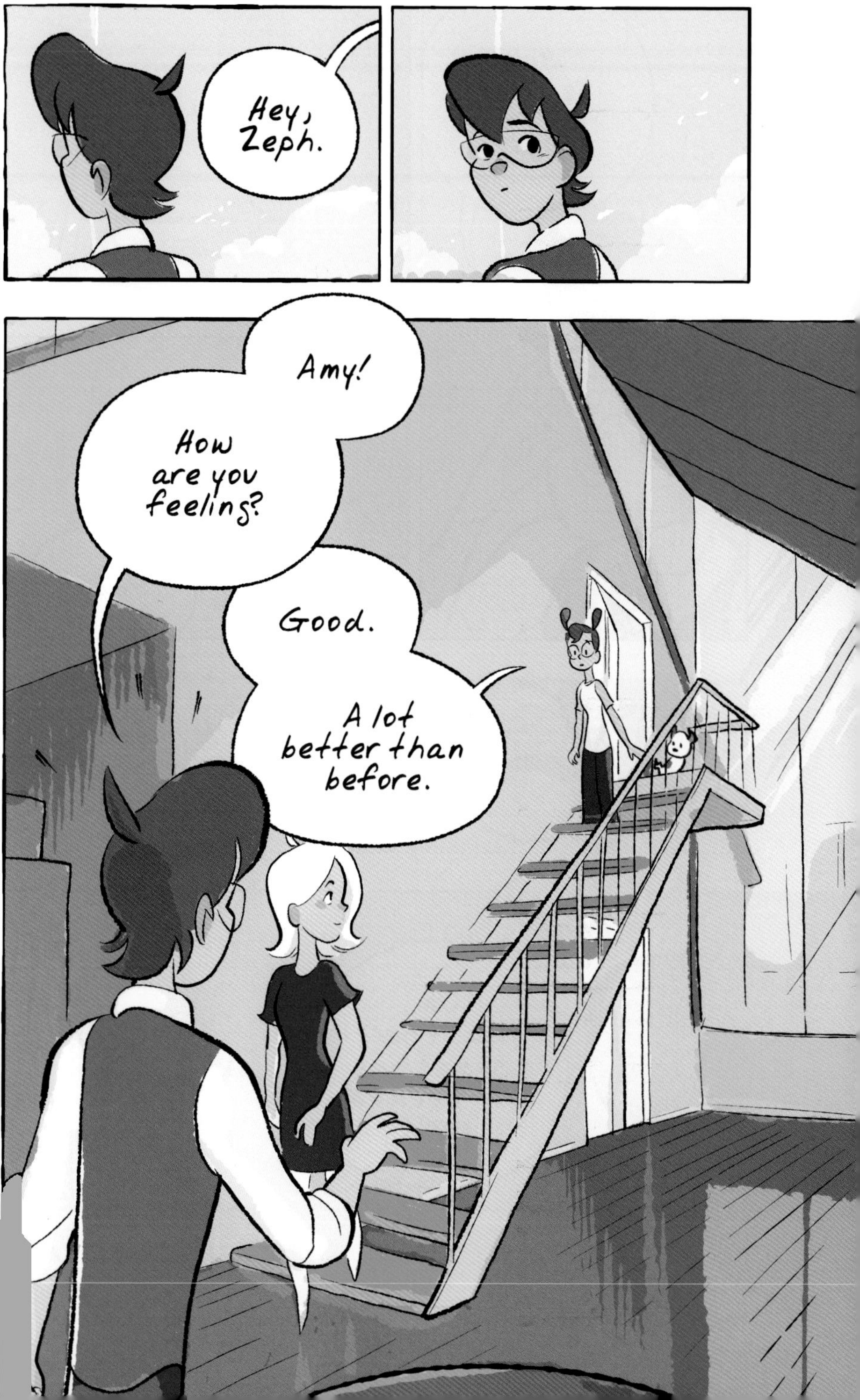
Hey, Zeph.
Amy!
How are you feeling?
Good.
A lot better than before.

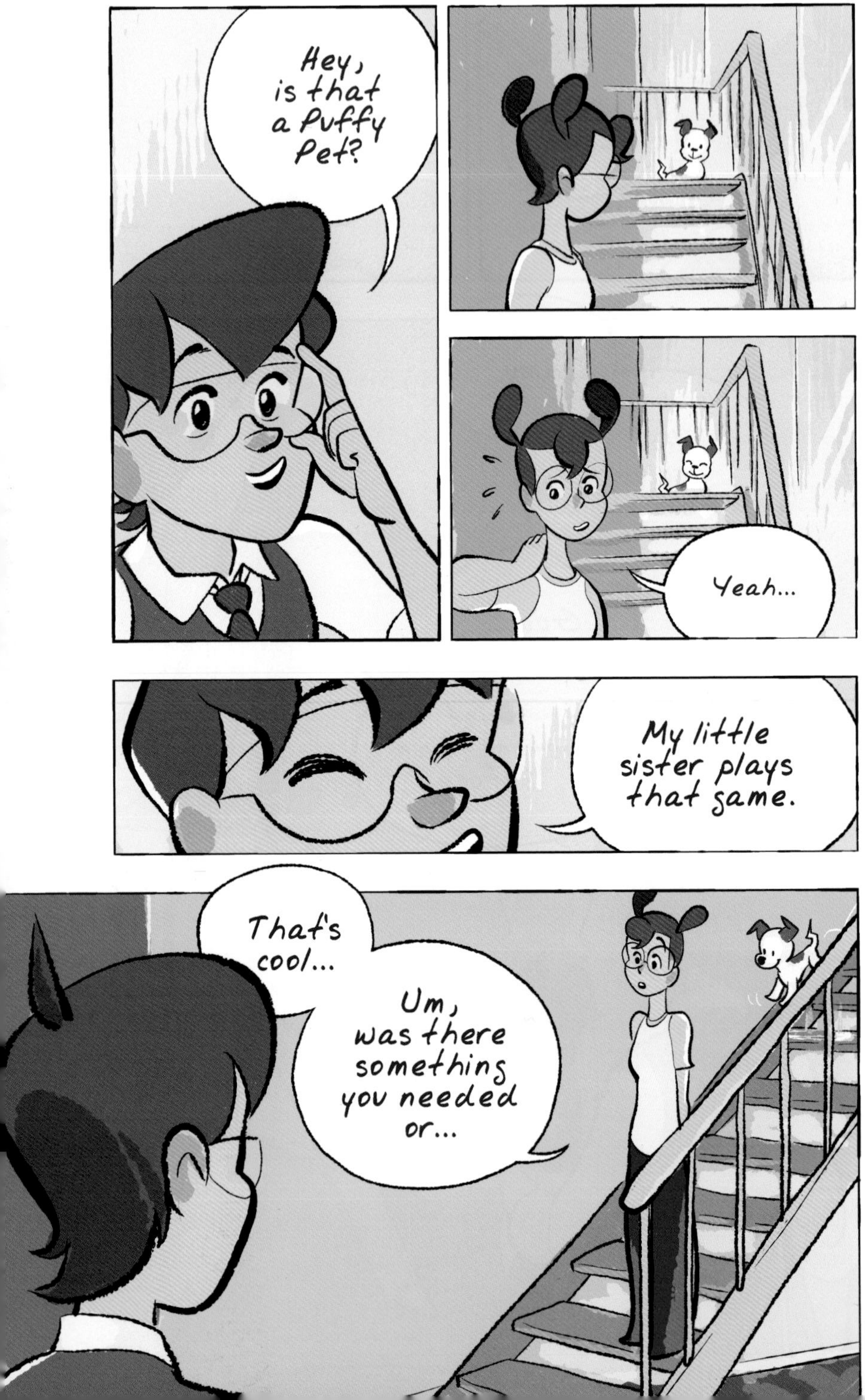
Hey, is that a Puffy Pet?
Yeah...
My little sister plays that game.
That's cool...
Um, was there something you needed or...

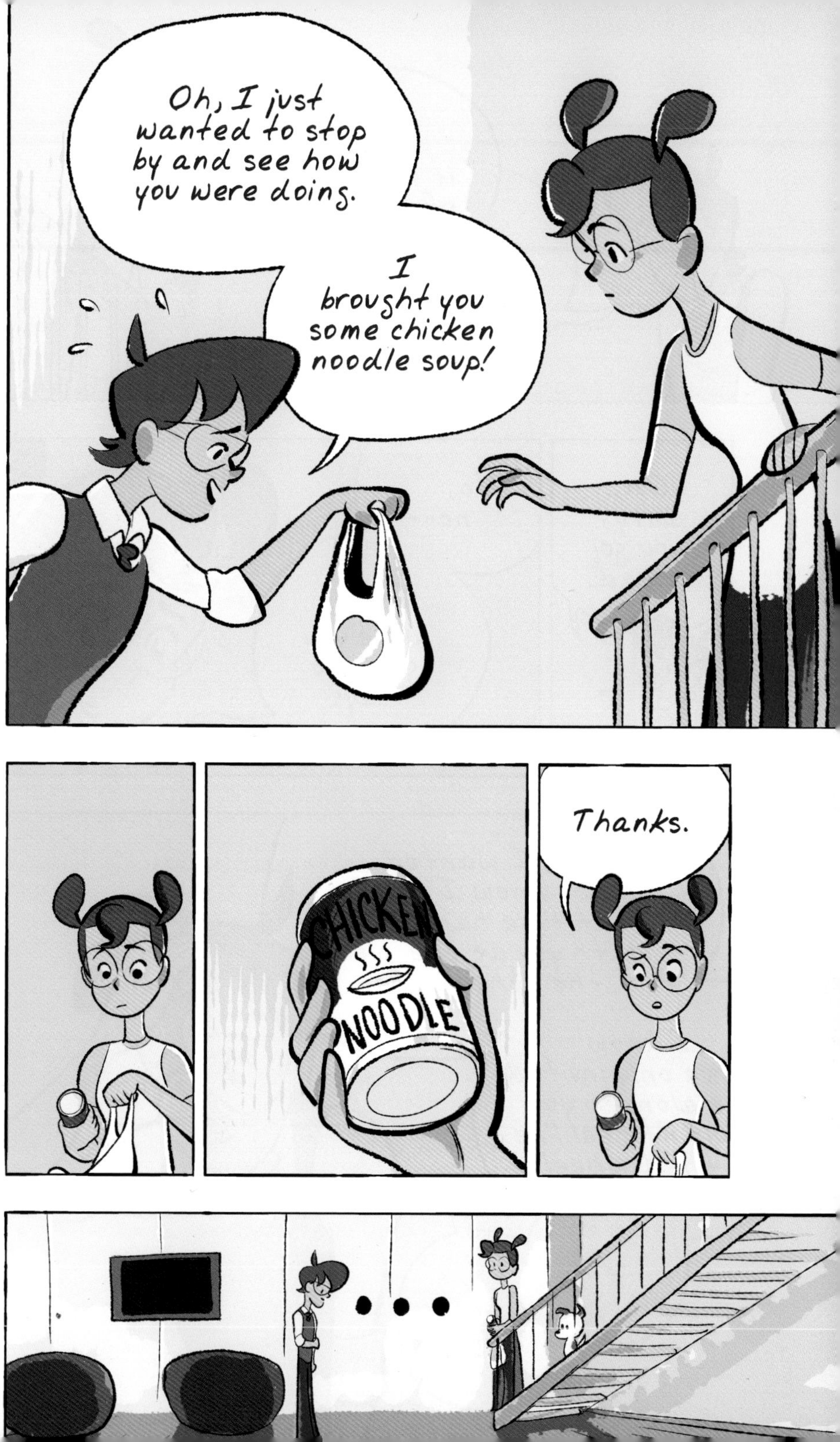
Oh, I just wanted to stop by and see how you were doing.
I brought you some chicken noodle soup!
CHICKEN NOODLE
Thanks.
...

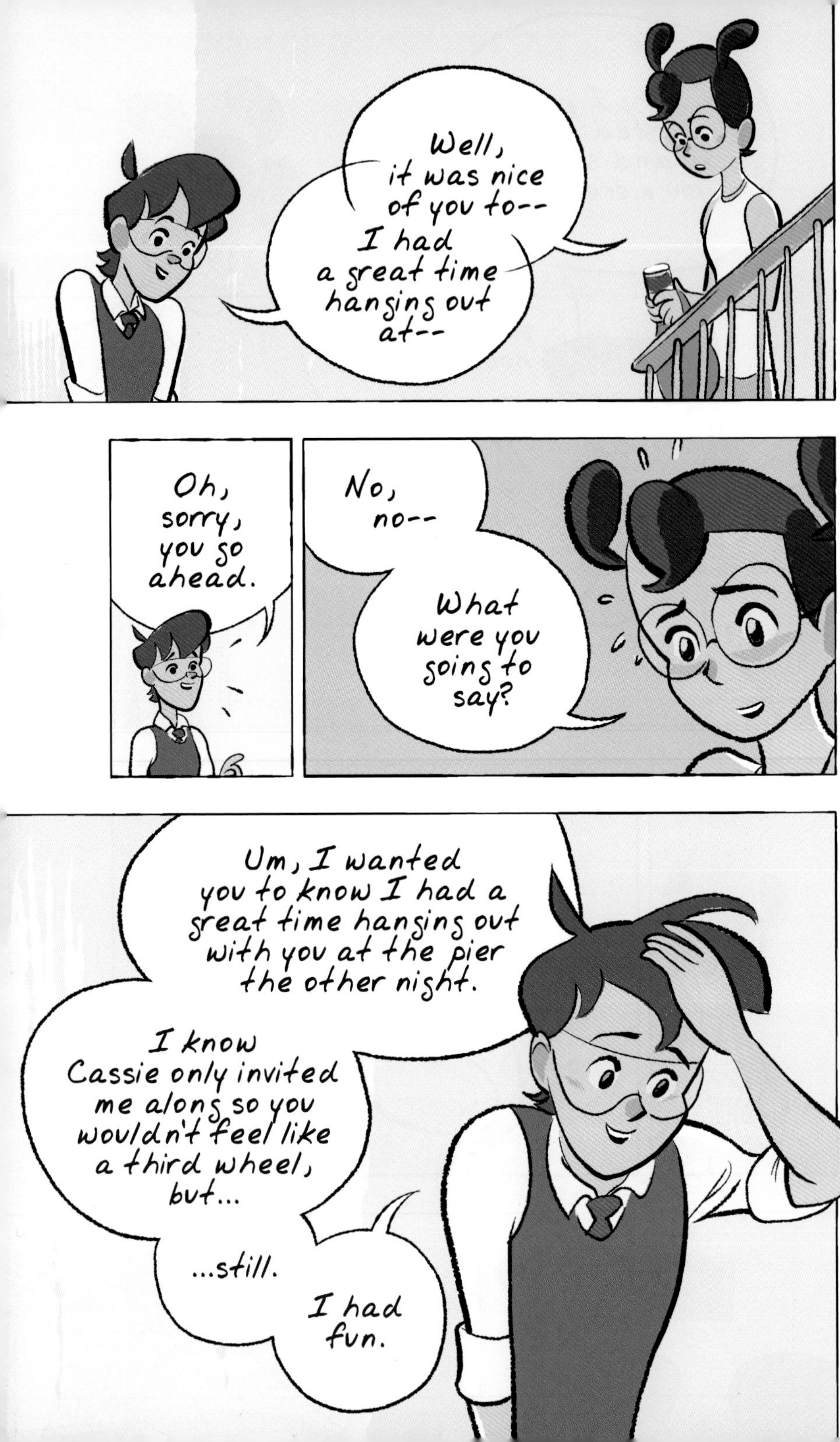
Well, it was nice of you to--
I had a great time hanging out at--
Oh, sorry, you go ahead.
No, no--
What were you going to say?
Um, I wanted you to know I had a great time hanging out with you at the pier the other night.
I know Cassie only invited me along so you wouldn't feel like a third wheel, but...
...still.
I had fun.

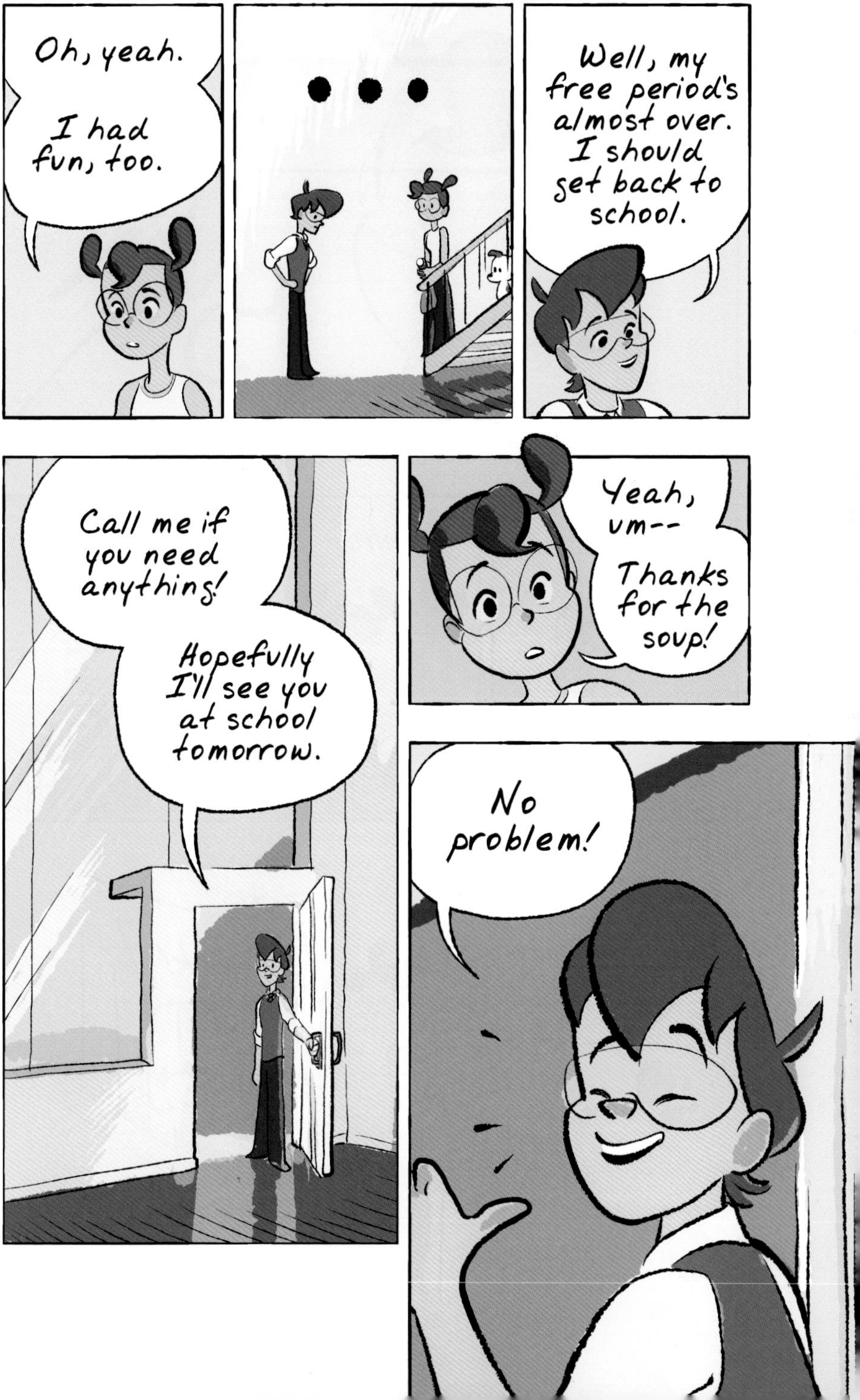
Oh, yeah.
I had fun, too.
Well, my free period's almost over. I should get back to school.
Call me if you need anything!
Hopefully I'll see you at school tomorrow.
Yeah, um--
Thanks for the soup!
No problem!

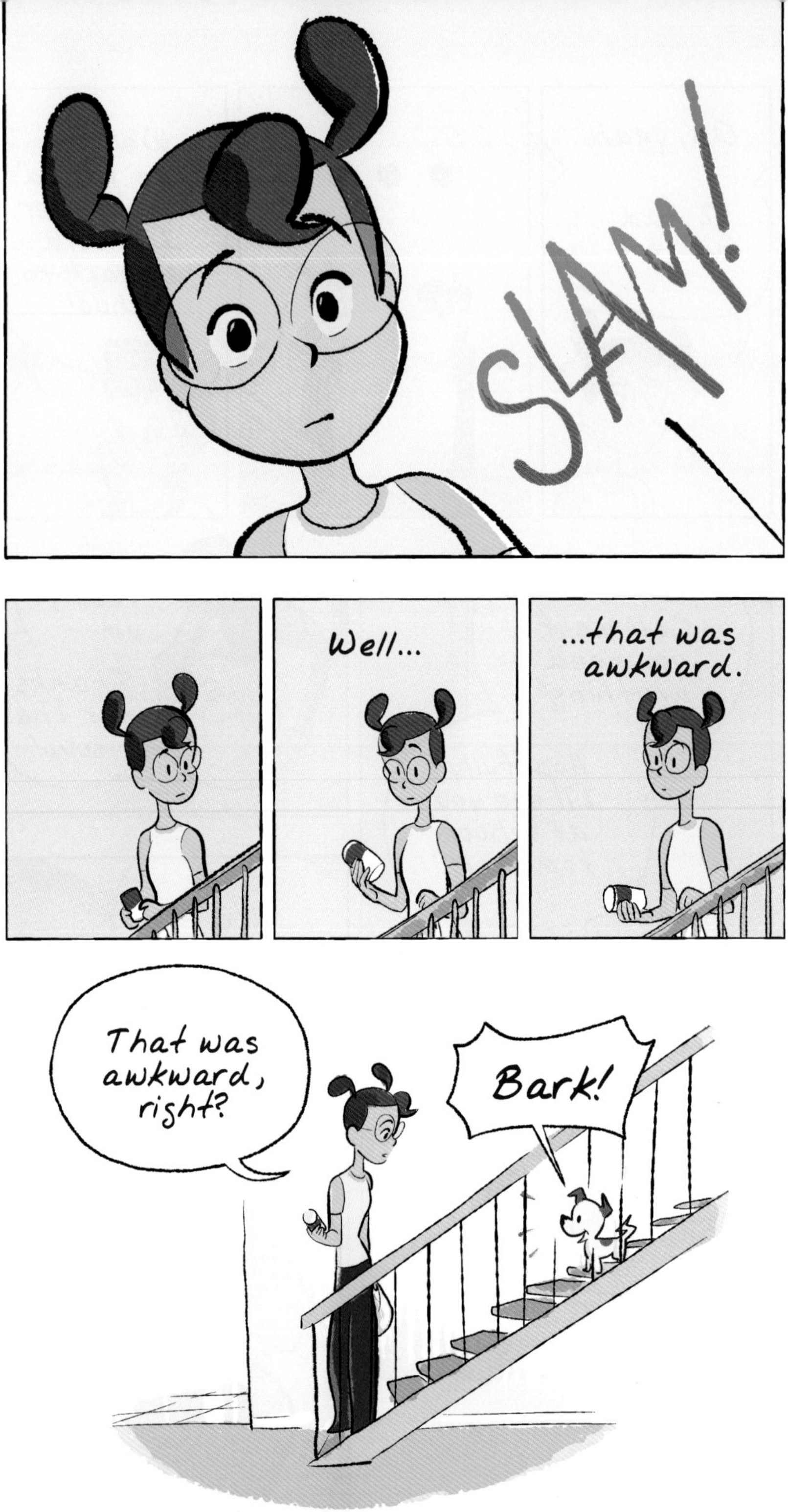
SLAM!
Well...
...that was awkward.
That was awkward, right?
Bark!

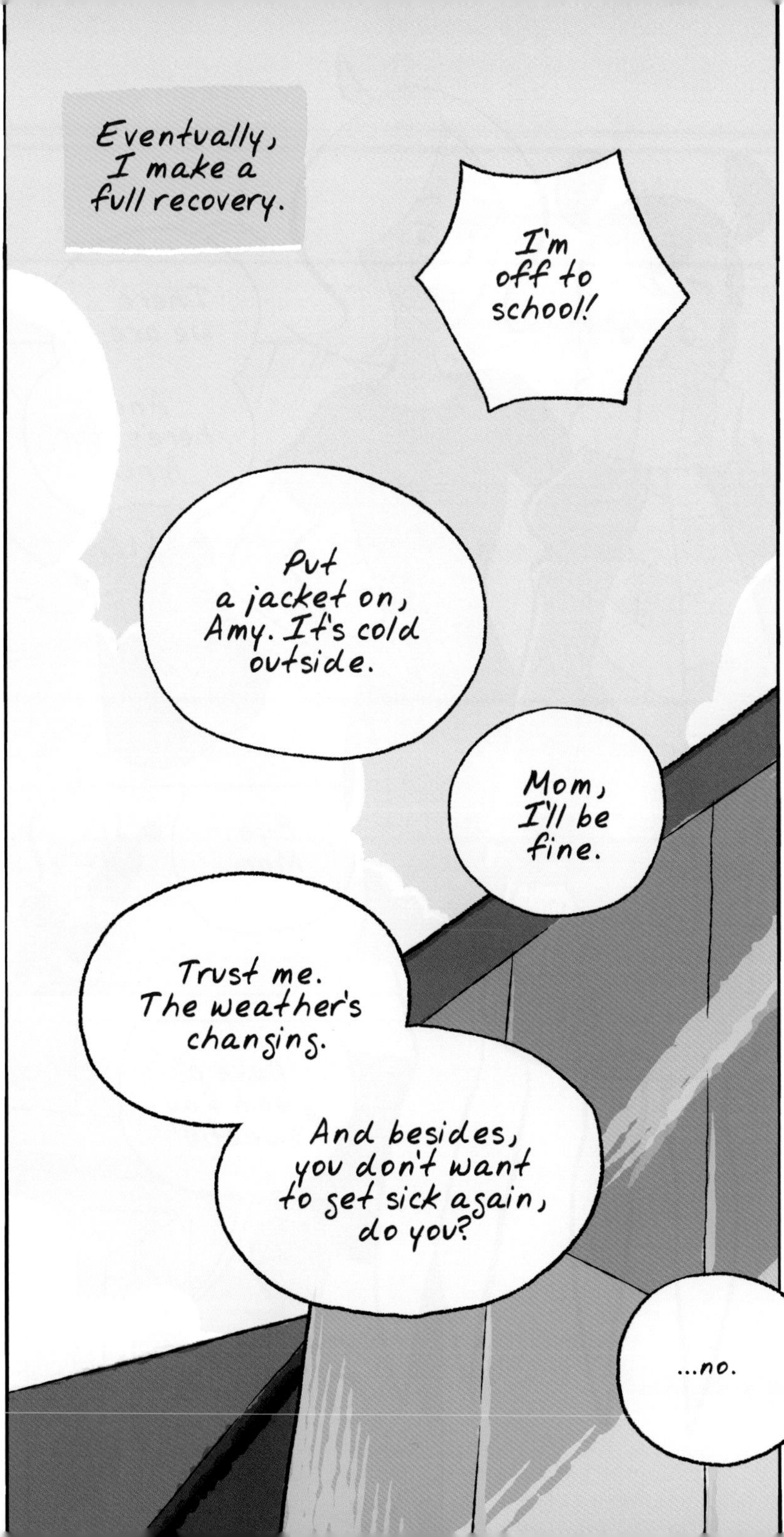
Eventually, I make a full recovery.
I'm off to school!
Put a jacket on, Amy. It's cold outside.
Mom, I'll be fine.
Trust me. The weather's changing.
And besides, you don't want to get sick again, do you?
...no.

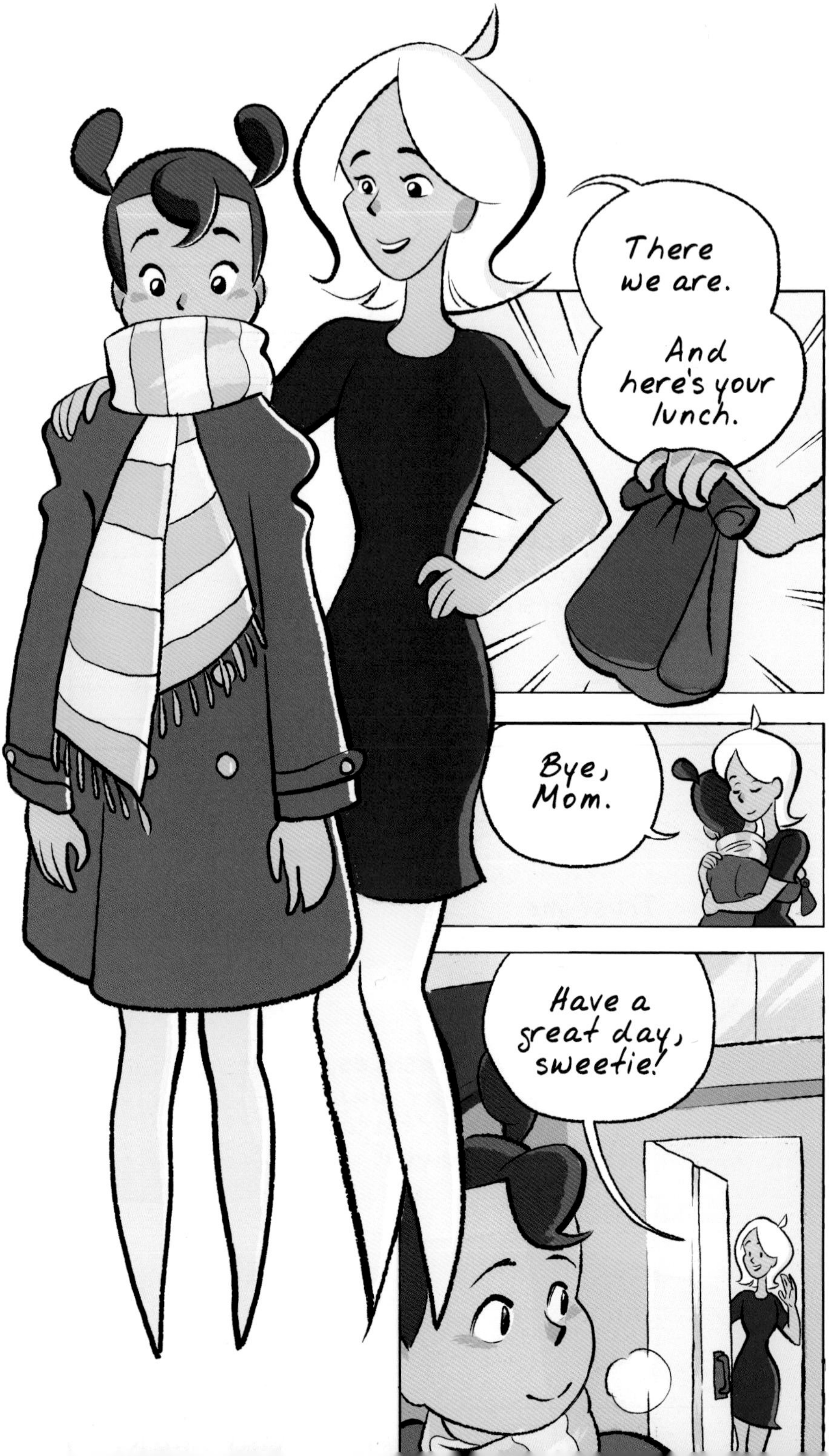
There we are.
And here's your lunch.
Bye, Mom.
Have a great day, sweetie!

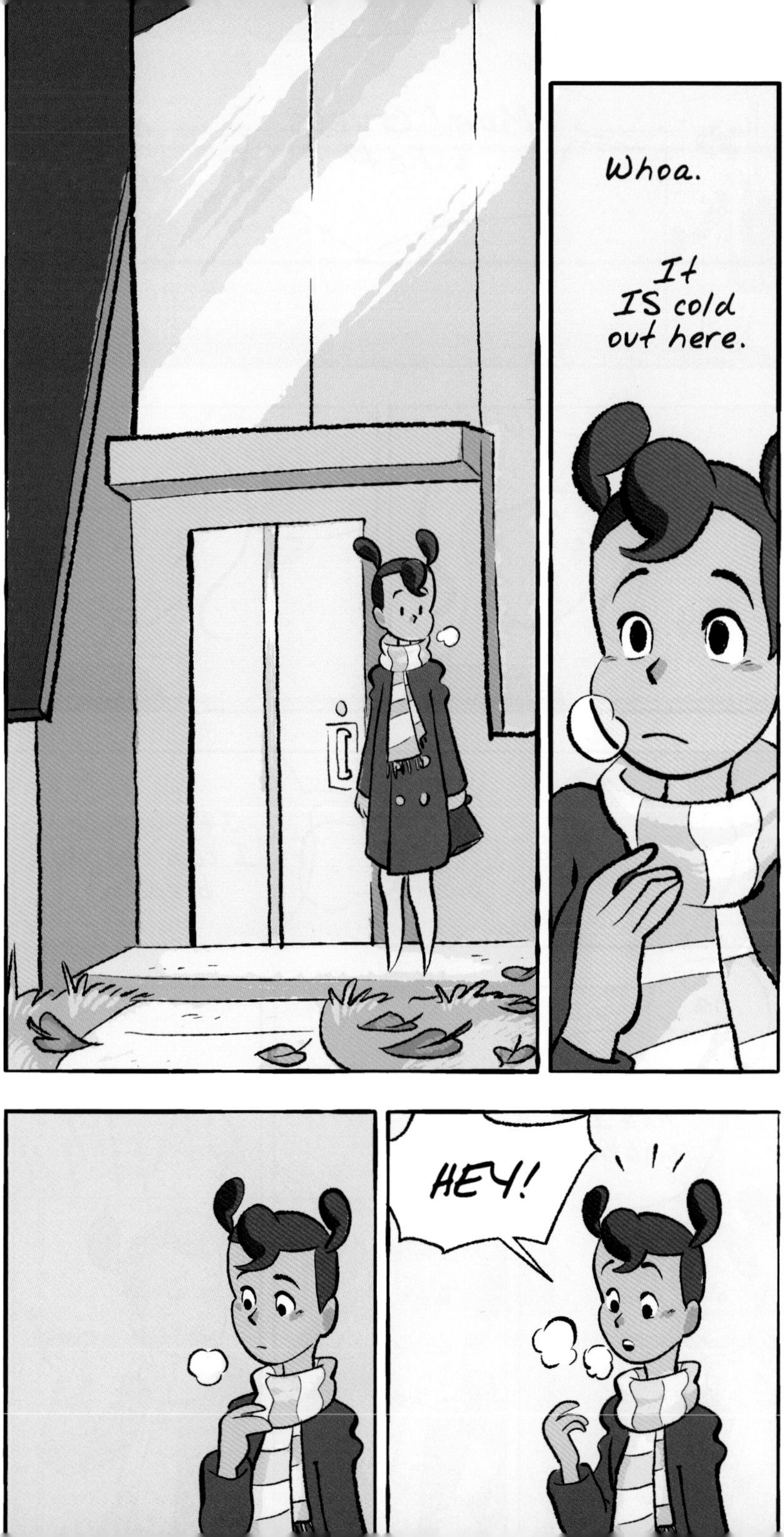
Whoa.
It IS cold out here.
HEY!

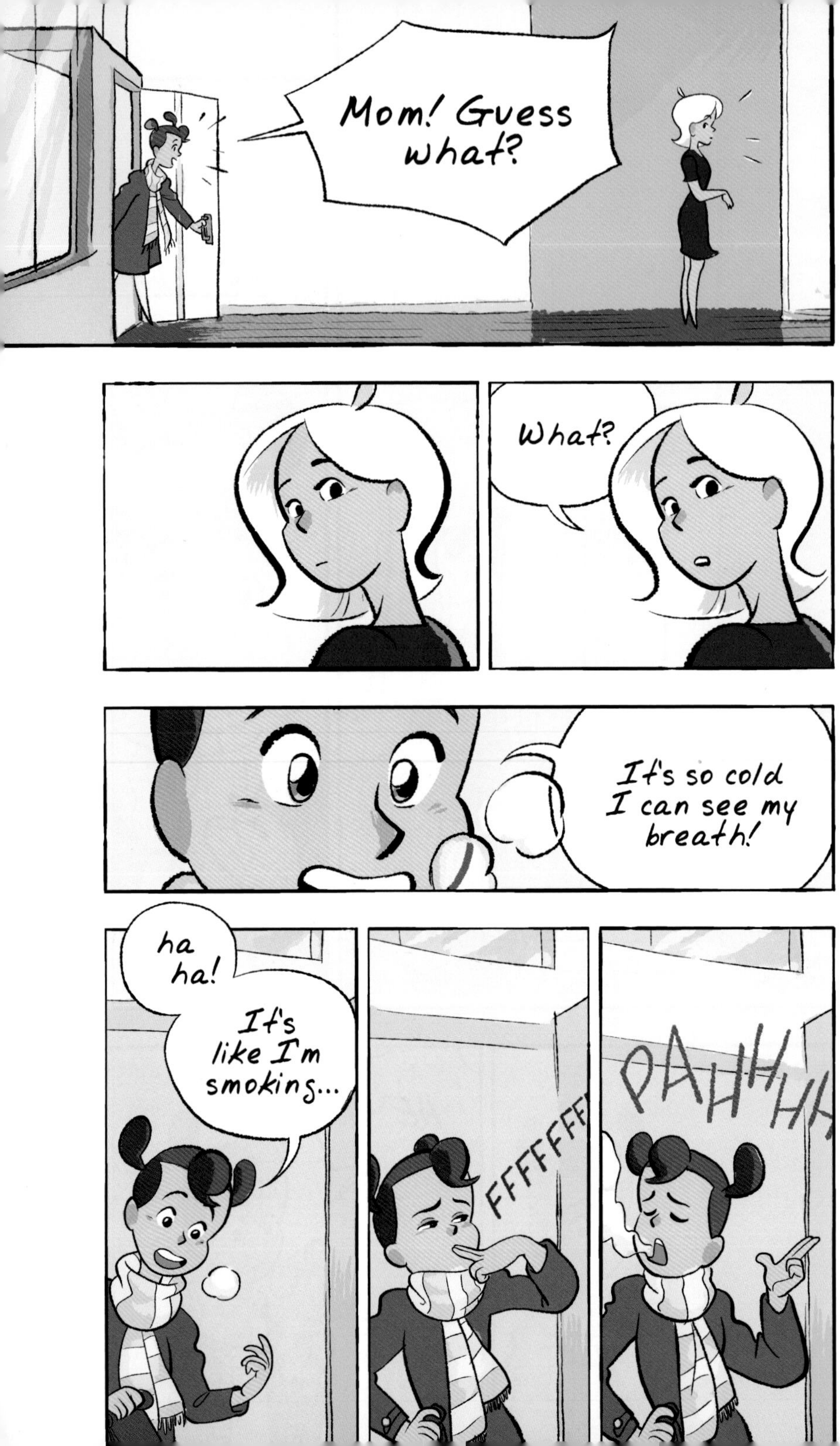
Mom! Guess what?
What?
It's so cold I can see my breath!
ha ha!
It's like I'm smoking...
FFFFFFF
PAHHHH

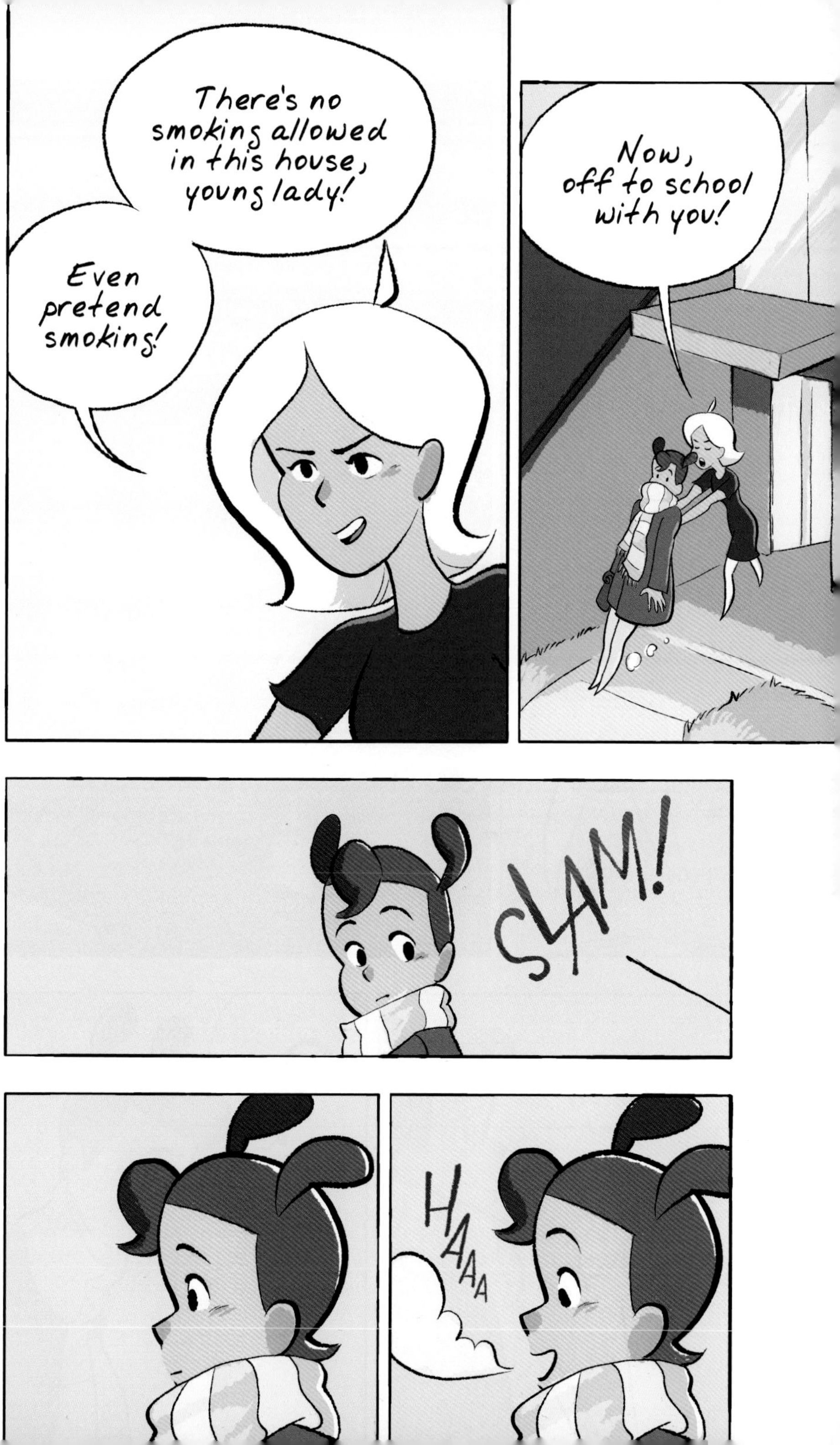
There's no smoking allowed in this house, young lady!
Even pretend smoking!
Now, off to school with you!
SLAM!
HAAAA

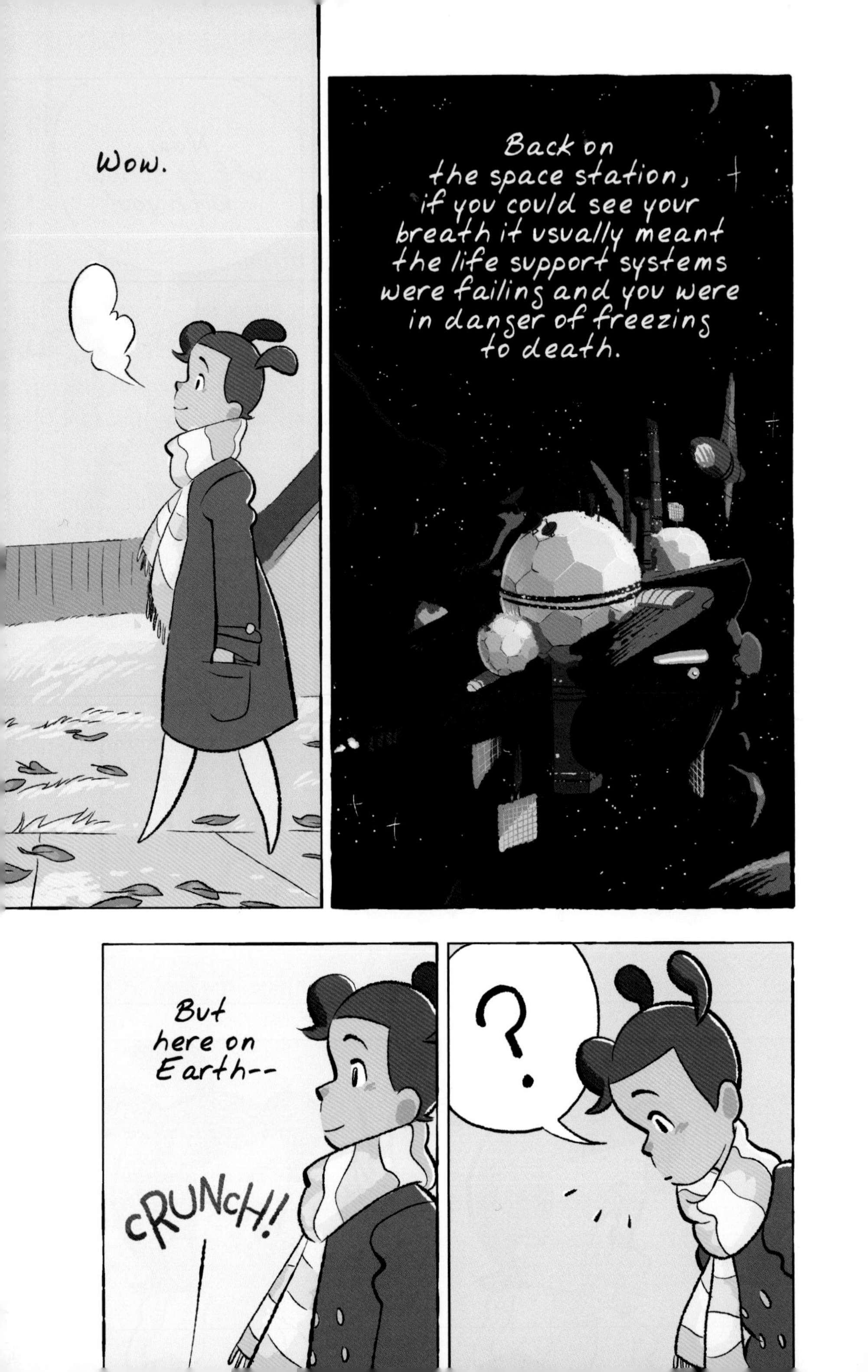
Wow.
Back on the space station, if you could see your breath it usually meant the life support systems were failing and you were in danger of freezing to death.
But here on Earth--
CRUNCH!
?

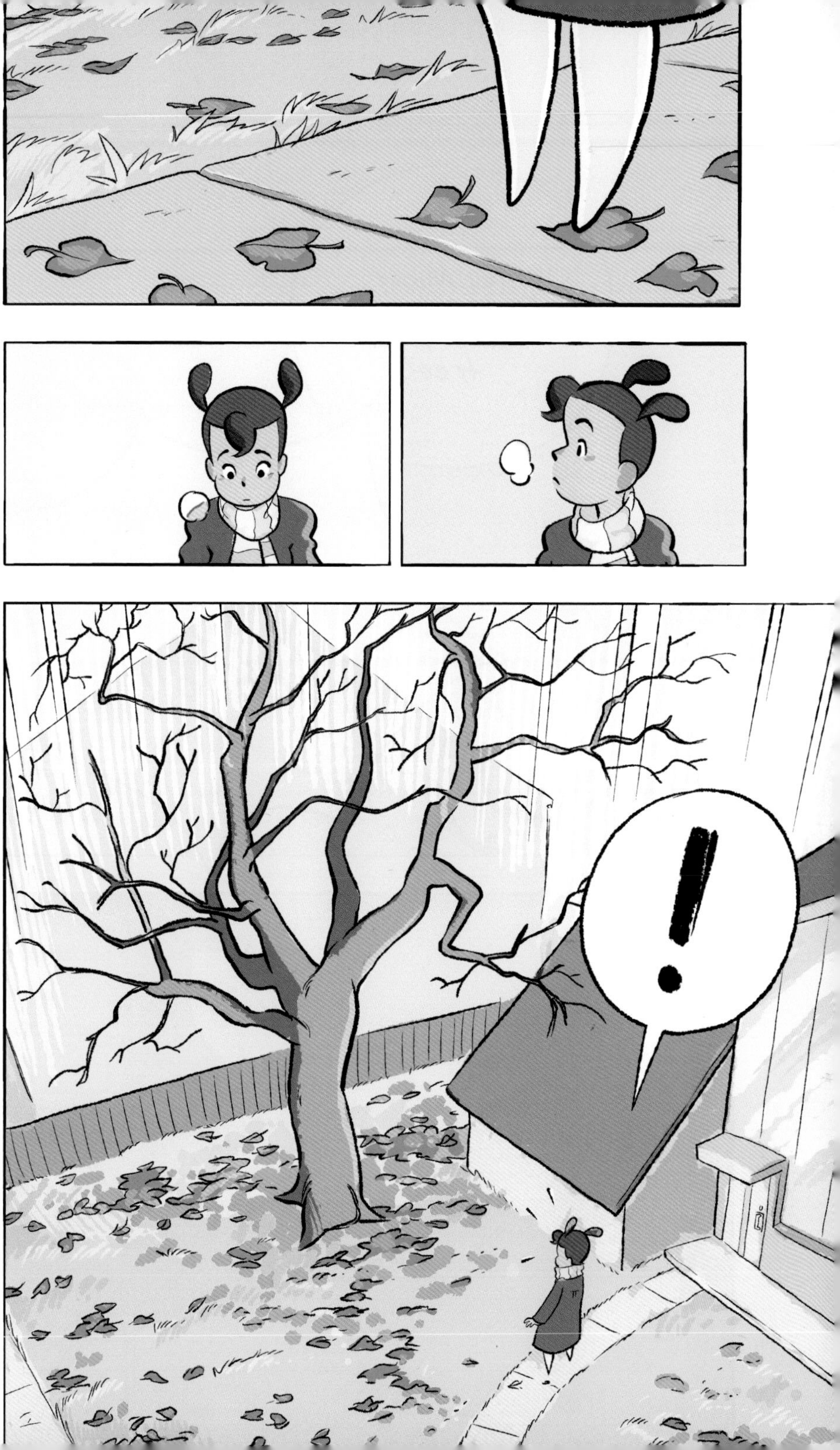
!

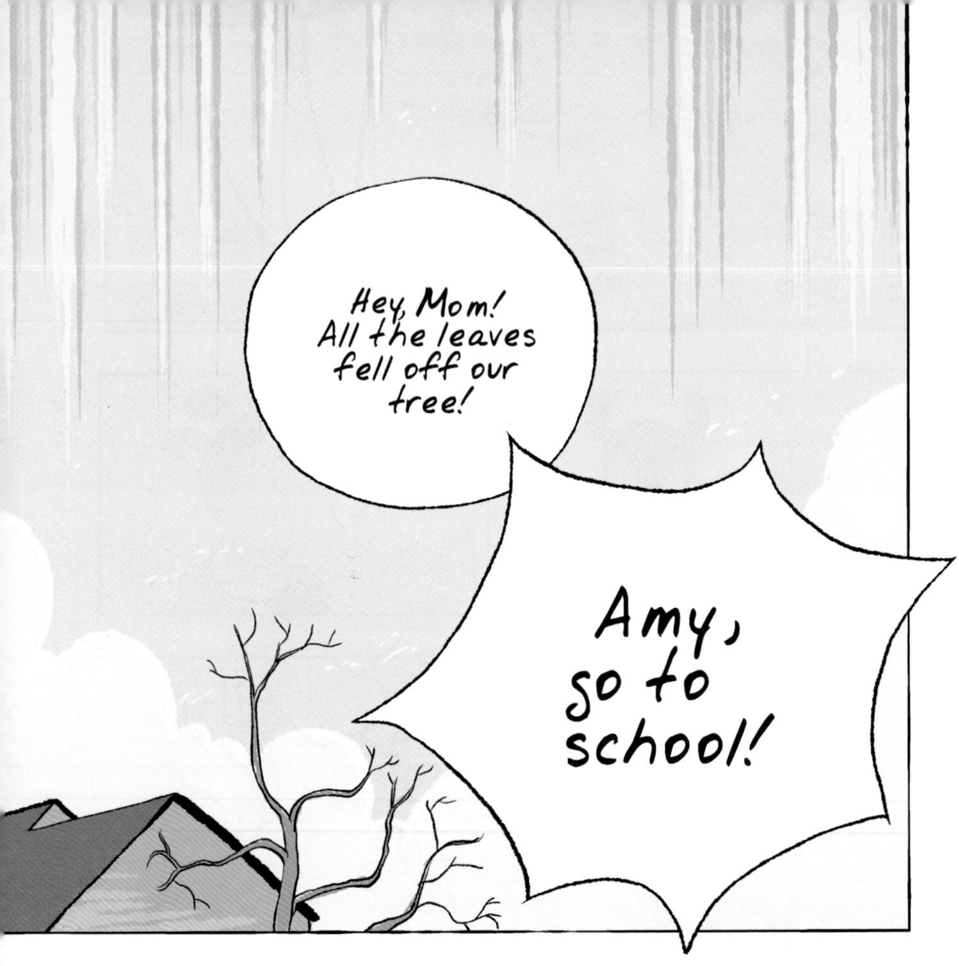
Hey, Mom! All the leaves fell off our tree!
Amy, go to school!

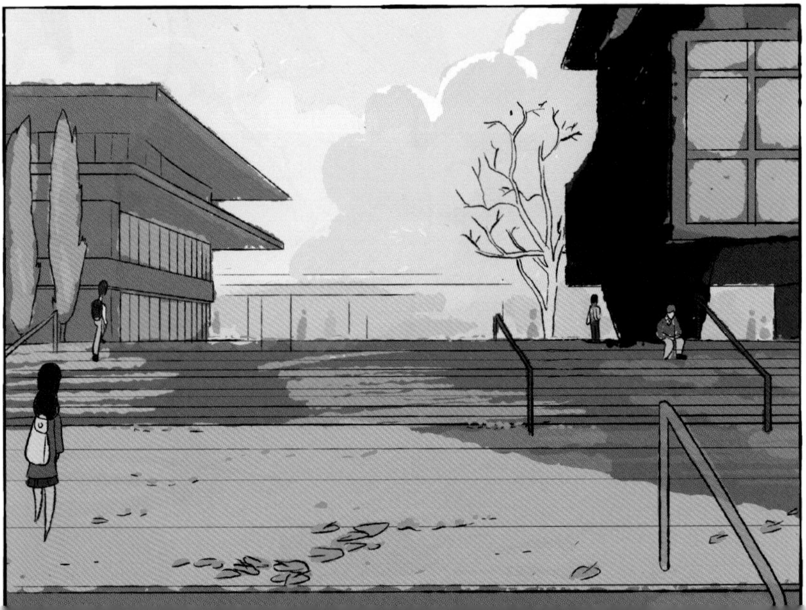

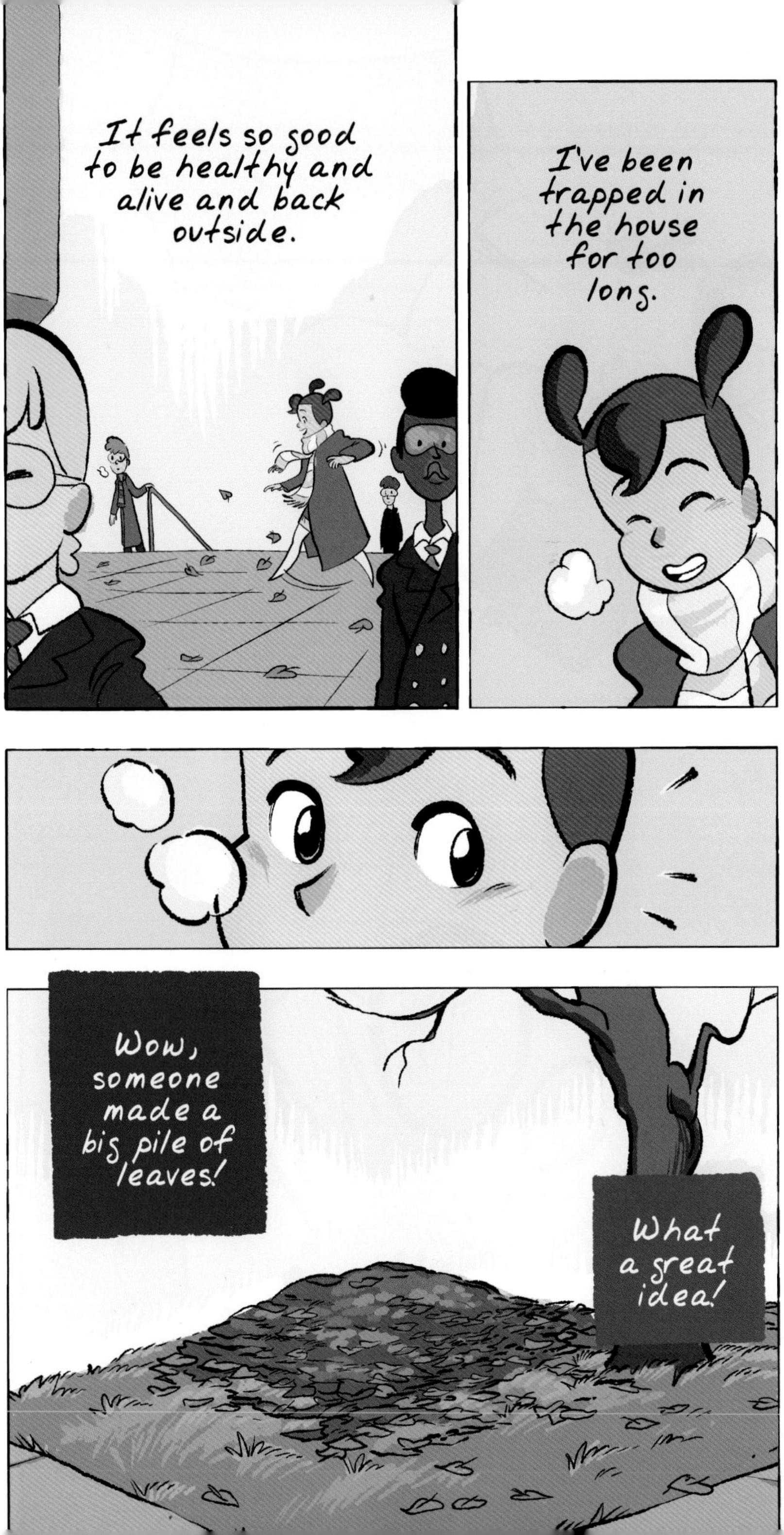
It feels so good to be healthy and alive and back outside.
I've been trapped in the house for too long.
Wow, someone made a big pile of leaves!
What a great idea!

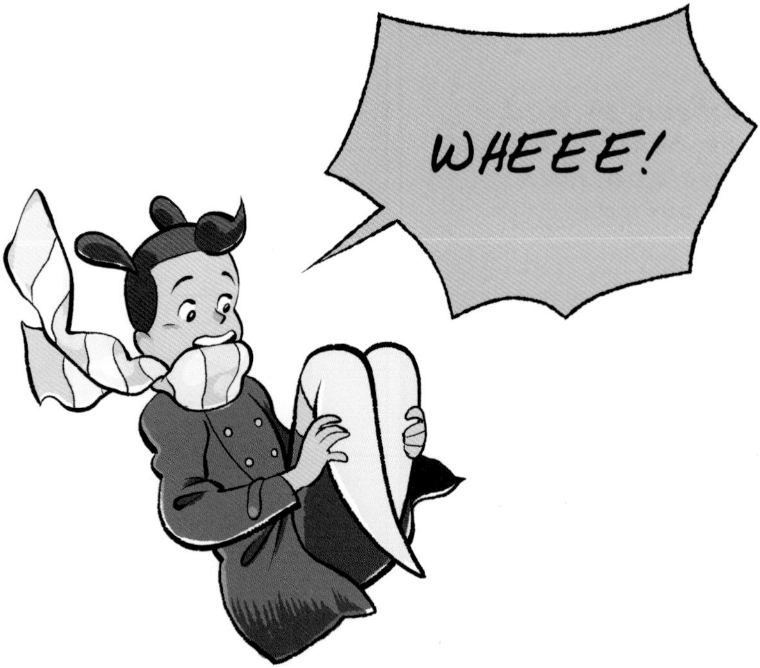
WHEEE!

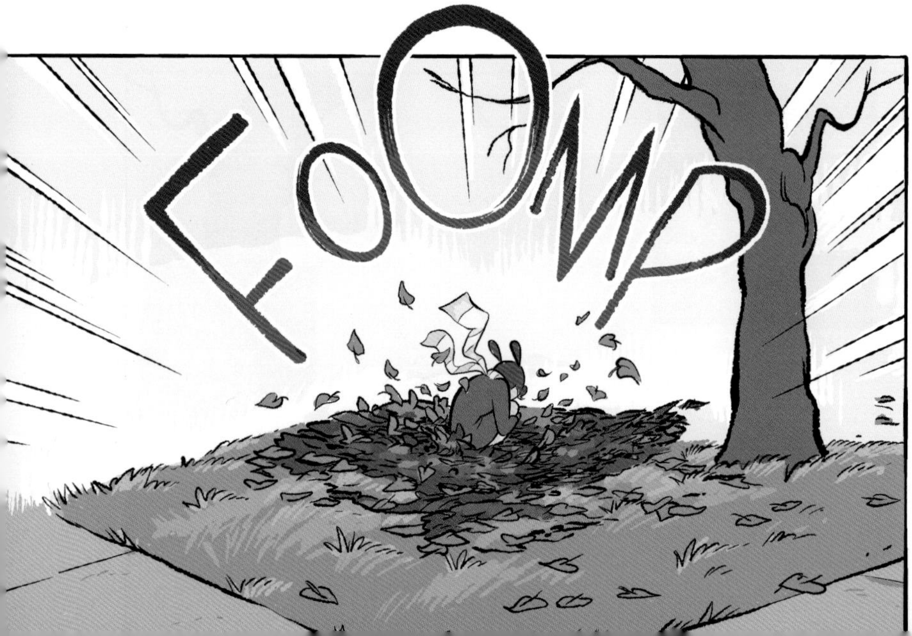
FOOMP

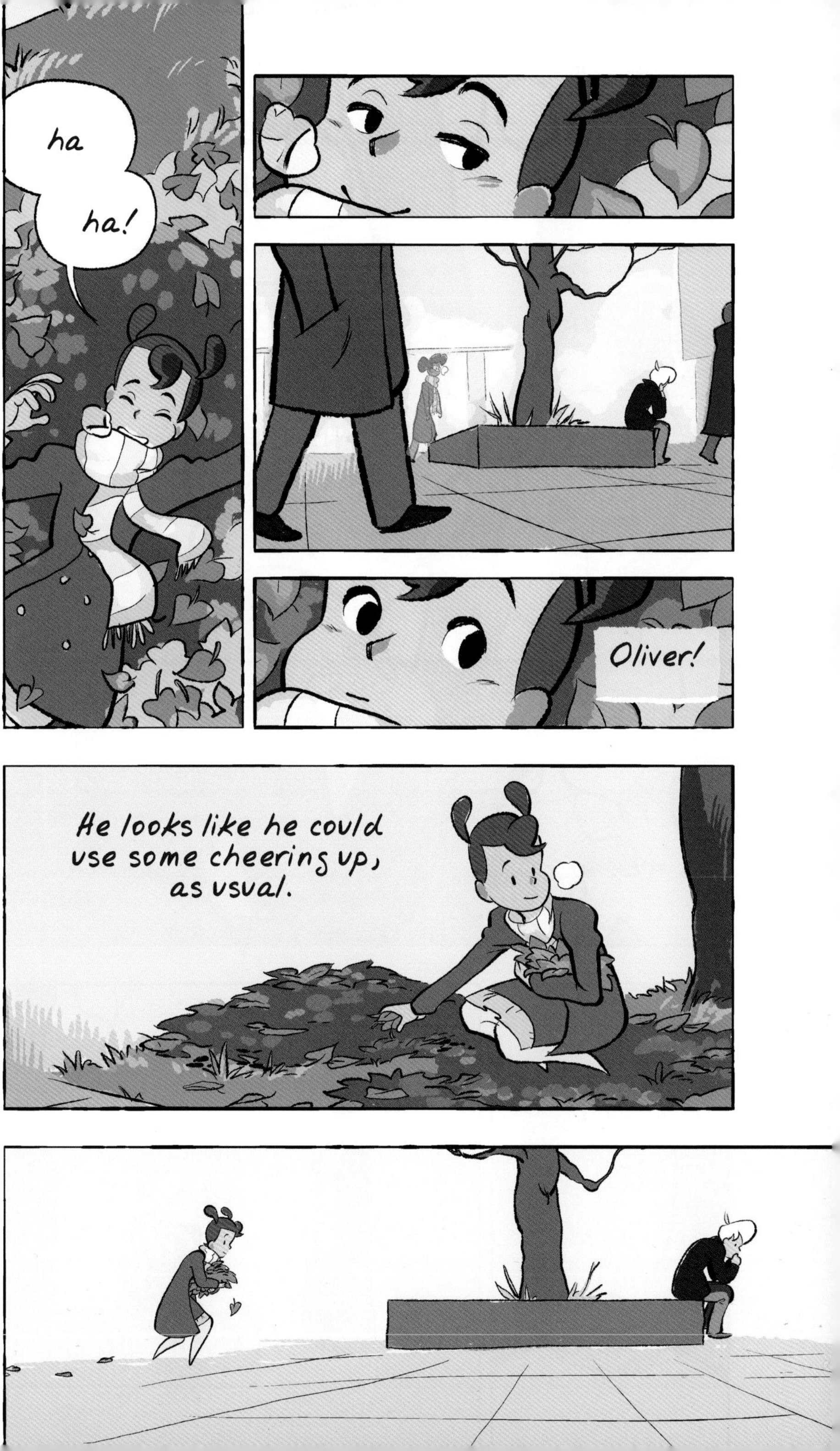
ha
ha!
Oliver!
He looks like he could use some cheering up, as usual.

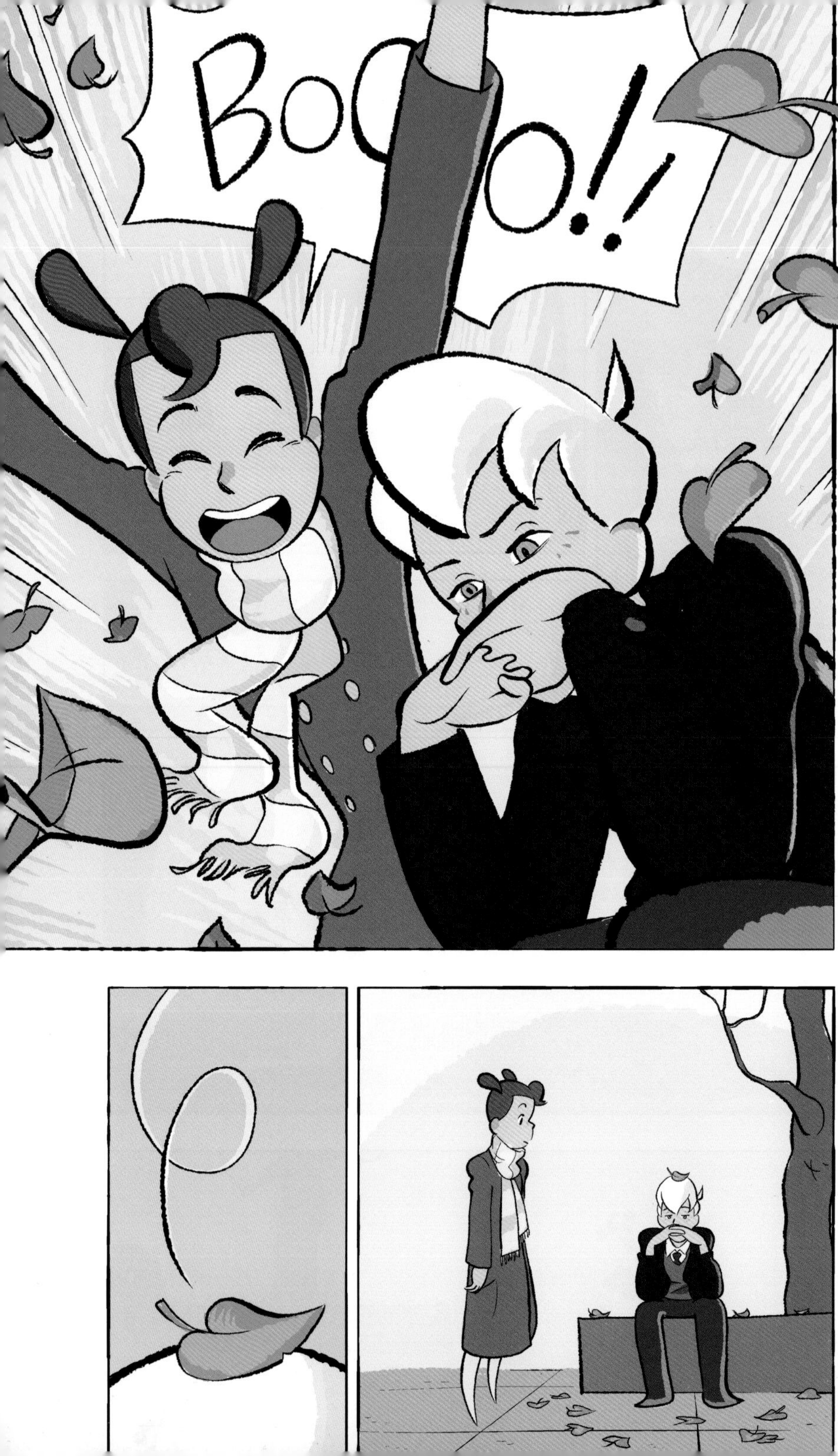
BOOO!!

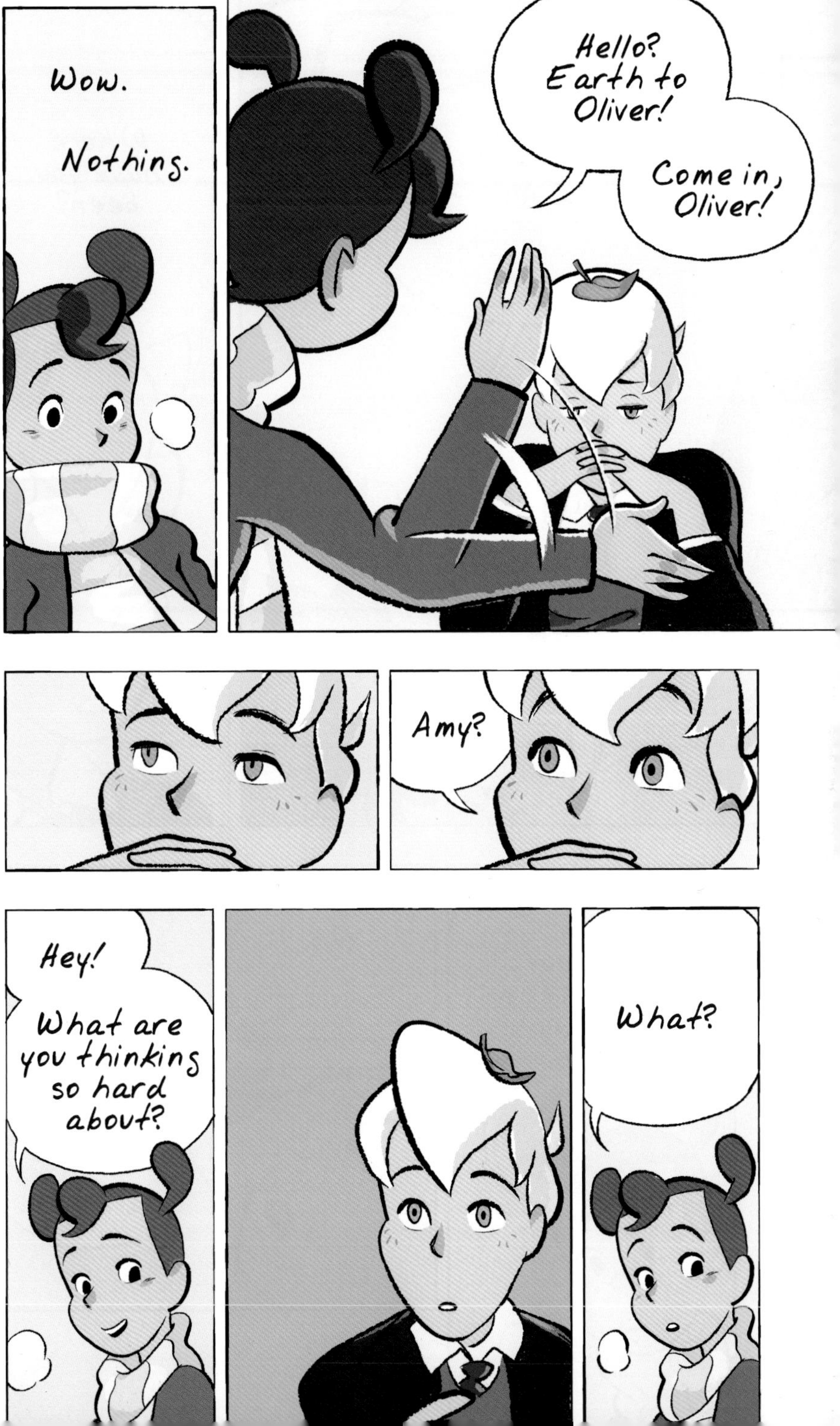
Wow.
Nothing.
Hello? Earth to Oliver!
Come in, Oliver!
Amy?
Hey!
What are you thinking so hard about?
What?

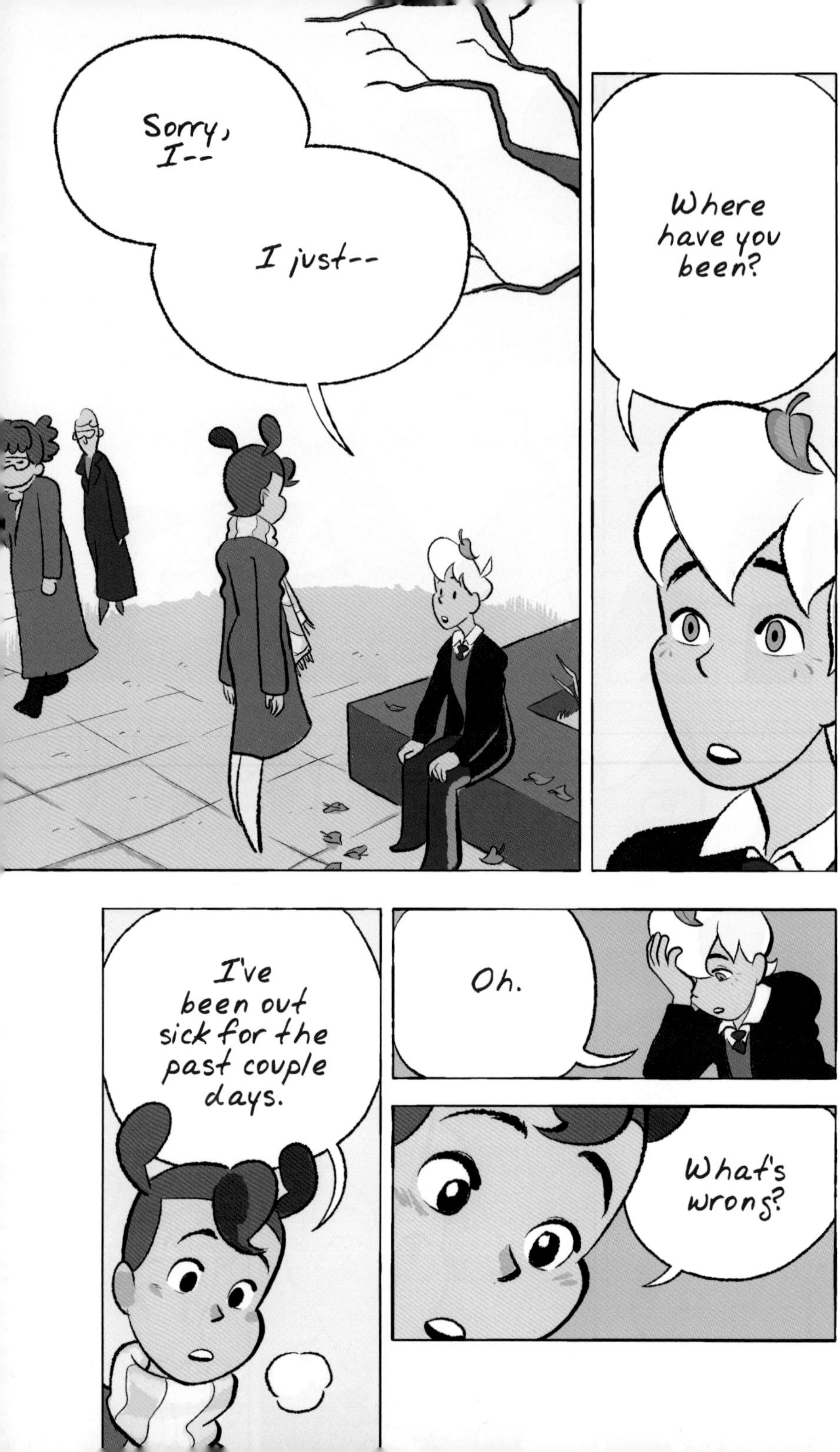
Sorry, I--
I just--
Where have you been?
I've been out sick for the past couple days.
Oh.
What's wrong?

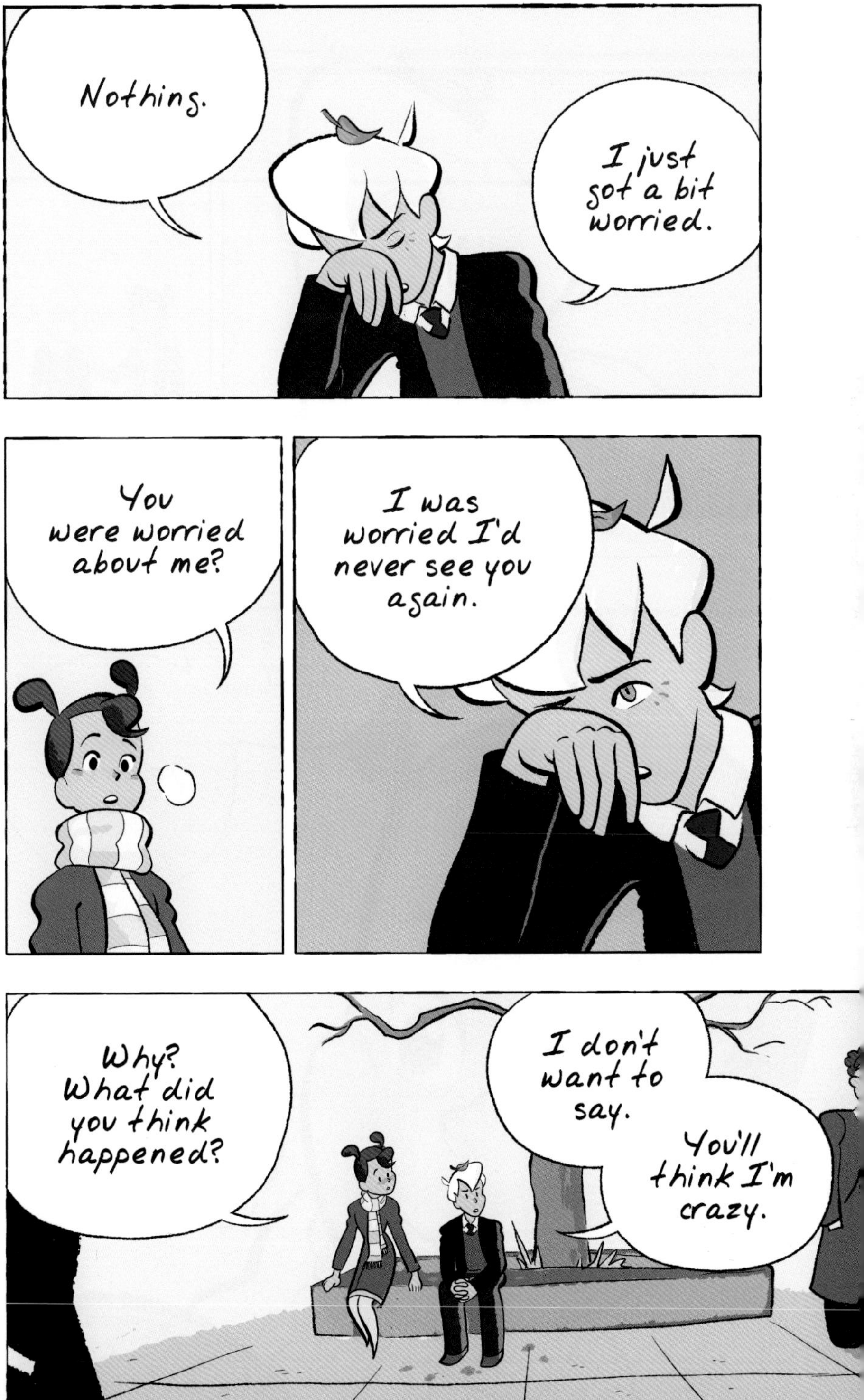
Nothing.
I just got a bit worried.
You were worried about me?
I was worried I'd never see you again.
Why? What did you think happened?
I don't want to say.
You'll think I'm crazy.

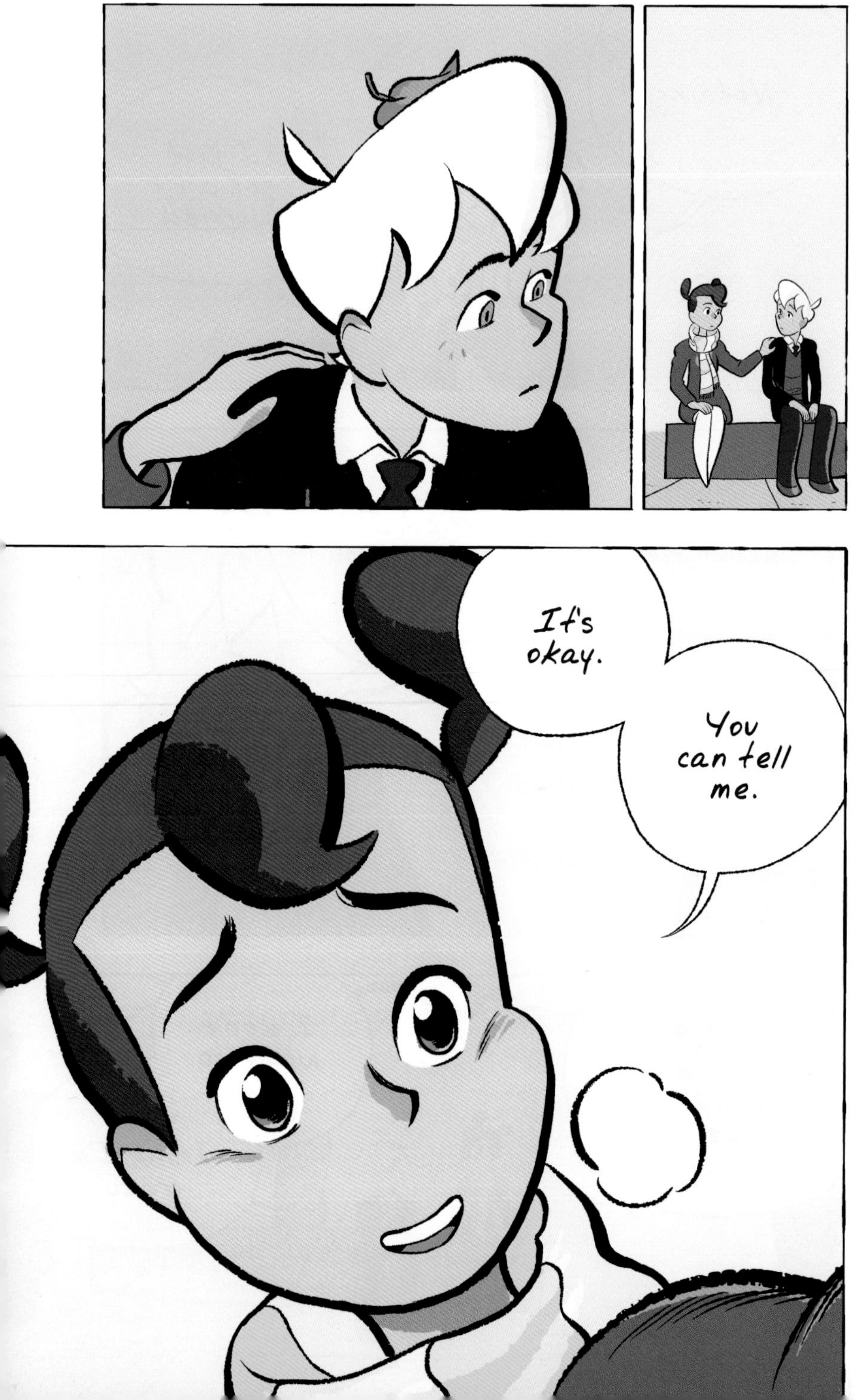
It's okay.
You can tell me.

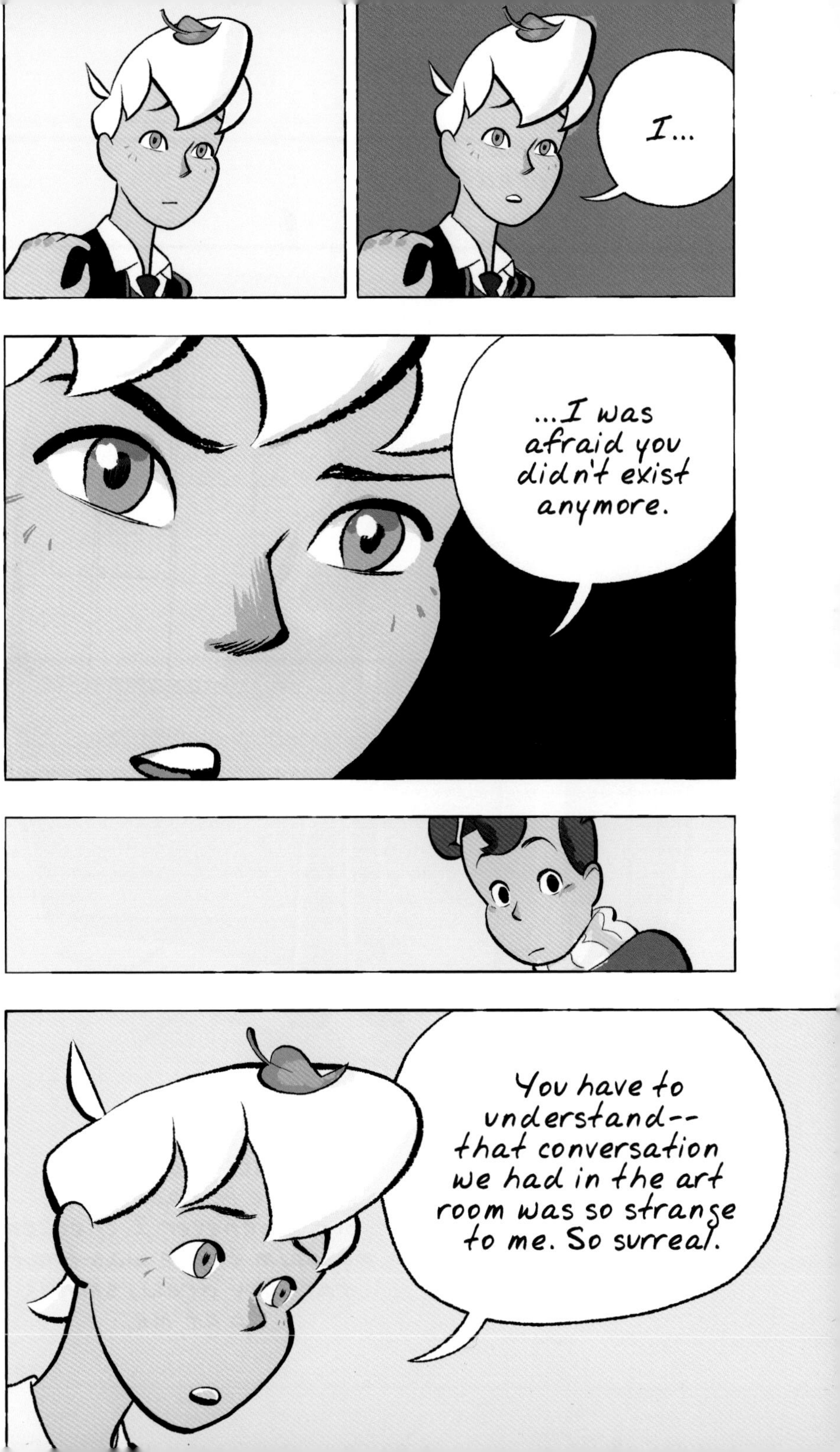
I...
...I was afraid you didn't exist anymore.
You have to understand-- that conversation we had in the art room was so strange to me. So surreal.

"You appeared out of nowhere and then disappeared just as quick.

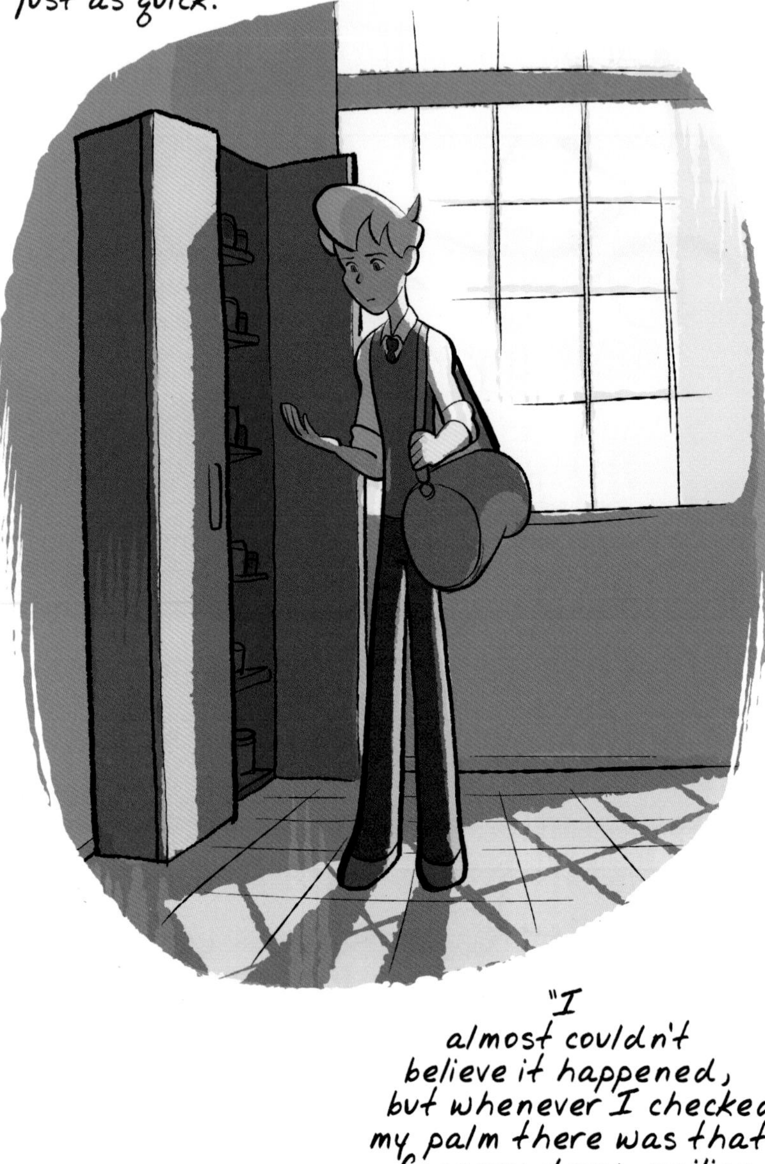

"I almost couldn't believe it happened, but whenever I checked my palm there was that face you drew, smiling up at me.

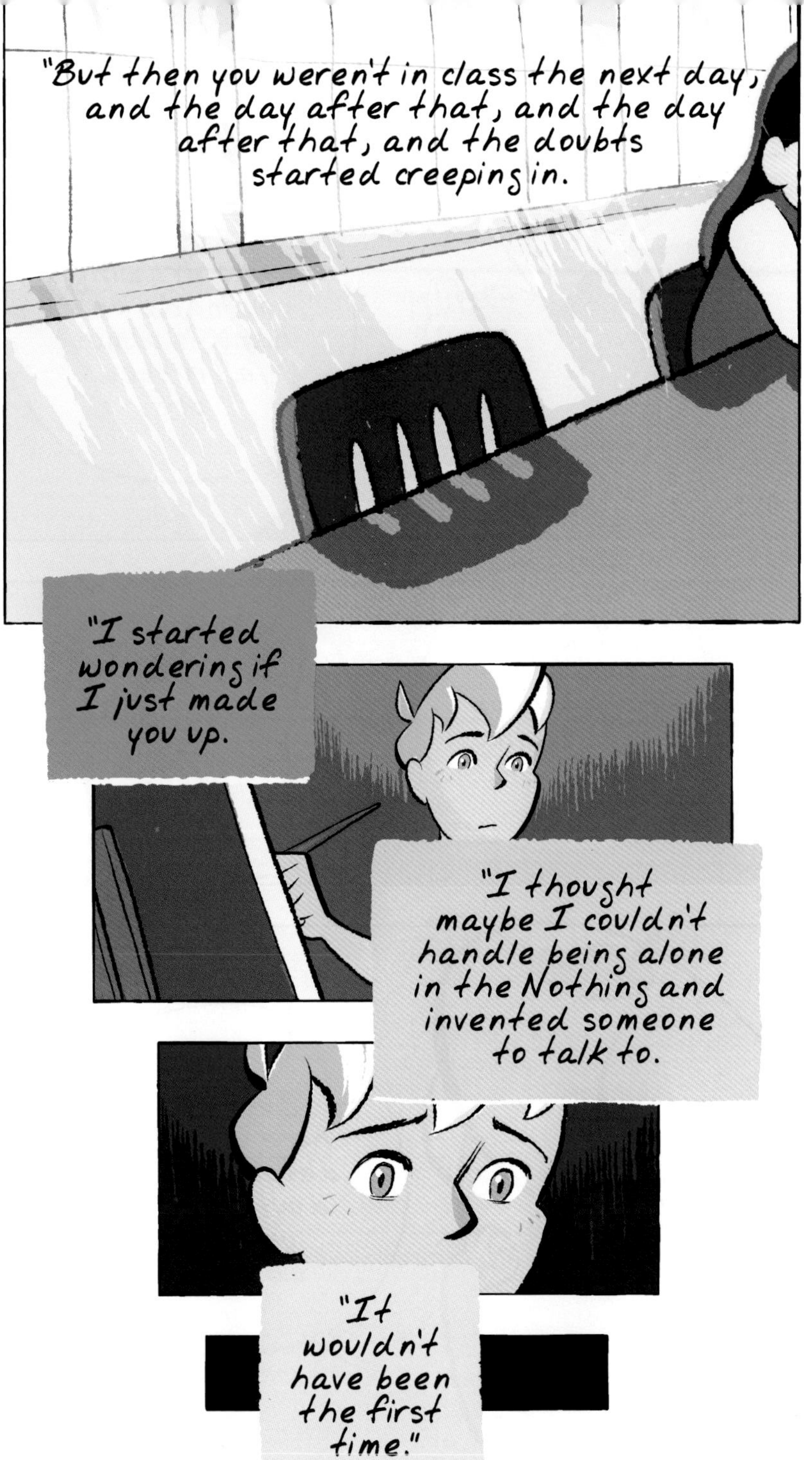
"But then you weren't in class the next day, and the day after that, and the day after that, and the doubts started creeping in.
"I started wondering if I just made you up.
"I thought maybe I couldn't handle being alone in the Nothing and invented someone to talk to.
"It wouldn't have been the first time."

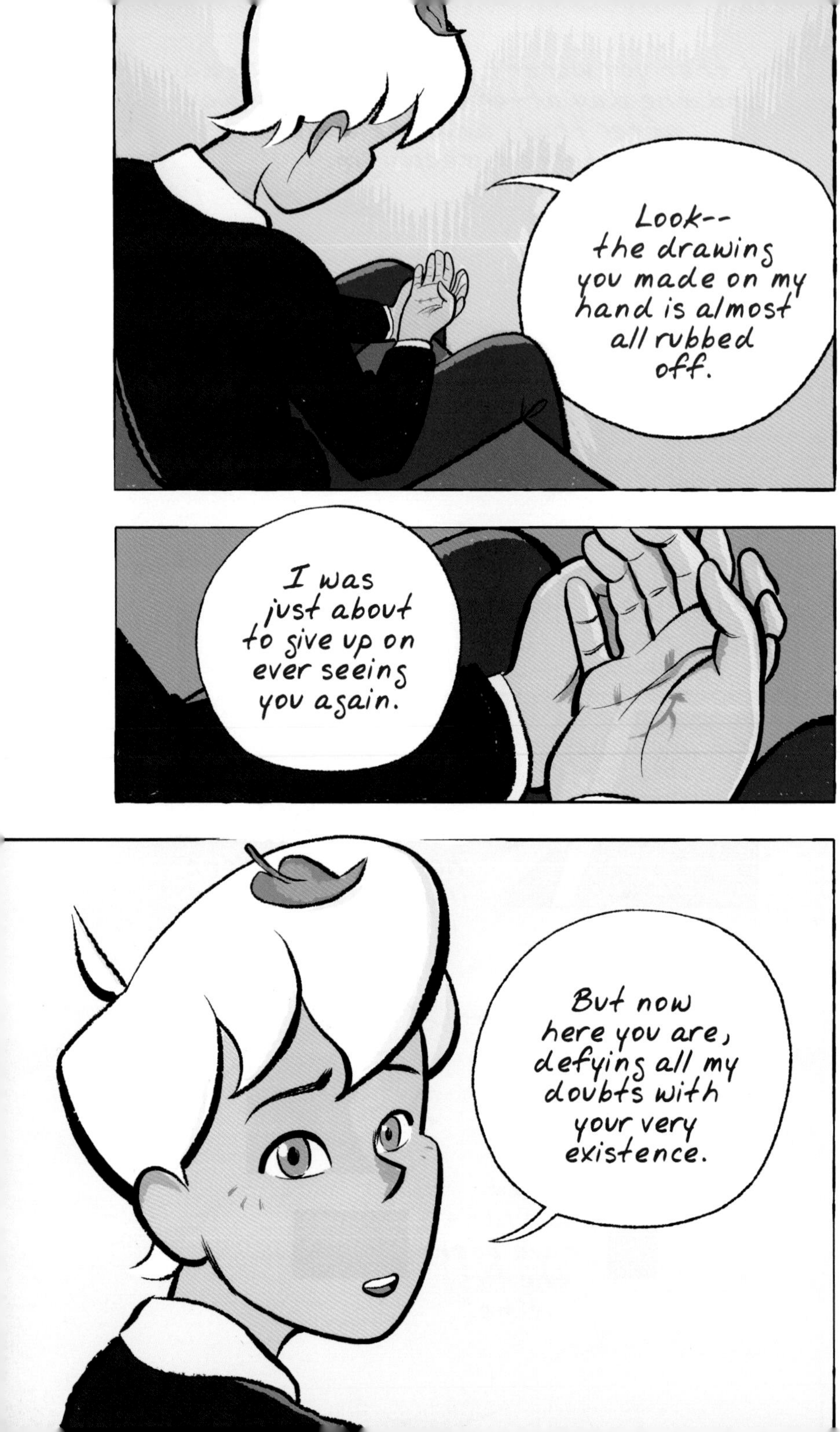
Look-- the drawings you made on my hand is almost all rubbed off.
I was just about to give up on ever seeing you again.
But now here you are, defying all my doubts with your very existence.

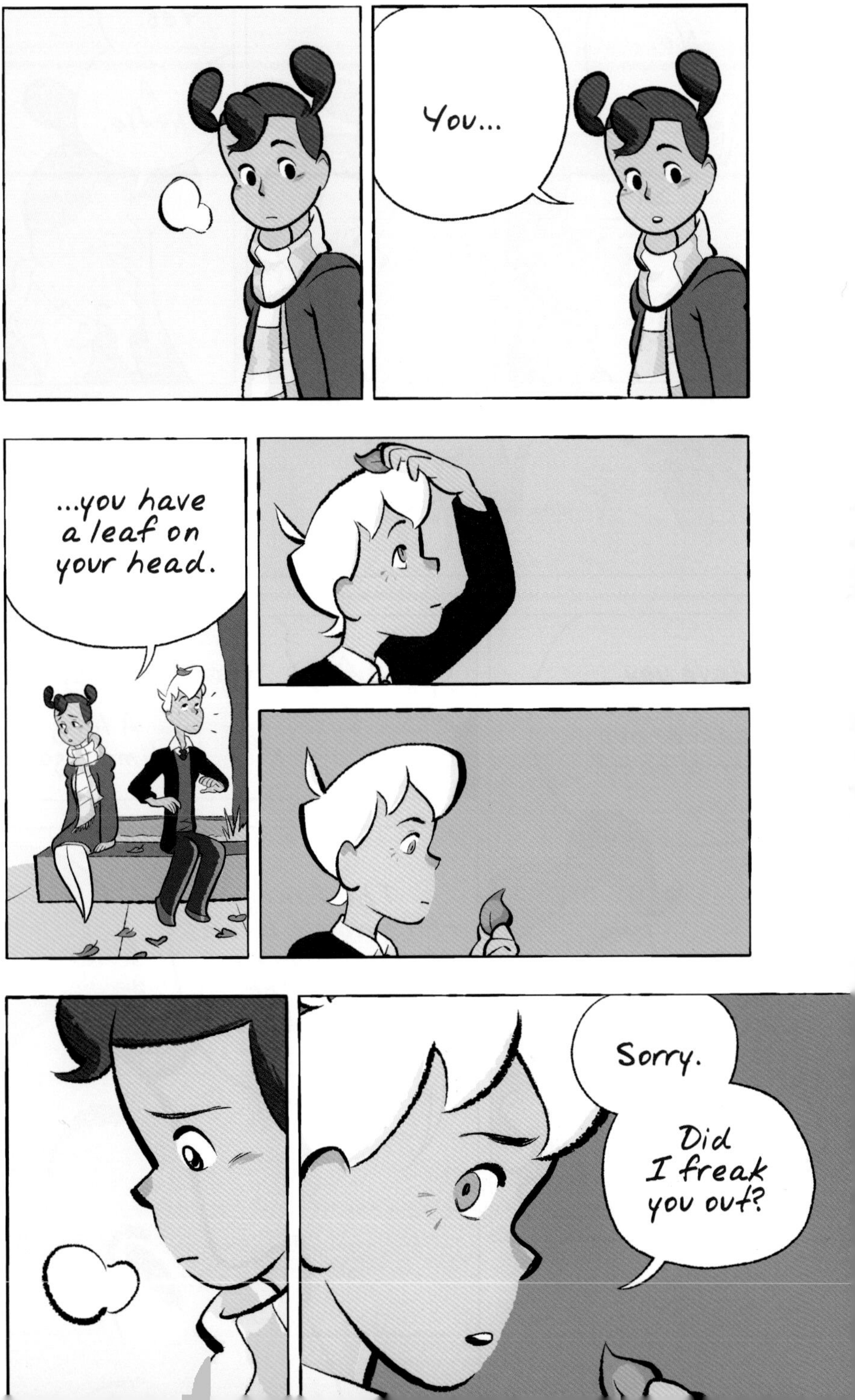
You...
...you have a leaf on your head.
Sorry.
Did I freak you out?

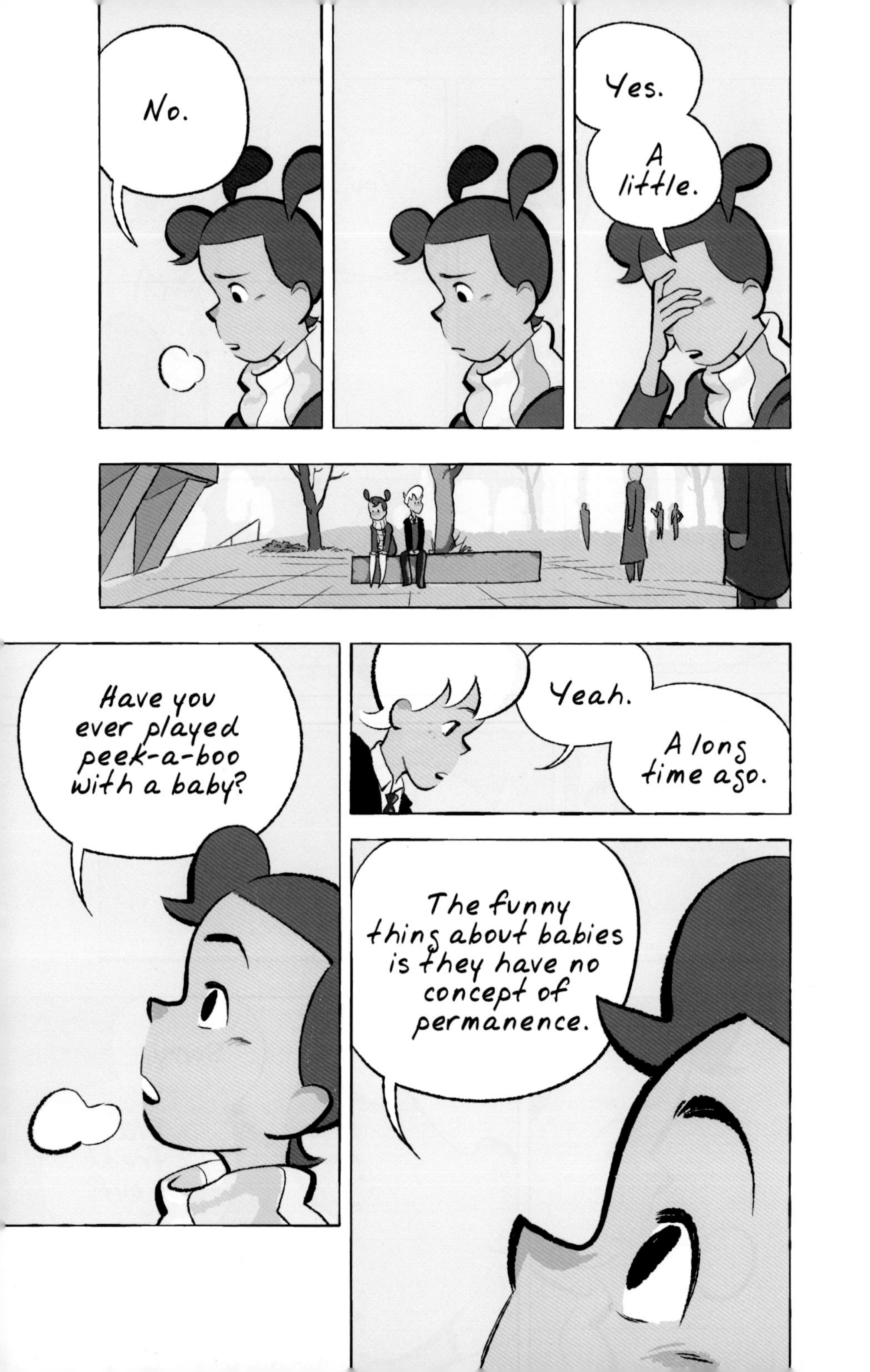
No.
Yes.
A little.
Have you ever played peek-a-boo with a baby?
Yeah.
A long time ago.
The funny thing about babies is they have no concept of permanence.

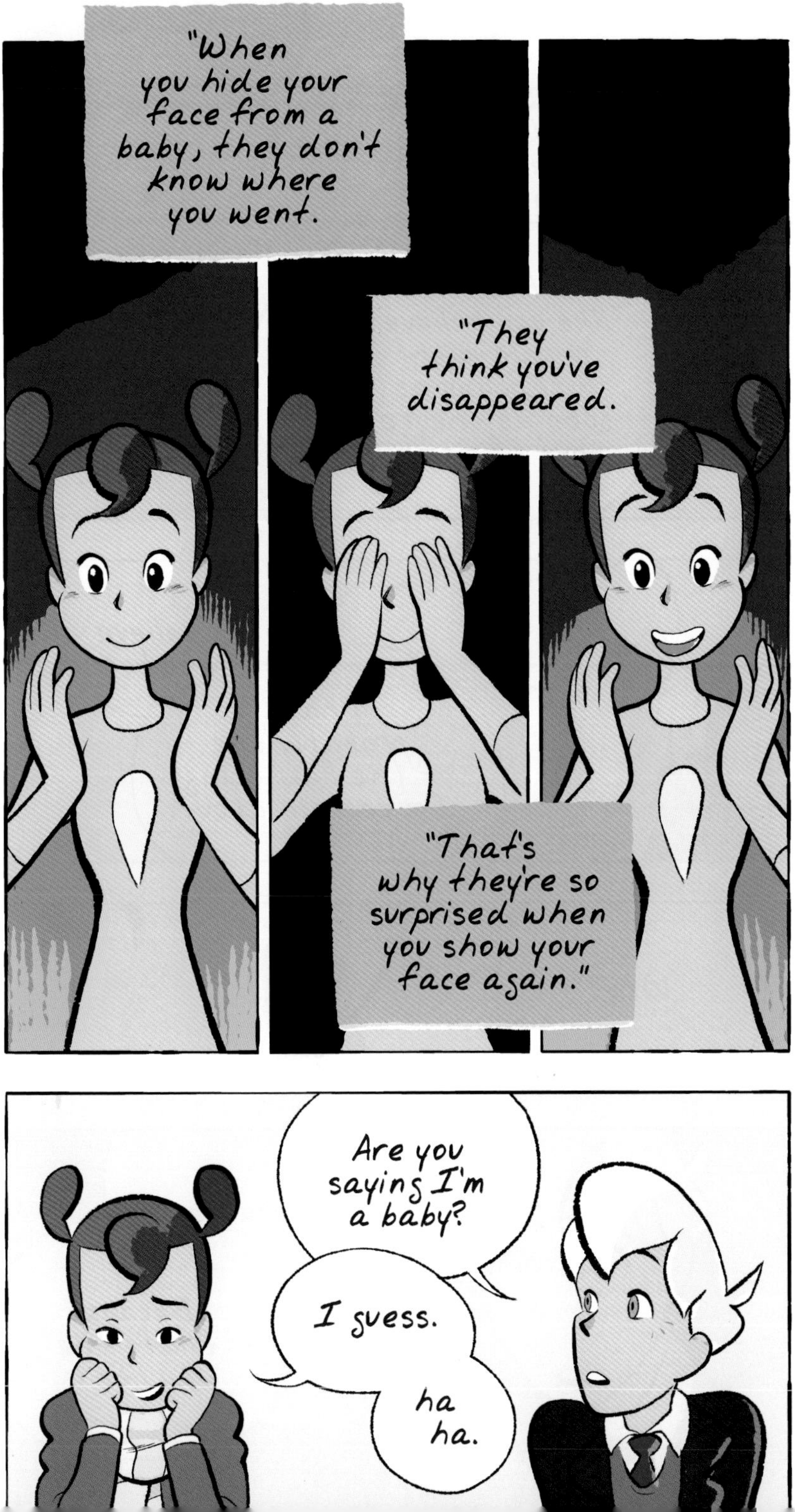
"When you hide your face from a baby, they don't know where you went.
"They think you've disappeared.
"That's why they're so surprised when you show your face again."
Are you saying I'm a baby?
I guess.
ha ha.

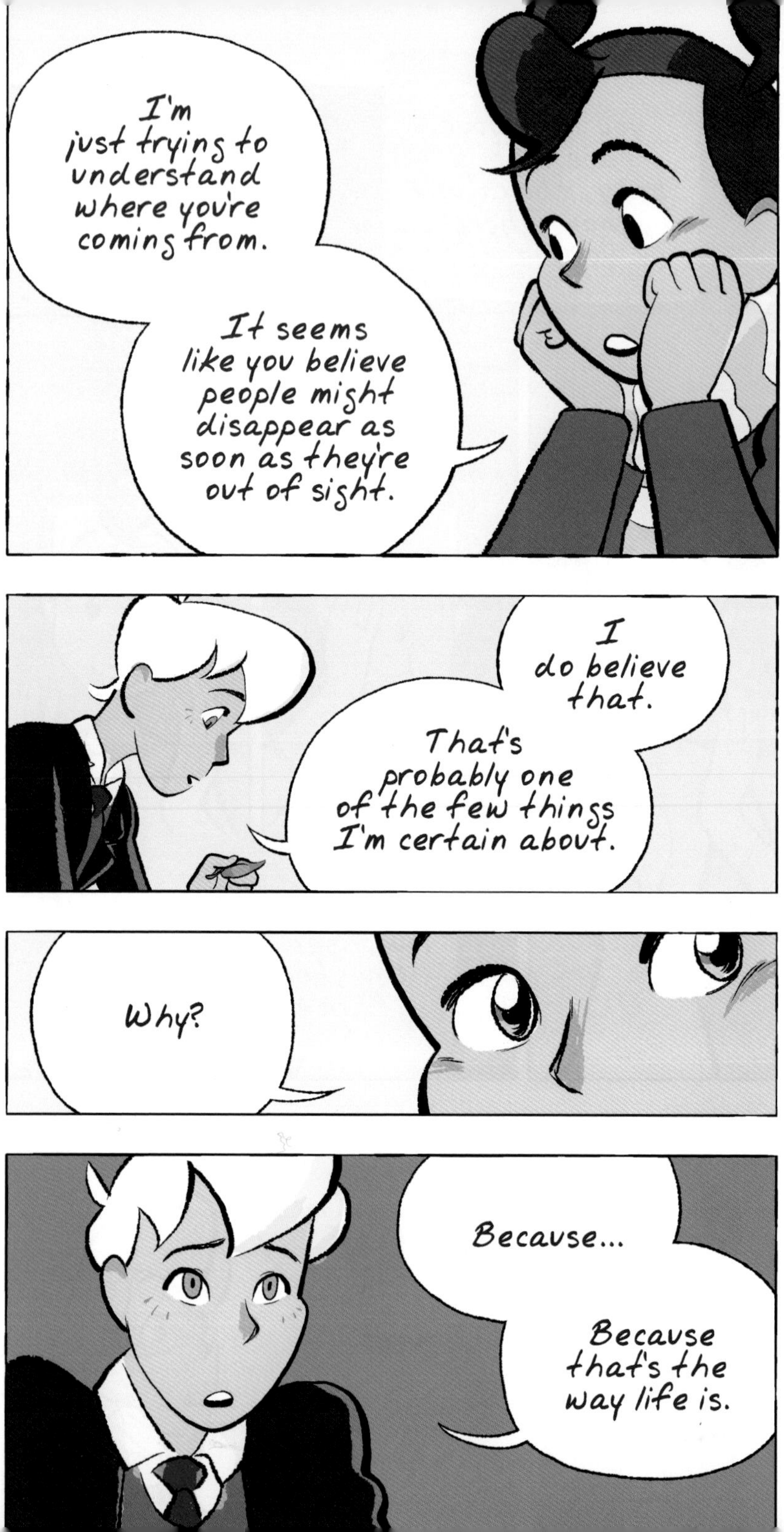
I'm just trying to understand where you're coming from.
It seems like you believe people might disappear as soon as they're out of sight.
I do believe that.
That's probably one of the few things I'm certain about.
Why?
Because...
Because that's the way life is.

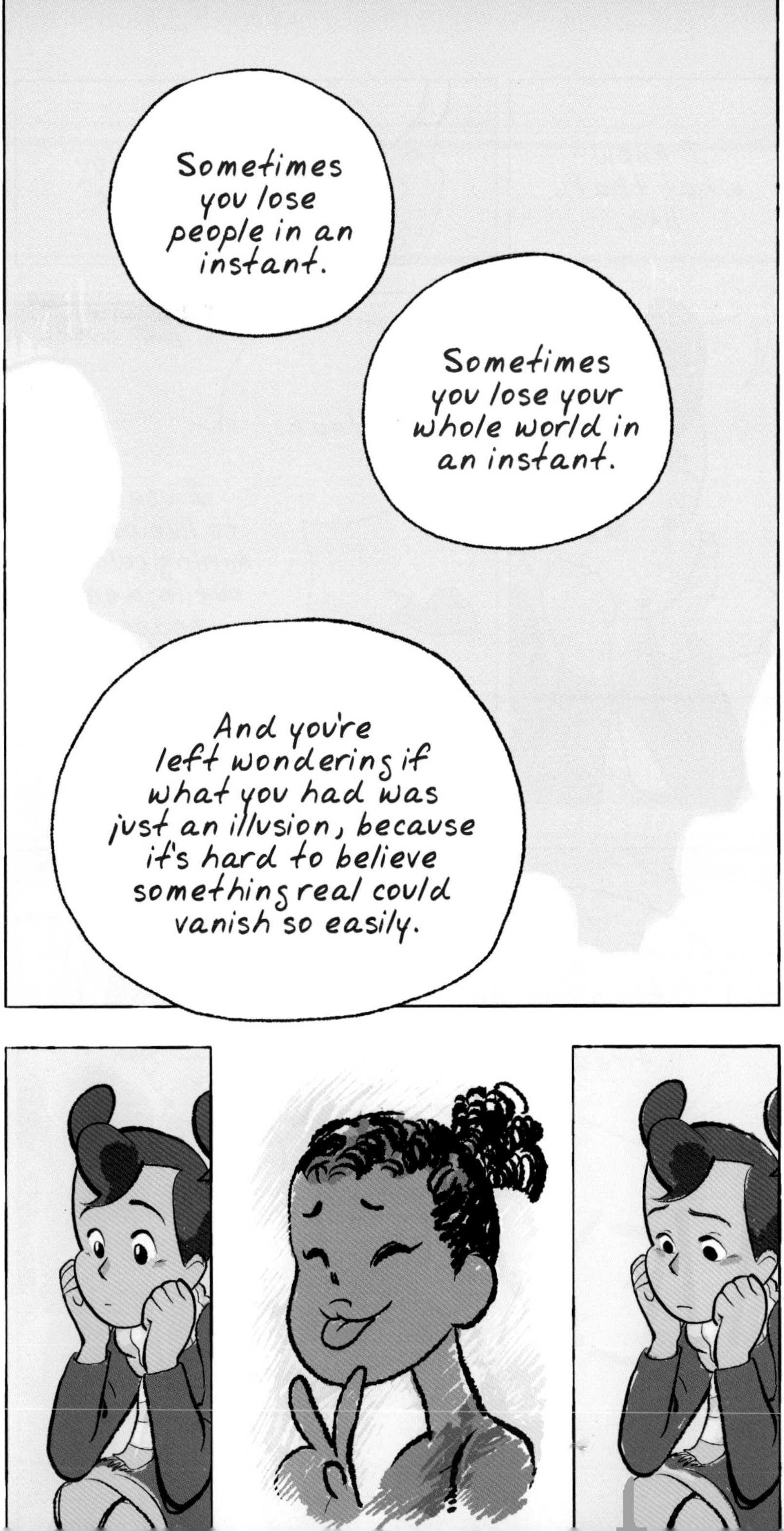
Sometimes you lose people in an instant.
Sometimes you lose your whole world in an instant.
And you're left wondering if what you had was just an illusion, because it's hard to believe something real could vanish so easily.

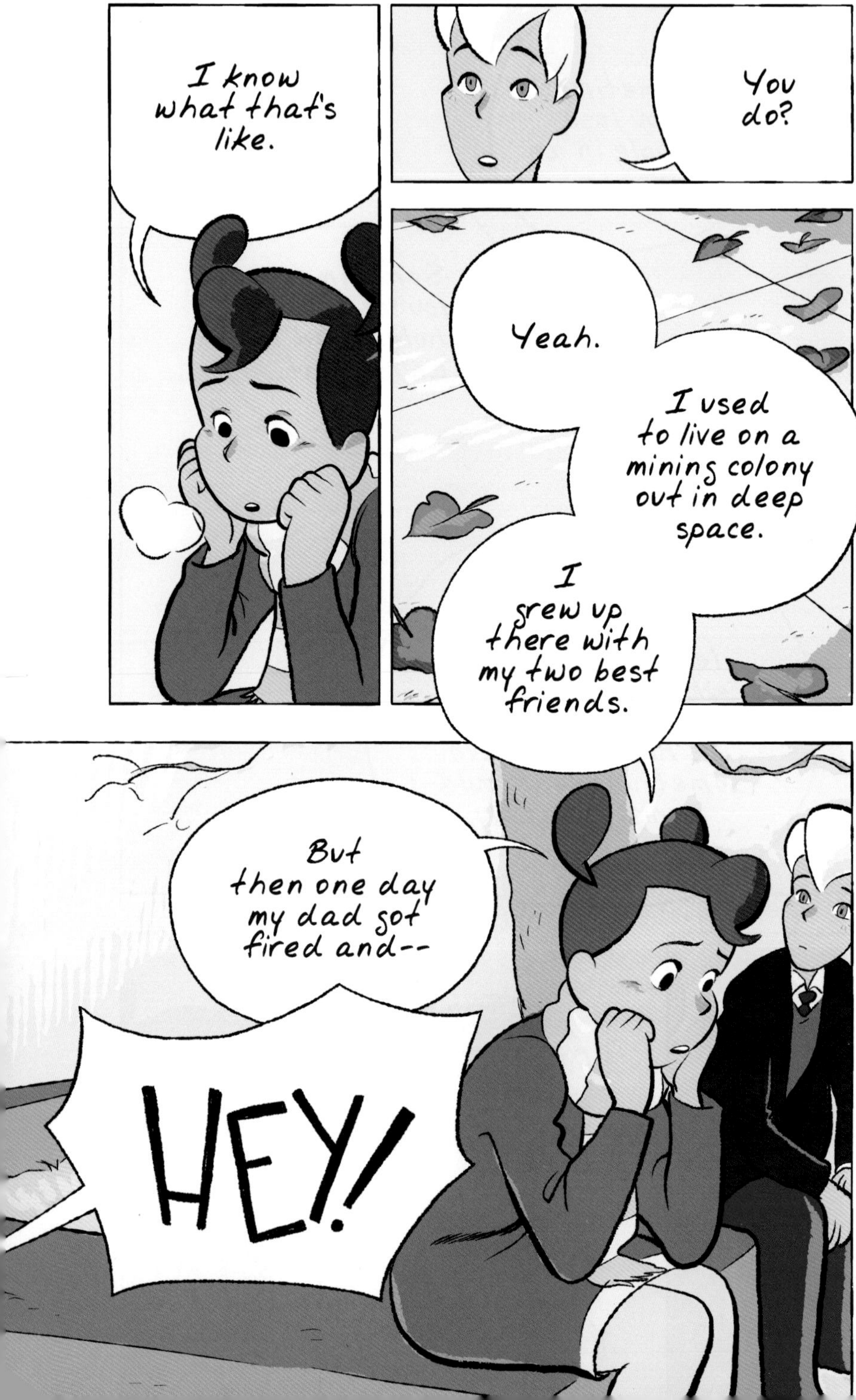
I know what that's like.
You do?
Yeah.
I used to live on a mining colony out in deep space.
I grew up there with my two best friends.
But then one day my dad got fired and--
HEY!!

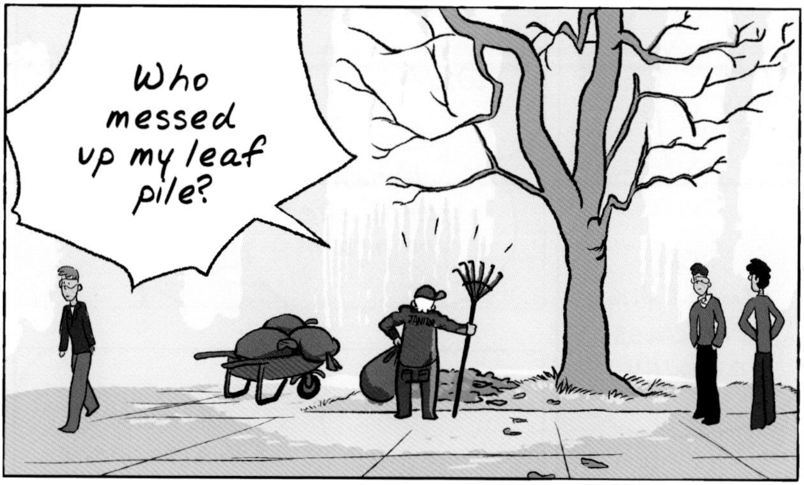
Who messed up my leaf pile?
JANITOR

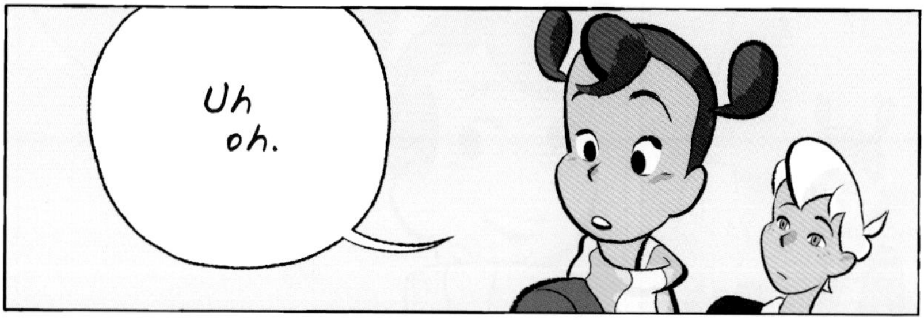
Uh oh.

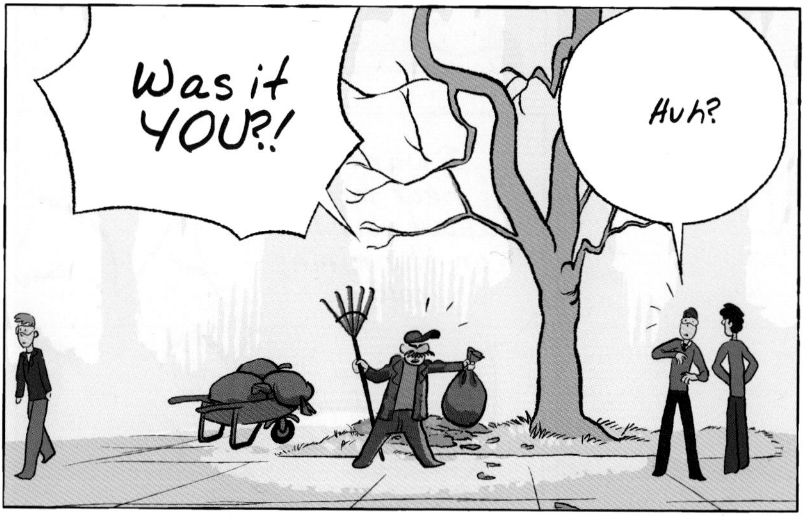
Was it YOU?!
Huh?

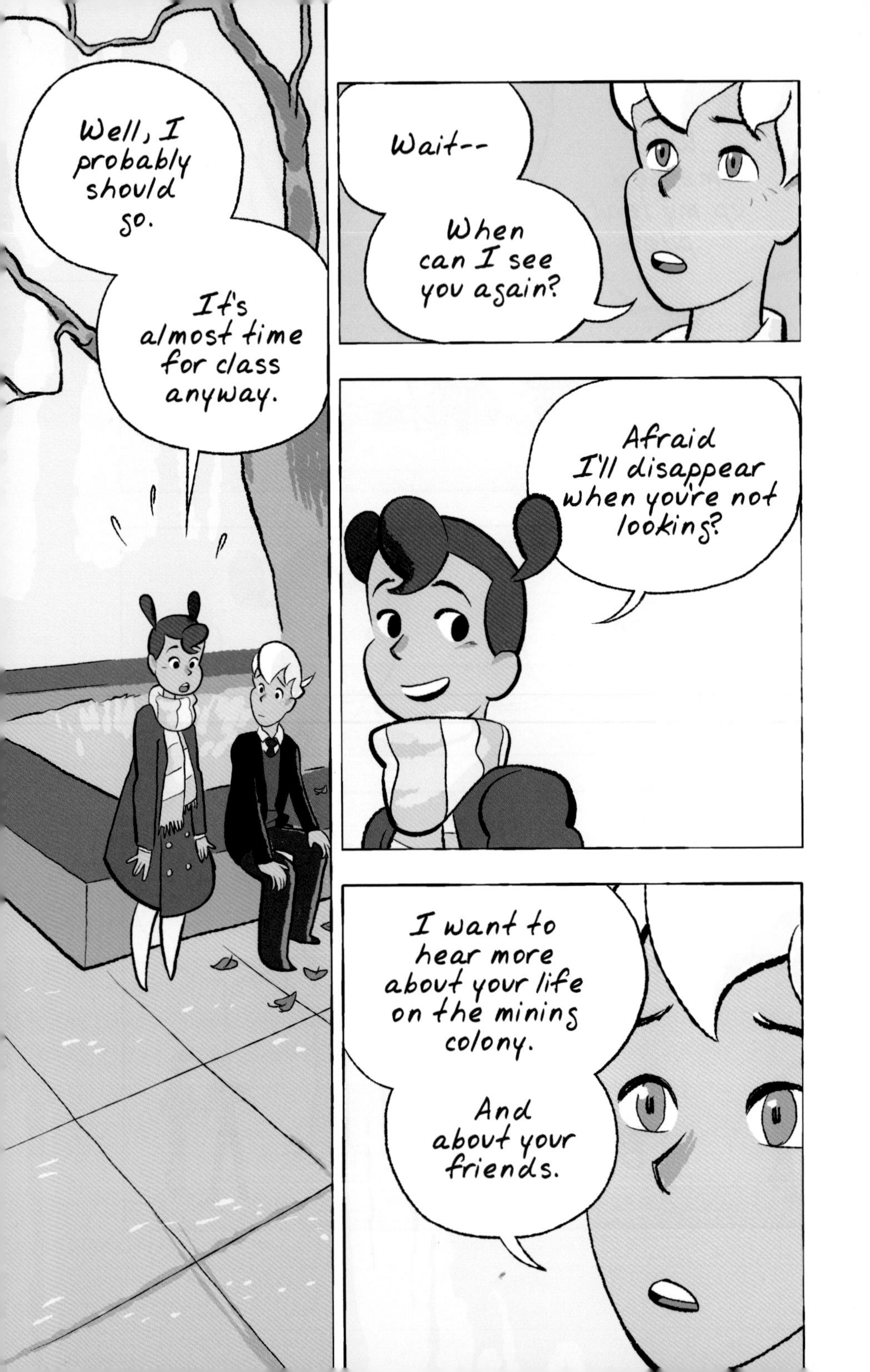
Well, I probably should go.
It's almost time for class anyway.
Wait--
When can I see you again?
Afraid I'll disappear when you're not looking?
I want to hear more about your life on the mining colony.
And about your friends.

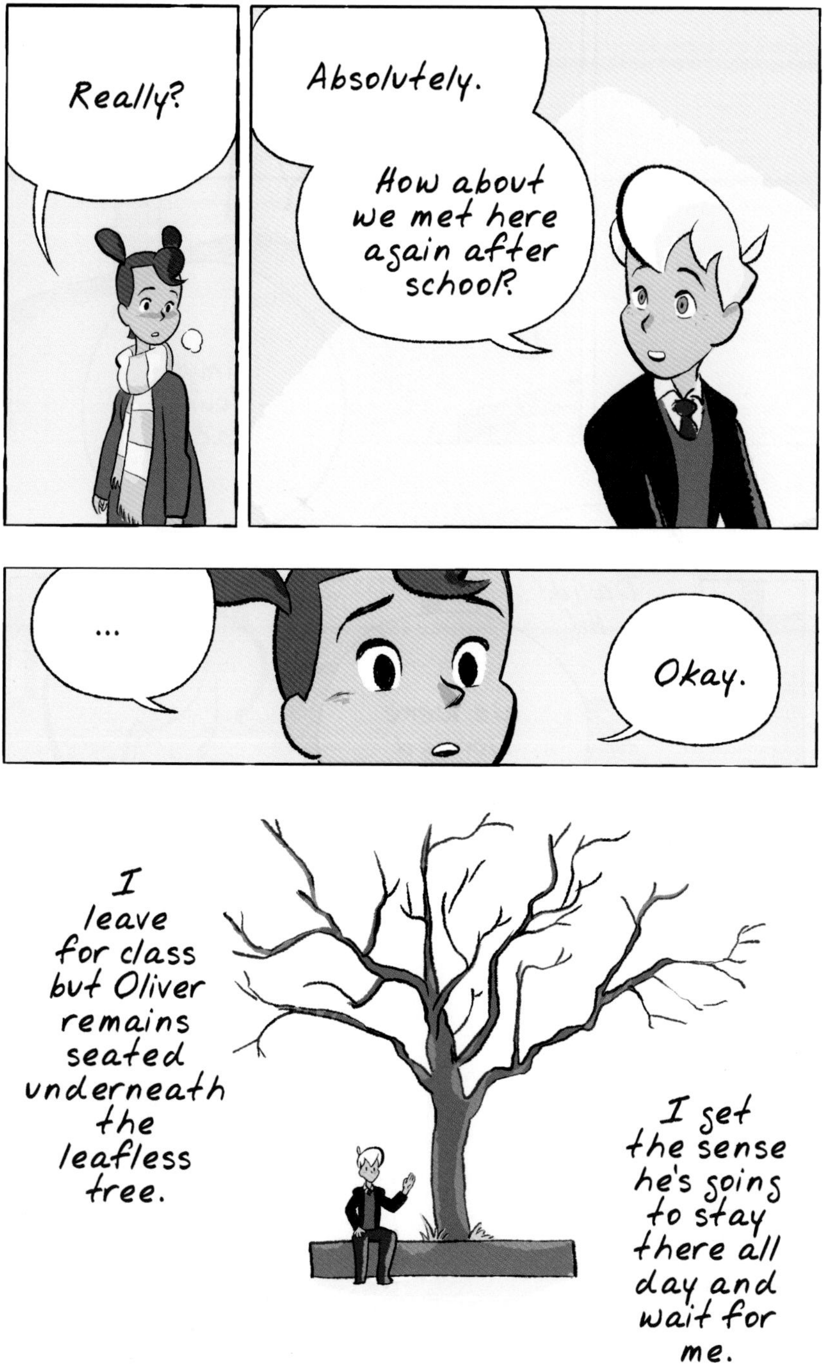
Really?
Absolutely.
How about we met here again after school?
...
Okay.
I leave for class but Oliver remains seated underneath the leafless tree.
I get the sense he's going to stay there all day and wait for me.

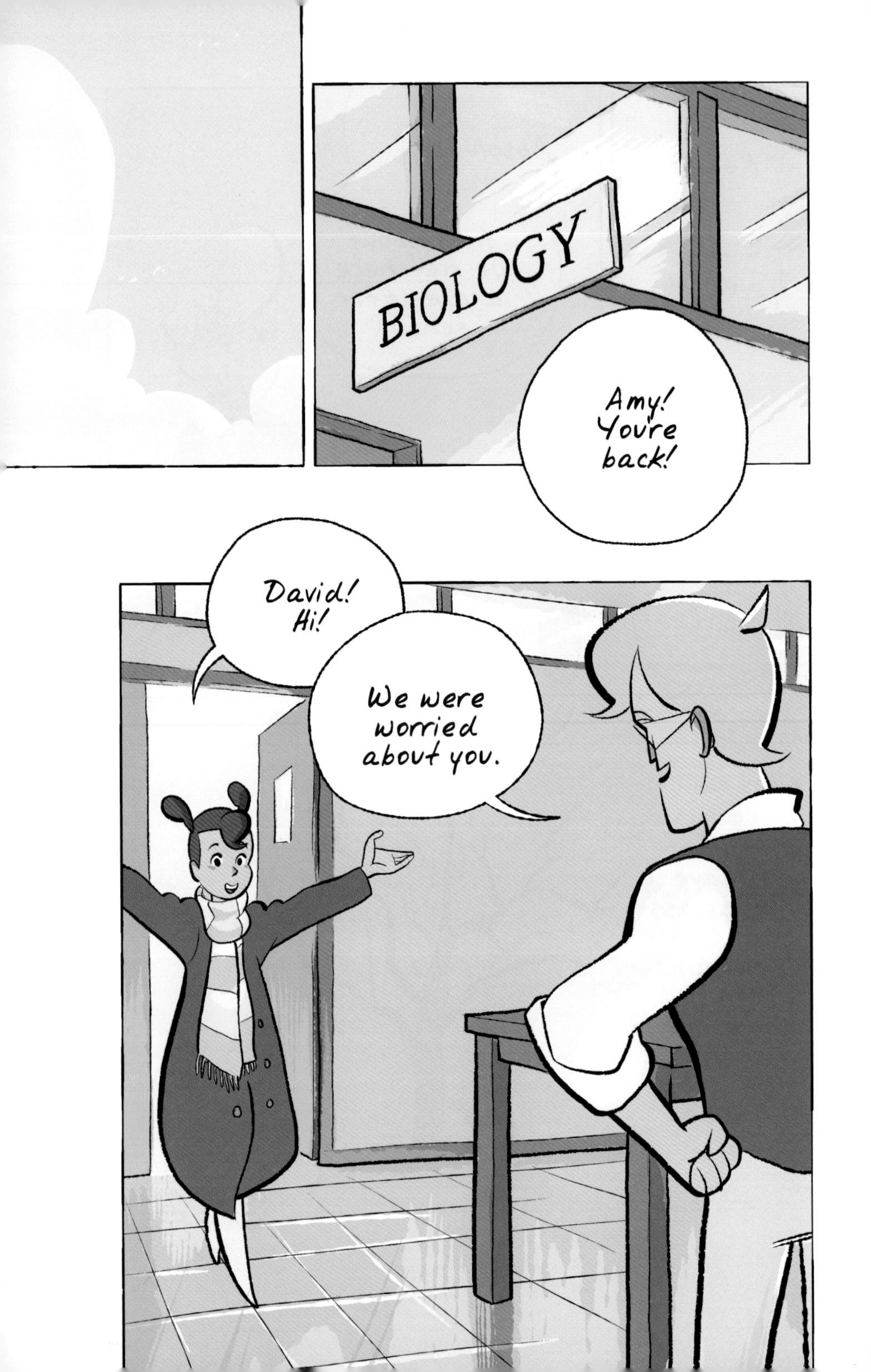
BIOLOGY
Amy! You're back!
David! Hi!
We were worried about you.

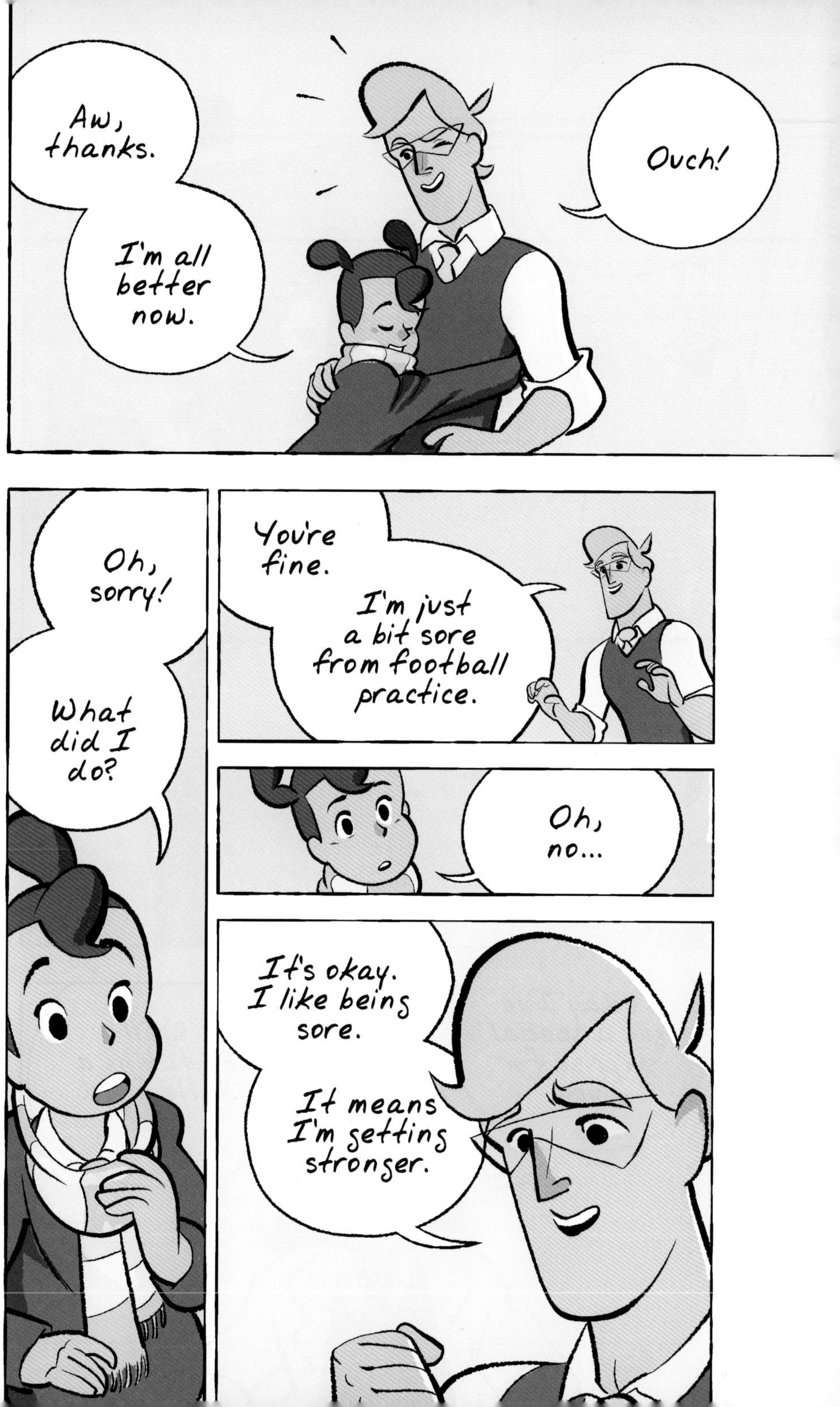
Aw, thanks.
I'm all better now.
Ouch!
Oh, sorry!
What did I do?
You're fine.
I'm just a bit sore from football practice.
Oh, no...
It's okay. I like being sore.
It means I'm getting stronger.

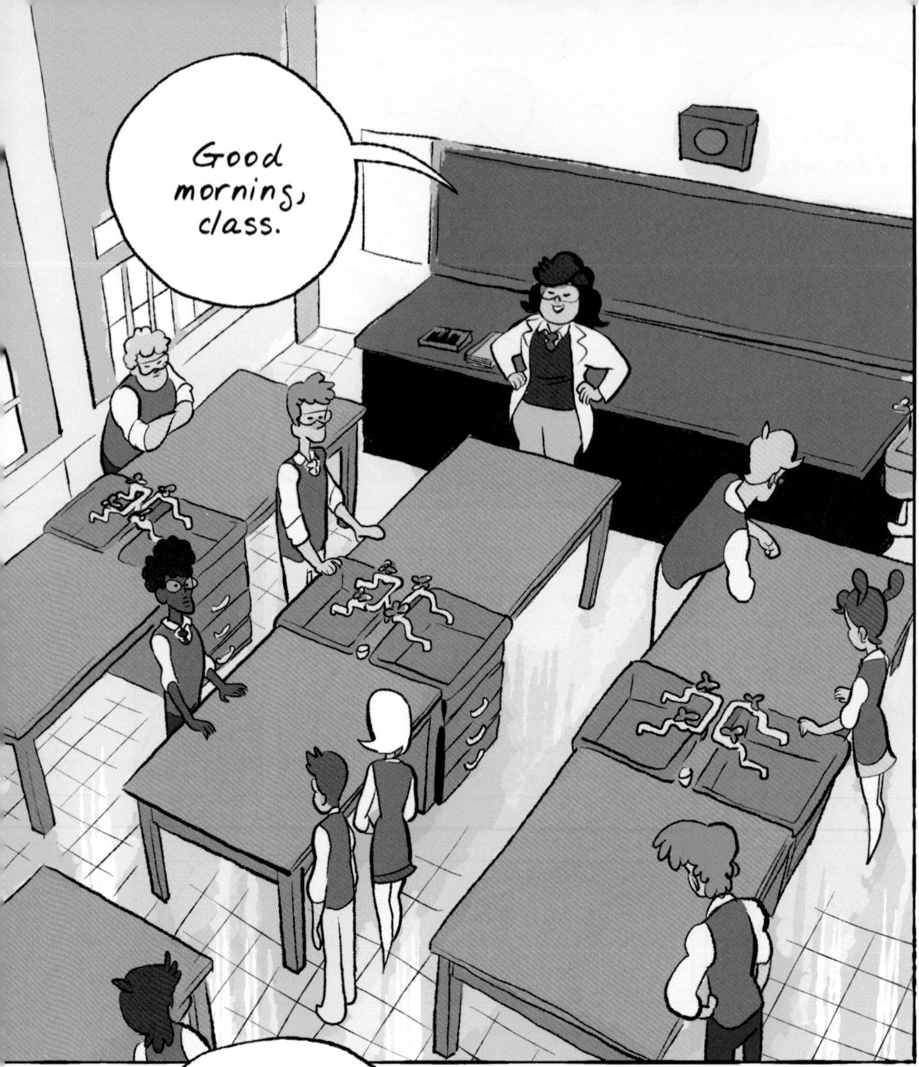
Good morning, class.

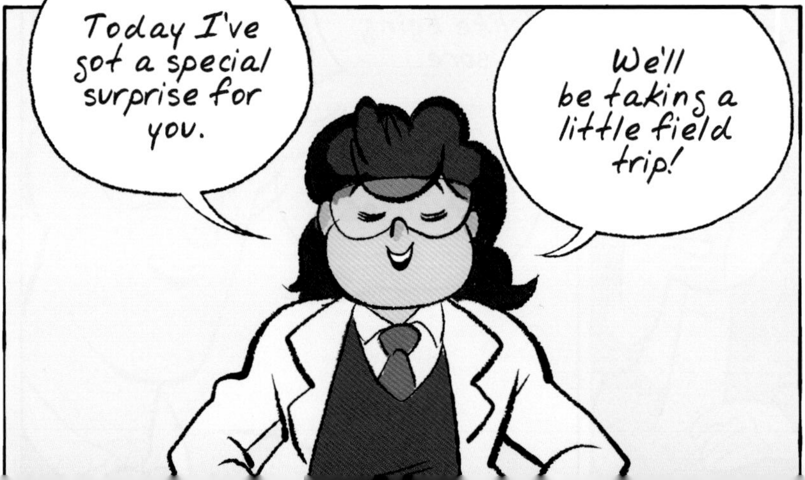
Today I've got a special surprise for you.
We'll be taking a little field trip!

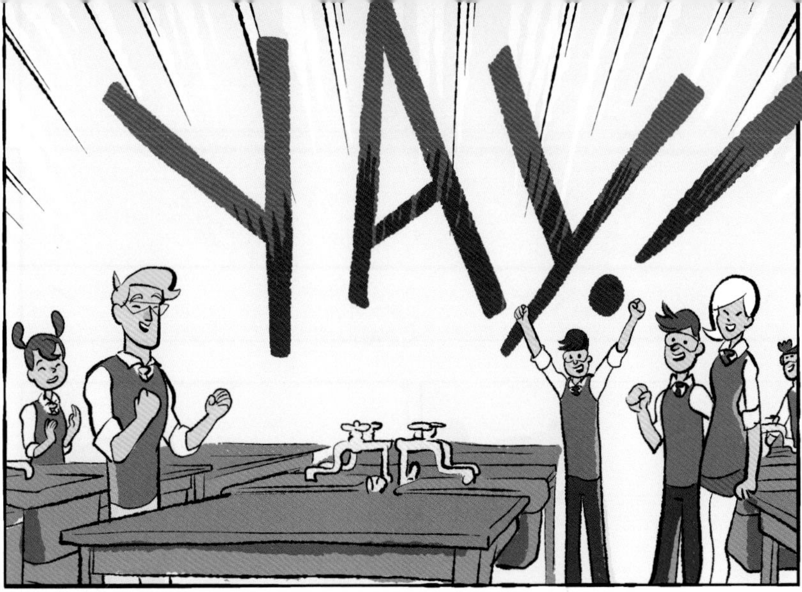
YAY!

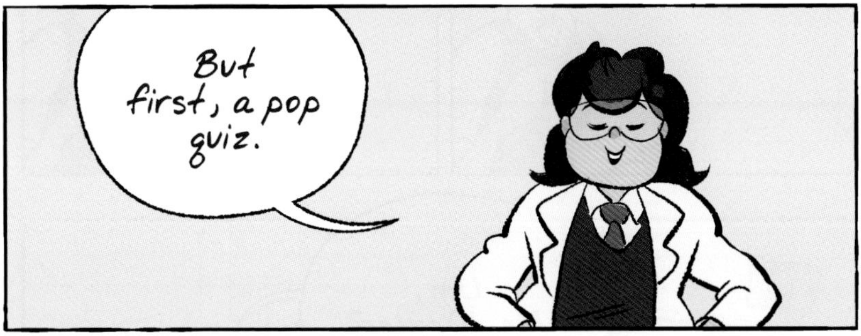
But first, a pop quiz.

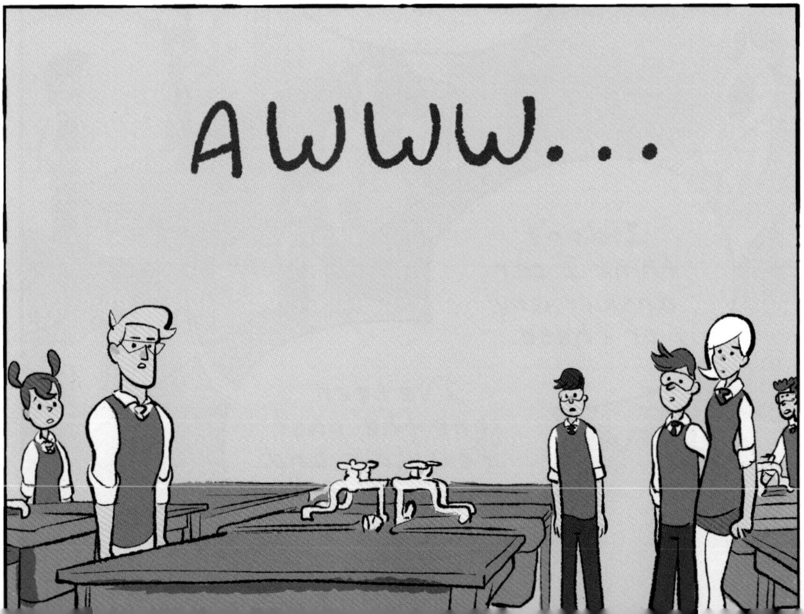
AWWW...

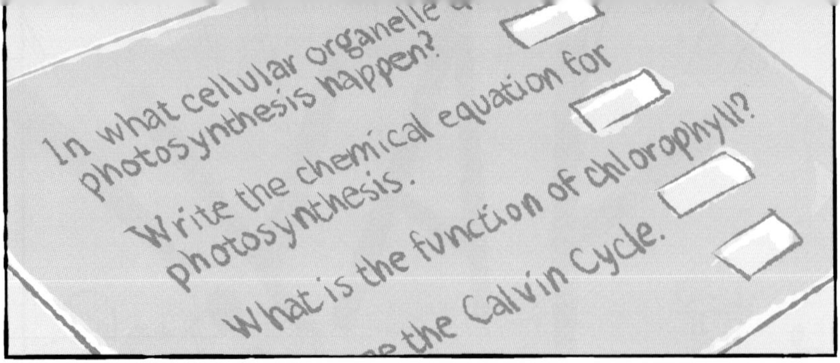
In what cellular organelle
photosynthesis happen?
Write the chemical equation for
photosynthesis.
What is the function of chlorophyll?
the Calvin Cycle.

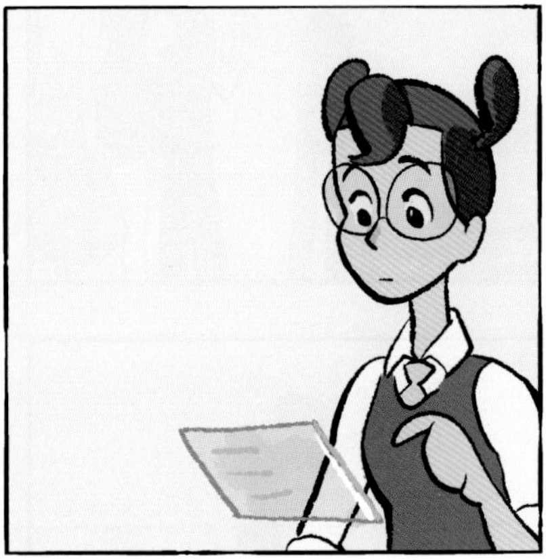

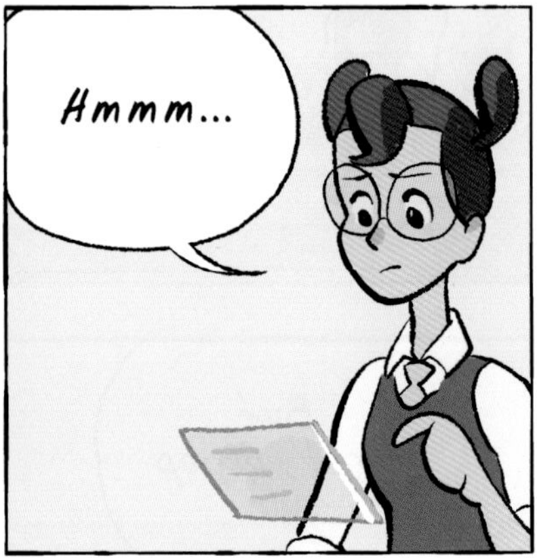
Hmmm...

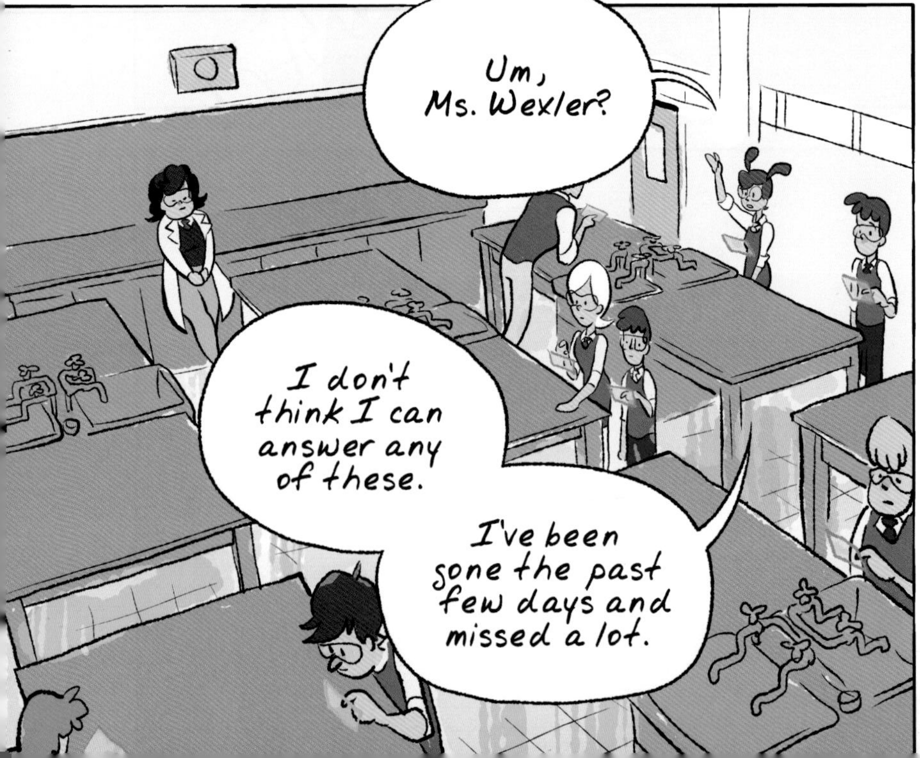
Um, Ms. Wexler?
I don't think I can answer any of these.
I've been gone the past few days and missed a lot.

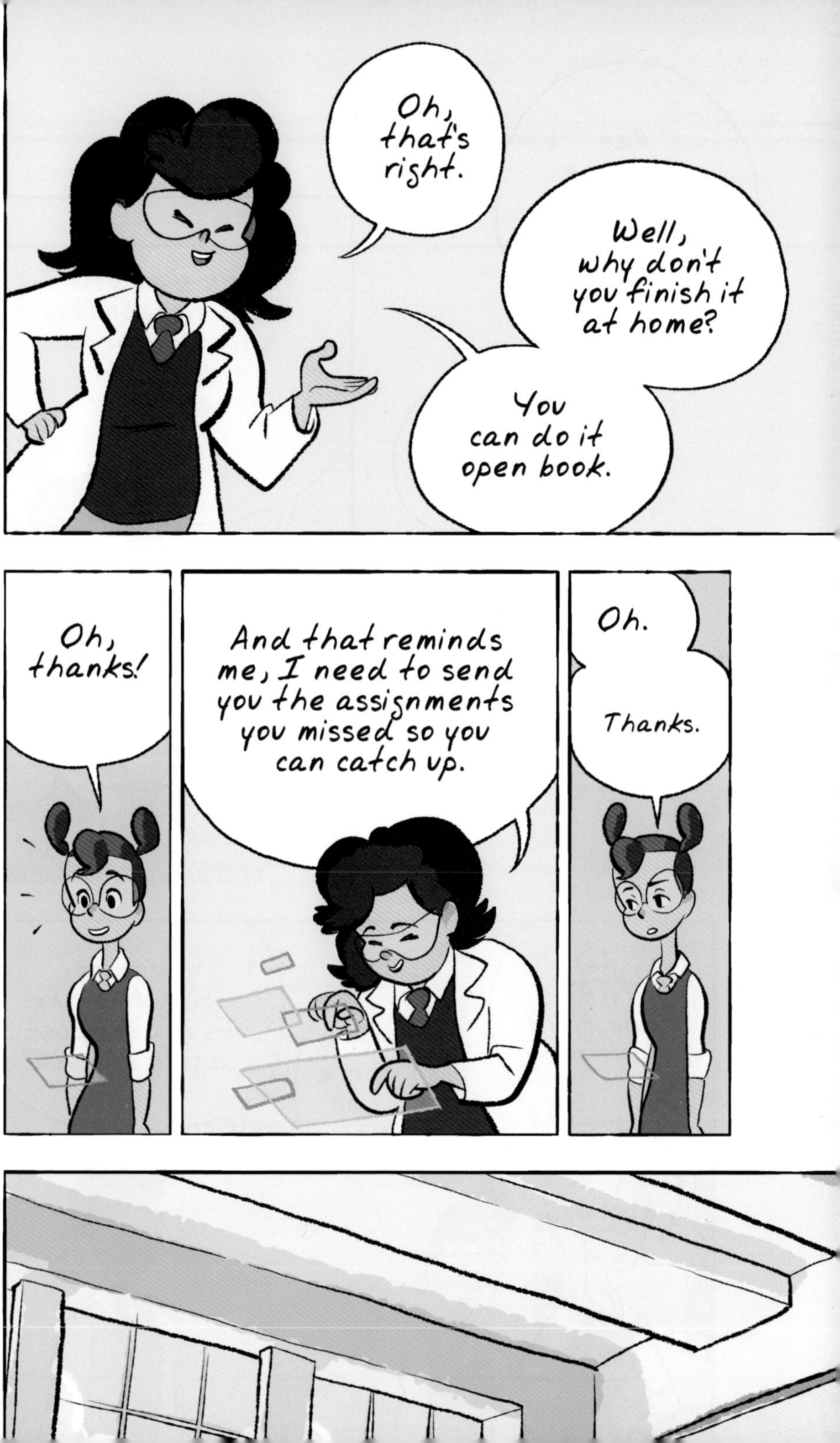
Oh, that's right.
Well, why don't you finish it at home?
You can do it open book.
Oh, thanks!
And that reminds me, I need to send you the assignments you missed so you can catch up.
Oh.
Thanks.

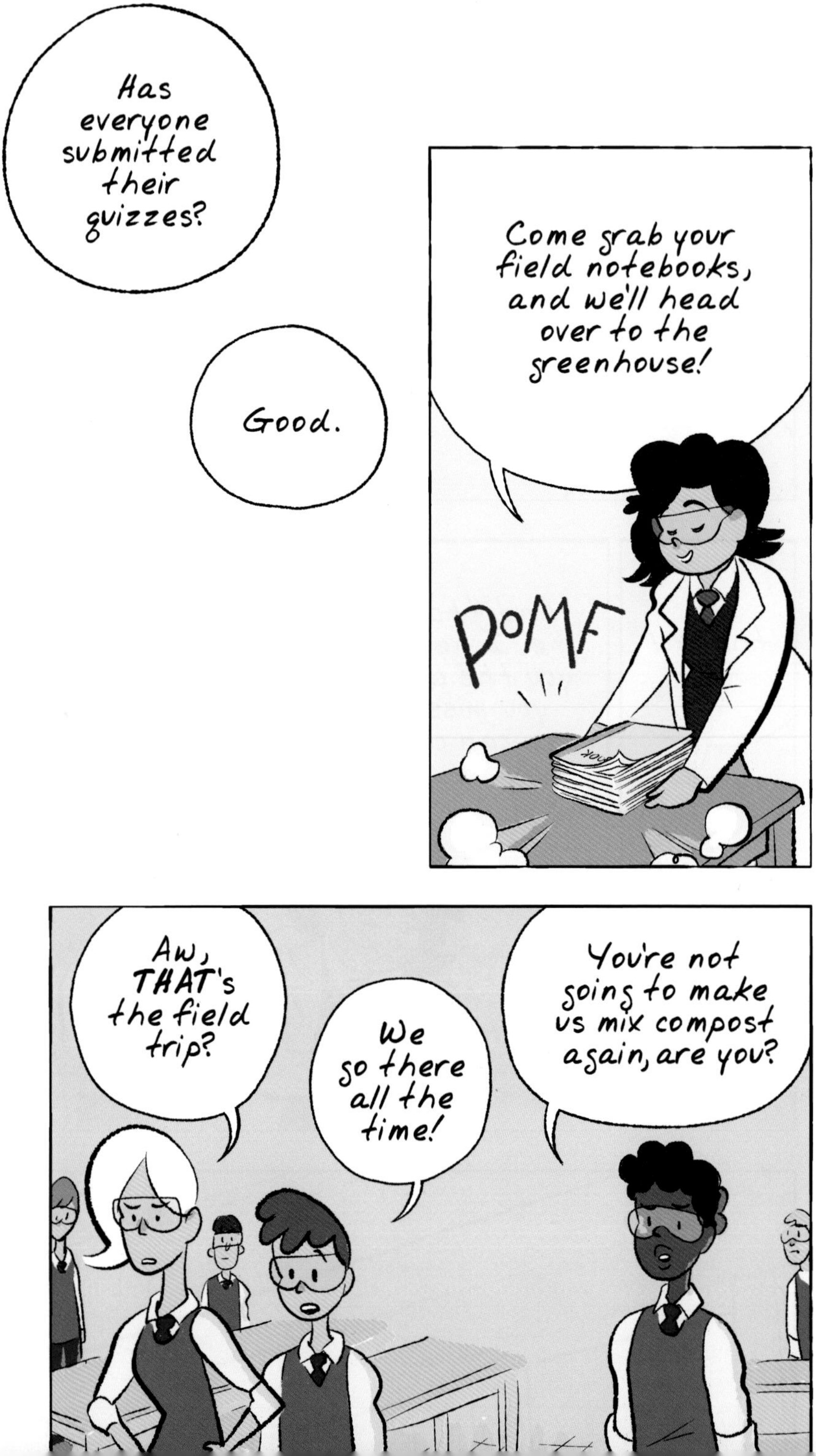
Has everyone submitted their quizzes?
Good.
Come grab your field notebooks, and we'll head over to the greenhouse!
POMF
Aw, THAT's the field trip?
We go there all the time!
You're not going to make us mix compost again, are you?

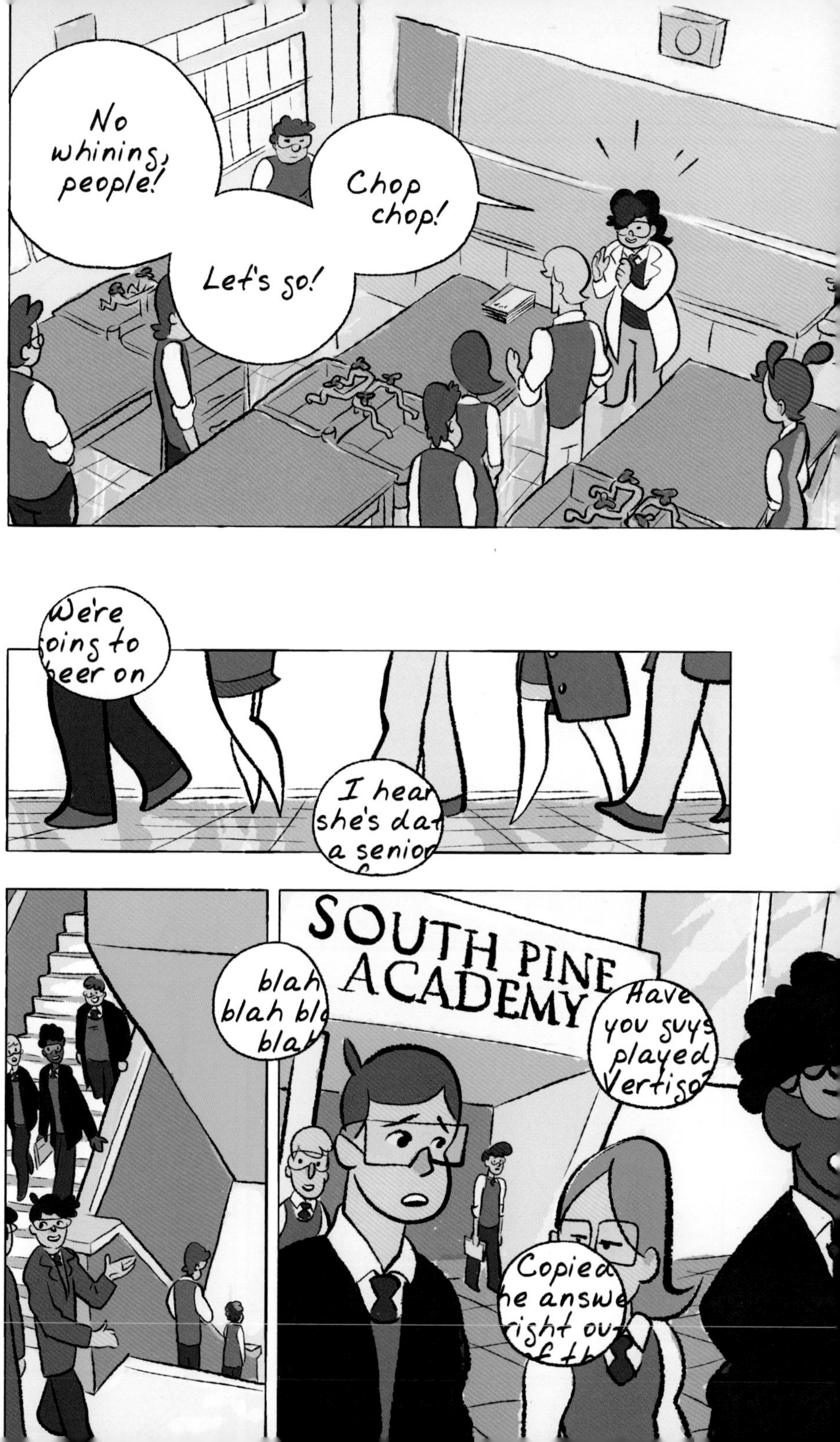
No whining, people!
Chop chop!
Let's go!
We're going to cheer on
I hear she's da a senio
SOUTH PINE ACADEMY
blah blah bl bla
Have you guys played Vertiso
Copied e answe ight ou

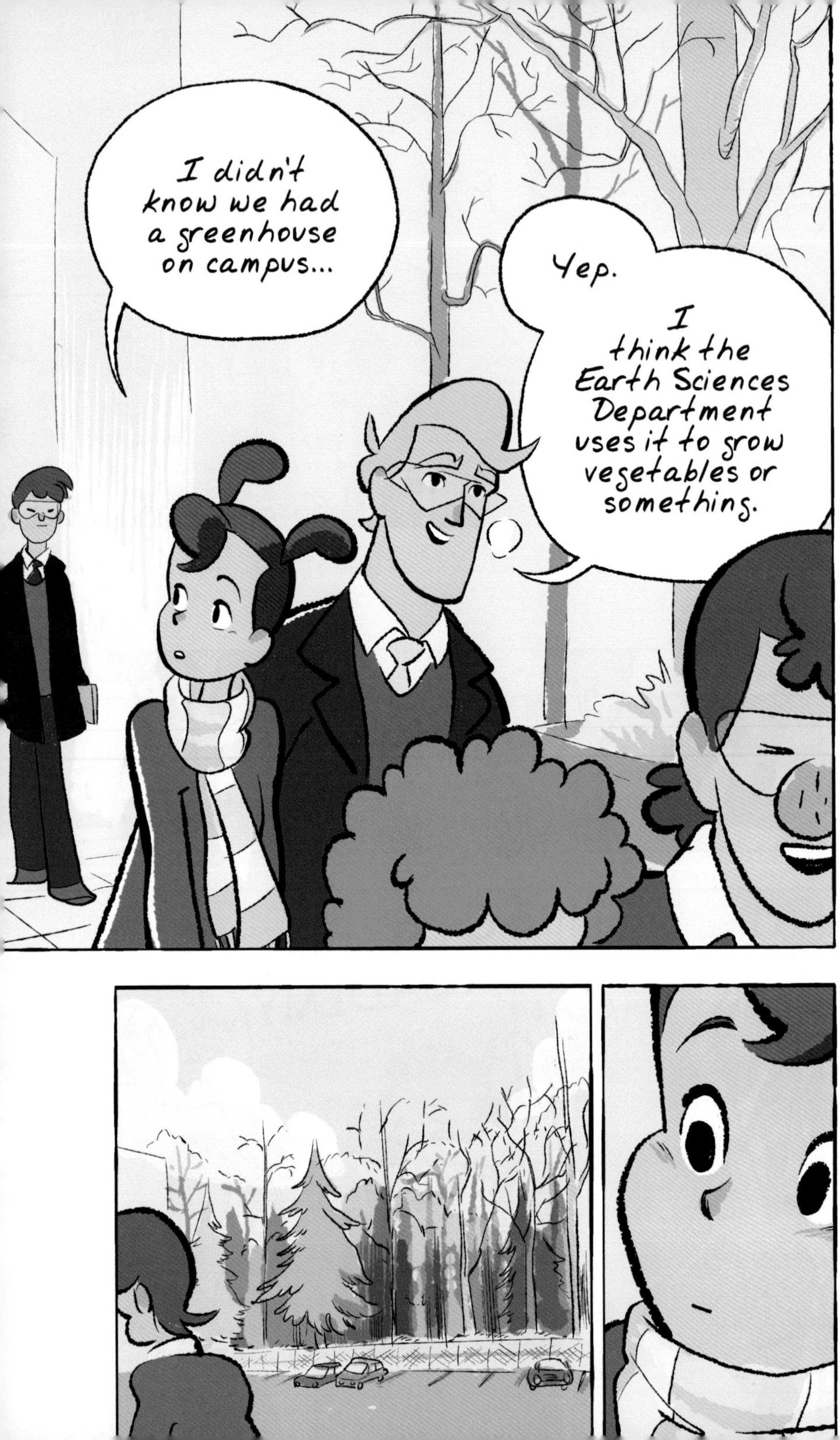
I didn't know we had a greenhouse on campus...
Yep.
I think the Earth Sciences Department uses it to grow vegetables or something.

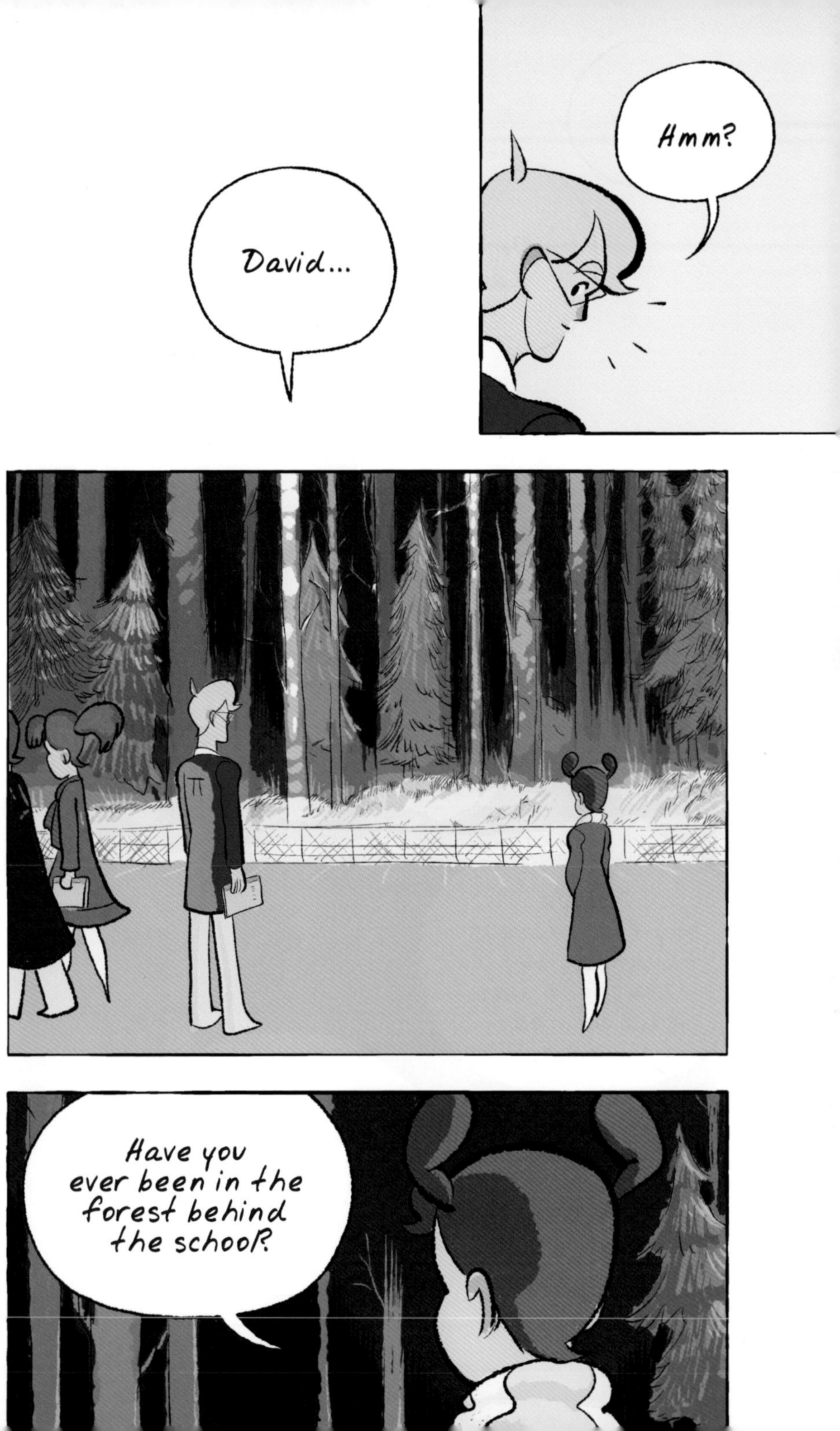
David...
Hmm?
Have you ever been in the forest behind the school?

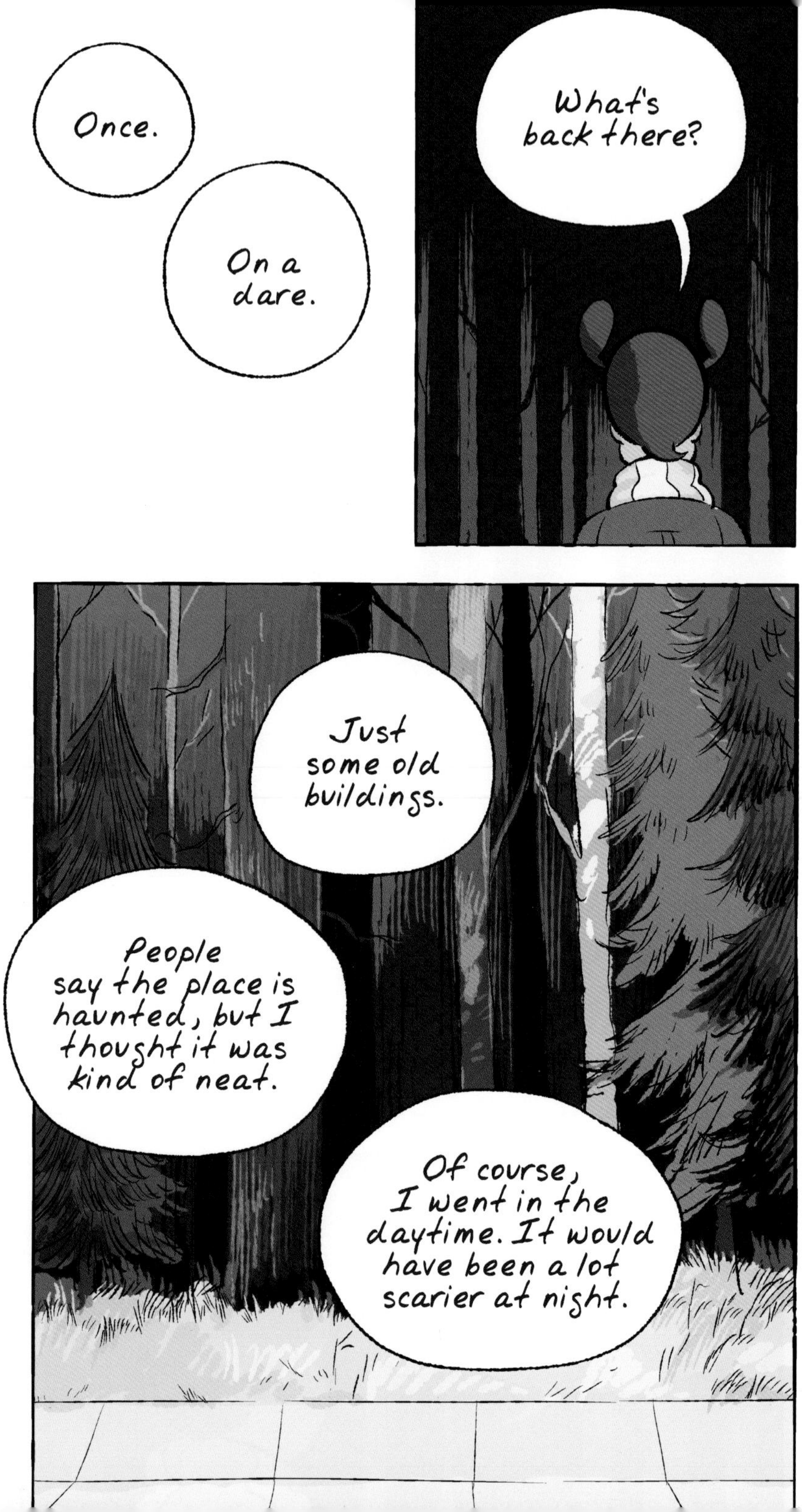
Once.
On a dare.
What's back there?
Just some old buildings.
People say the place is haunted, but I thought it was kind of neat.
Of course, I went in the daytime. It would have been a lot scarier at night.

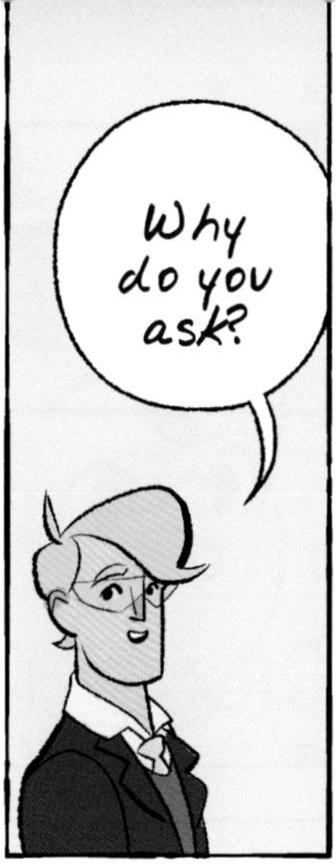
Why do you ask?

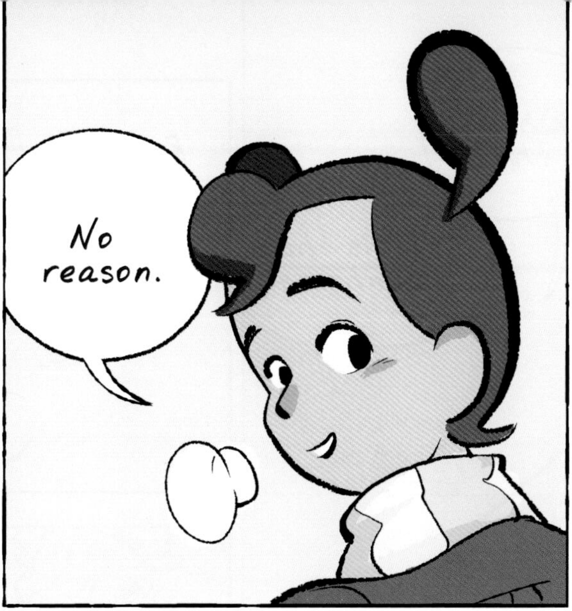
No reason.

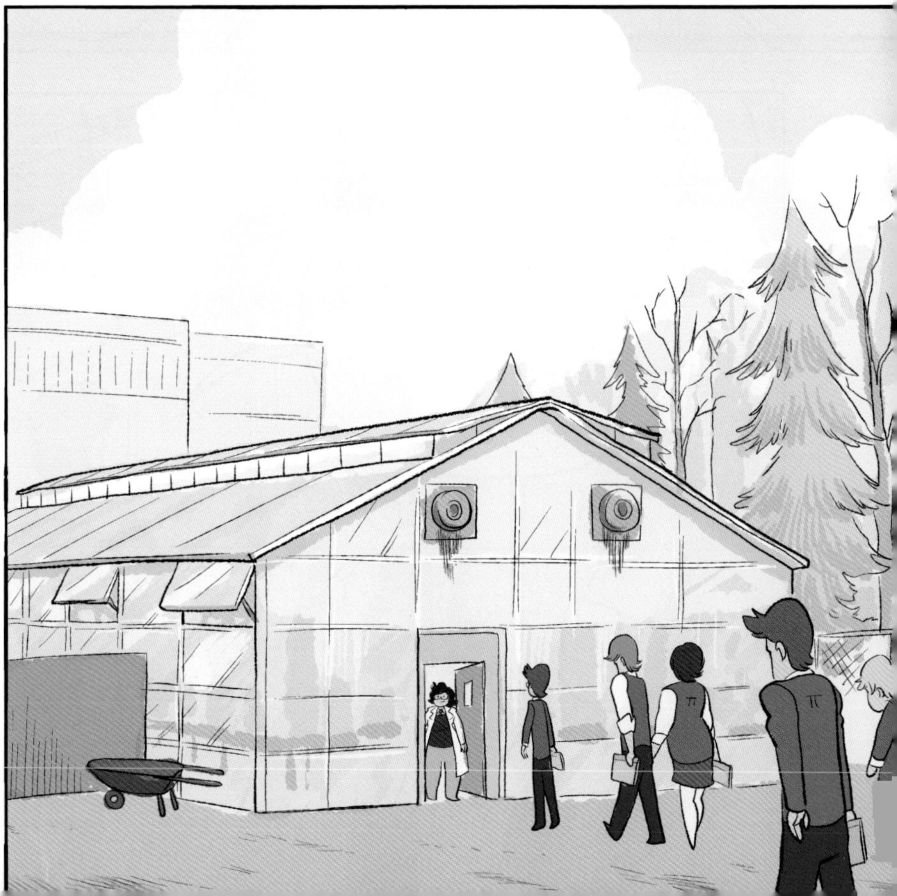

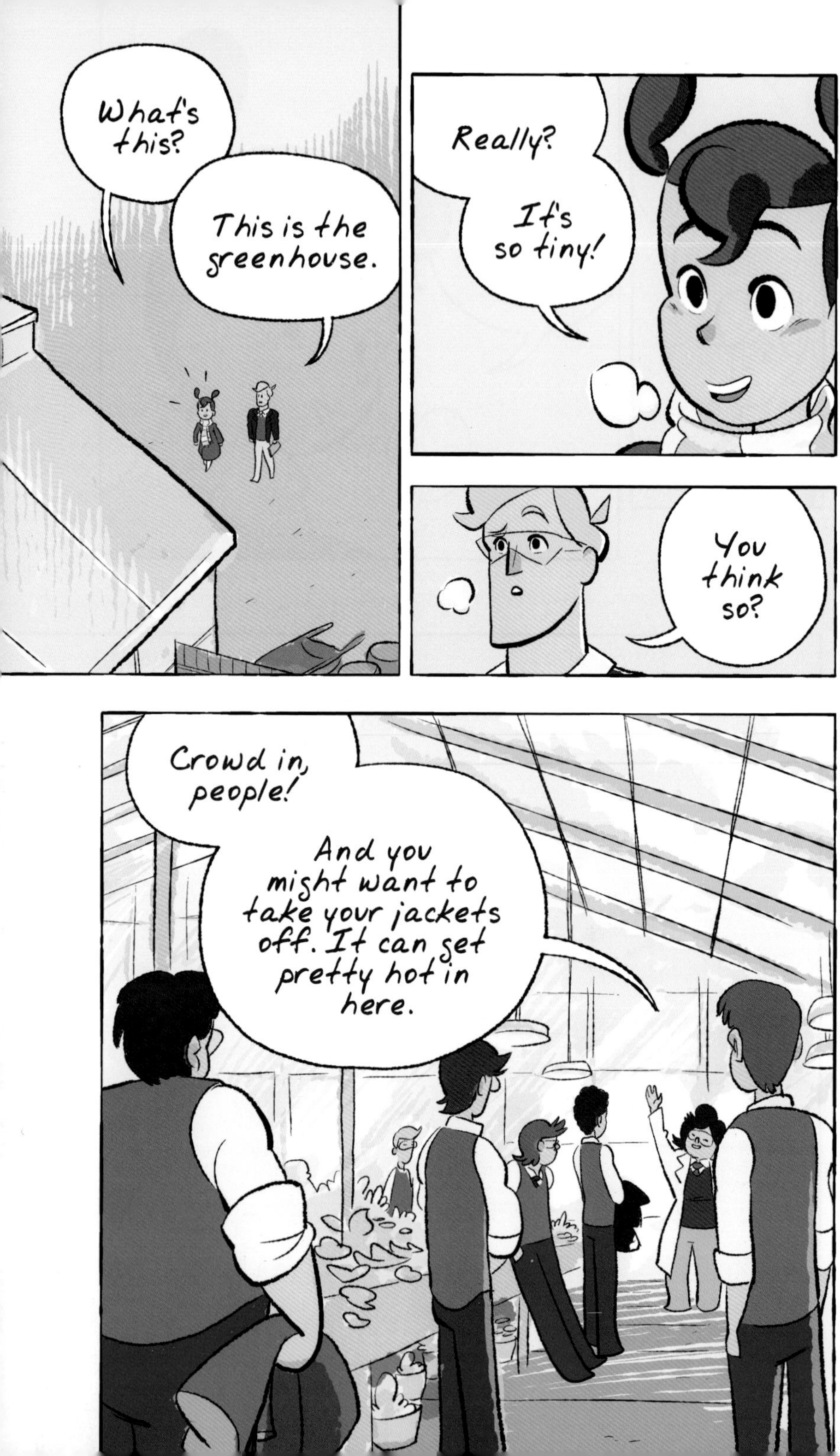
What's this?
This is the greenhouse.
Really?
It's so tiny!
You think so?
Crowd in, people!
And you might want to take your jackets off. It can get pretty hot in here.

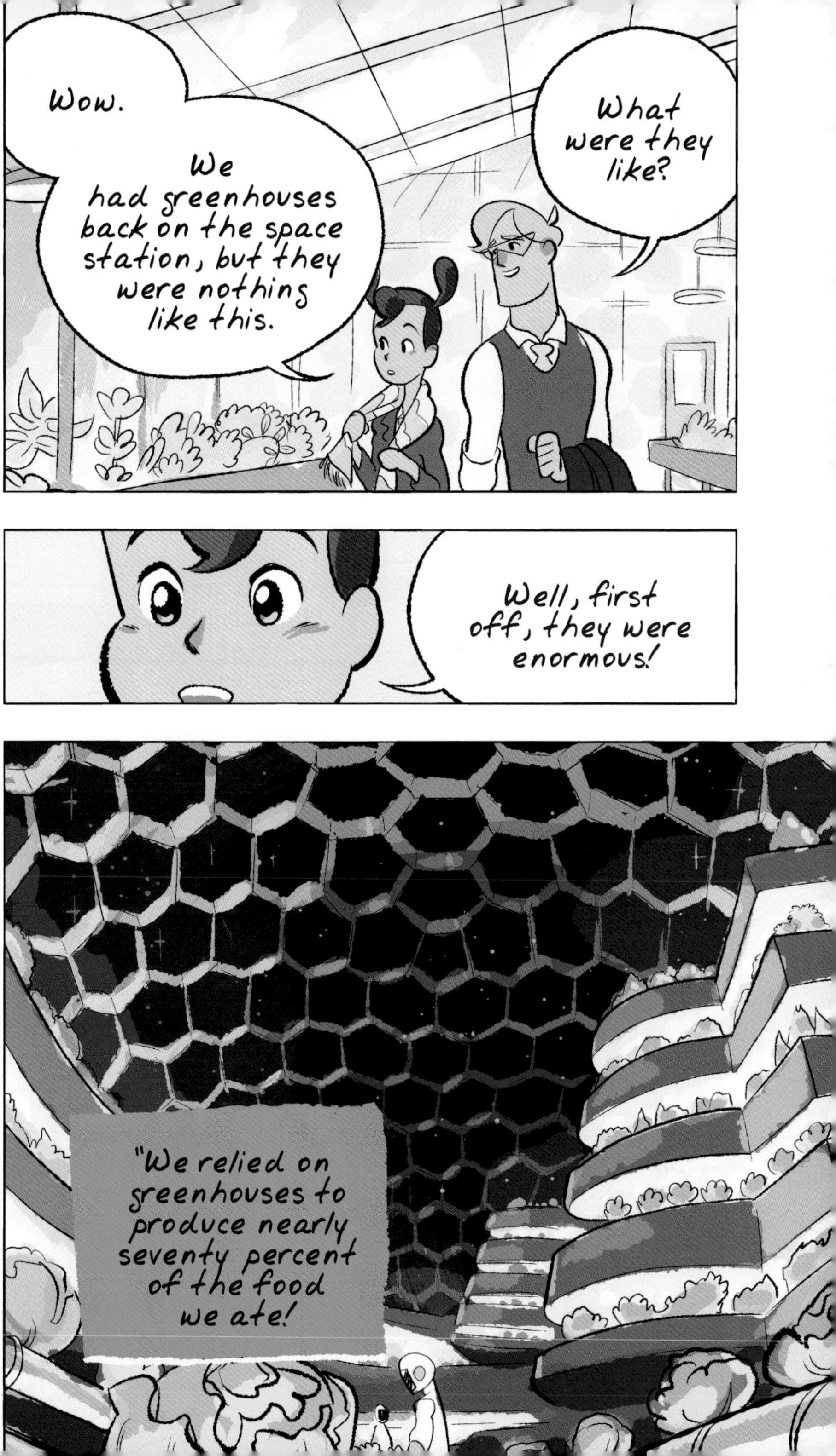
Wow.
We had greenhouses back on the space station, but they were nothing like this.
What were they like?
Well, first off, they were enormous!
"We relied on greenhouses to produce nearly seventy percent of the food we ate!

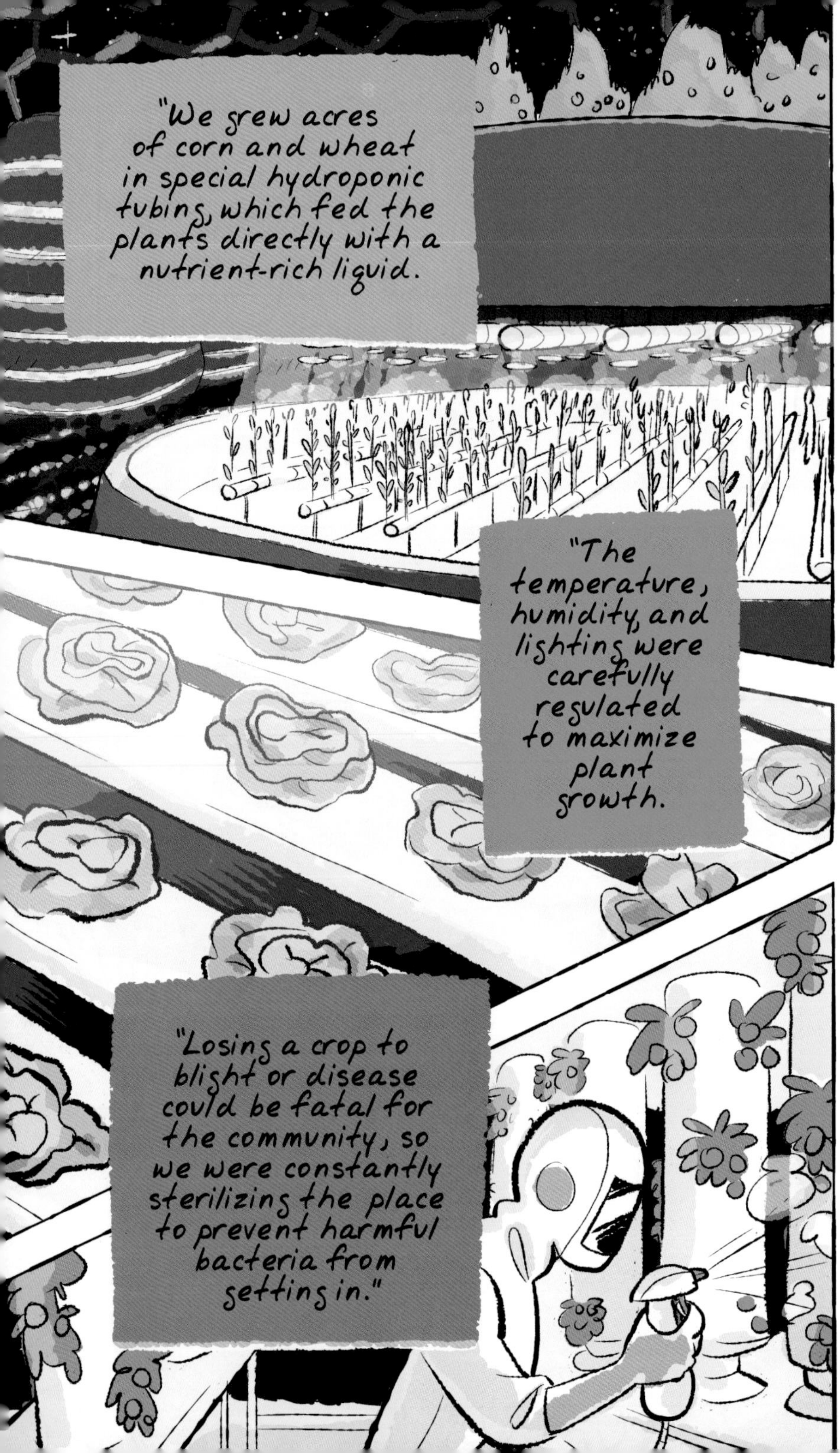
"We grew acres of corn and wheat in special hydroponic tubing, which fed the plants directly with a nutrient-rich liquid.
"The temperature, humidity, and lighting were carefully regulated to maximize plant growth.
"Losing a crop to blight or disease could be fatal for the community, so we were constantly sterilizing the place to prevent harmful bacteria from getting in."

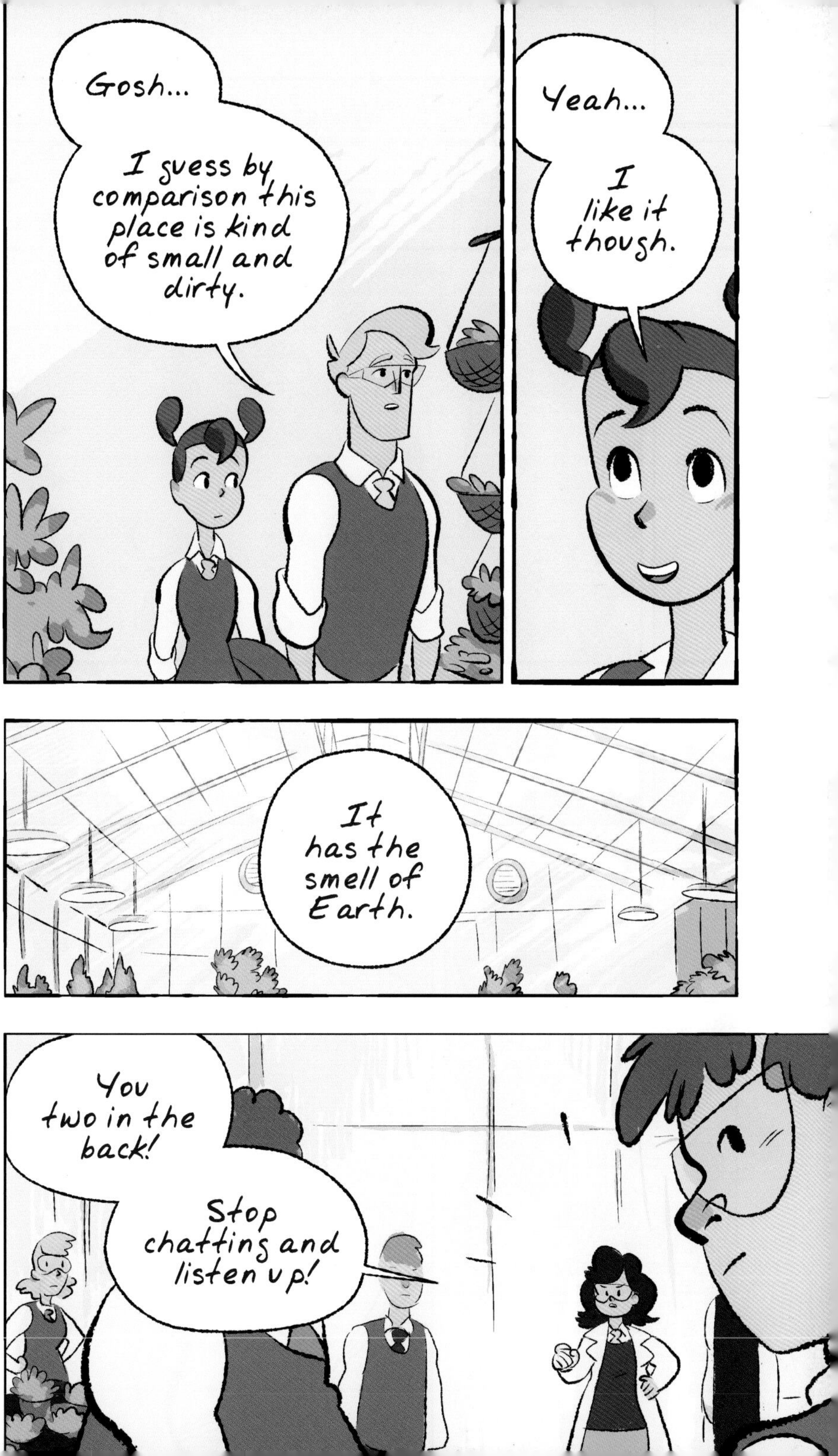
Gosh... I guess by comparison this place is kind of small and dirty.
Yeah... I like it though.
It has the smell of Earth.
You two in the back! Stop chatting and listen up!

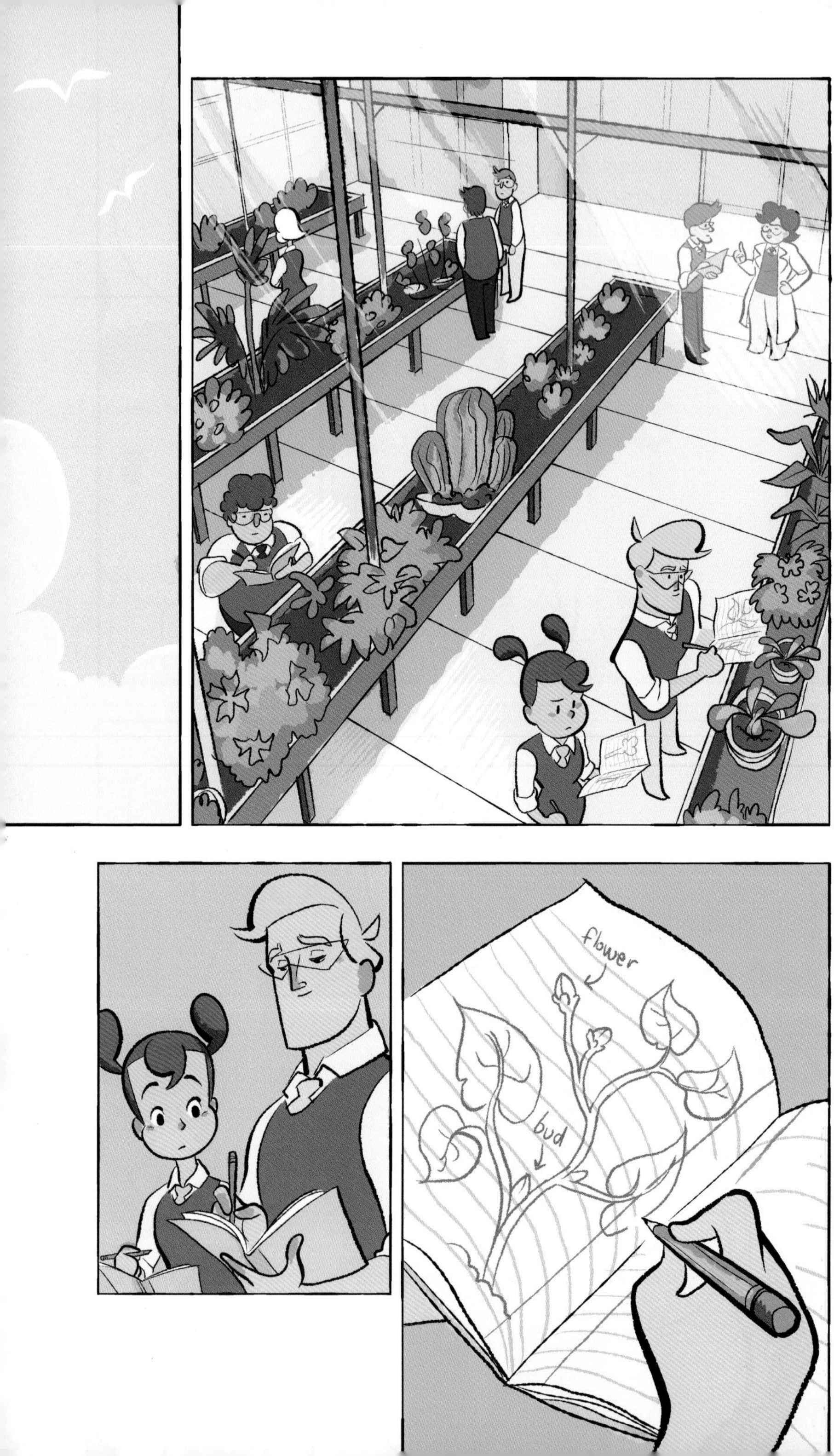
flower
bud

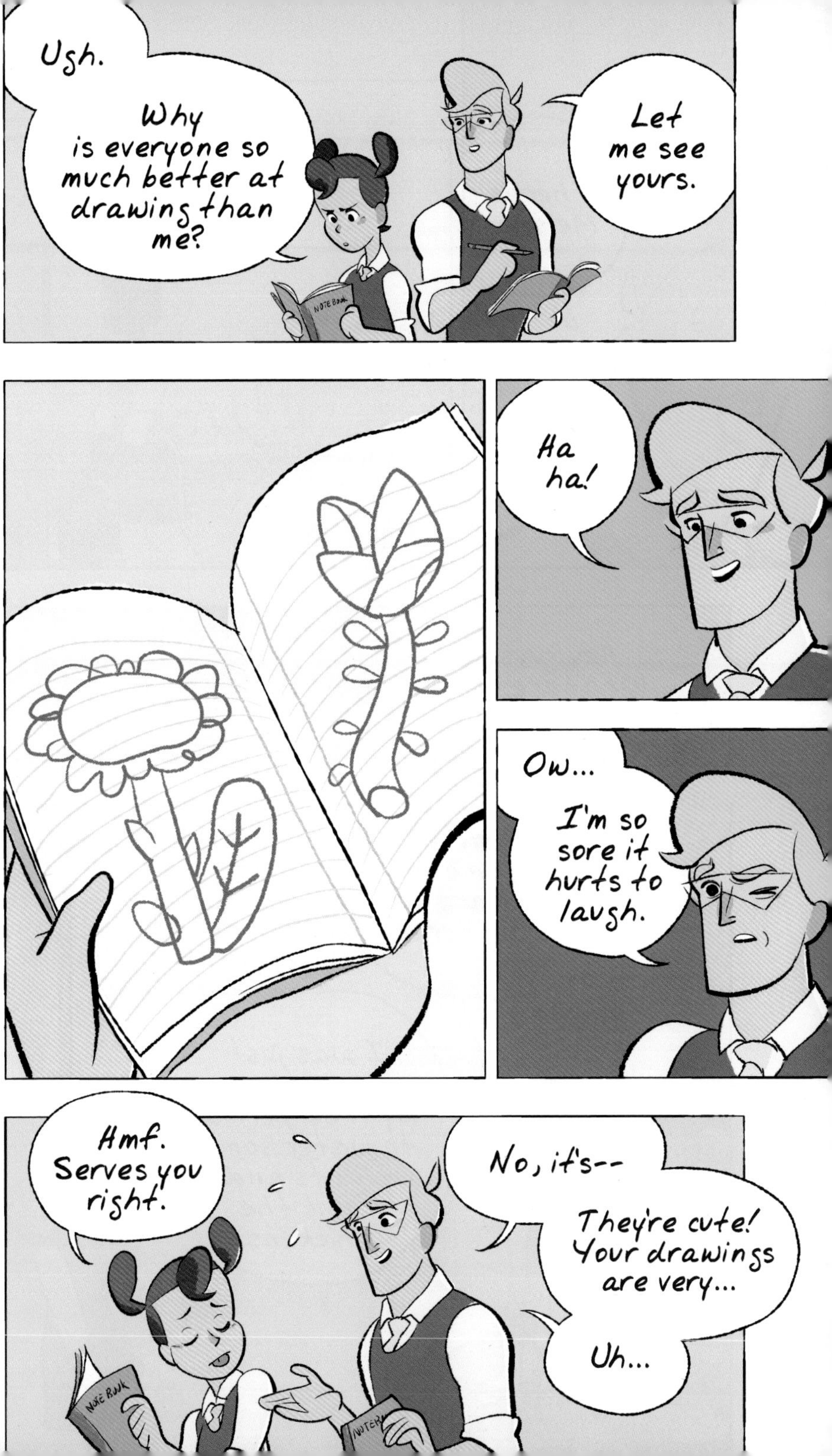
Ugh.
Why is everyone so much better at drawings than me?
Let me see yours.
NOTEBOOK
Ha ha!
Ow...
I'm so sore it hurts to laugh.
Hmf. Serves you right.
No, it's--
They're cute! Your drawings are very...
Uh...
NOTEBOOK

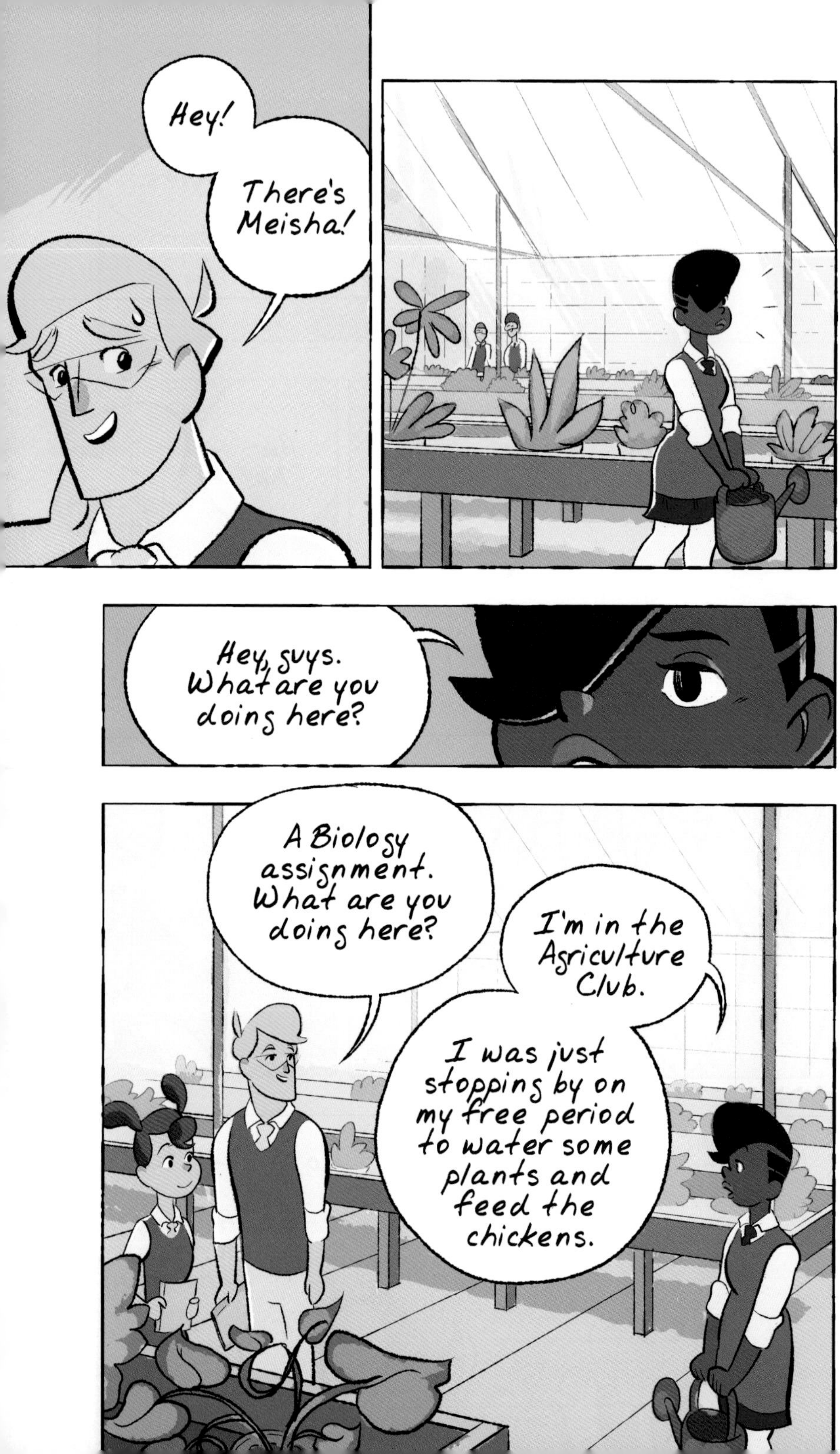
Hey!
There's Meisha!
Hey, guys. What are you doing here?
A Biology assignment. What are you doing here?
I'm in the Agriculture Club.
I was just stopping by on my free period to water some plants and feed the chickens.

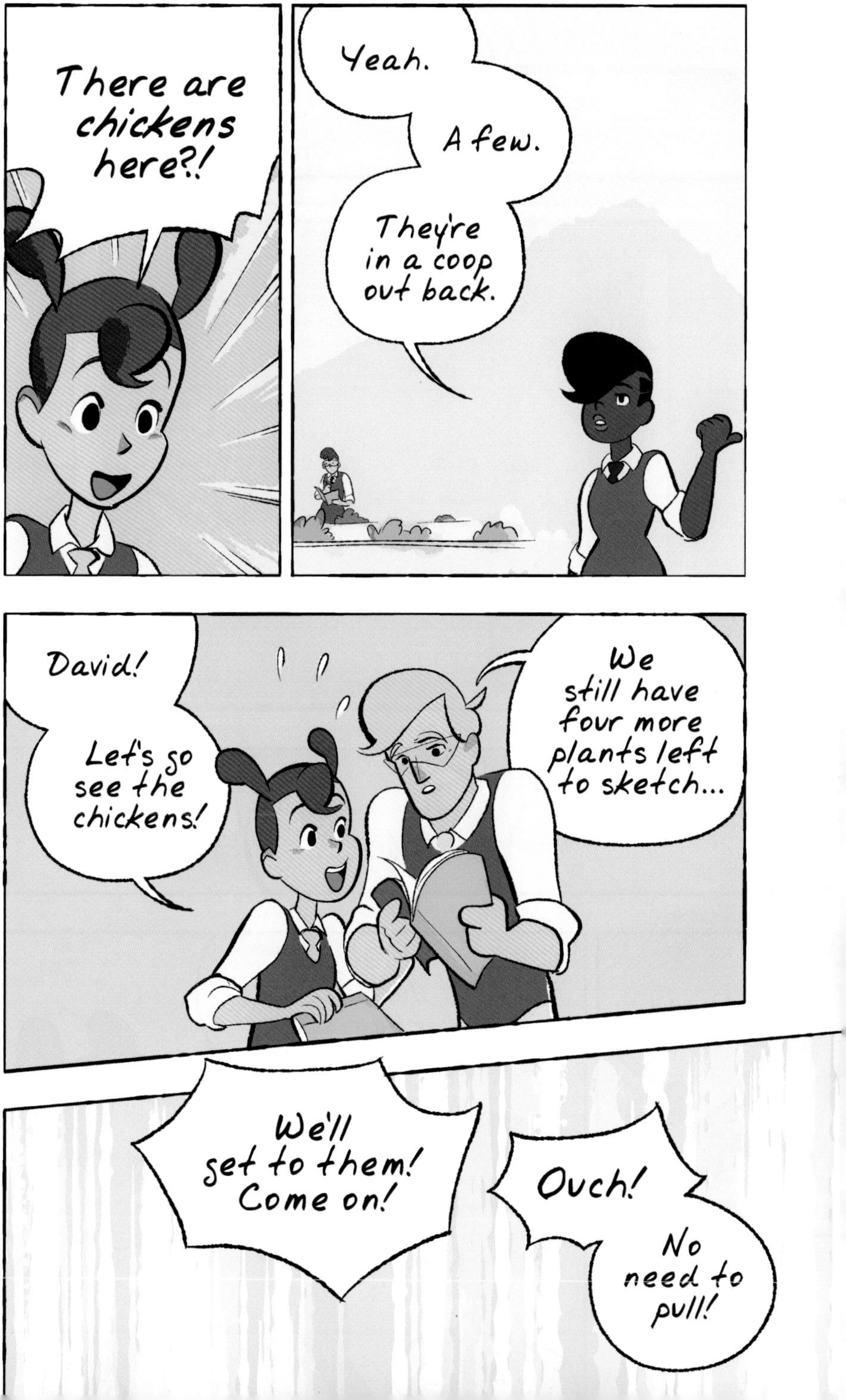
There are chickens here?!
Yeah.
A few.
They're in a coop out back.
David!
Let's go see the chickens!
We still have four more plants left to sketch...
We'll get to them! Come on!
Ouch!
No need to pull!

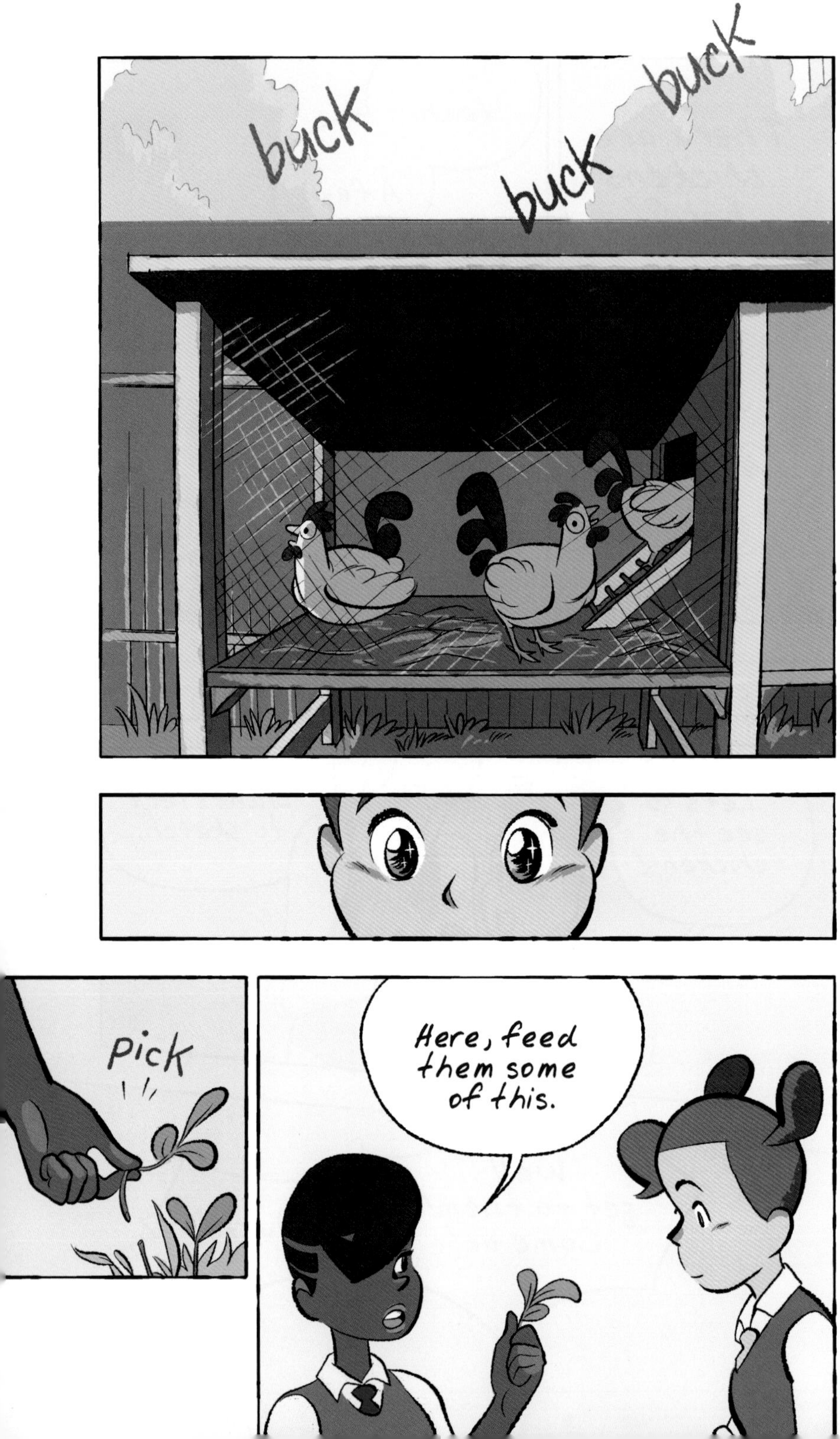
buck
buck
buck
pick
Here, feed them some of this.

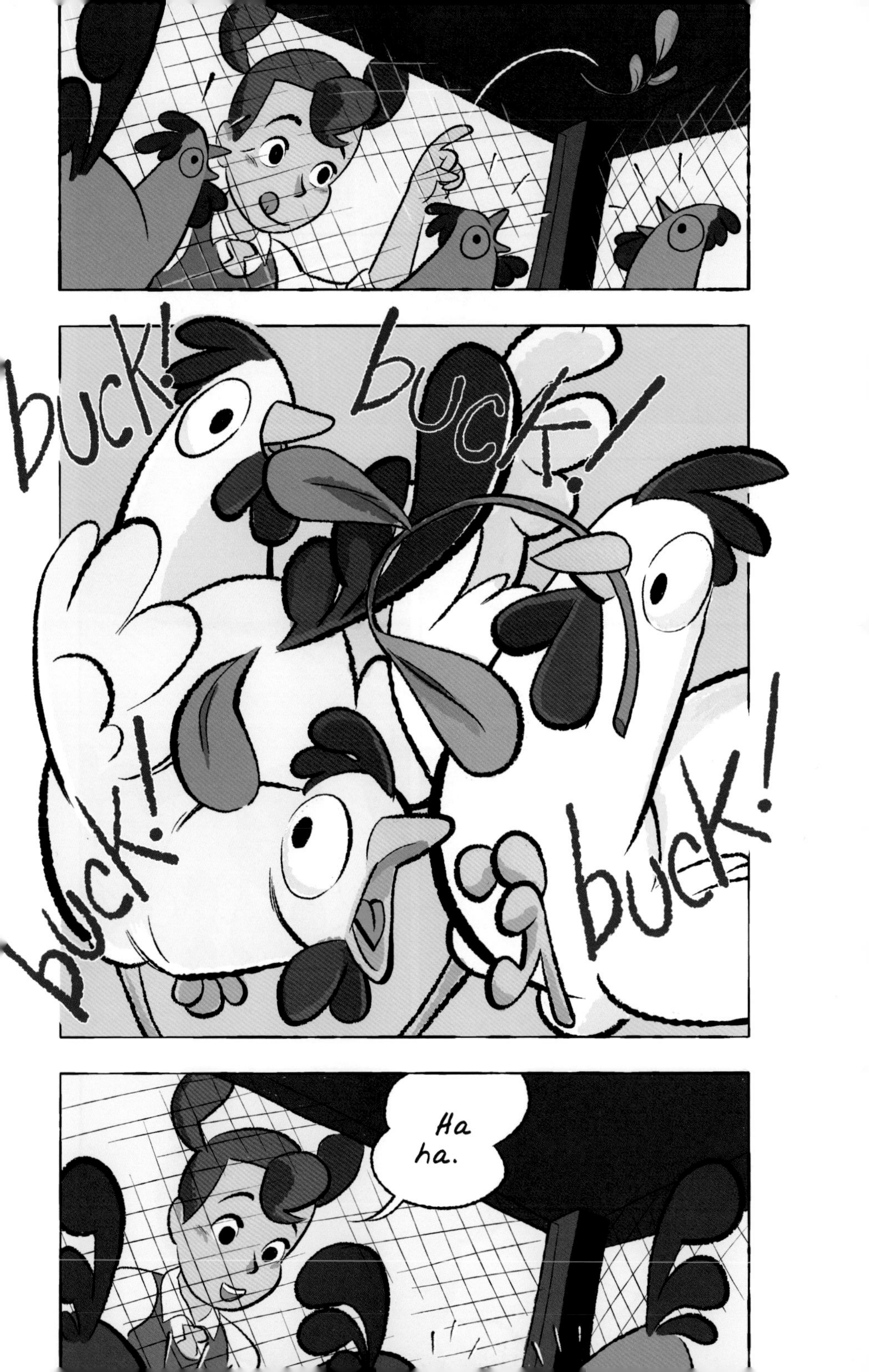
buck!
buck!
buck!
buck!
Ha ha.

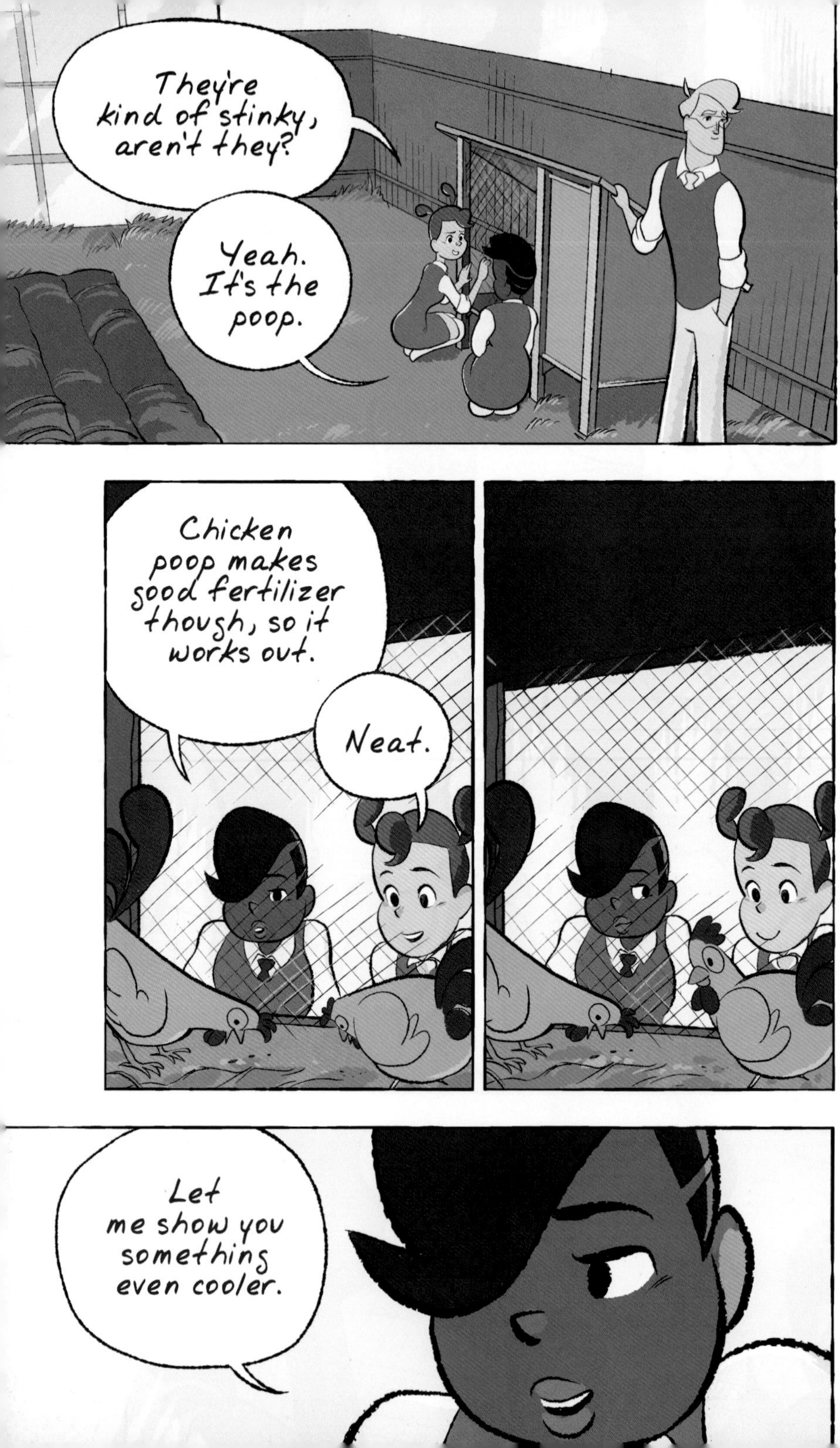
They're kind of stinky, aren't they?
Yeah. It's the poop.
Chicken poop makes good fertilizer though, so it works out.
Neat.
Let me show you something even cooler.

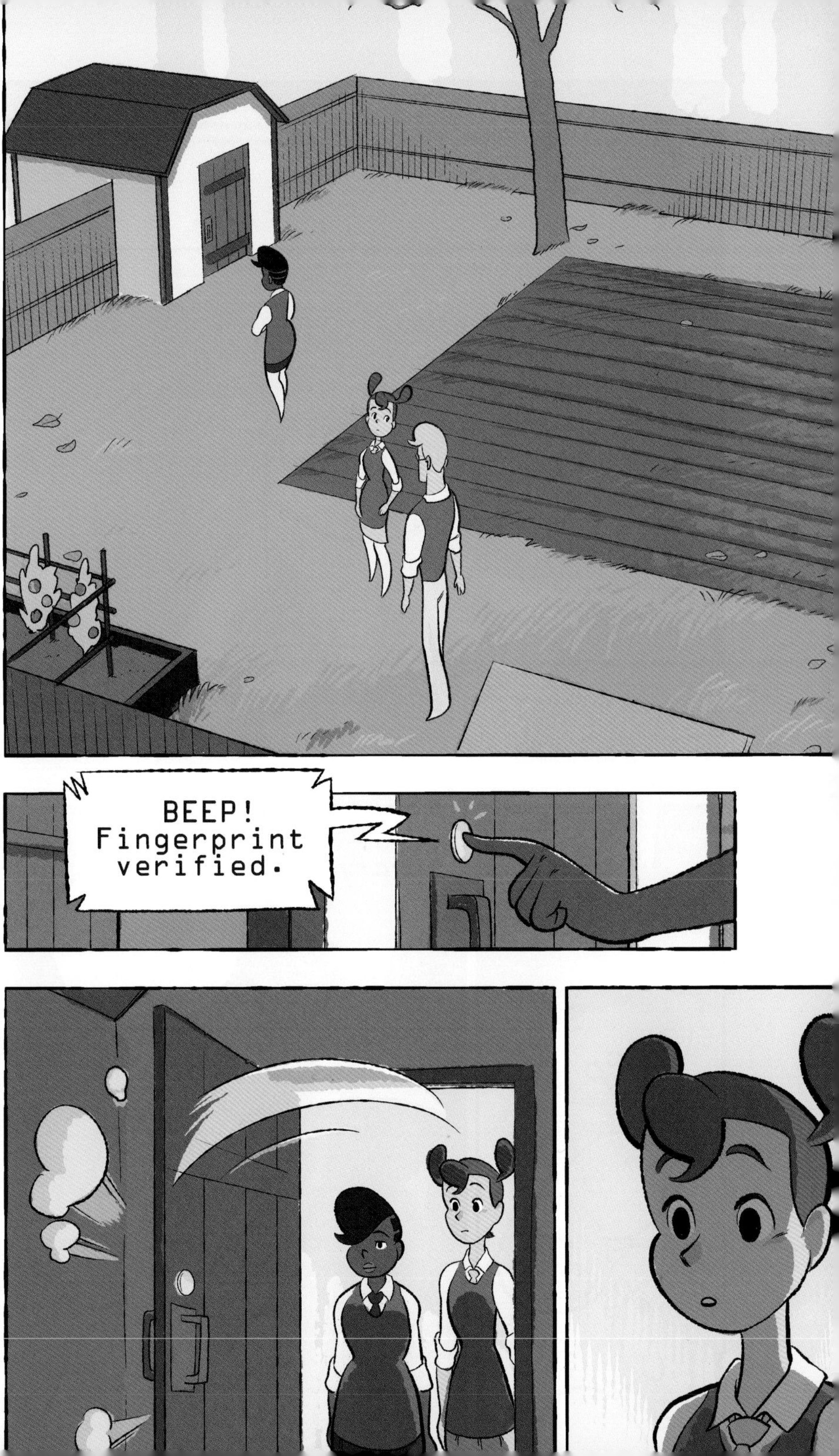
BEEP! Fingerprint verified.

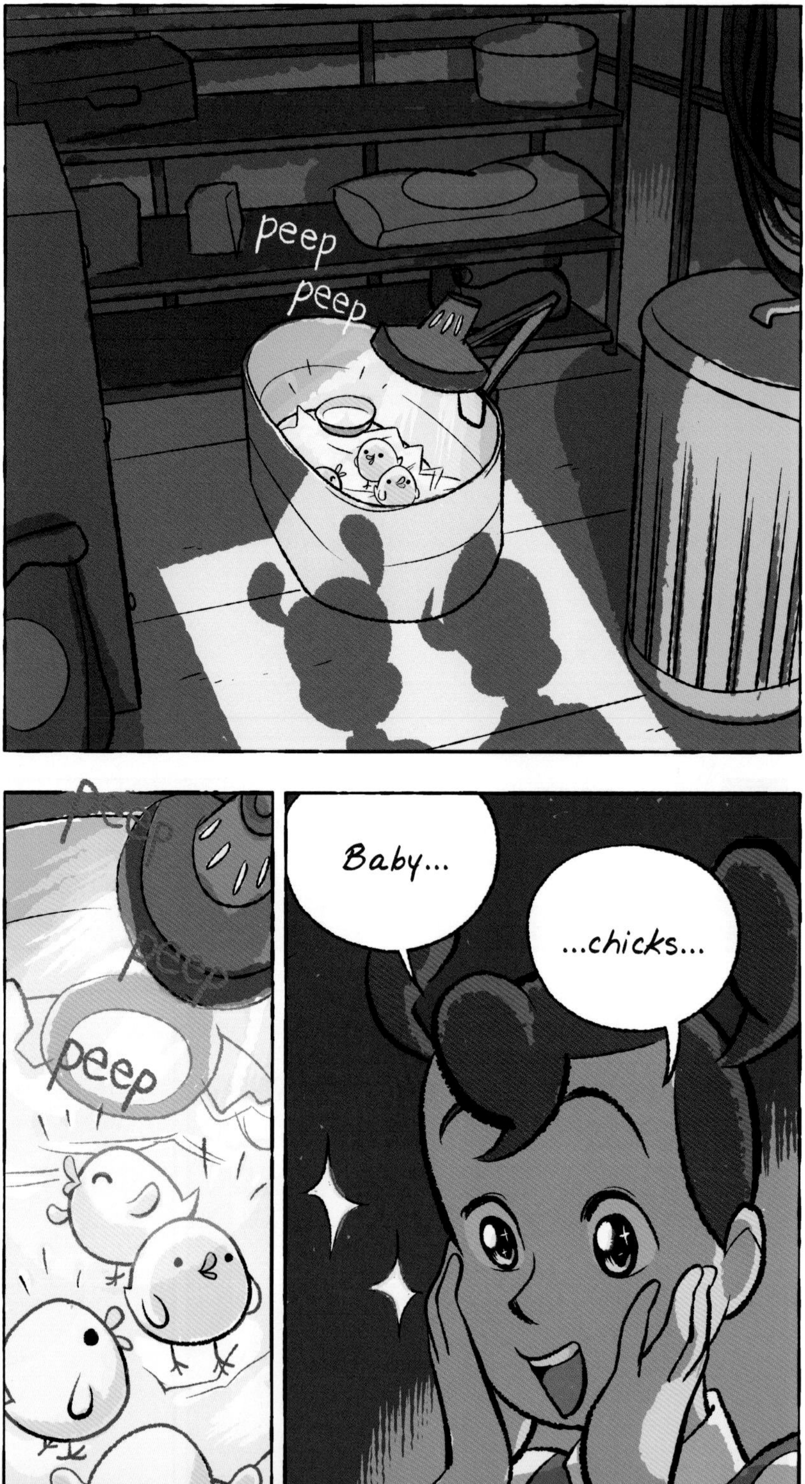
peep
peep
peep
peep
peep
Baby...
...chicks...

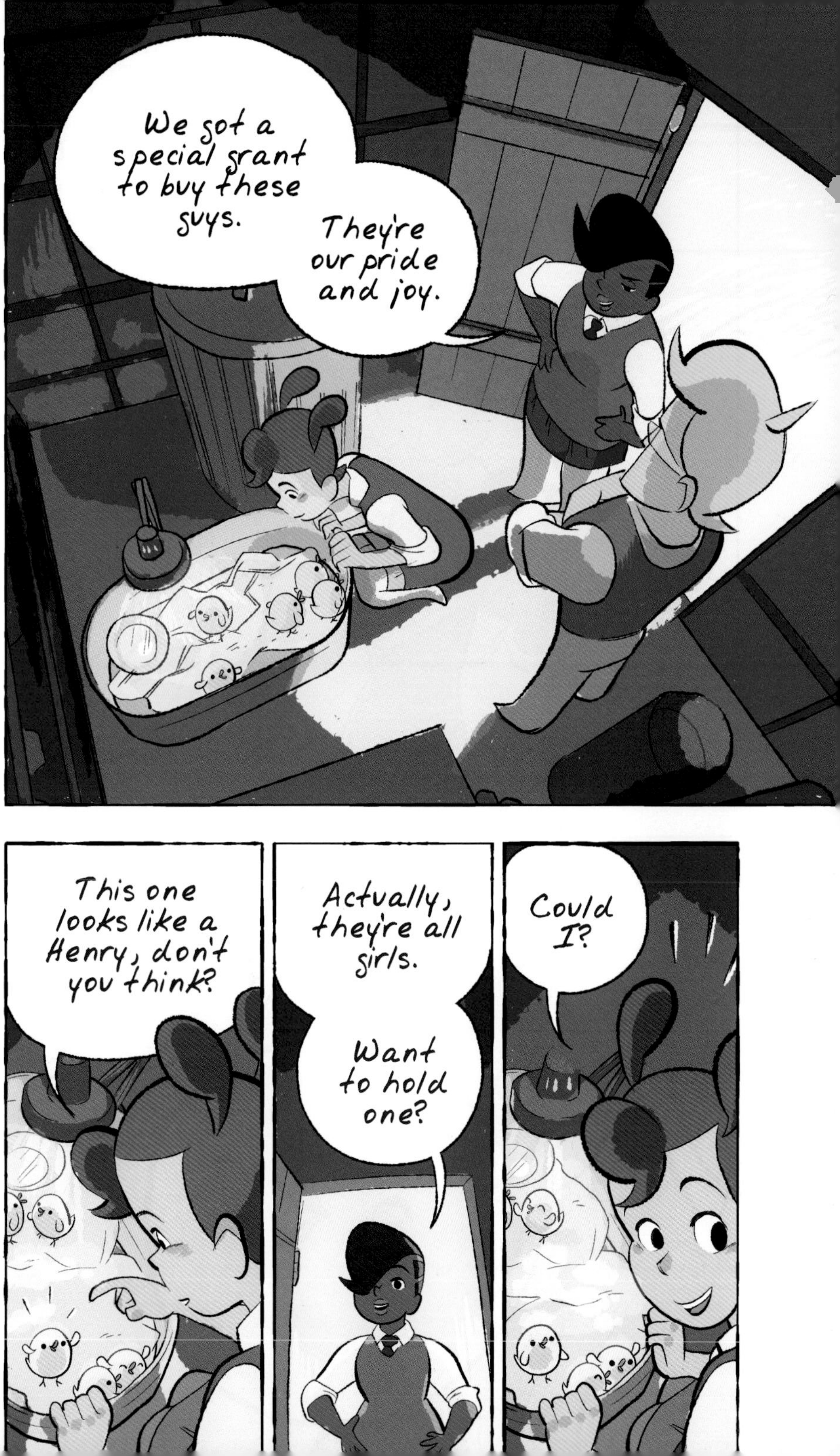
We got a special grant to buy these guys.
They're our pride and joy.
This one looks like a Henry, don't you think?
Actually, they're all girls.
Want to hold one?
Could I?

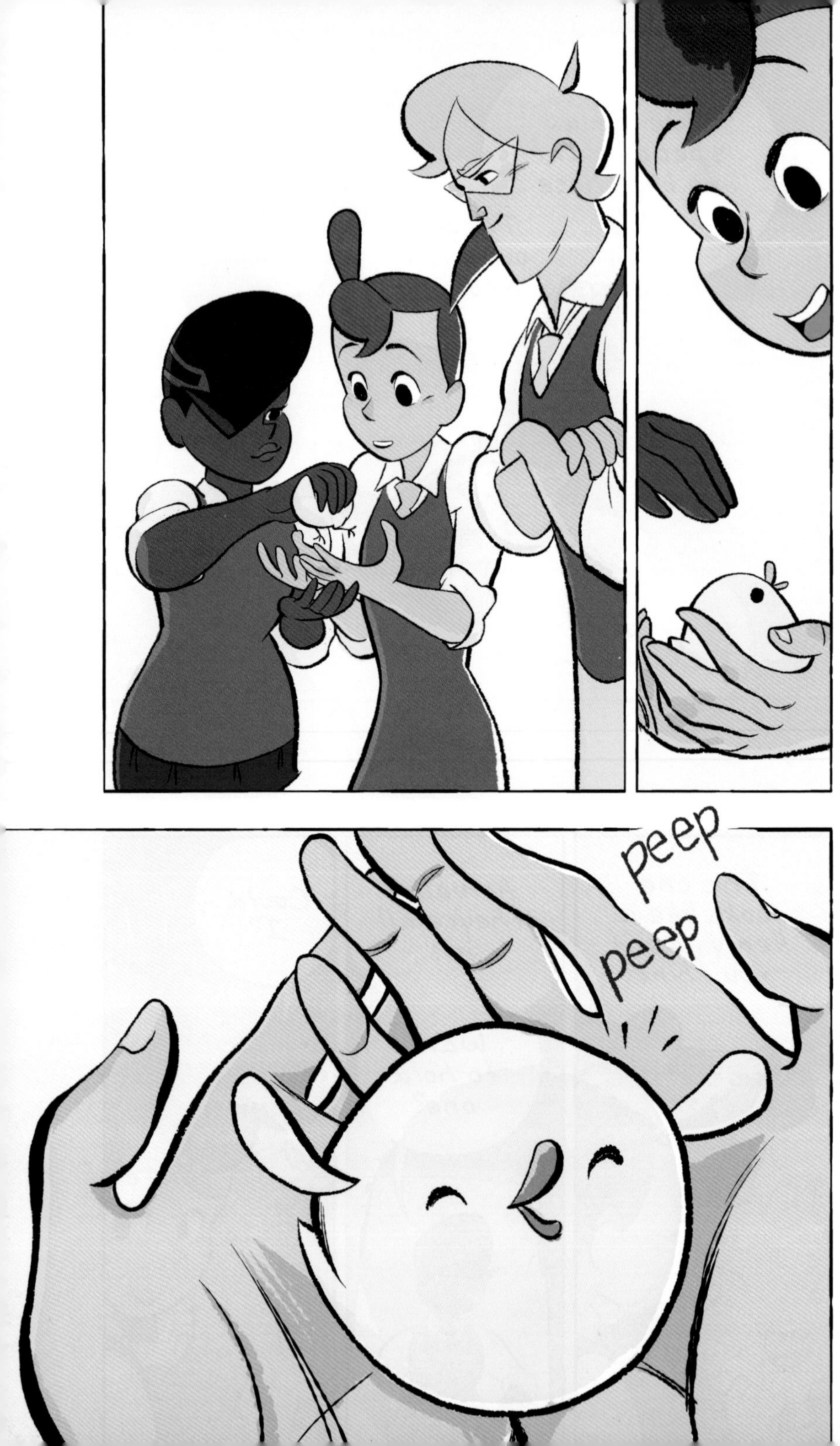
peep
peep

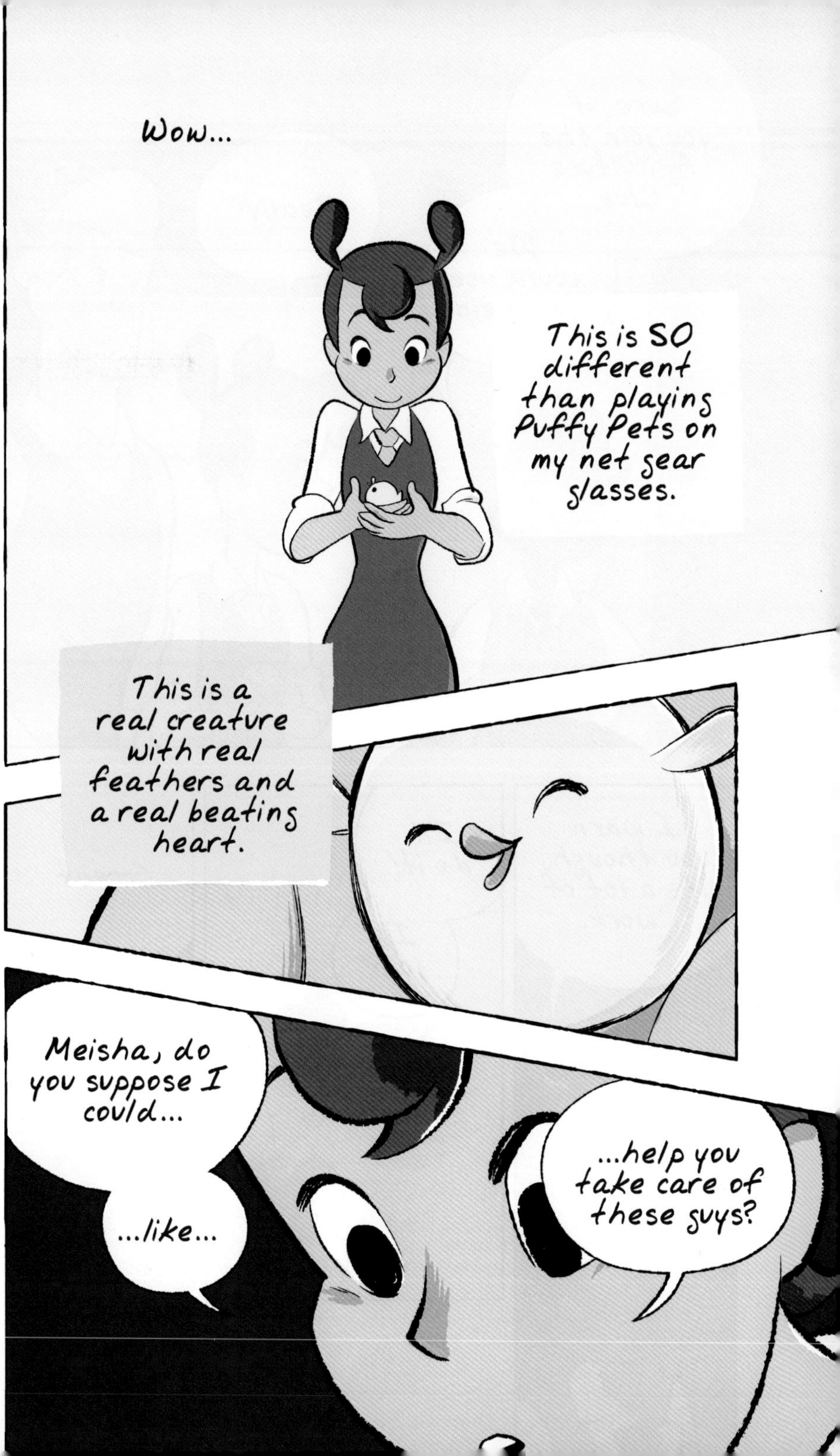
Wow...
This is SO different than playing Puffy Pets on my net gear glasses.
This is a real creature with real feathers and a real beating heart.
Meisha, do you suppose I could...
...like...
...help you take care of these guys?

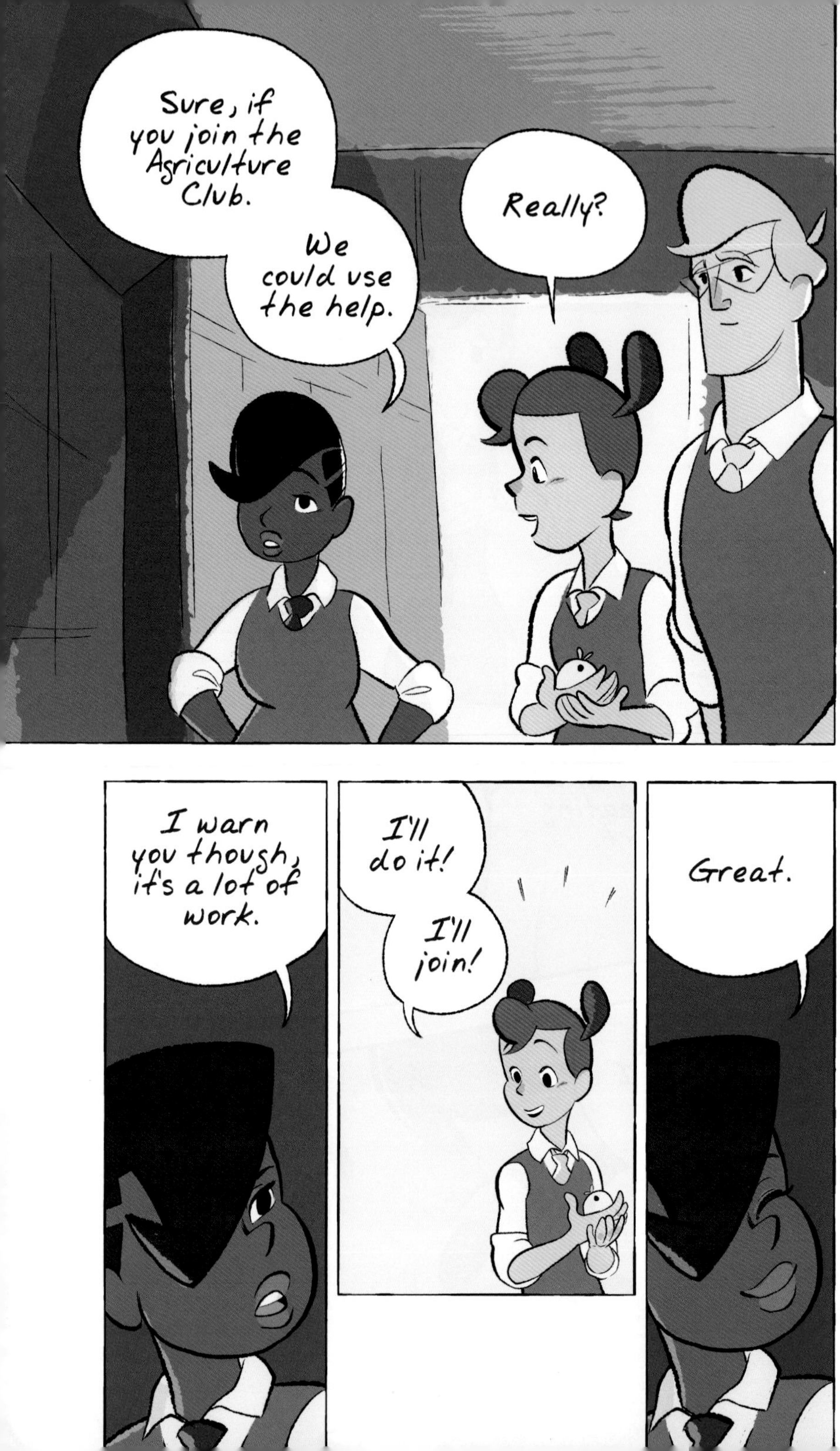
Sure, if you join the Agriculture Club.
We could use the help.
Really?
I warn you though, it's a lot of work.
I'll do it!
I'll join!
Great.

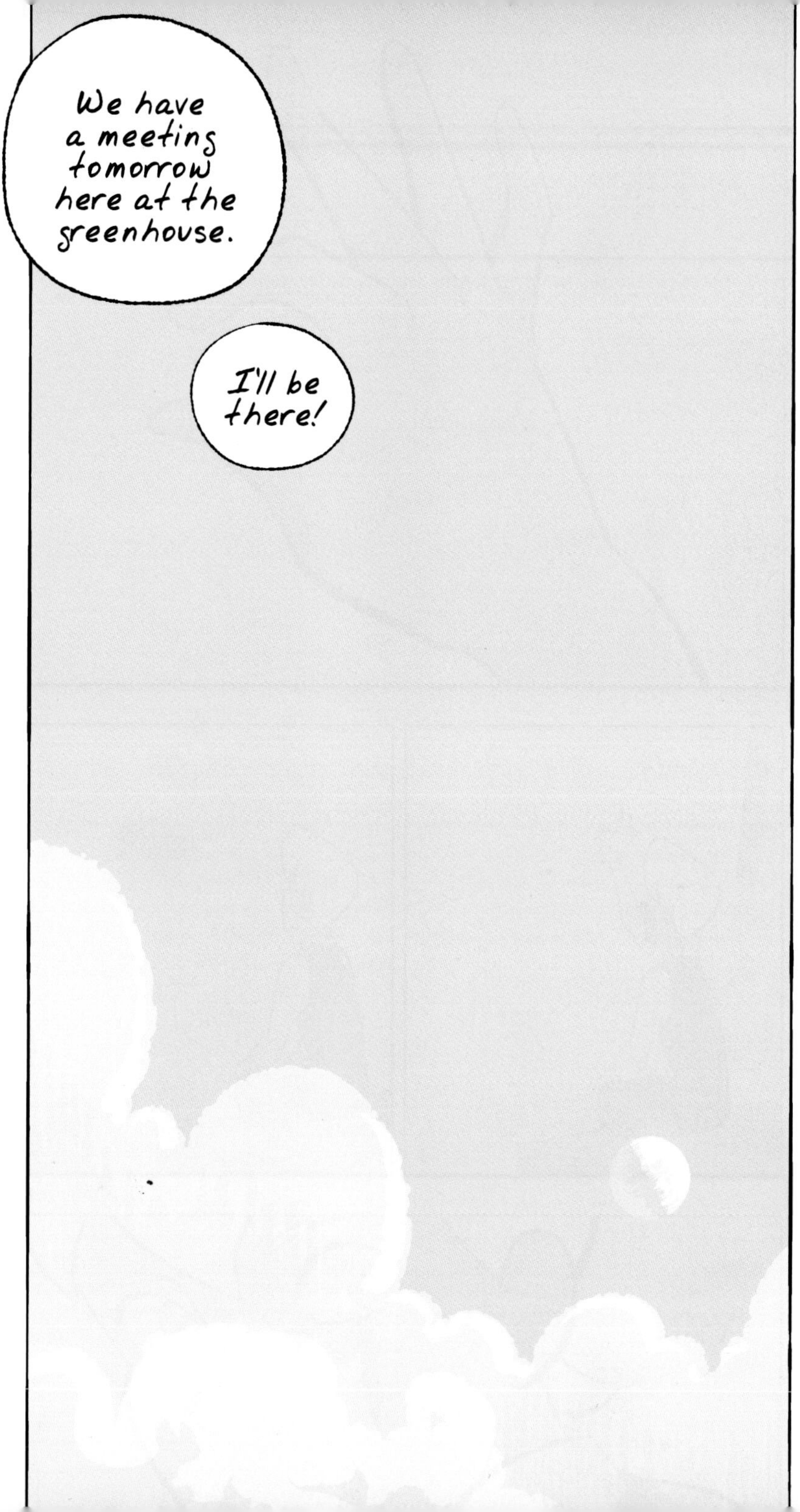
We have a meeting tomorrow here at the greenhouse.
I'll be there!

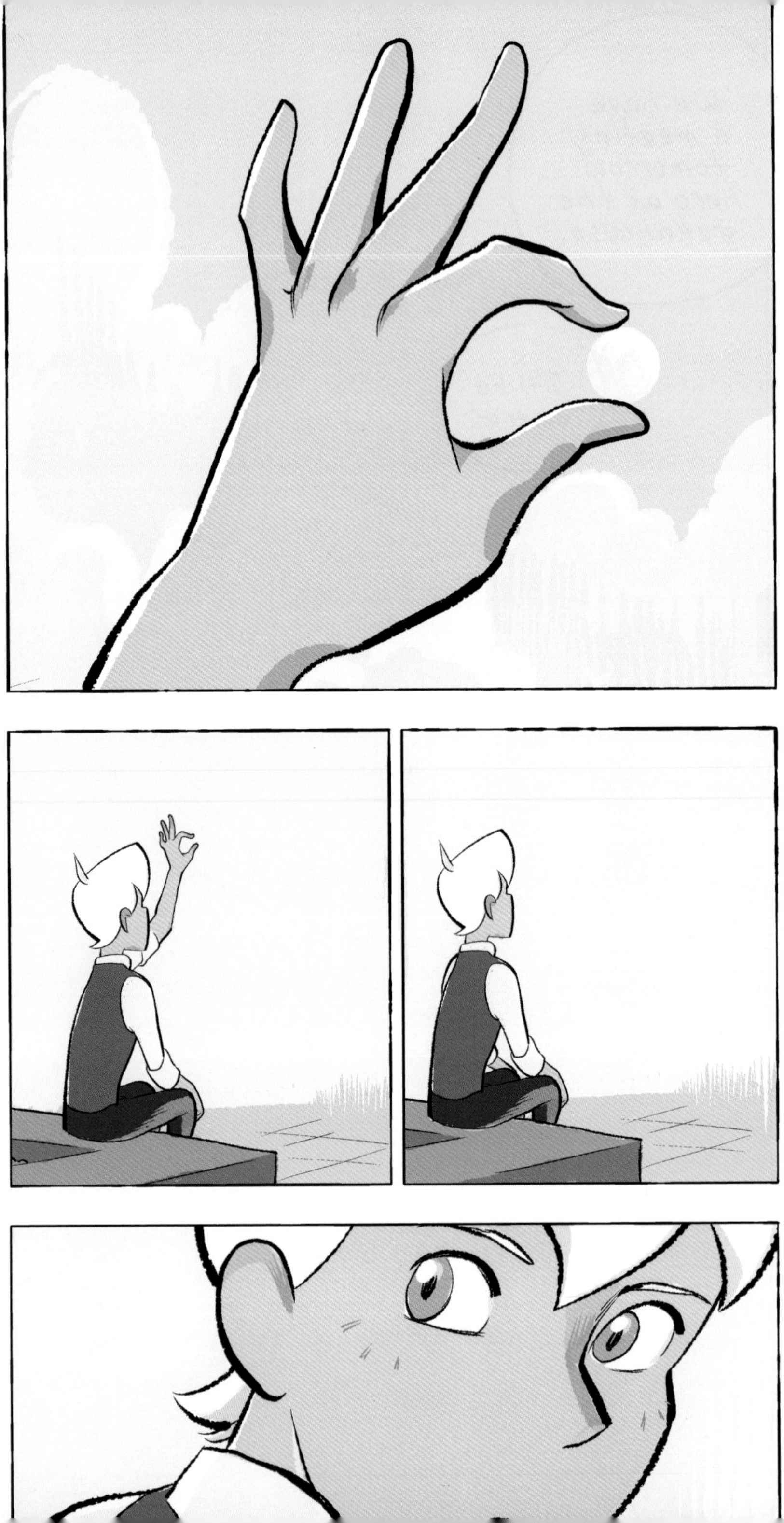

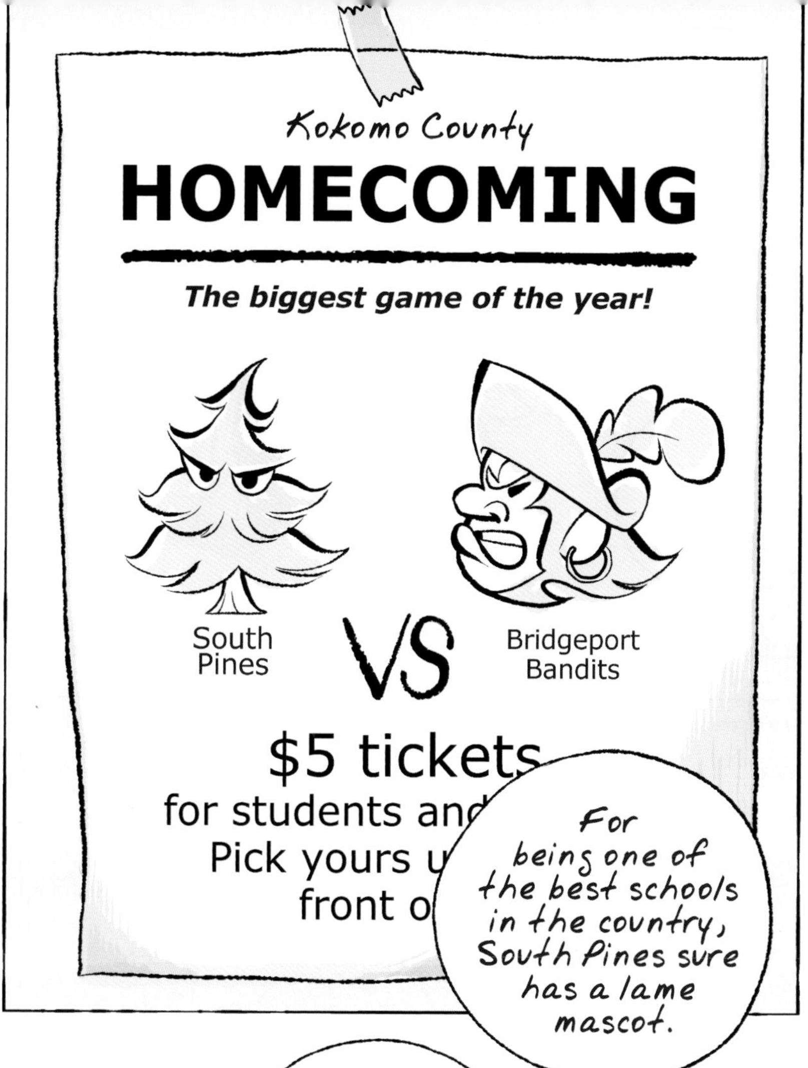
Kokomo County
HOMECOMING
The biggest game of the year!
South Pines
VS
Bridgeport Bandits
$5 tickets
for students and
Pick yours u
front o
For being one of the best schools in the country, South Pines sure has a lame mascot.

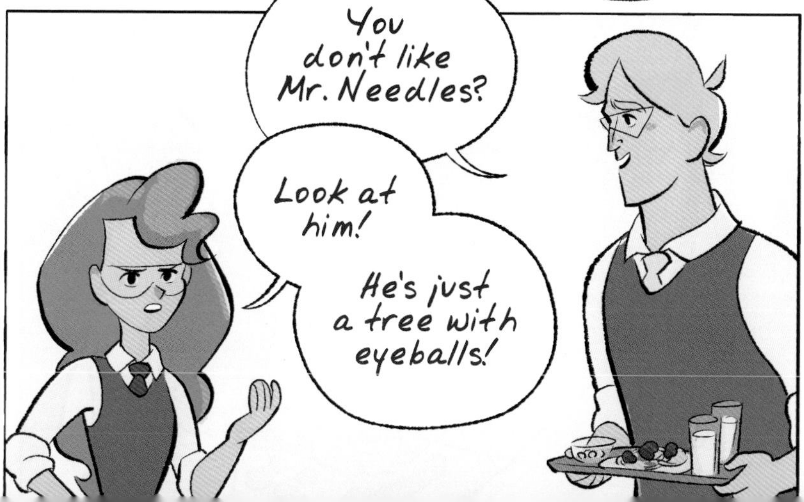
You don't like Mr. Needles?
Look at him!
He's just a tree with eyeballs!

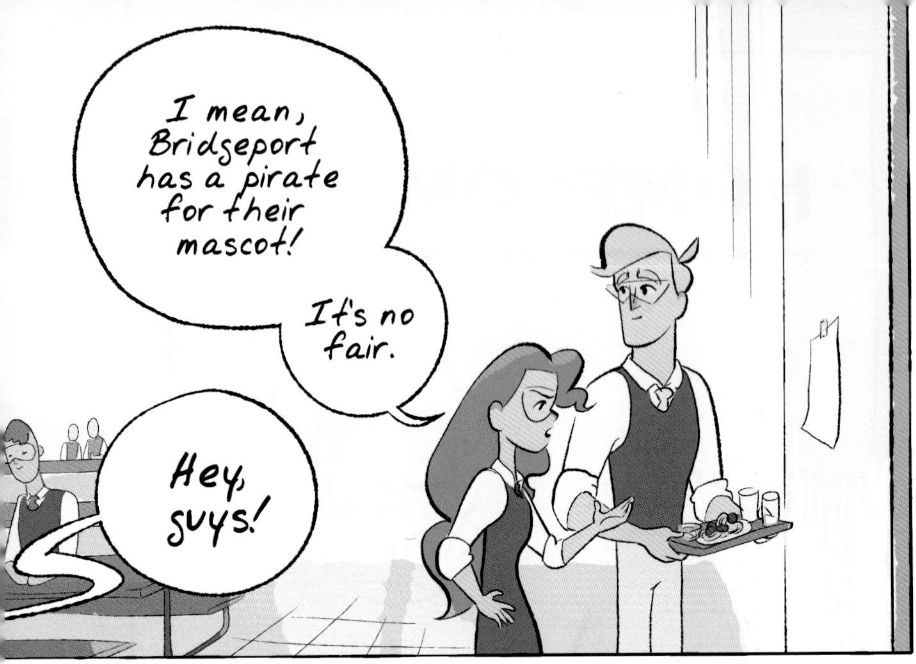
I mean, Bridgeport has a pirate for their mascot!
It's no fair.
Hey, guys!

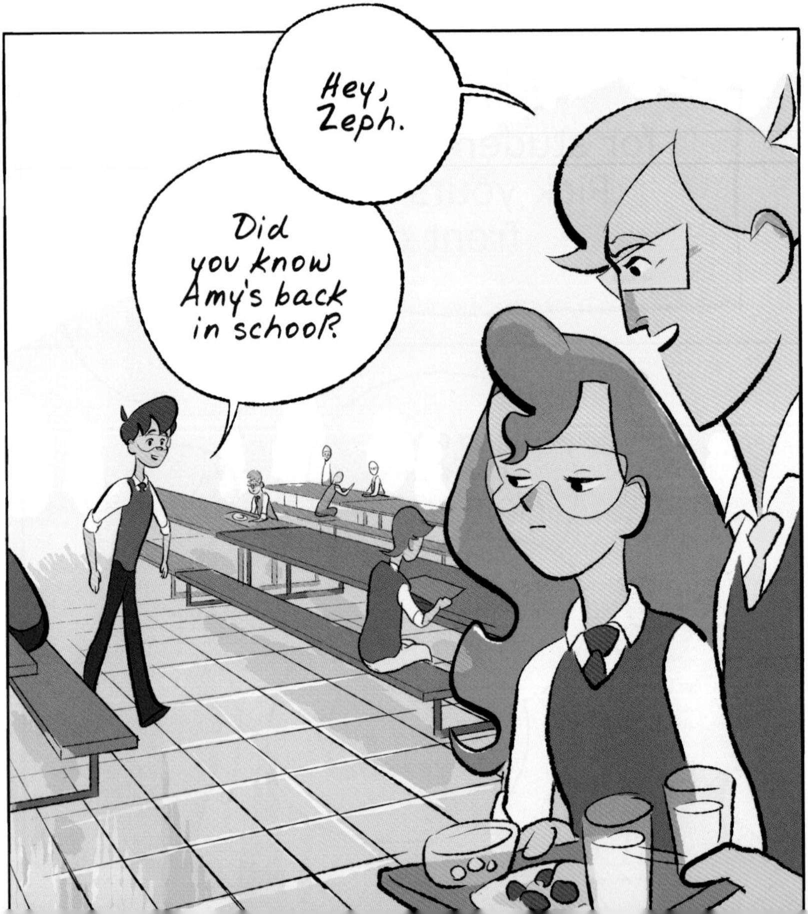
Hey, Zeph.
Did you know Amy's back in school?

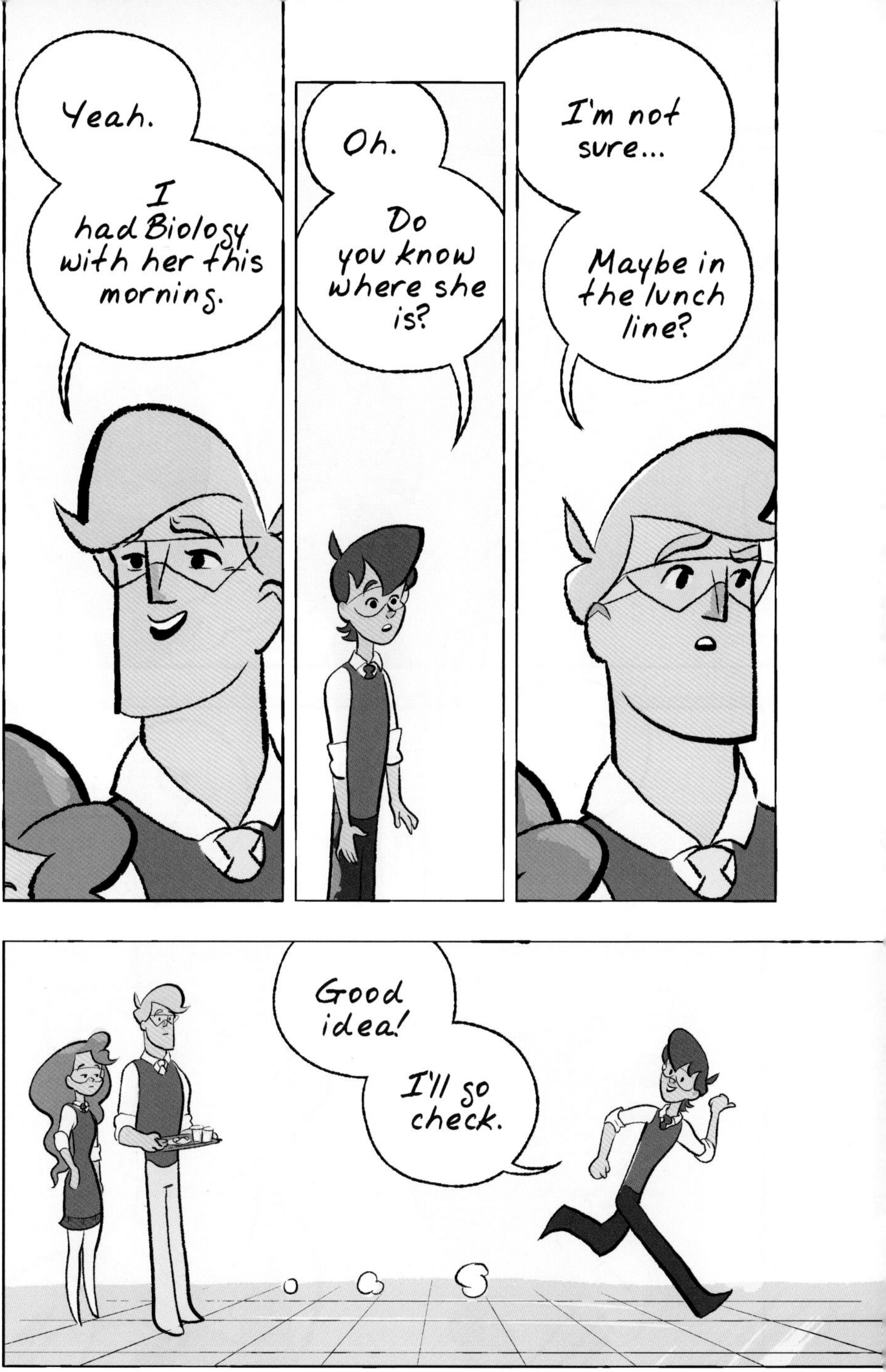
Yeah.
I had Biology with her this morning.
Oh.
Do you know where she is?
I'm not sure...
Maybe in the lunch line?
Good idea!
I'll go check.

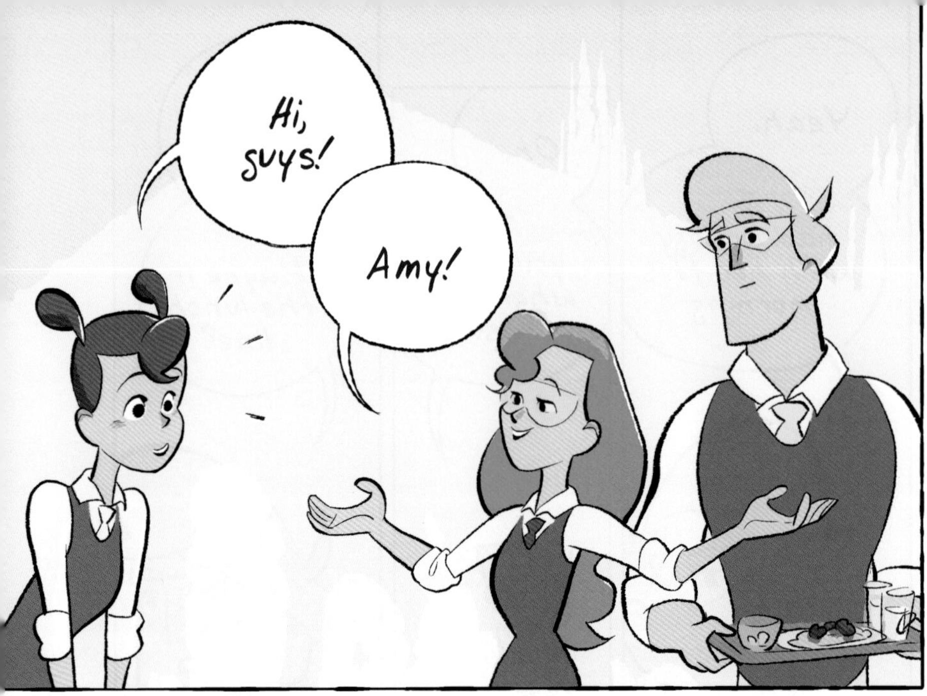
Hi, guys!
Amy!
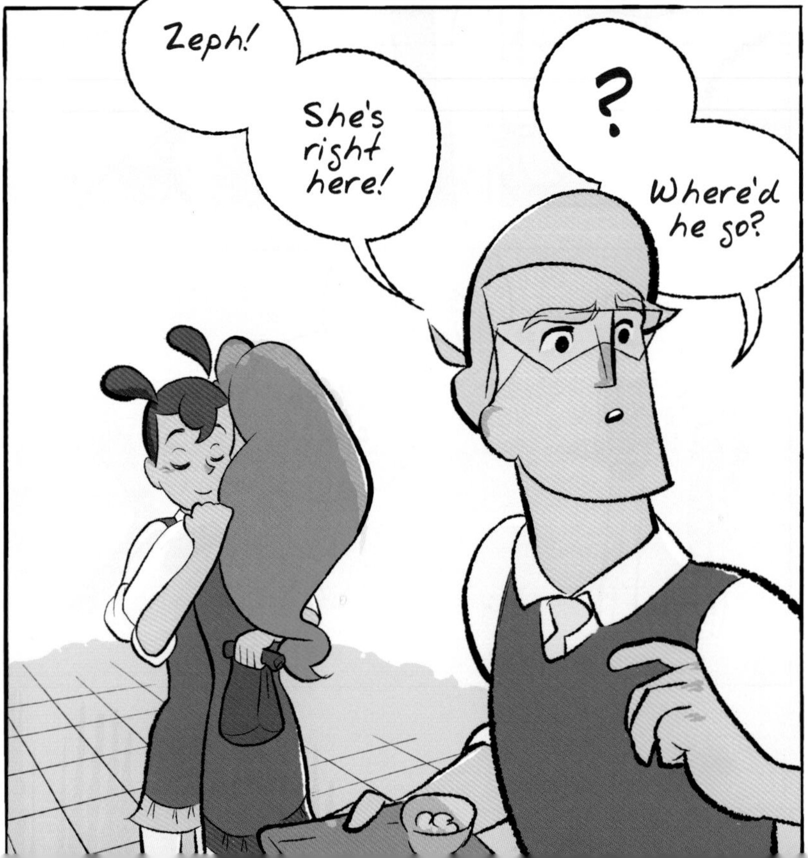
Zeph!
She's right here!
?
Where'd he go?

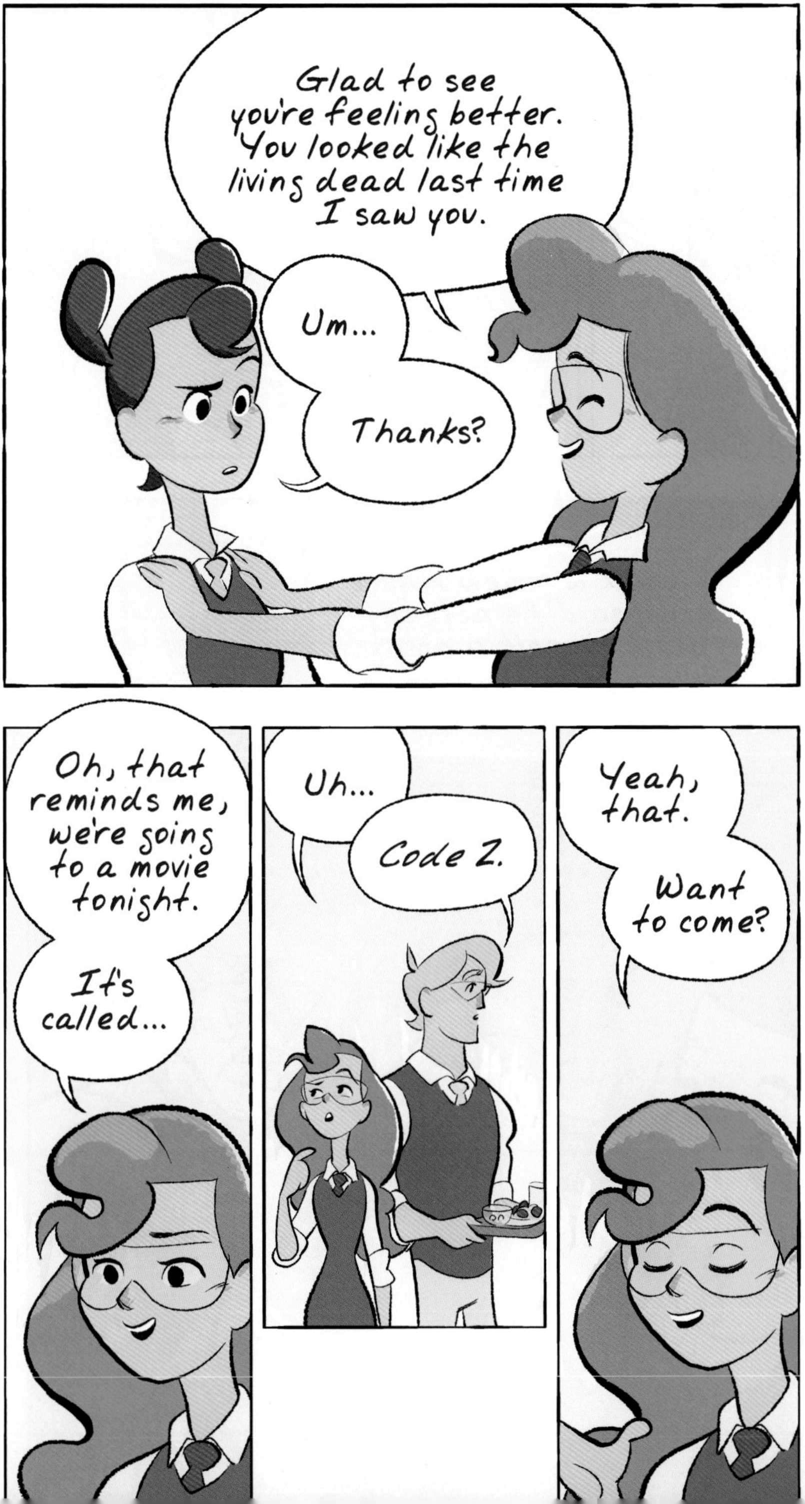
Glad to see you're feeling better. You looked like the living dead last time I saw you.
Um...
Thanks?
Oh, that reminds me, we're going to a movie tonight.
It's called...
Uh...
Code Z.
Yeah, that.
Want to come?

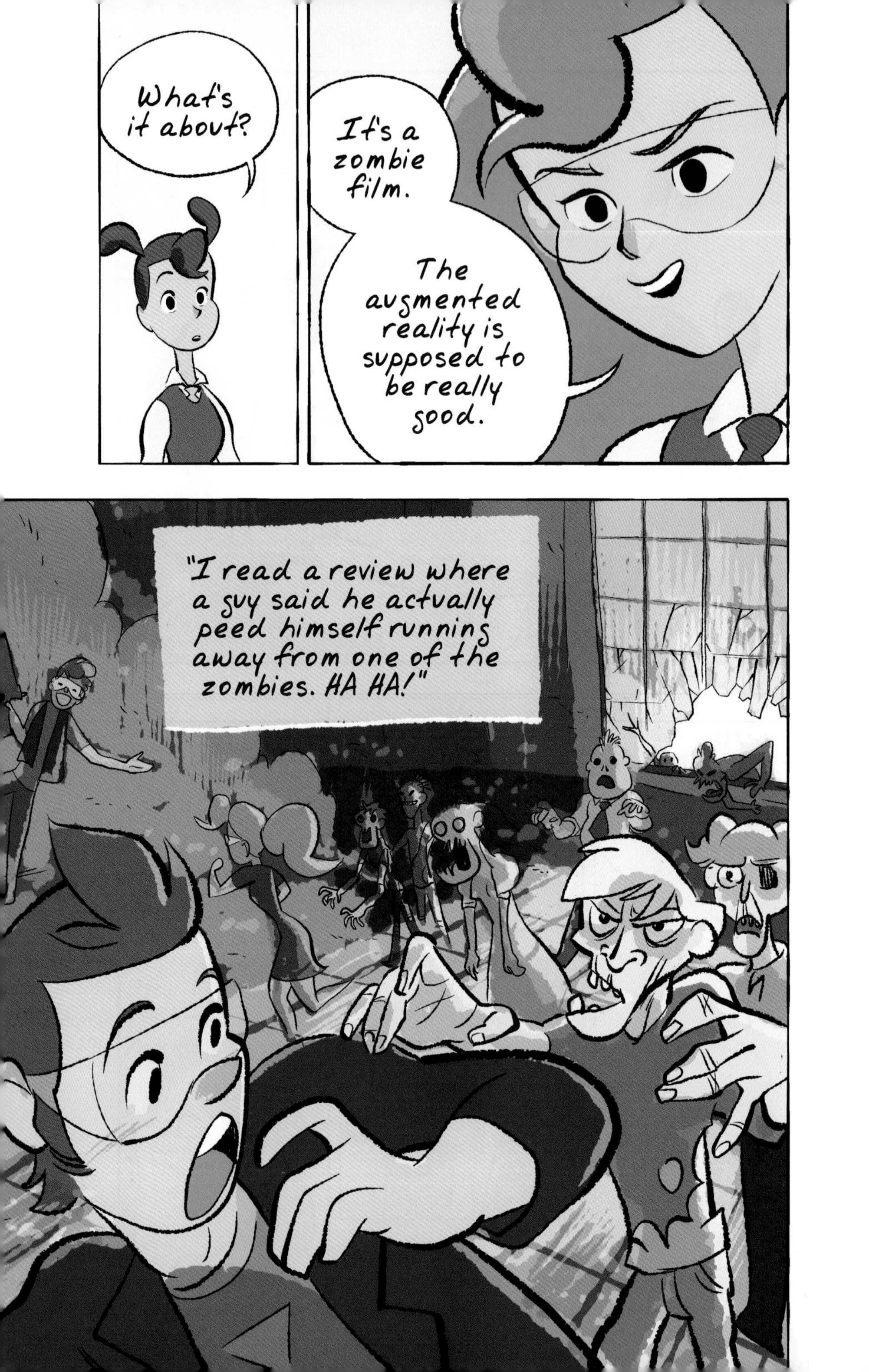
What's it about?
It's a zombie film.
The augmented reality is supposed to be really good.
"I read a review where a guy said he actually peed himself running away from one of the zombies. HA HA!"

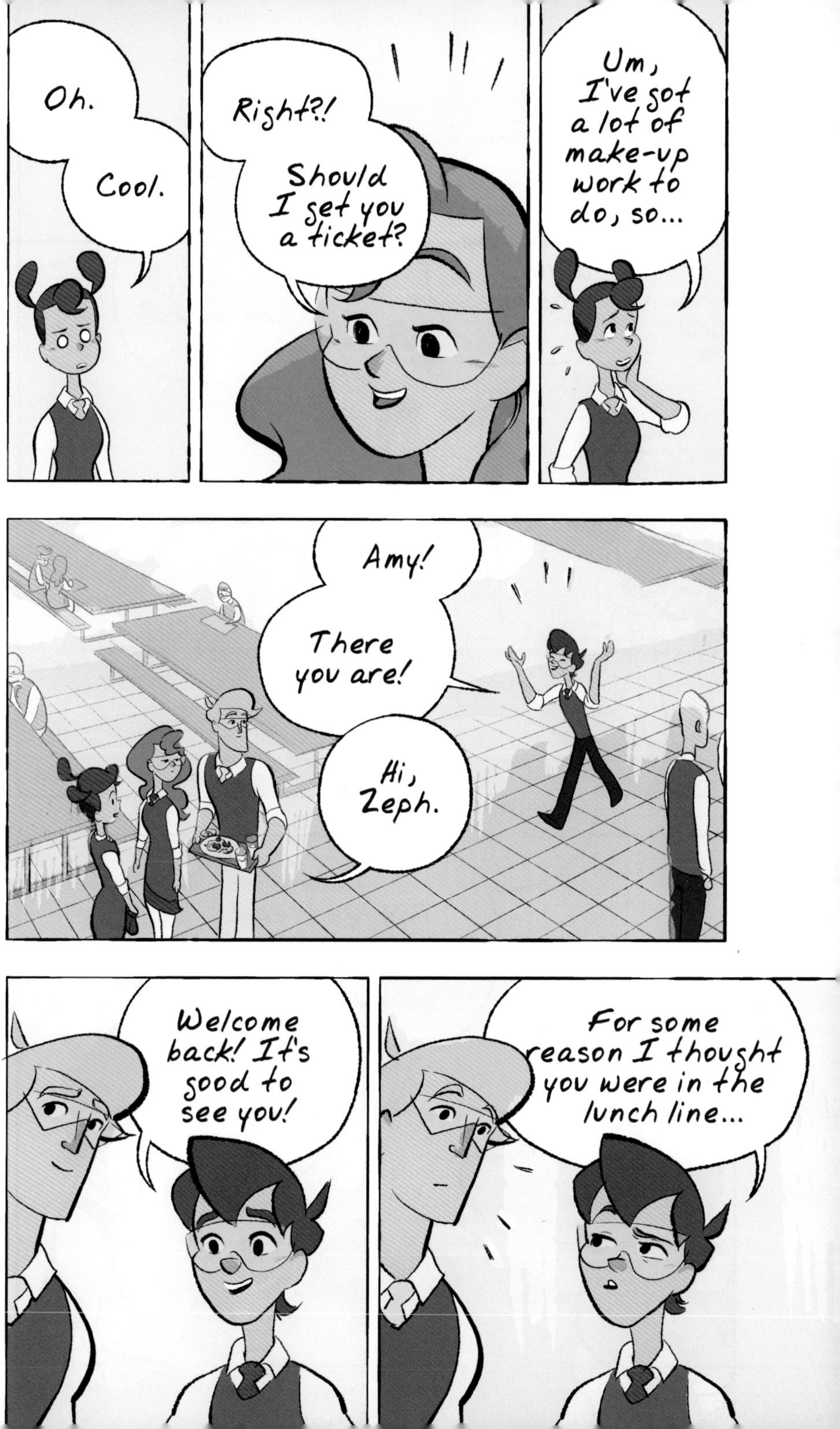
Oh.
Cool.
Right?!
Should I get you a ticket?
Um, I've got a lot of make-up work to do, so...
Amy!
There you are!
Hi, Zeph.
Welcome back! It's good to see you!
For some reason I thought you were in the lunch line...

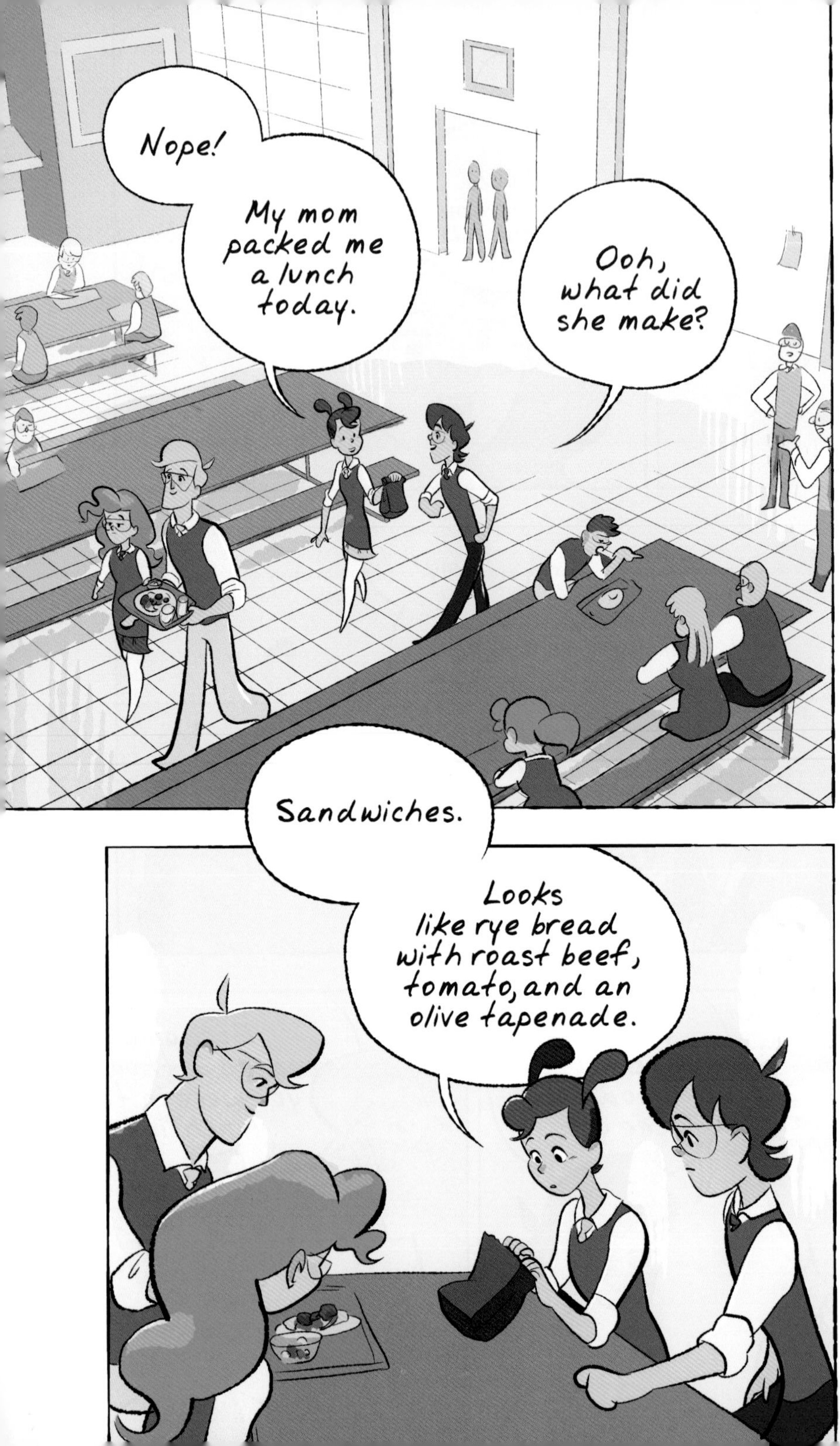
Nope!
My mom packed me a lunch today.
Ooh, what did she make?
Sandwiches.
Looks like rye bread with roast beef, tomato, and an olive tapenade.

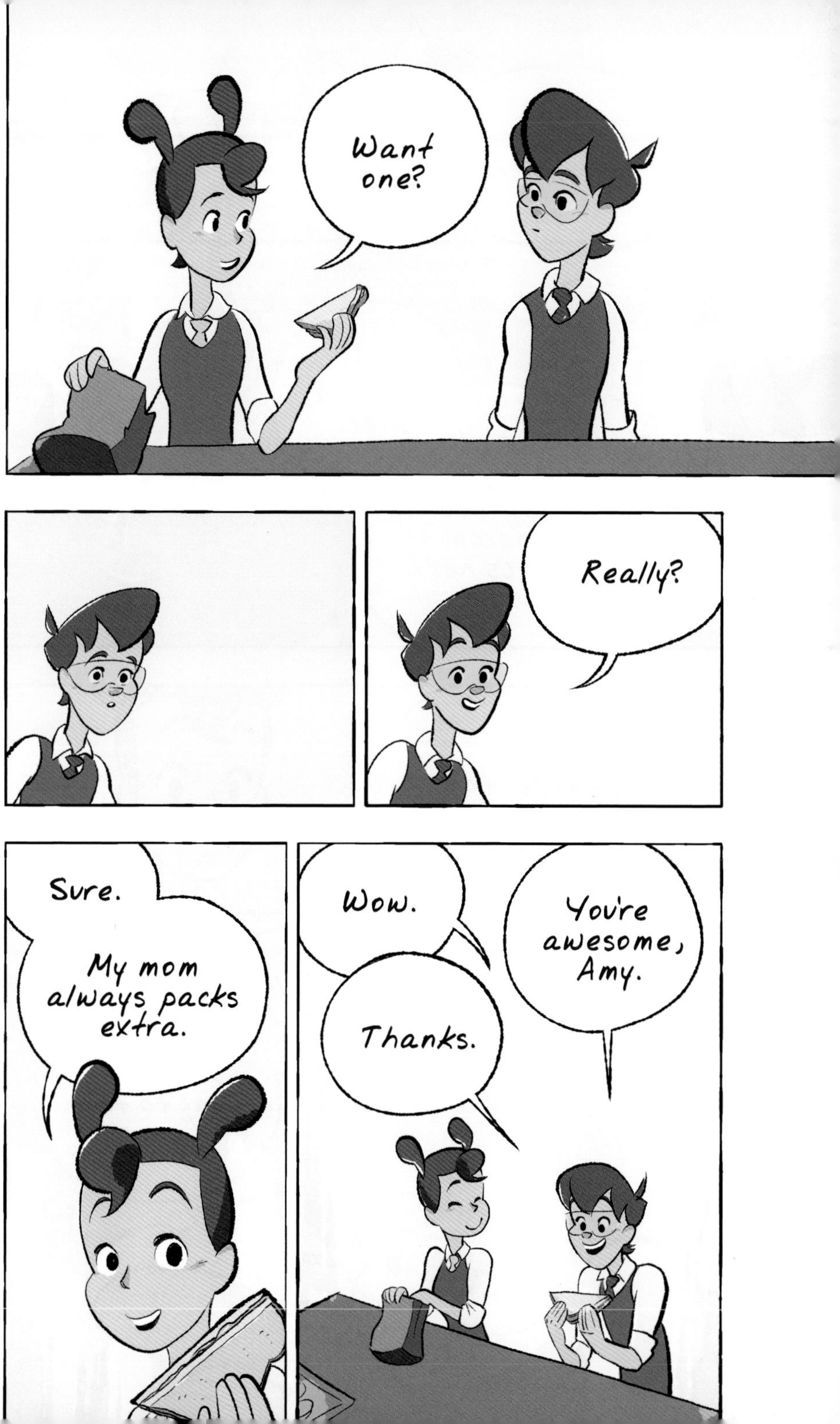
Want one?
Really?
Sure.
My mom always packs extra.
Wow.
You're awesome, Amy.
Thanks.

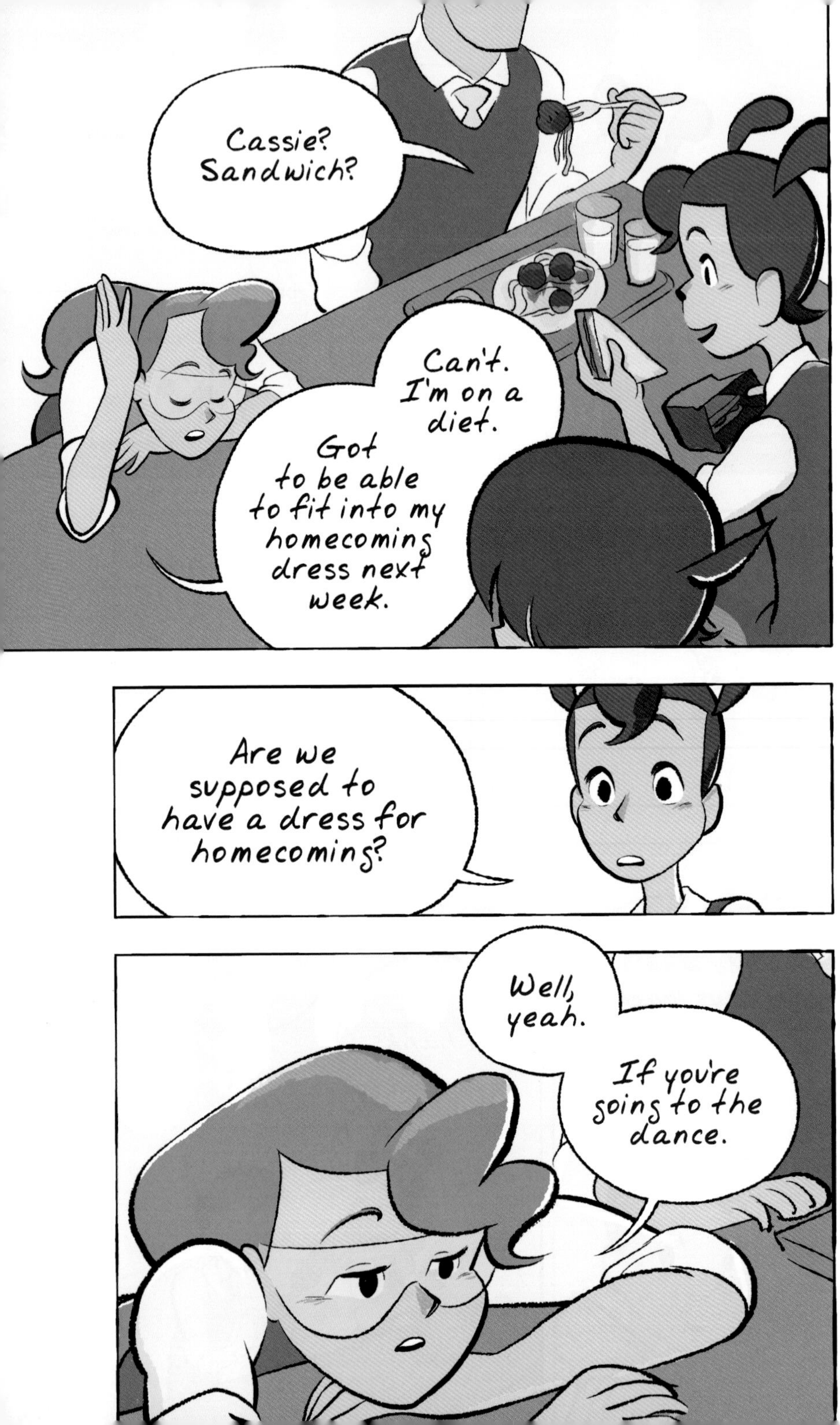
Cassie? Sandwich?
Can't. I'm on a diet.
Got to be able to fit into my homecoming dress next week.
Are we supposed to have a dress for homecoming?
Well, yeah.
If you're going to the dance.

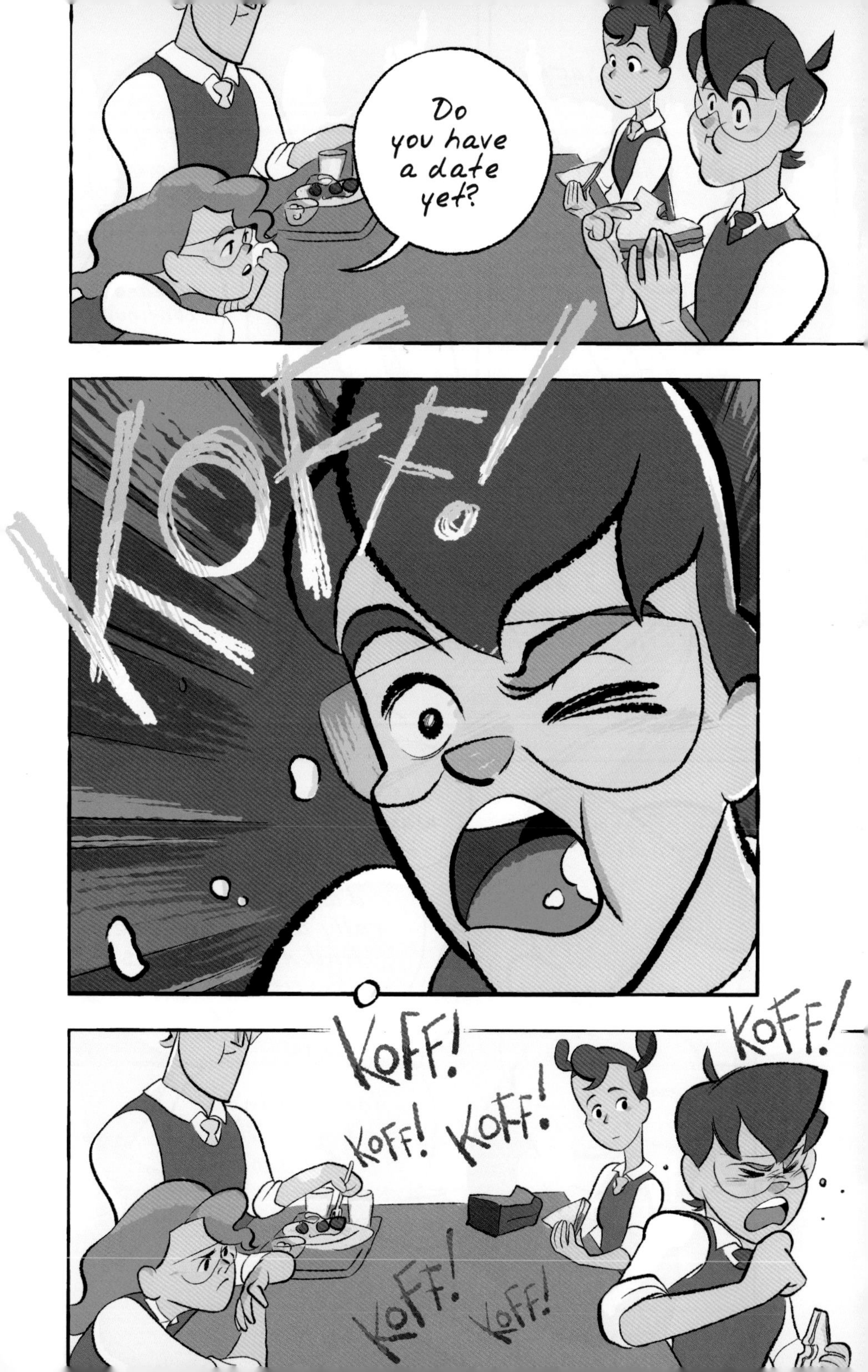
Do you have a date yet?
KOFF!
KOFF!
KOFF!
KOFF!
KOFF!
KOFF!
KOFF!

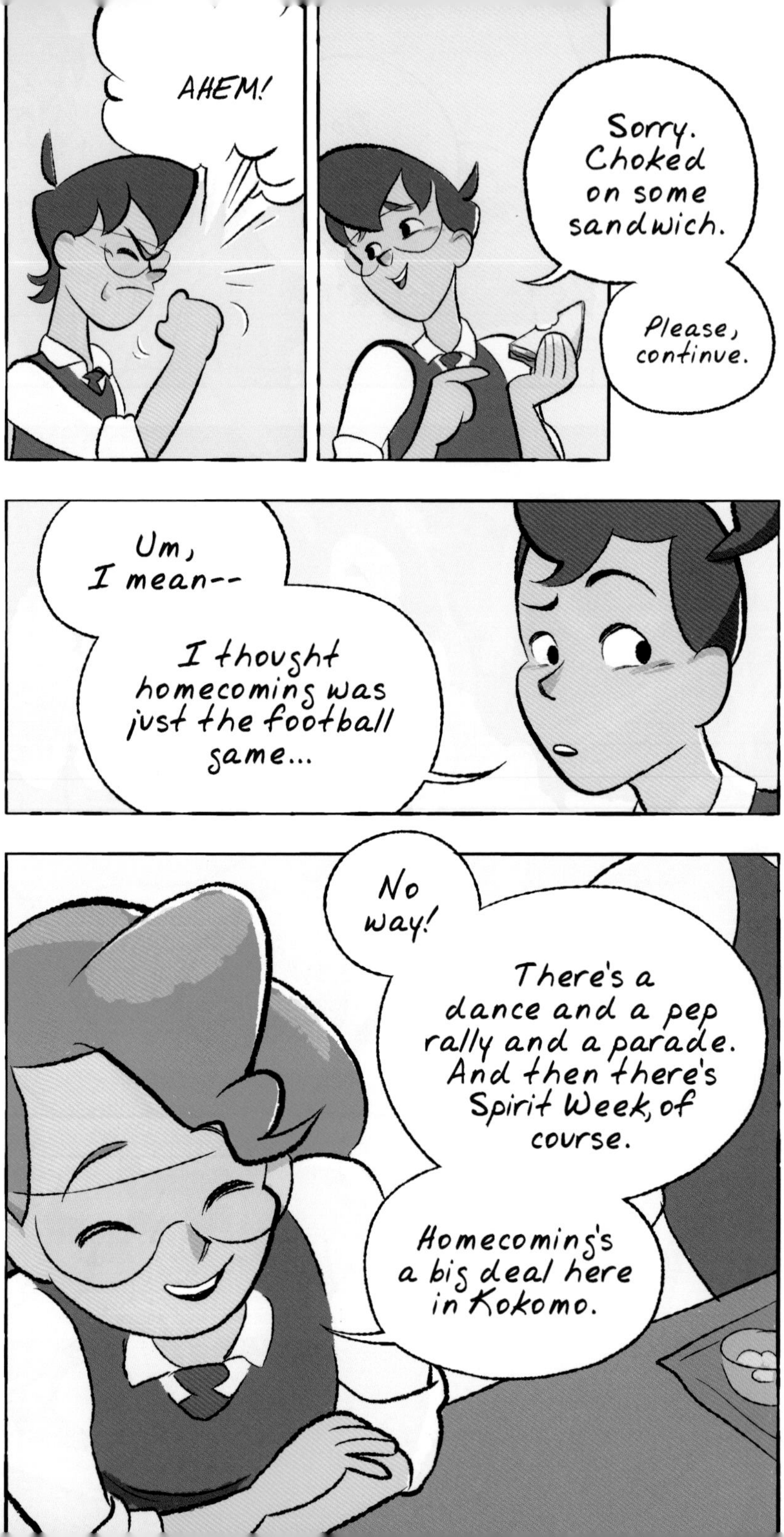
AHEM!
Sorry. Choked on some sandwich.
Please, continue.
Um, I mean--
I thought homecoming was just the football game...
No way!
There's a dance and a pep rally and a parade. And then there's Spirit Week, of course.
Homecoming's a big deal here in Kokomo.

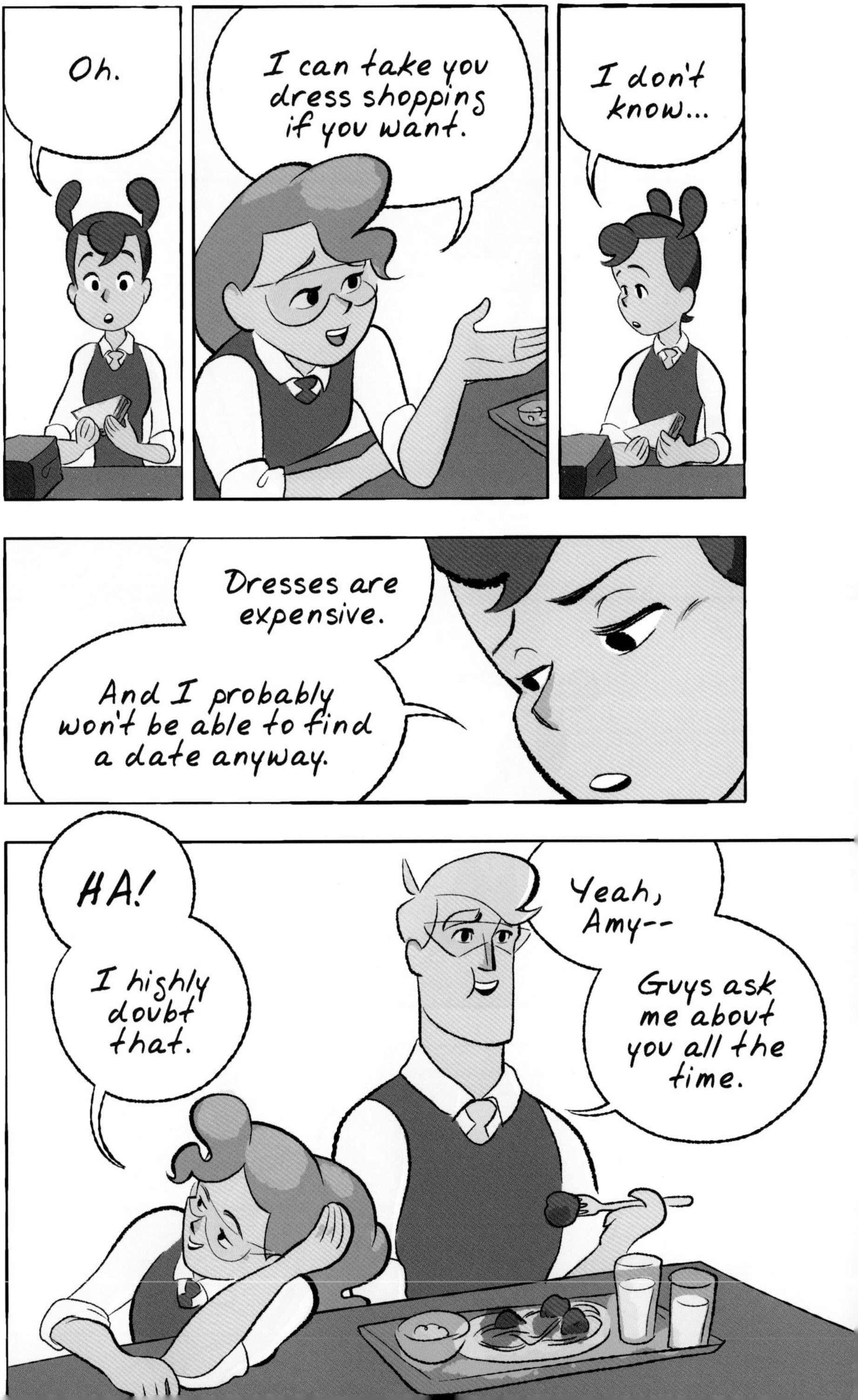
Oh.
I can take you dress shopping if you want.
I don't know...
Dresses are expensive.
And I probably won't be able to find a date anyway.
HA!
I highly doubt that.
Yeah, Amy--
Guys ask me about you all the time.

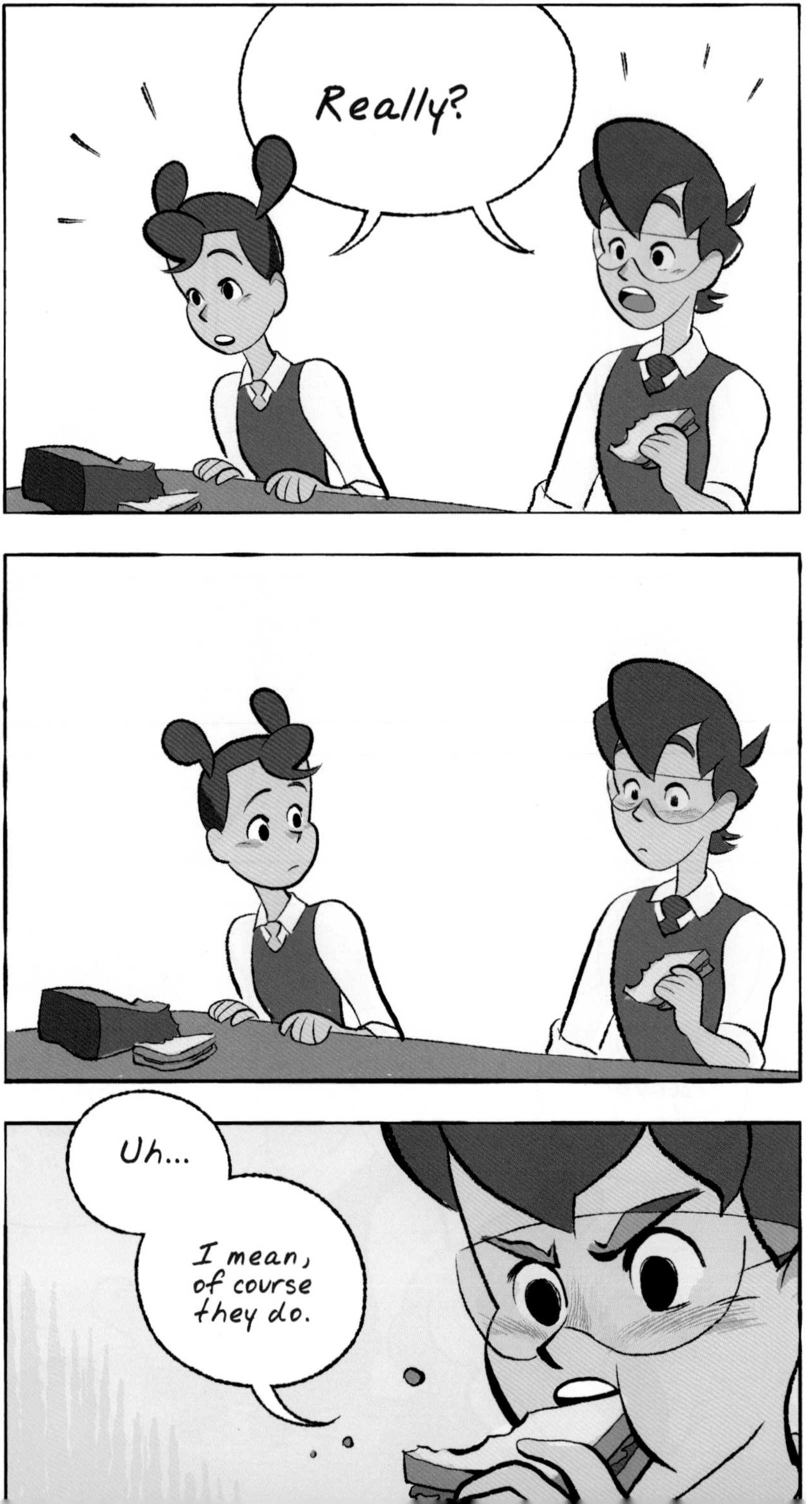
Really?
Uh...
I mean, of course they do.

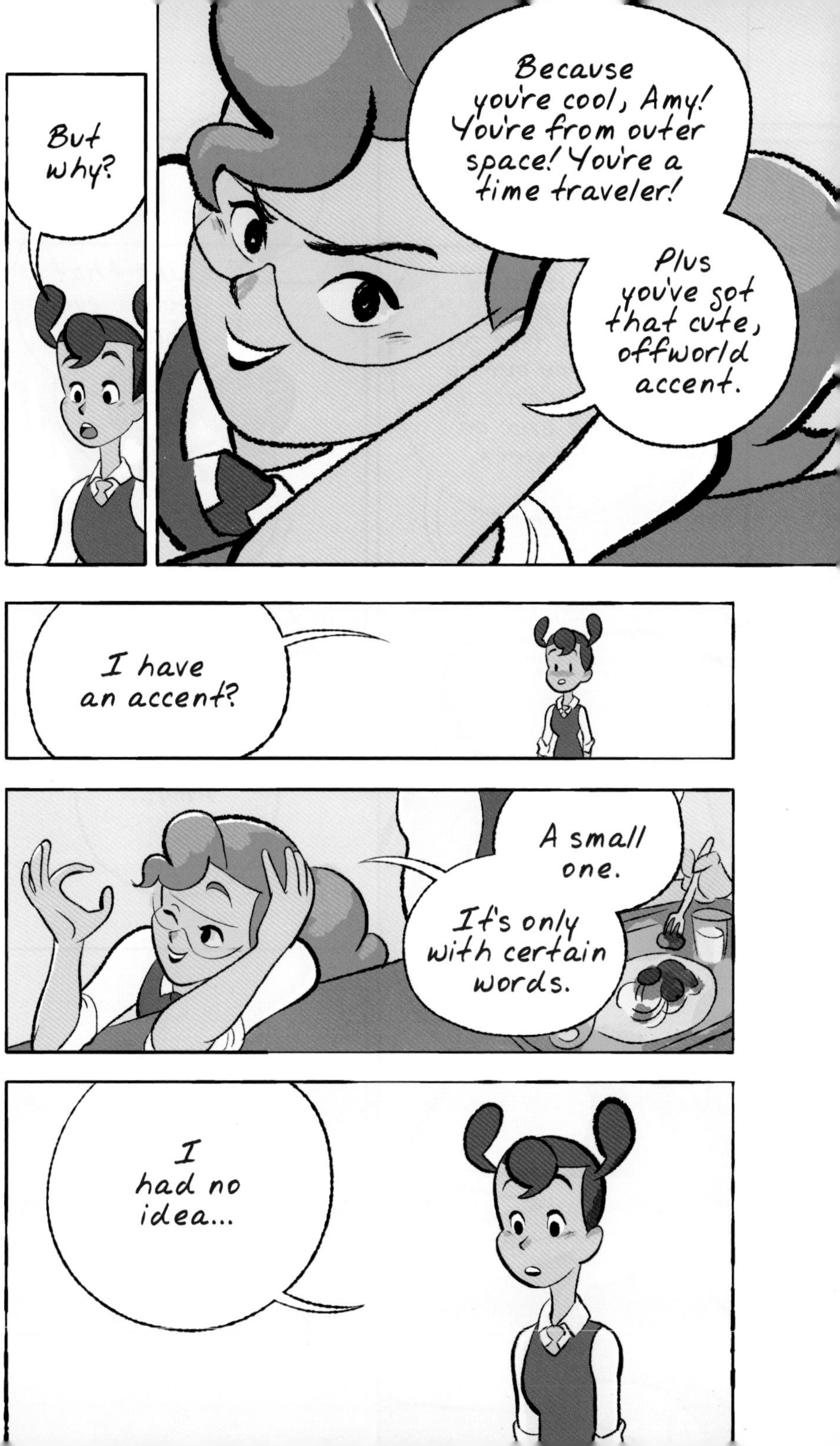
But why?
Because you're cool, Amy! You're from outer space! You're a time traveler!
Plus you've got that cute, offworld accent.
I have an accent?
A small one.
It's only with certain words.
I had no idea...

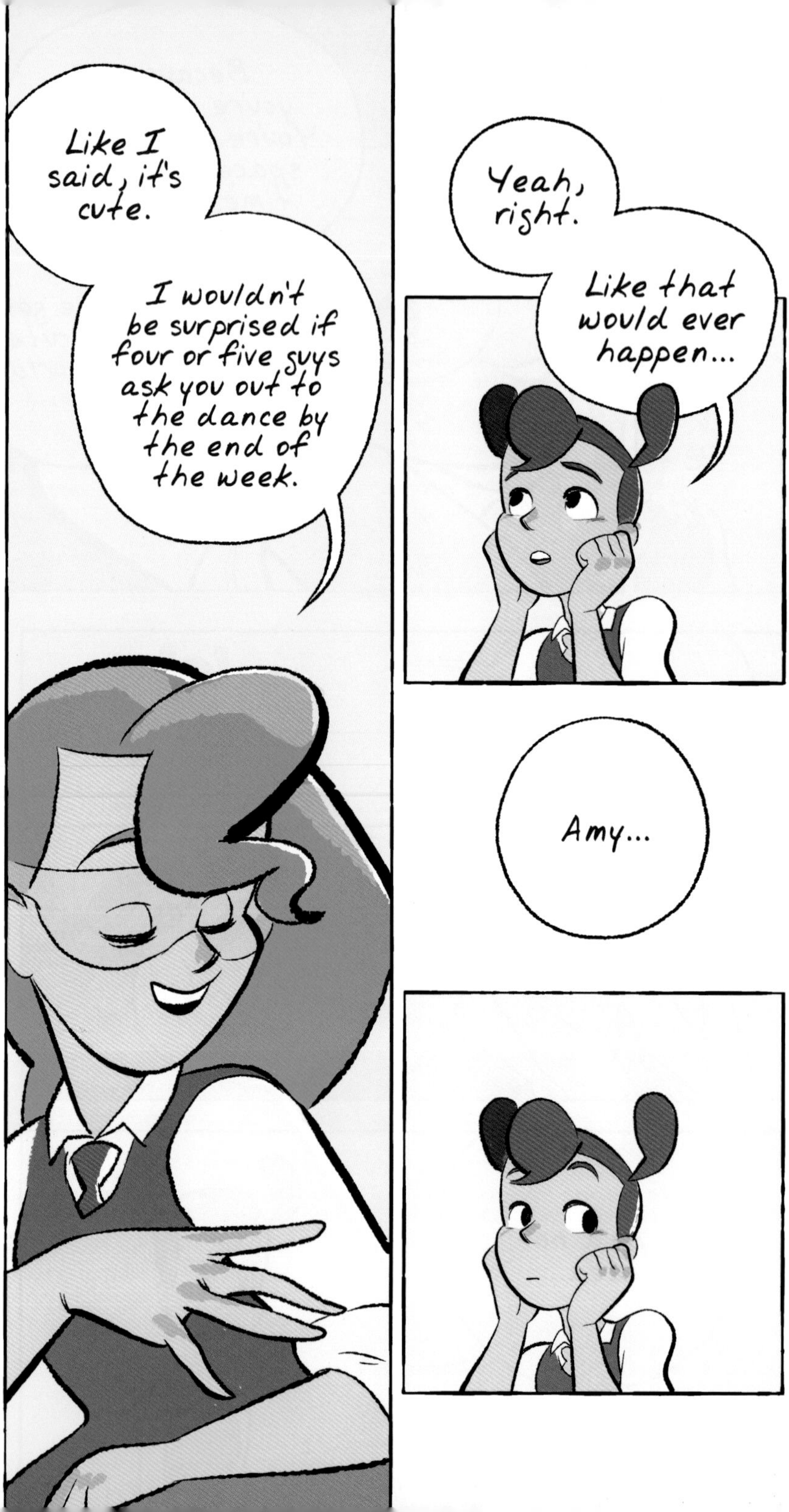
Like I said, it's cute.
I wouldn't be surprised if four or five guys ask you out to the dance by the end of the week.
Yeah, right.
Like that would ever happen...
Amy...

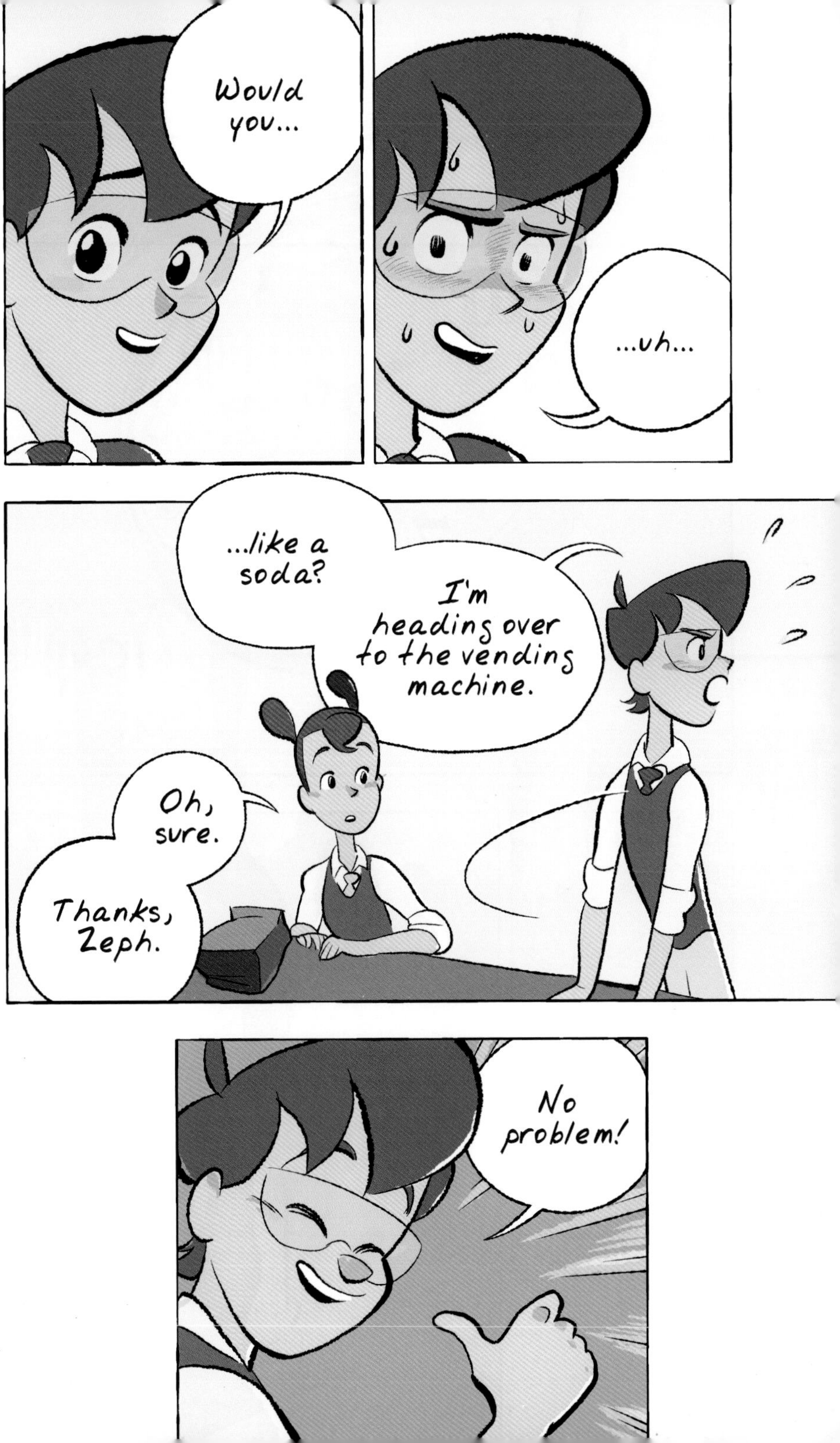
Would you...
...uh...
...like a soda?
I'm heading over to the vending machine.
Oh, sure.
Thanks, Zeph.
No problem!

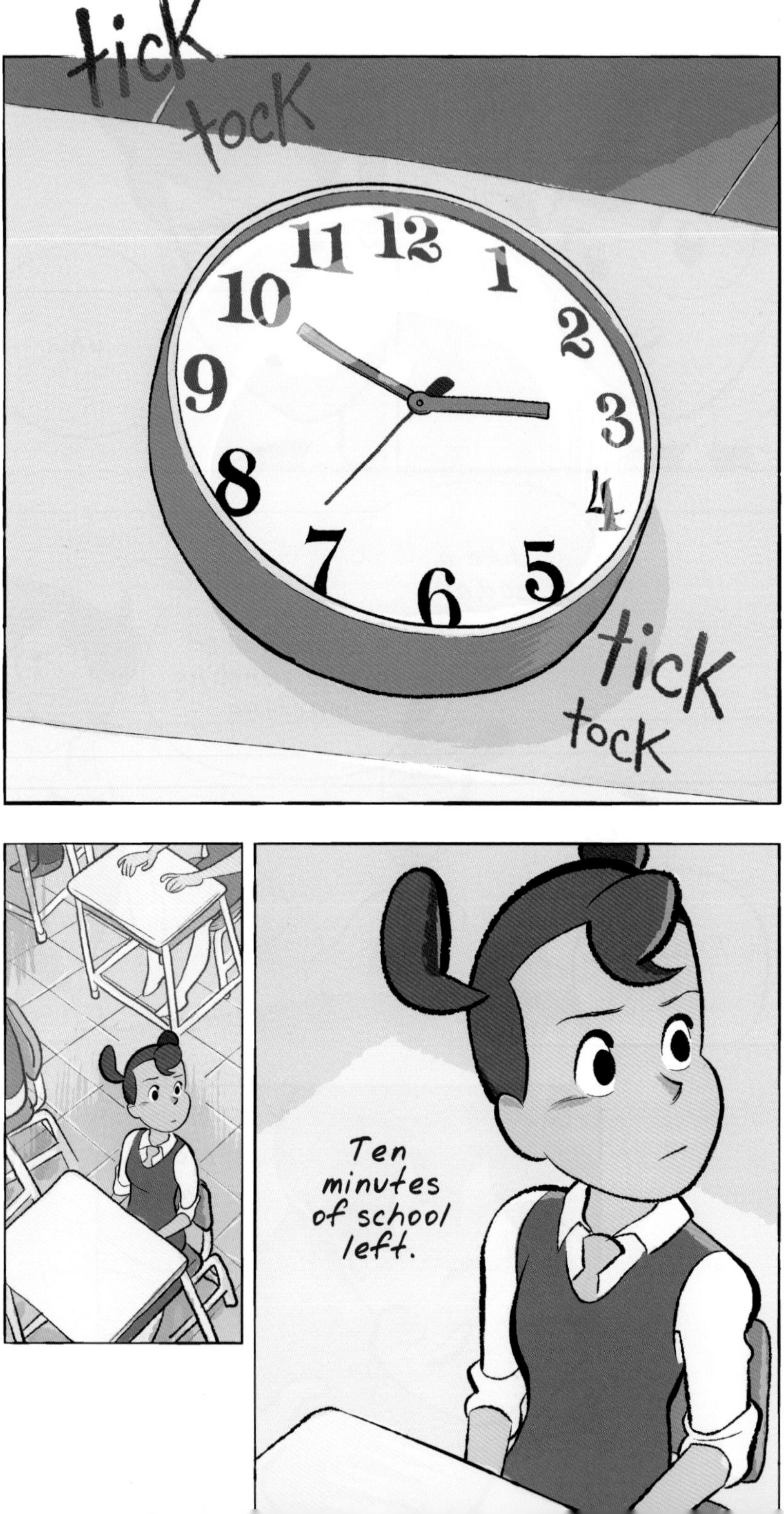
tick
tock
tick
tock
Ten minutes of school left.

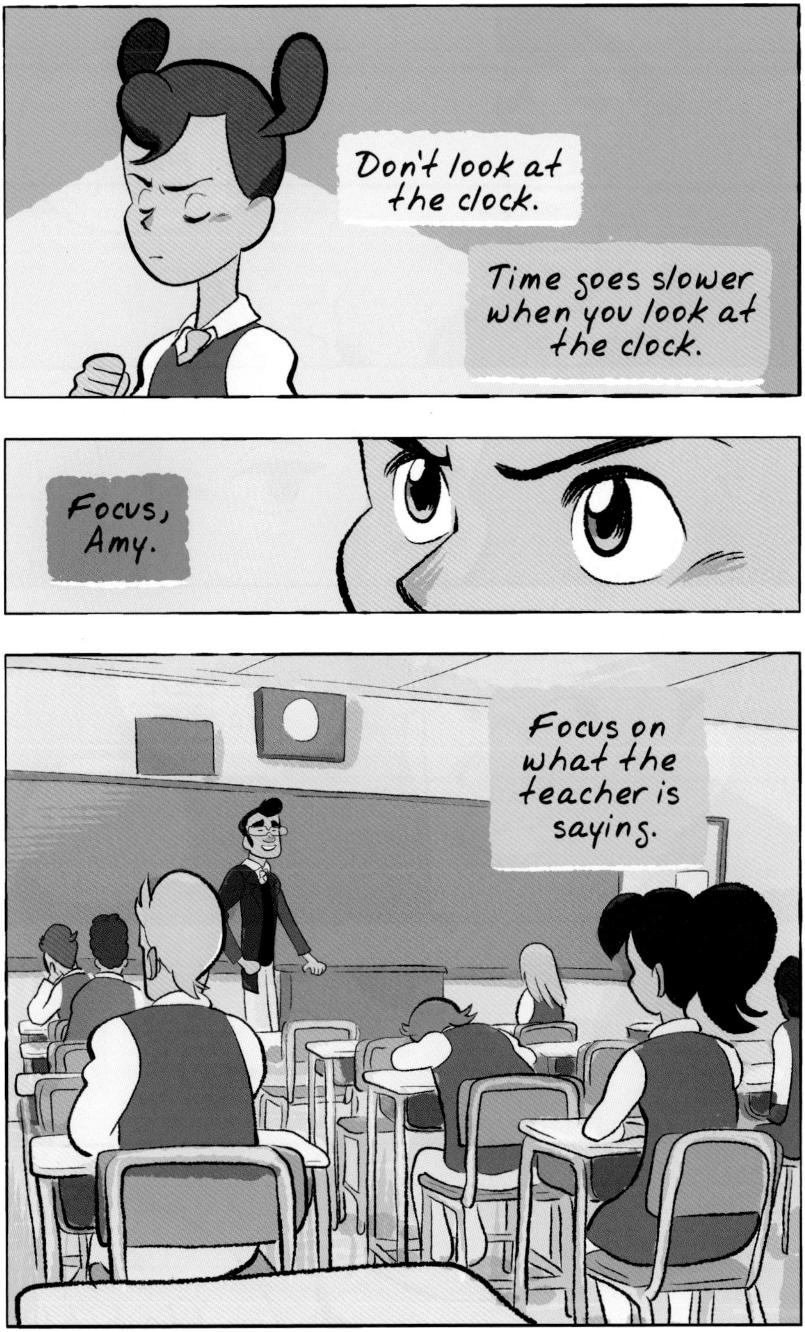

Don't look at the clock.
Time goes slower when you look at the clock.
Focus, Amy.
Focus on what the teacher is saying.

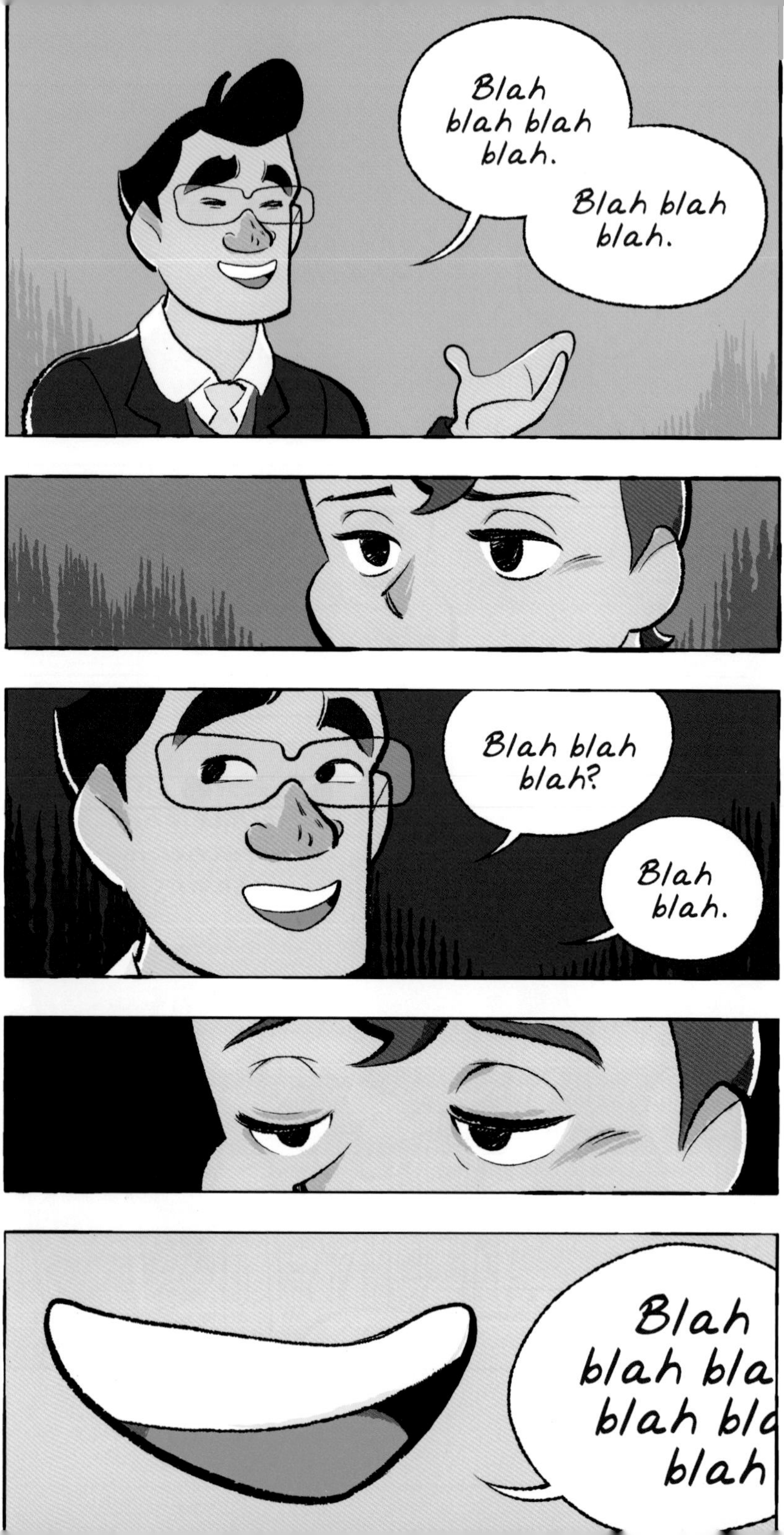
Blah blah blah blah.
Blah blah blah.
Blah blah blah?
Blah blah.
Blah blah blah bla blah bl blah

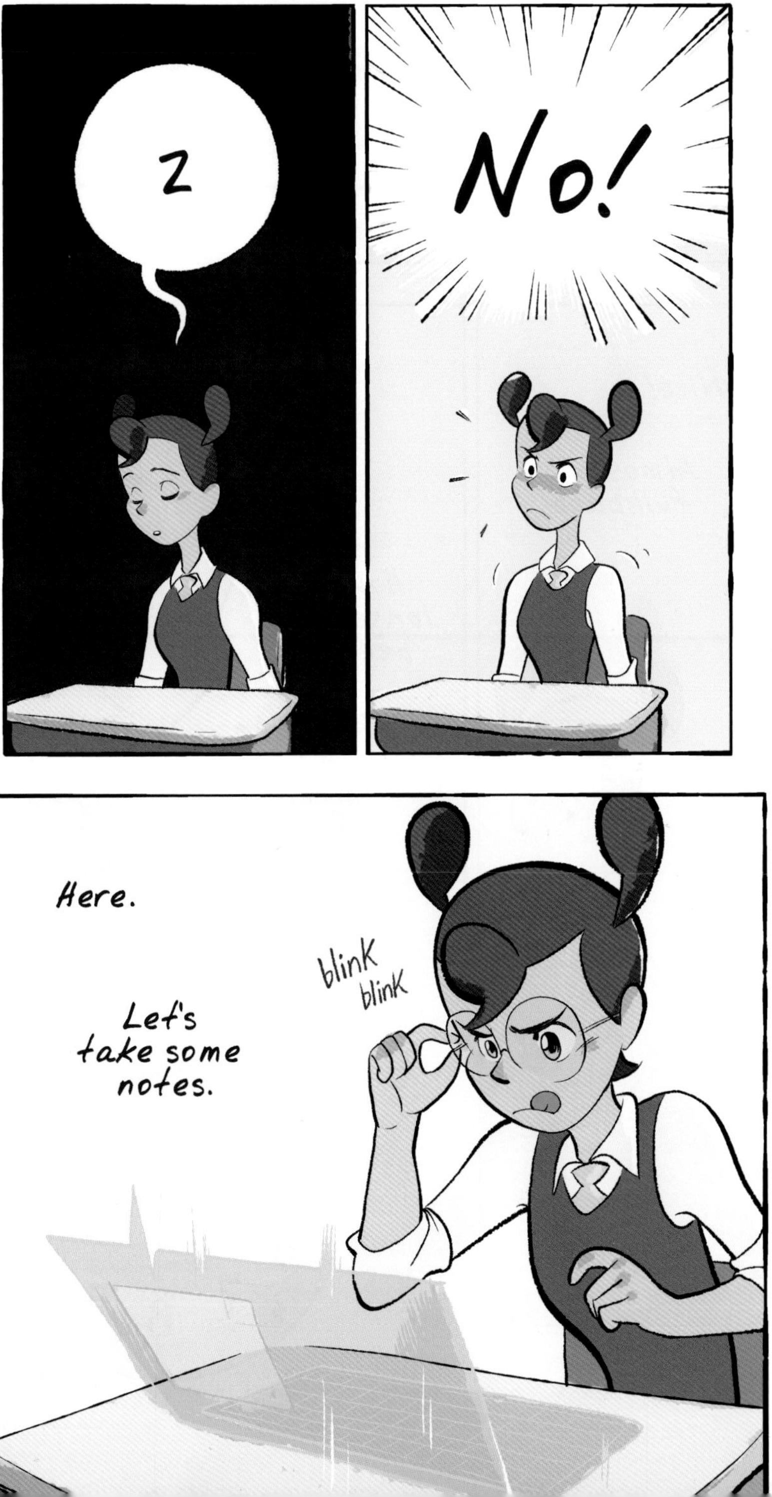
Z
No!
Here.
blink blink
Let's take some notes.

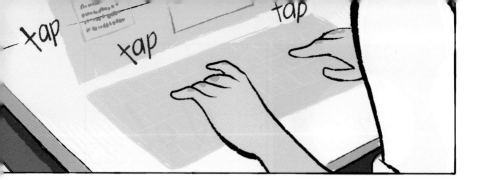

-tap _tap_ _tap_

Nice!

Almost a
full page!

How
long's it
been?

Feels like
I've been
working
forev--

tick

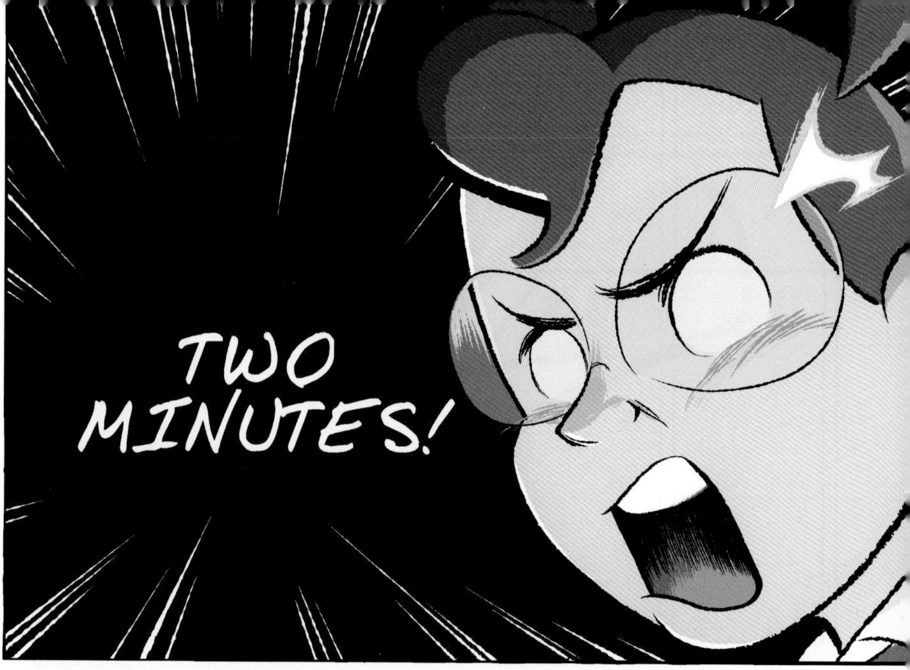
TWO MINUTES!

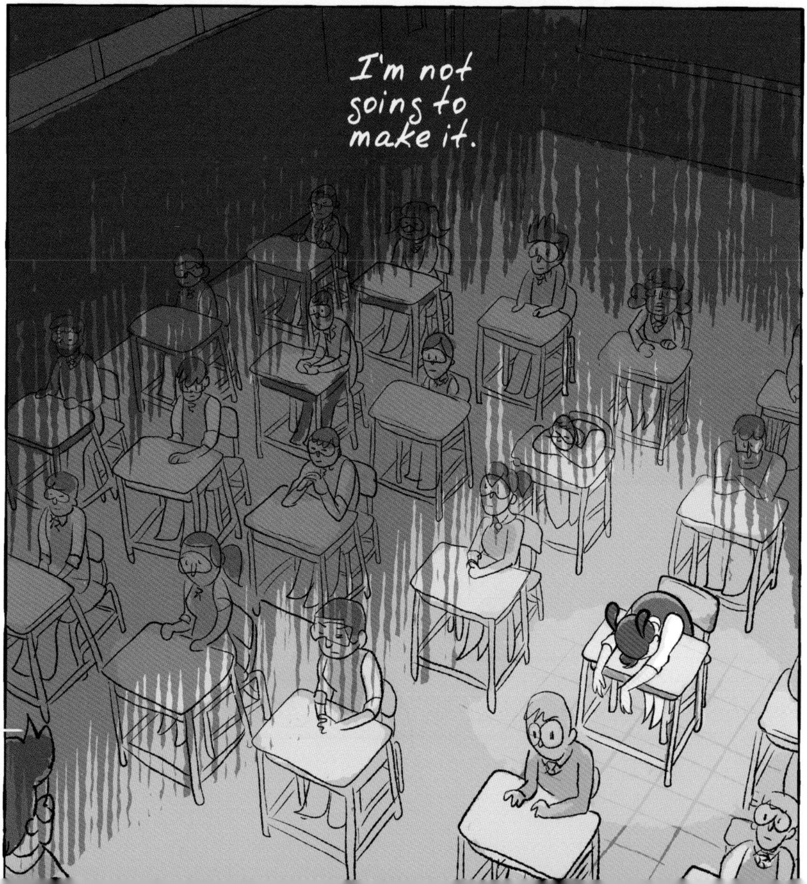
I'm not going to make it.

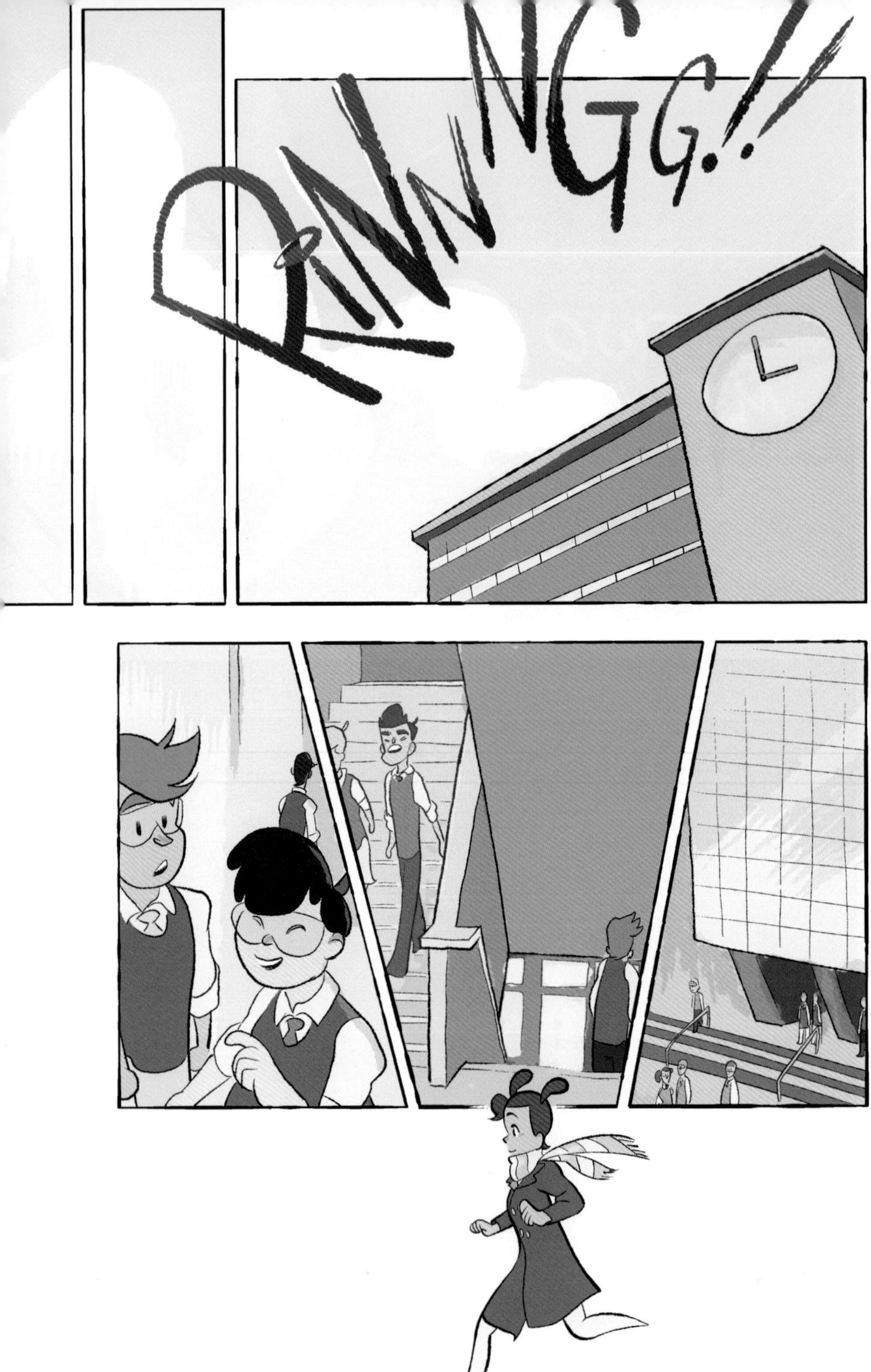
RINNNGG!!

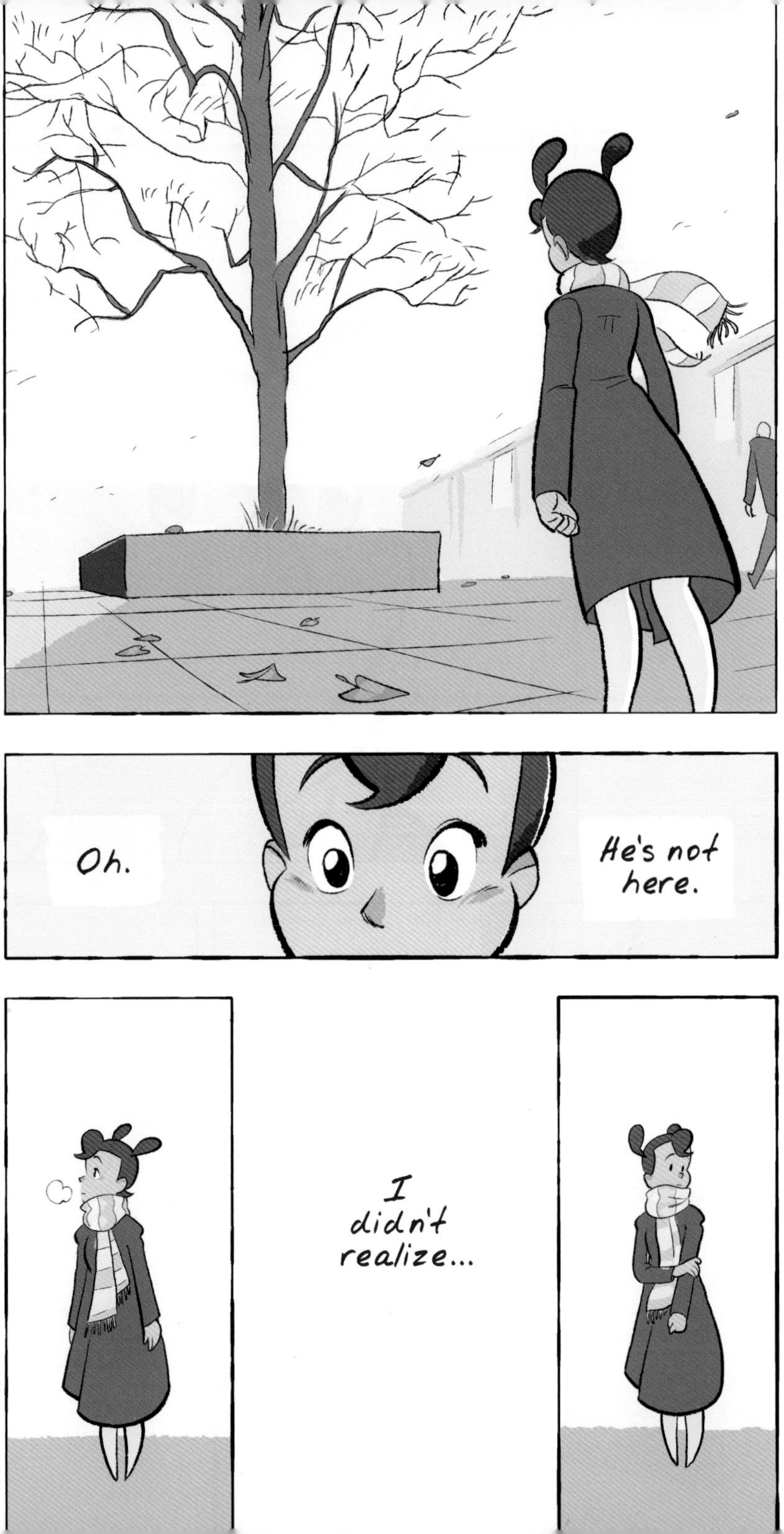
Oh.
He's not here.
I didn't realize...

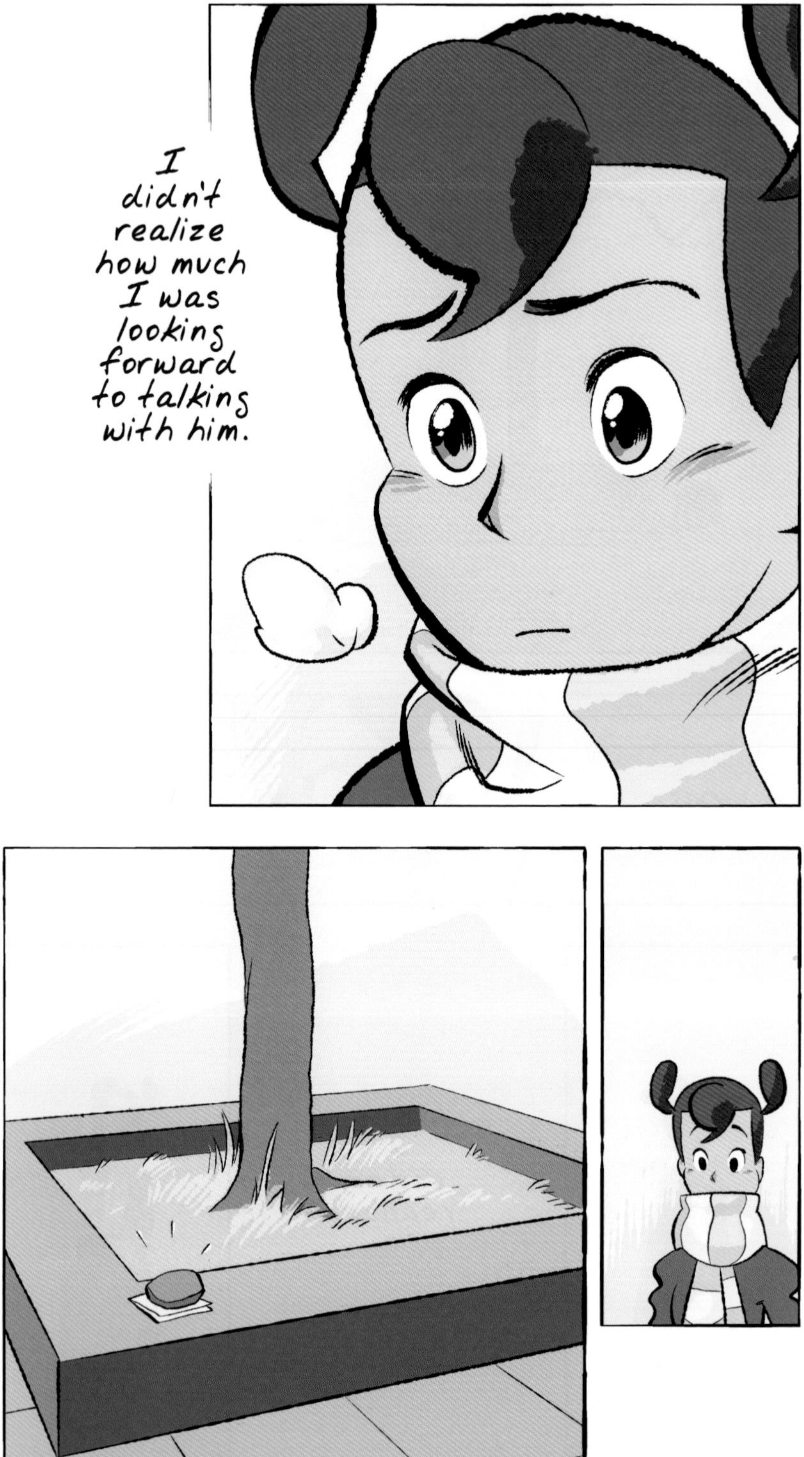
I didn't realize how much I was looking forward to talking with him.

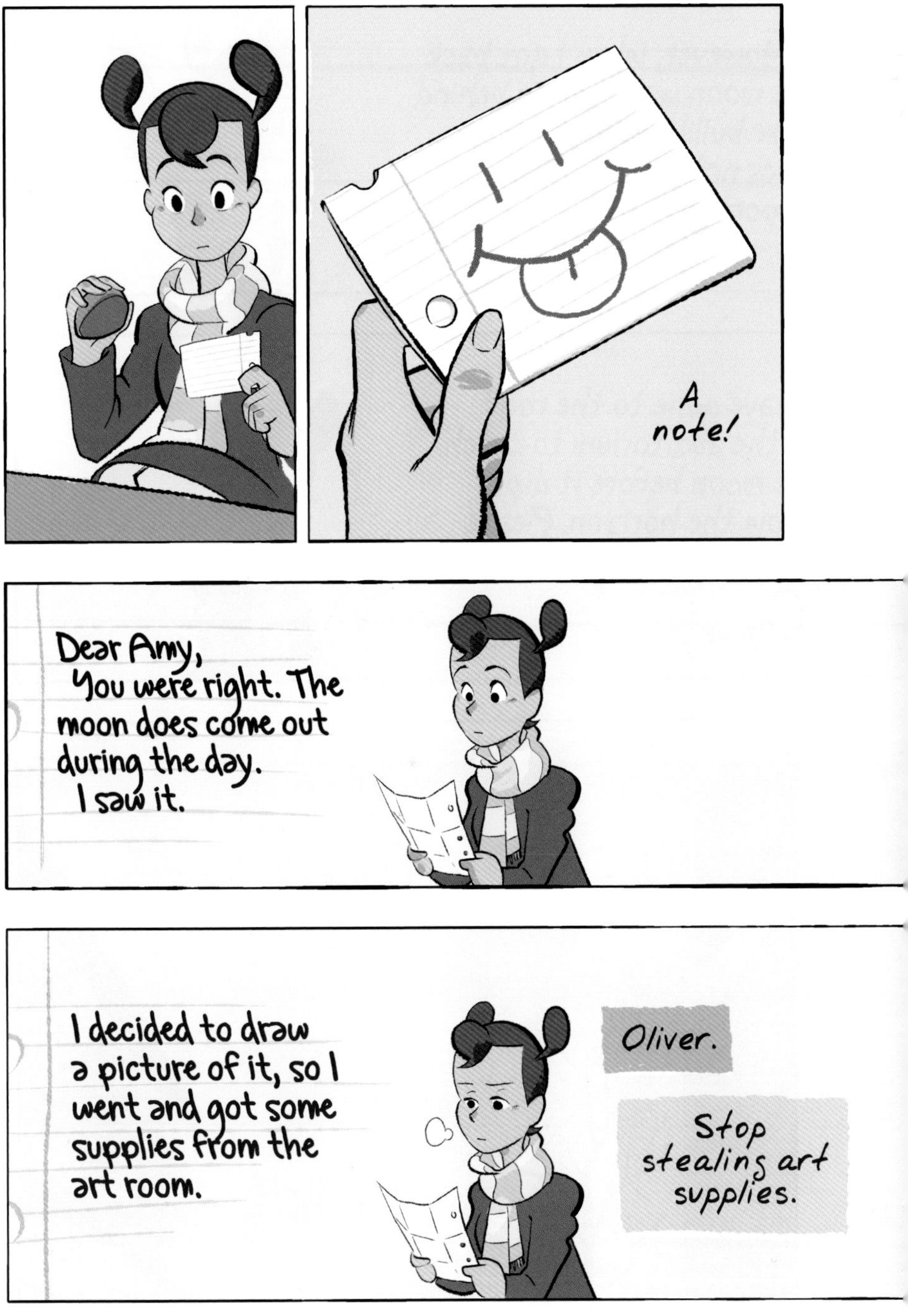
A note!
Dear Amy,
You were right. The moon does come out during the day.
I saw it.
I decided to draw a picture of it, so I went and got some supplies from the art room.
Oliver.
Stop stealing art supplies.

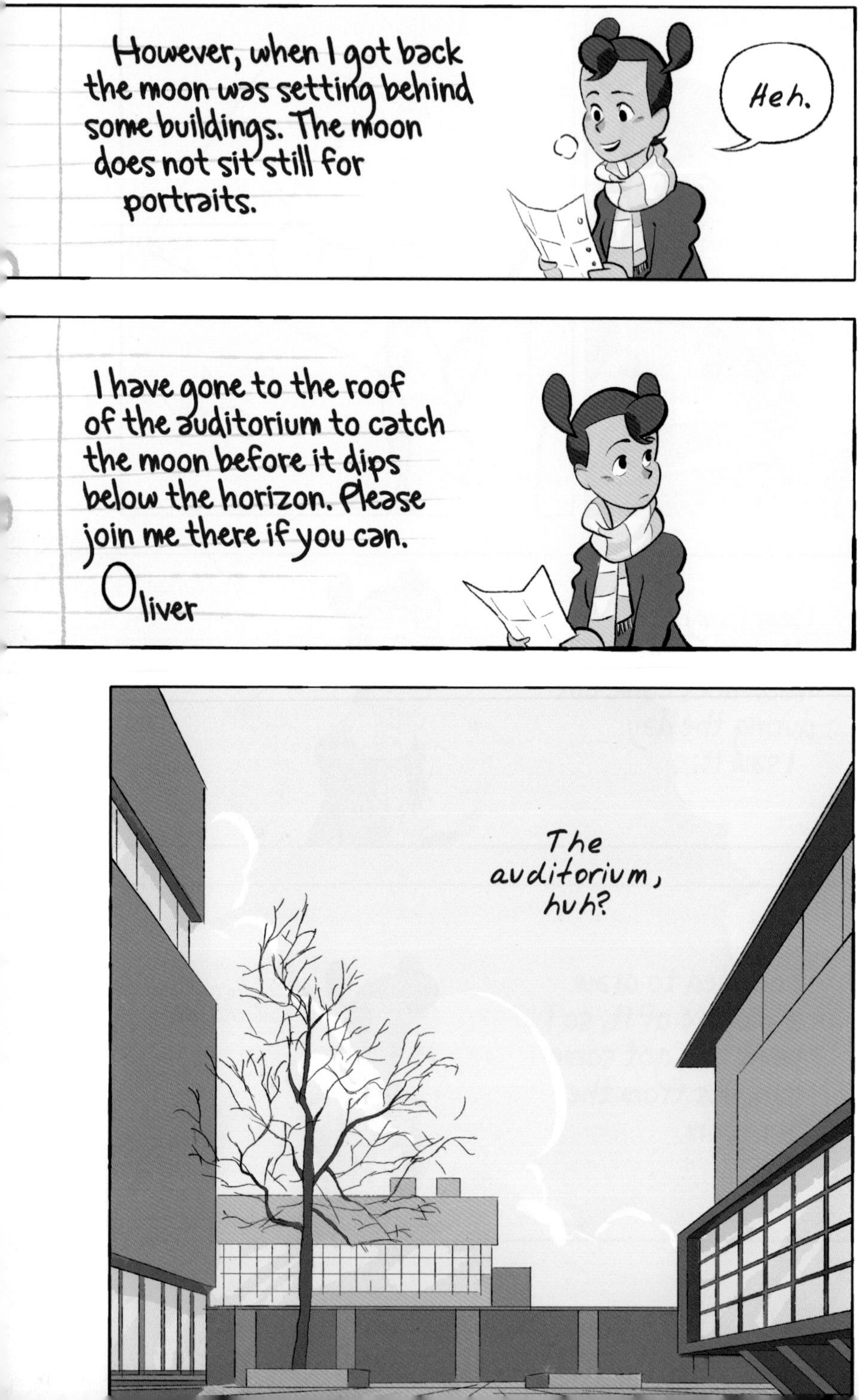
However, when I got back the moon was setting behind some buildings. The moon does not sit still for portraits.
Heh.
I have gone to the roof of the auditorium to catch the moon before it dips below the horizon. Please join me there if you can.
Oliver
The auditorium, huh?

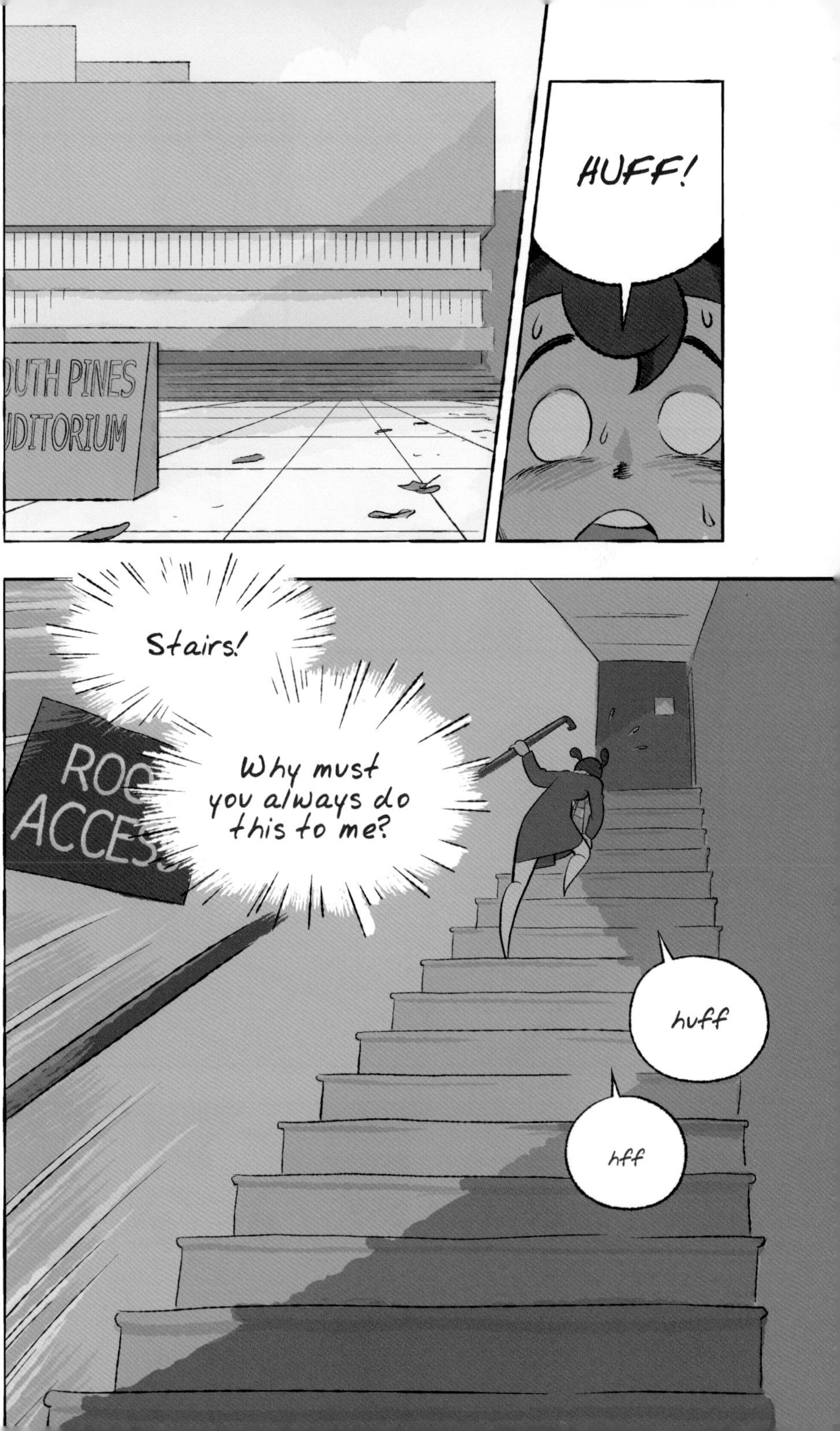
OUTH PINES
UDITORIUM
HUFF!
Stairs!
ROO
ACCES
Why must you always do this to me?
huff
hff

huff

huff

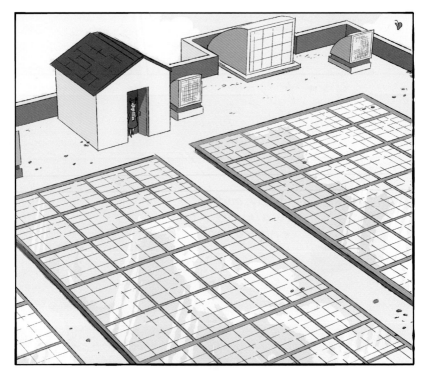

Wow...

Look
at all these
solar panels...

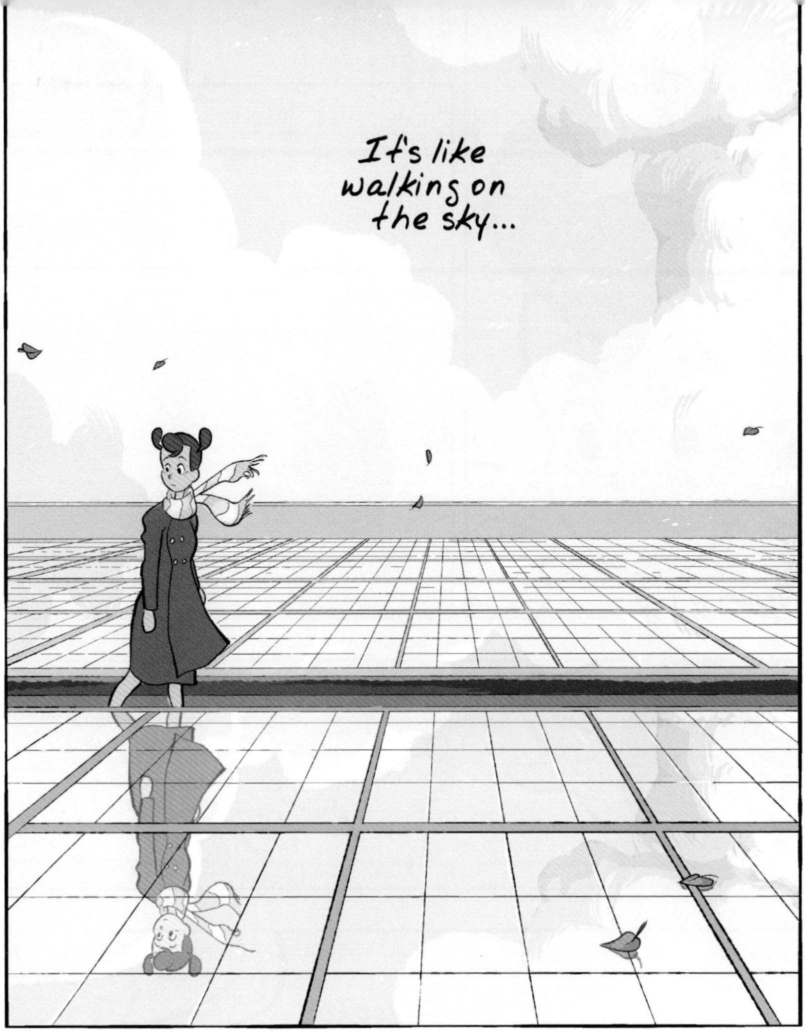
It's like walking on the sky...

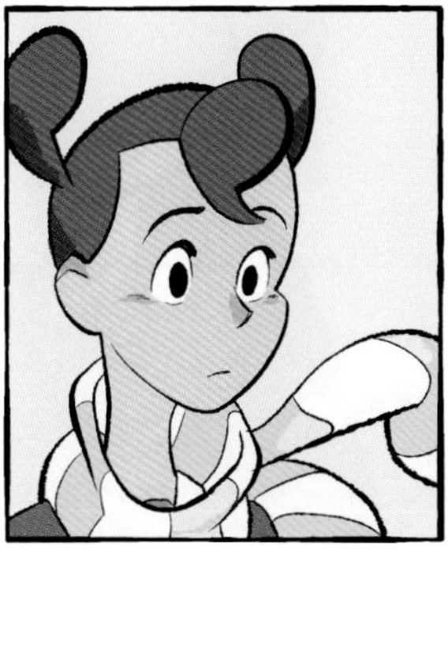

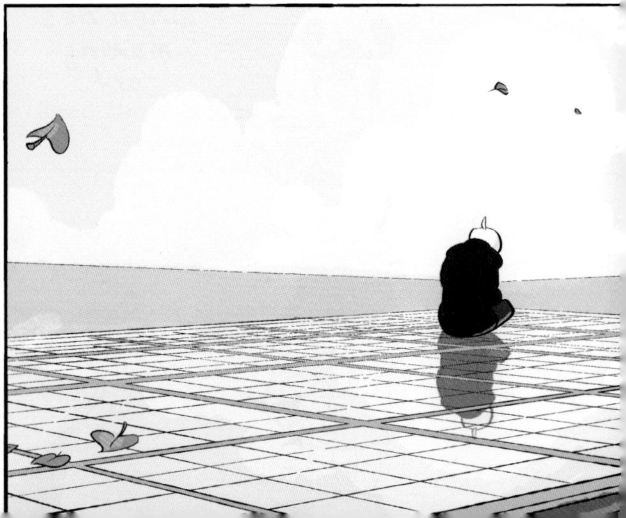

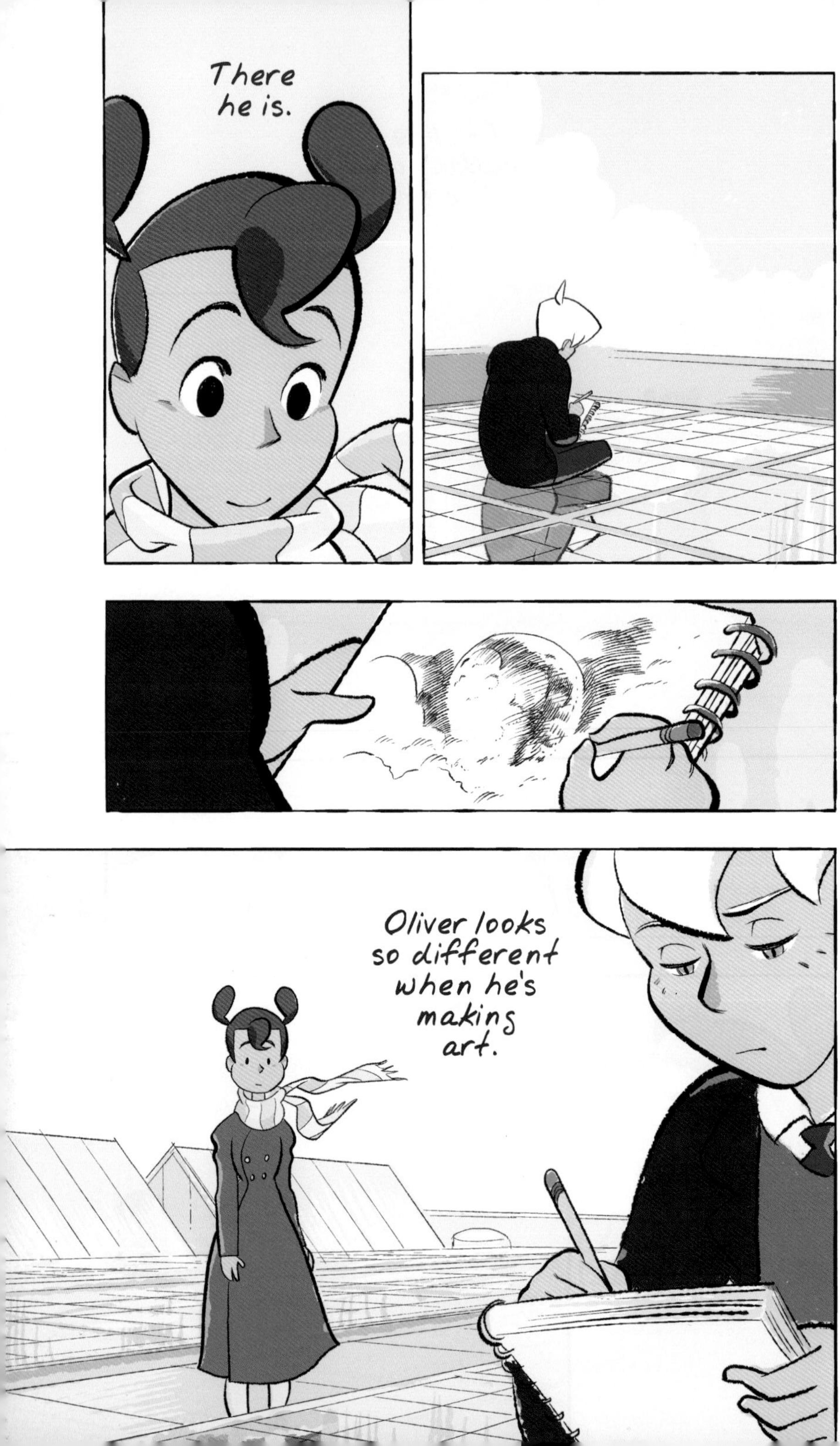
There he is.
Oliver looks so different when he's making art.

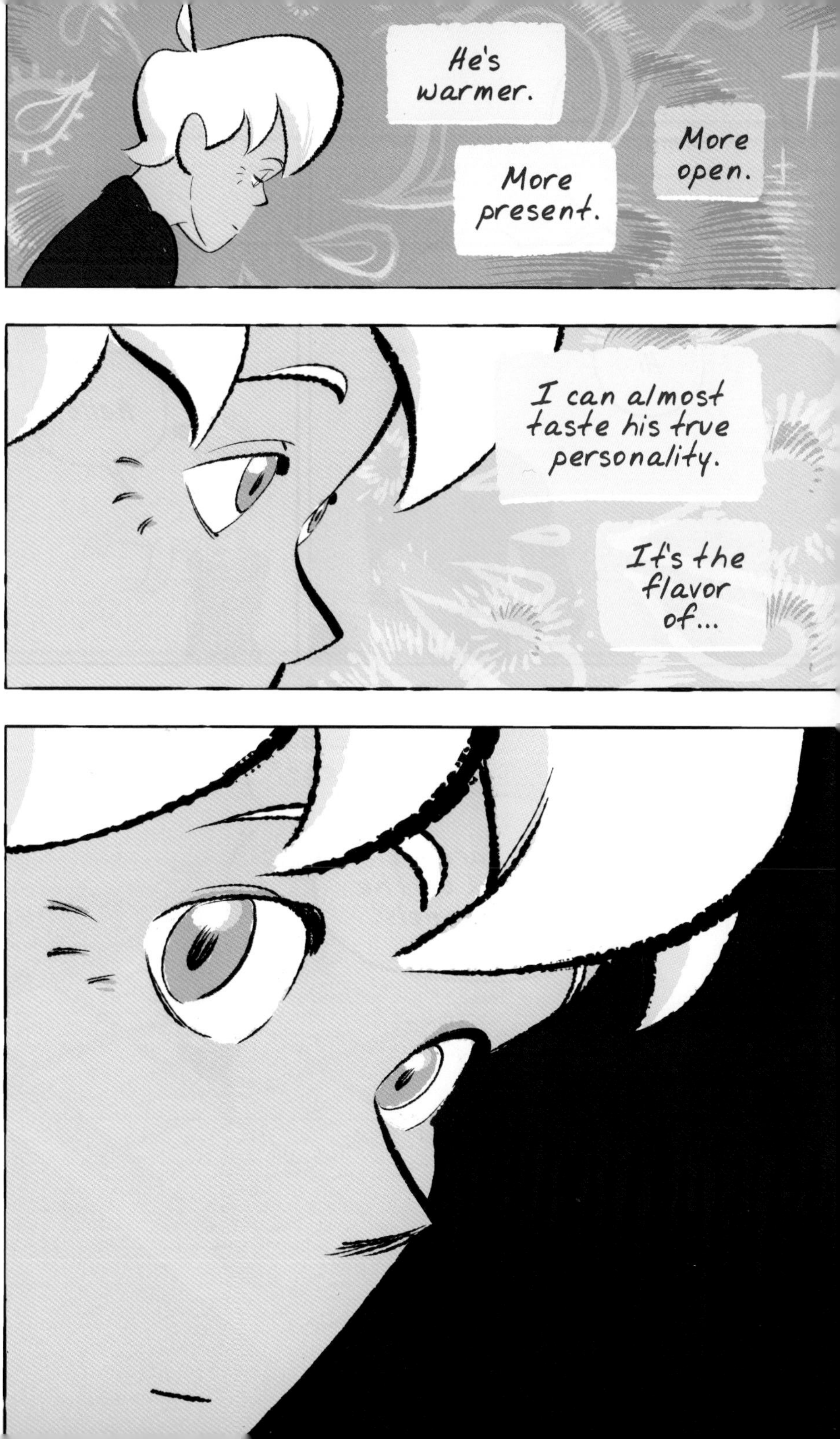
He's warmer.
More present.
More open.
I can almost taste his true personality.
It's the flavor of...

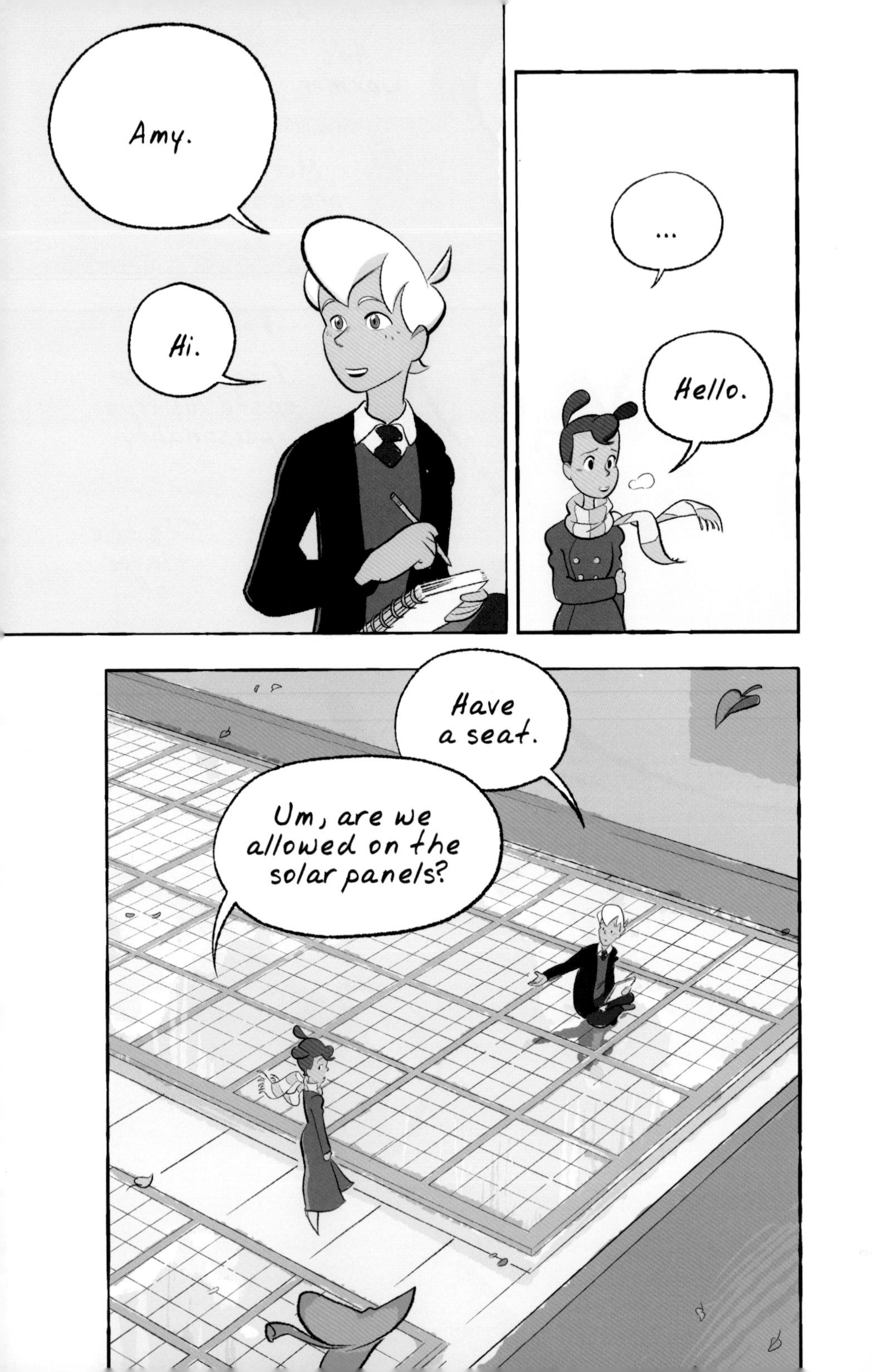
Amy.
Hi.
...
Hello.
Have a seat.
Um, are we allowed on the solar panels?

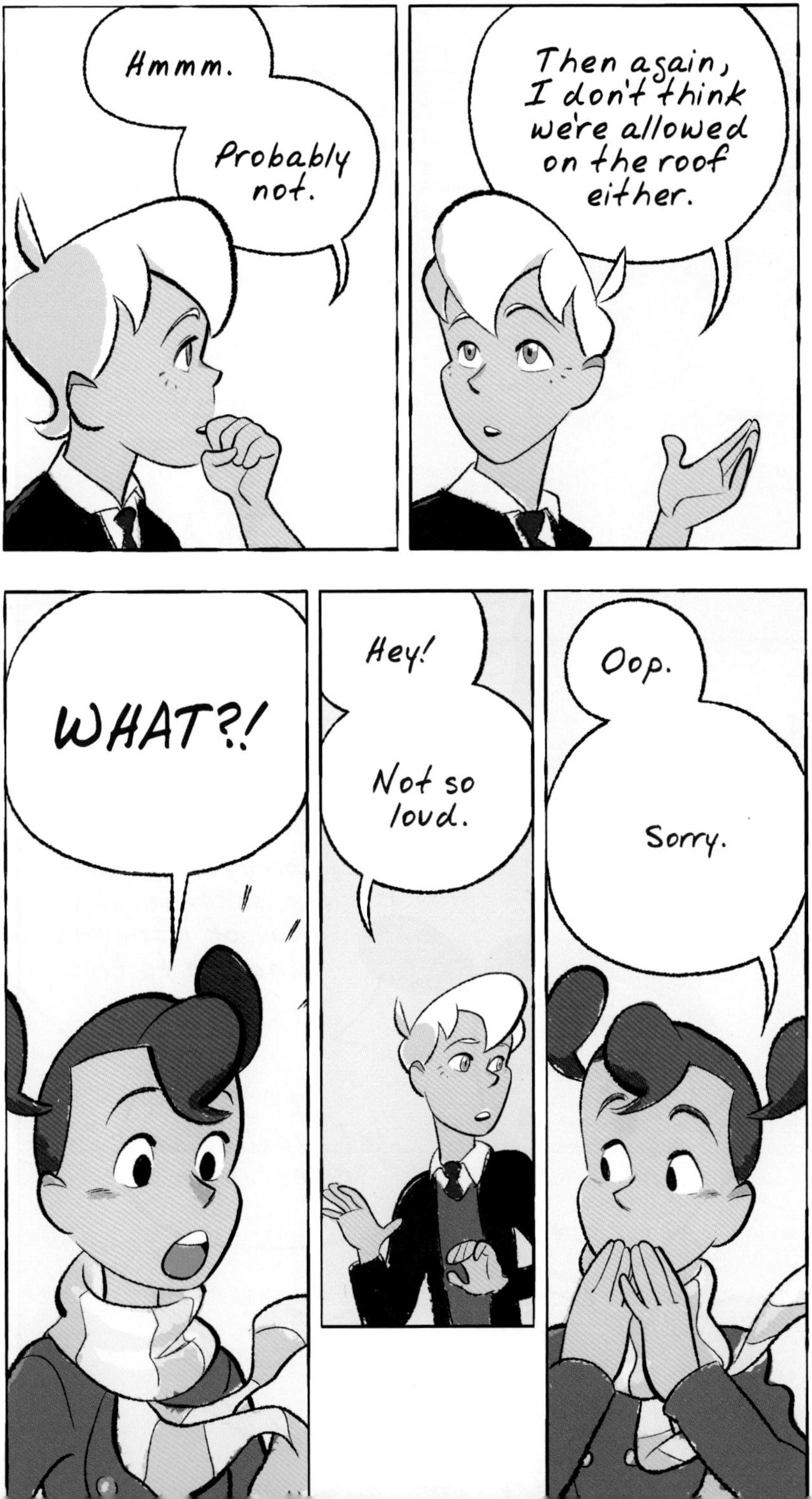
Hmmm.
Probably not.
Then again, I don't think we're allowed on the roof either.
WHAT?!
Hey!
Not so loud.
Oop.
Sorry.

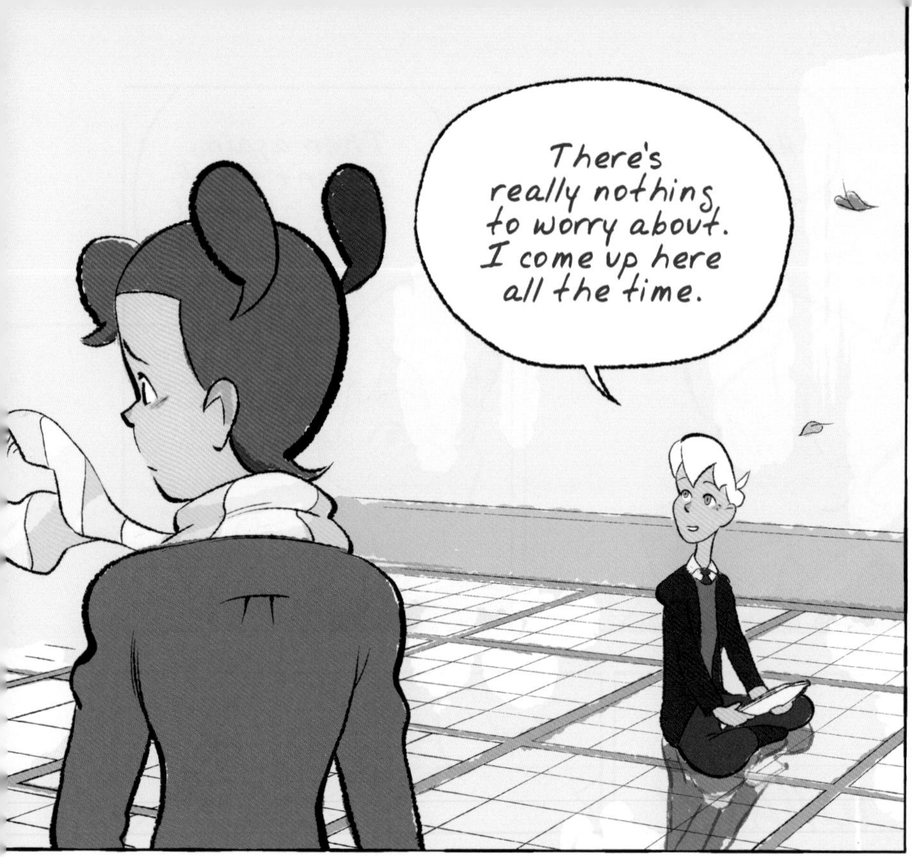
There's really nothing to worry about. I come up here all the time.

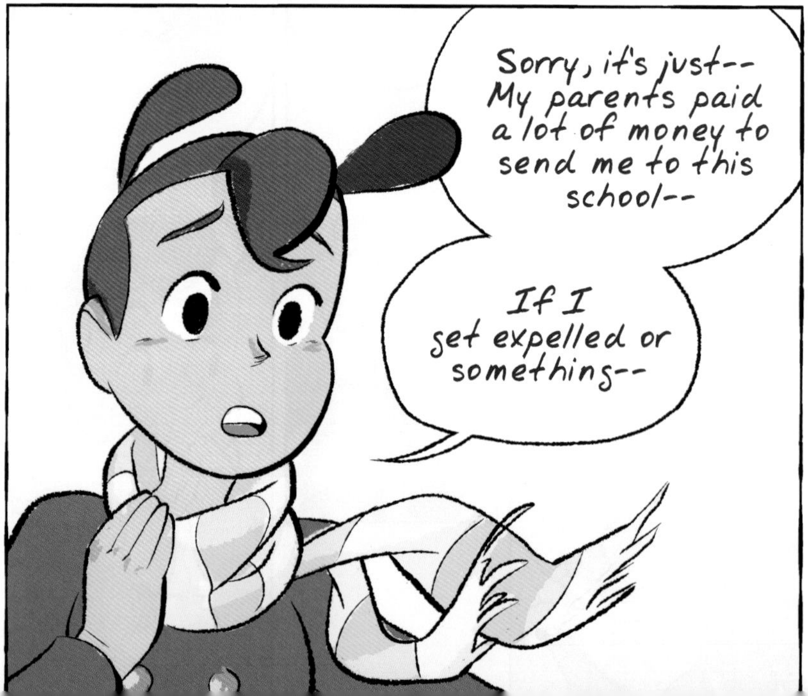
Sorry, it's just-- My parents paid a lot of money to send me to this school--
If I get expelled or something--

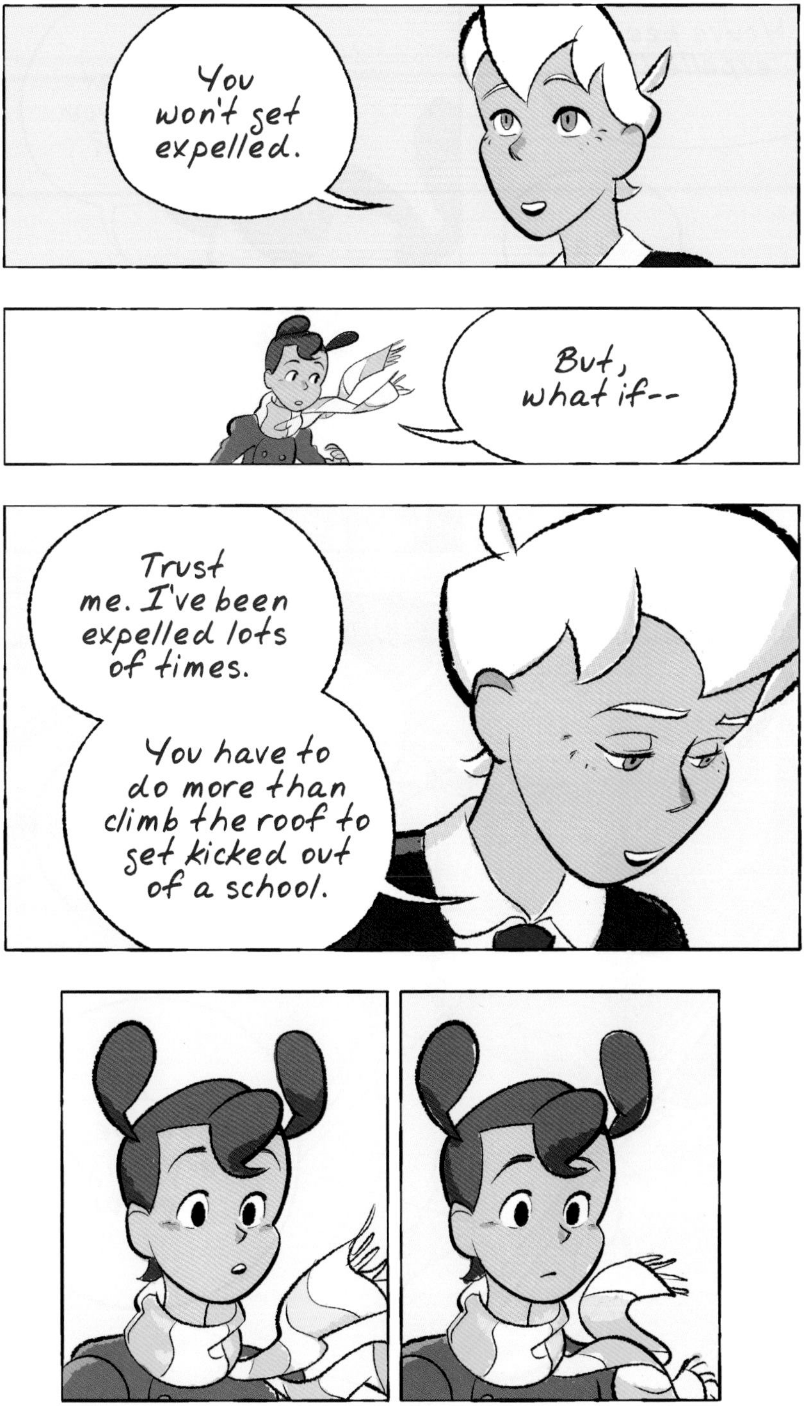
You won't get expelled.
But, what if--
Trust me. I've been expelled lots of times.
You have to do more than climb the roof to get kicked out of a school.

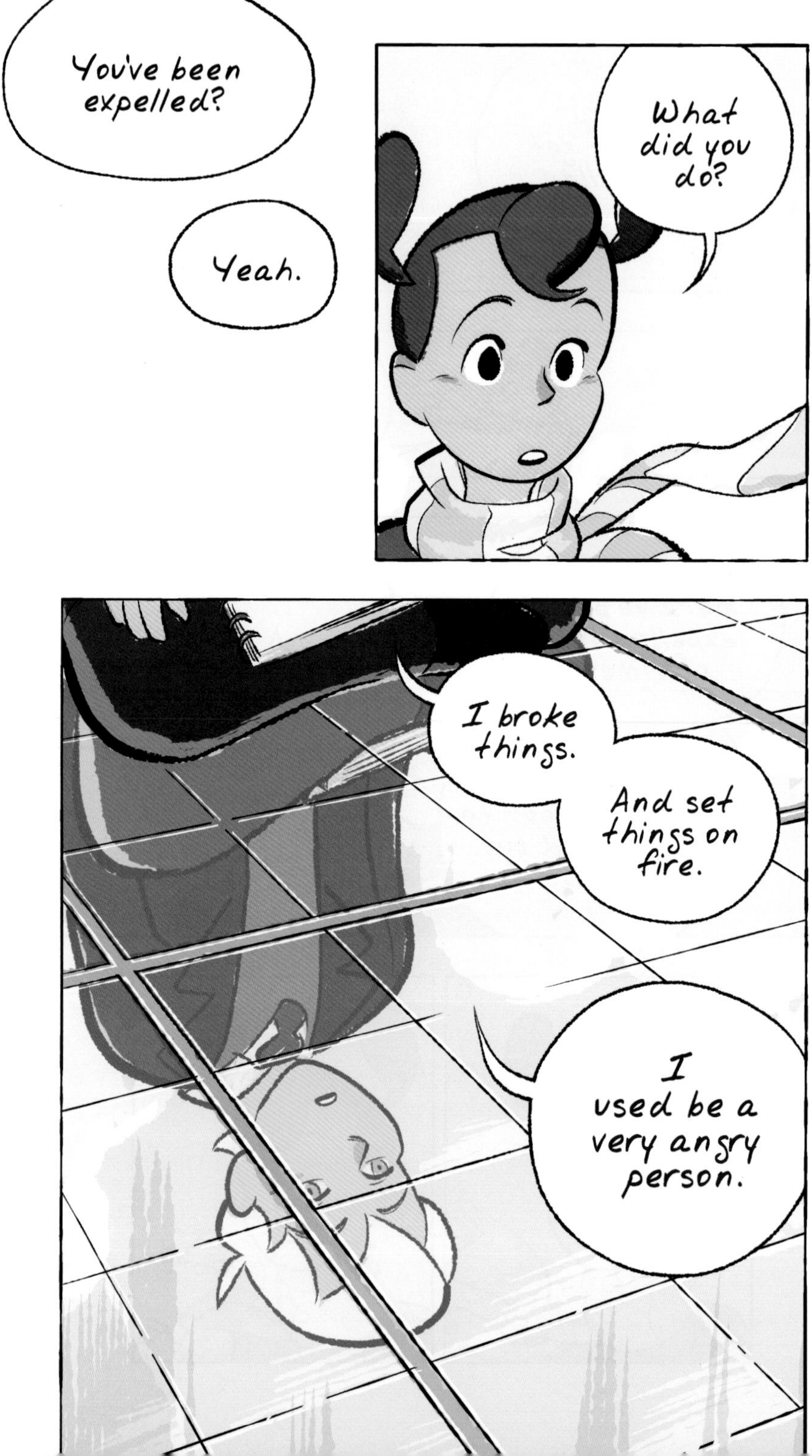
You've been expelled?
What did you do?
Yeah.
I broke things.
And set things on fire.
I used be a very angry person.

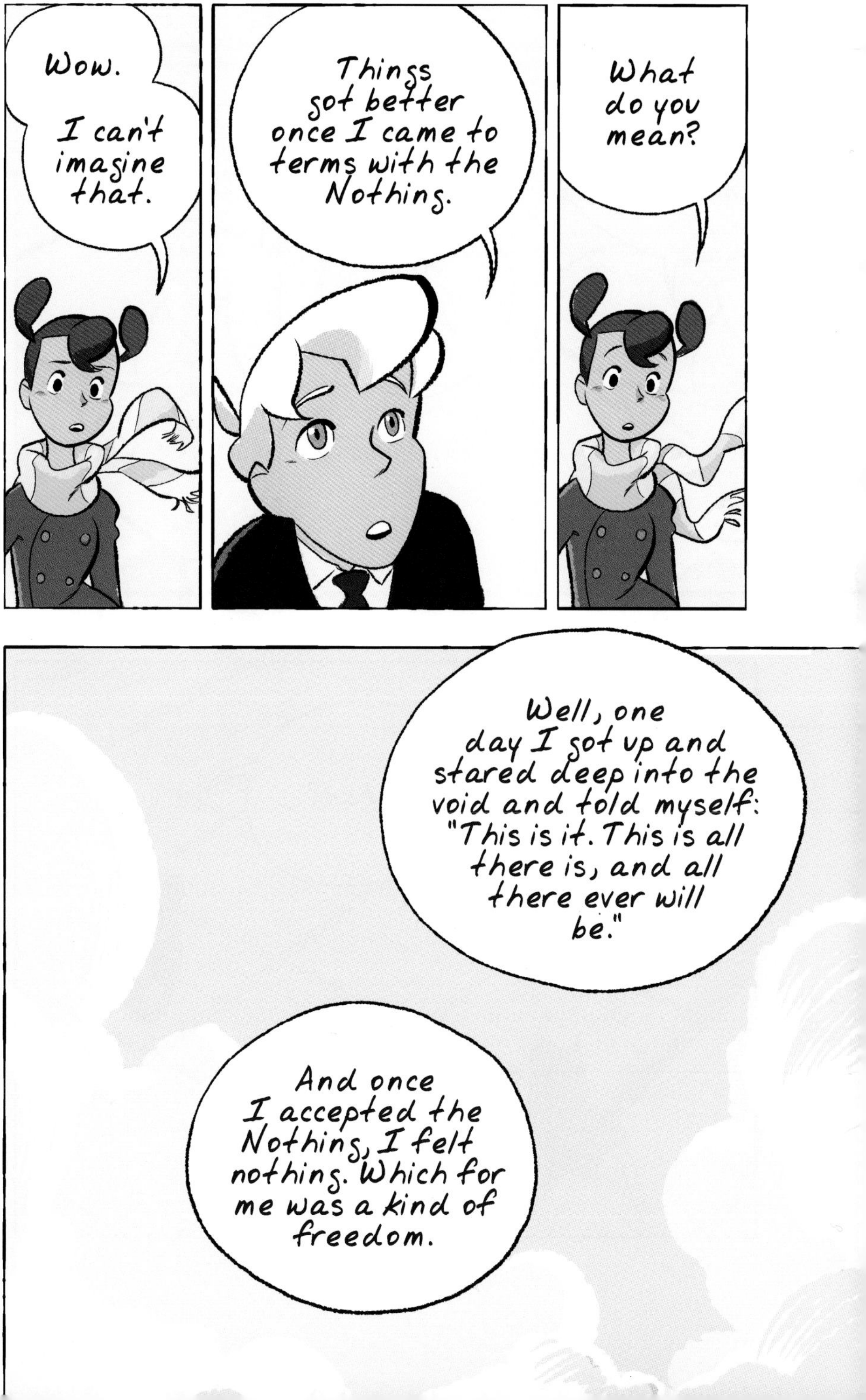
Wow.
I can't imagine that.
Things got better once I came to terms with the Nothing.
What do you mean?
Well, one day I got up and stared deep into the void and told myself: "This is it. This is all there is, and all there ever will be."
And once I accepted the Nothing, I felt nothing. Which for me was a kind of freedom.

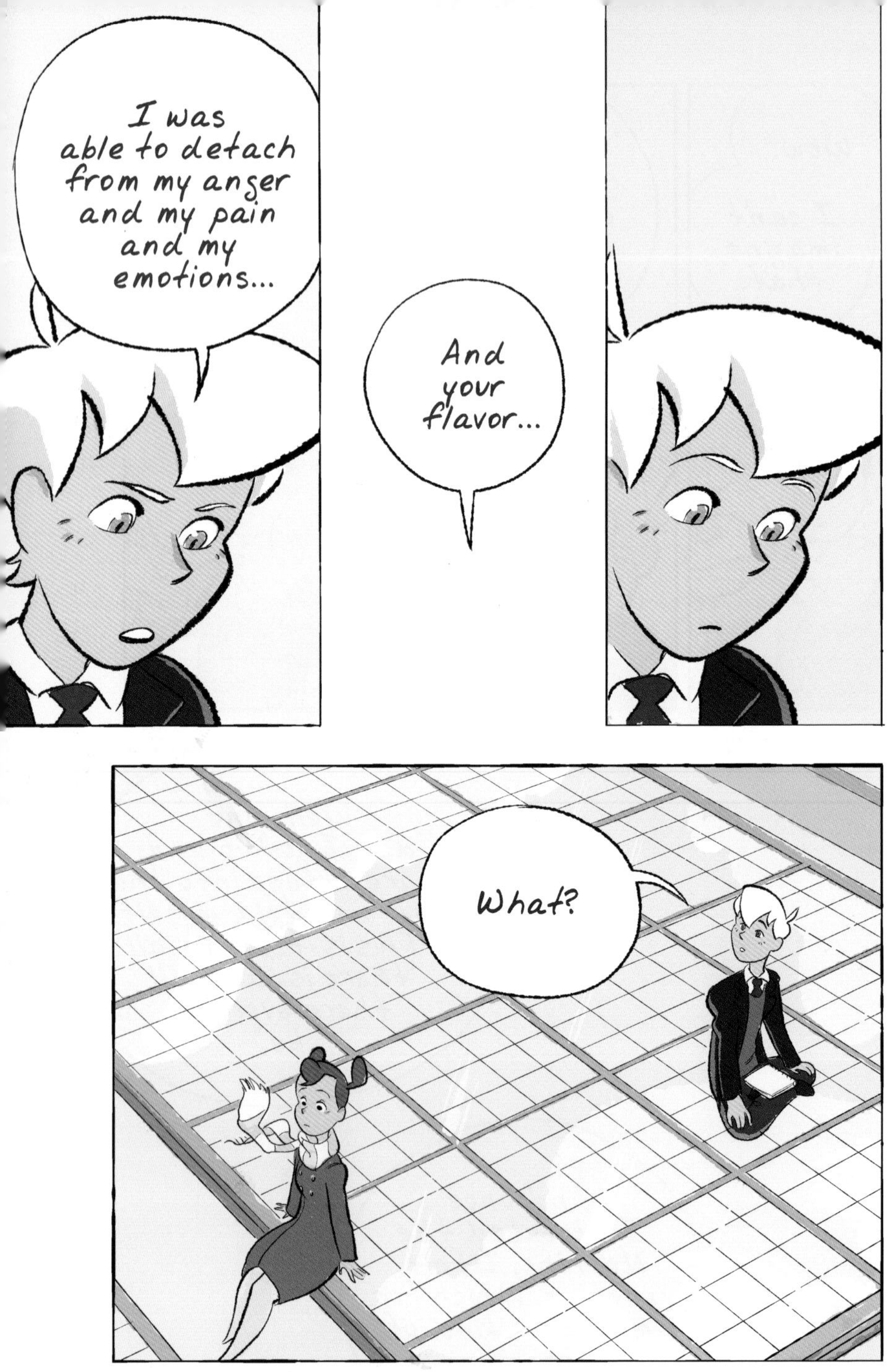
I was able to detach from my anger and my pain and my emotions...
And your flavor...
What?

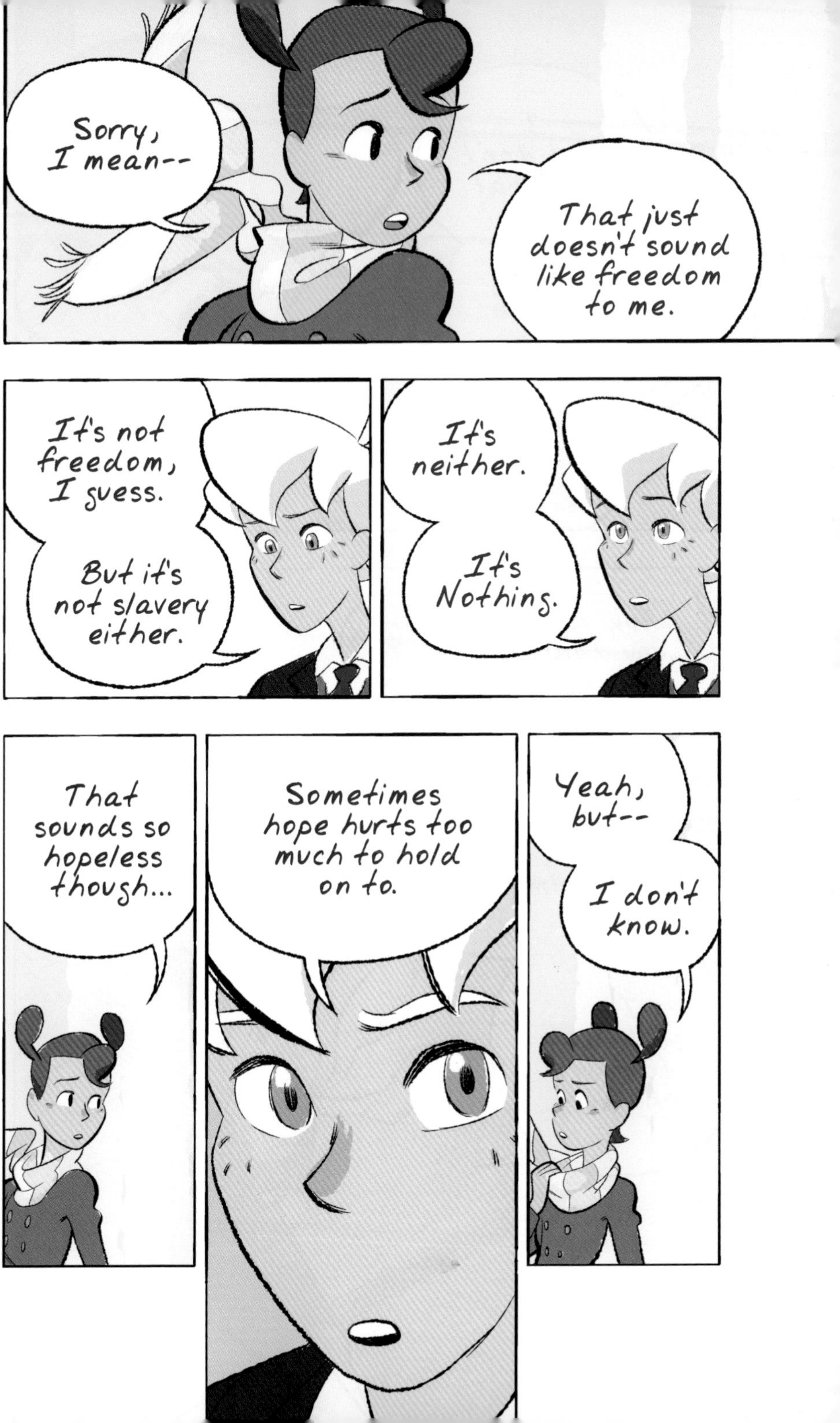

Sorry, I mean--
That just doesn't sound like freedom to me.
It's not freedom, I guess.
But it's not slavery either.
It's neither.
It's Nothing.
That sounds so hopeless though...
Sometimes hope hurts too much to hold on to.
Yeah, but--
I don't know.

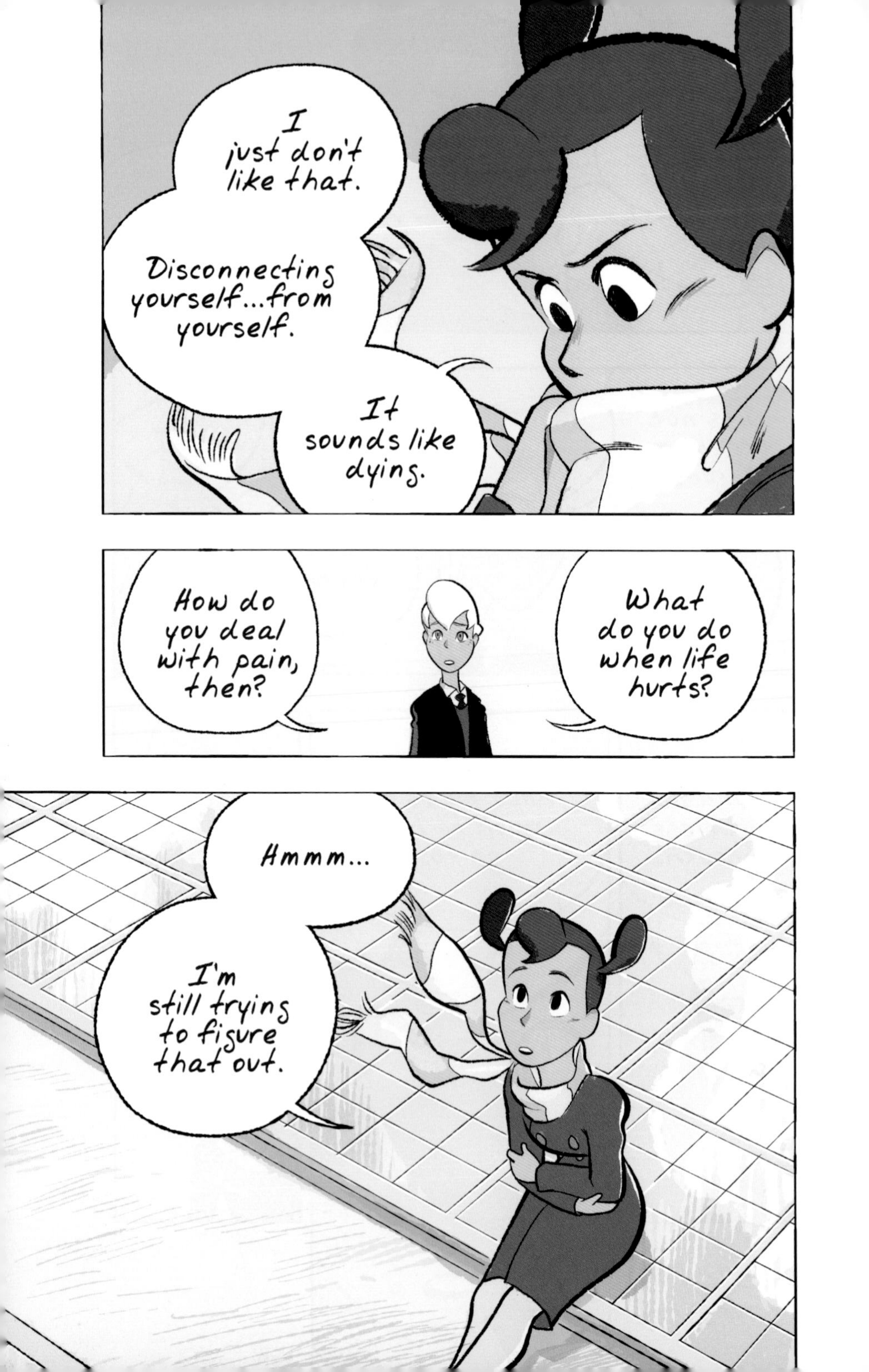
I just don't like that.
Disconnecting yourself...from yourself.
It sounds like dying.
How do you deal with pain, then?
What do you do when life hurts?
Hmmm...
I'm still trying to figure that out.

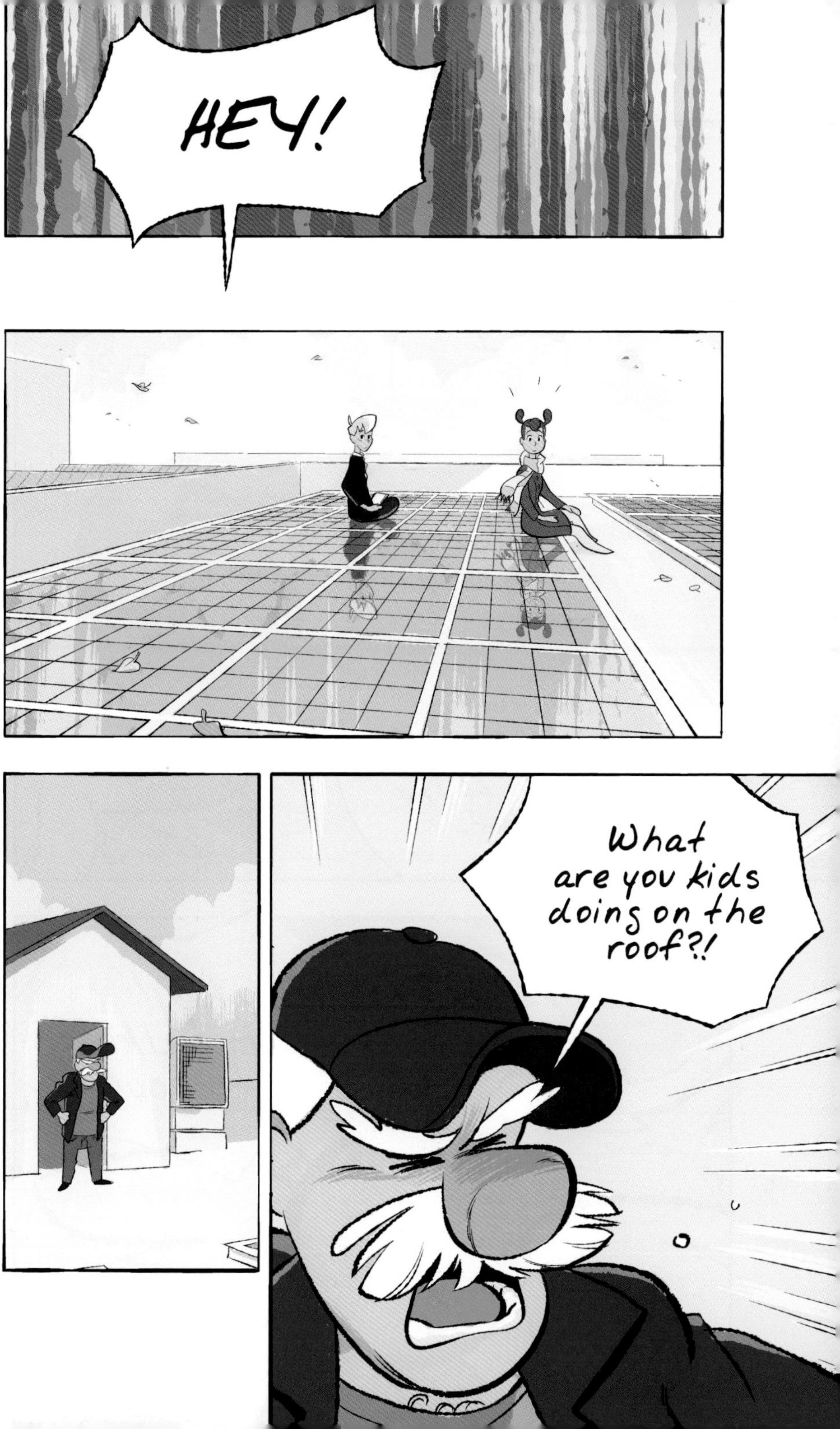
HEY!
What are you kids doing on the roof?!

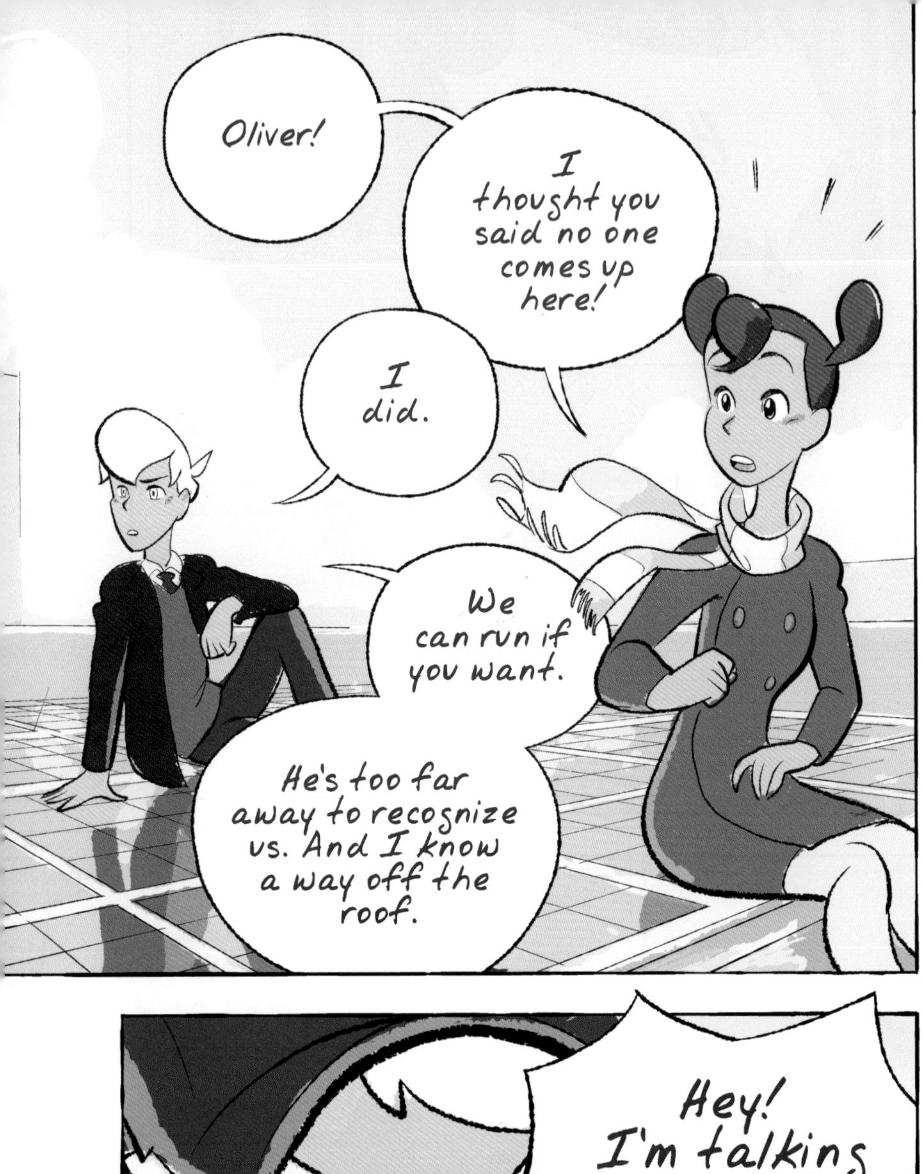
Oliver!
I thought you said no one comes up here!
I did.
We can run if you want.
He's too far away to recognize us. And I know a way off the roof.
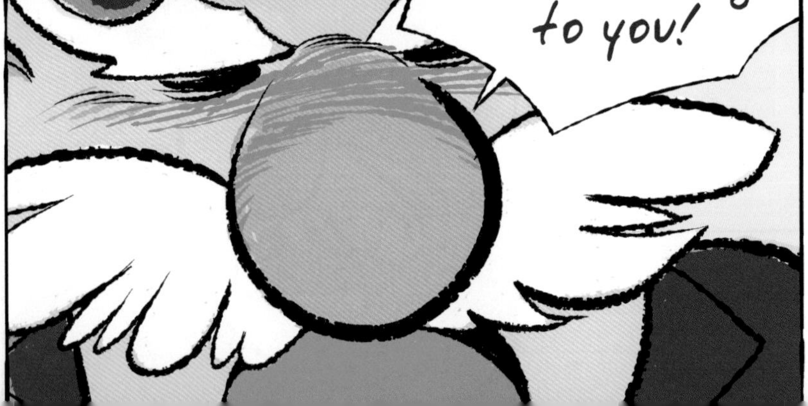
Hey! I'm talking to you!

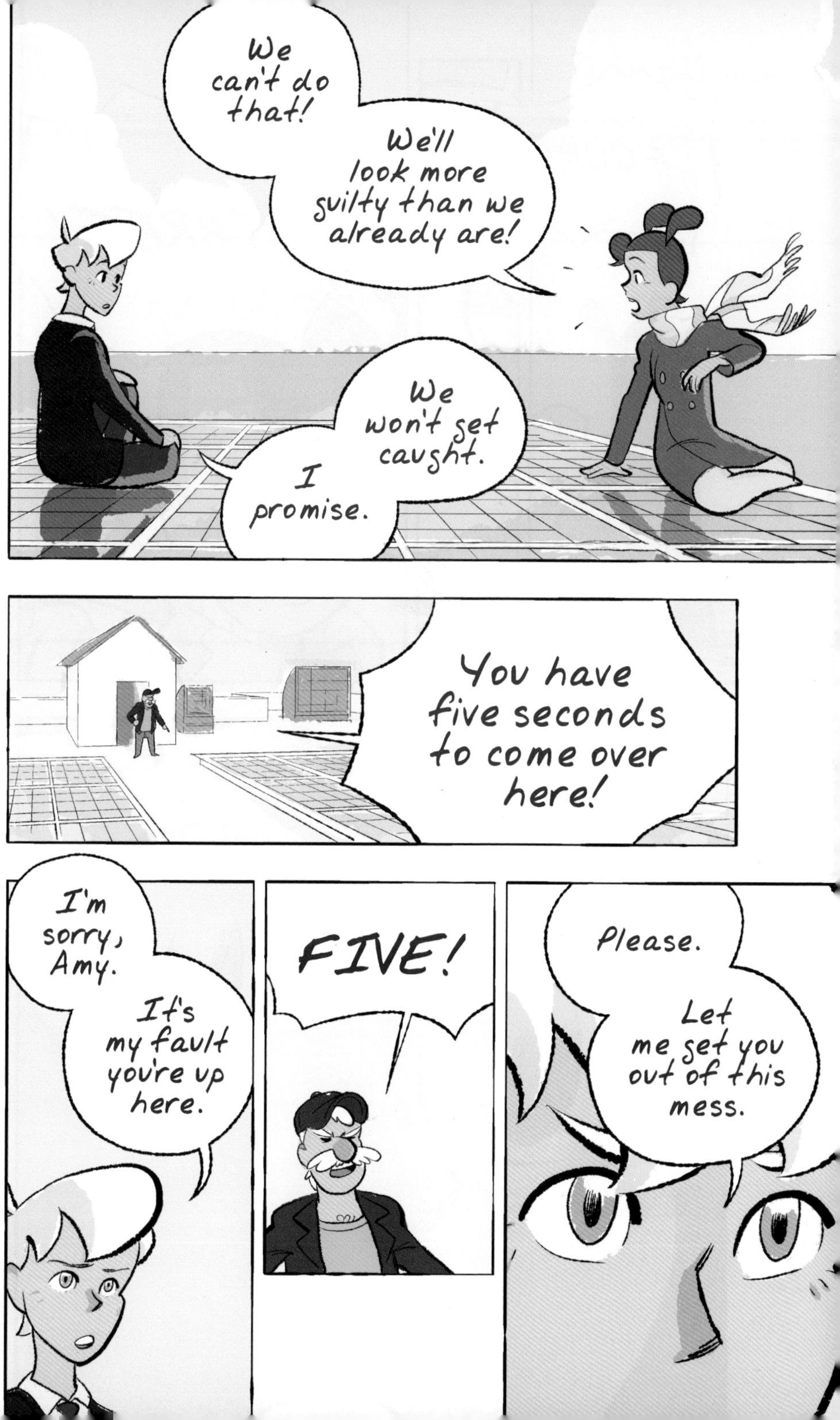
We can't do that!
We'll look more guilty than we already are!
We won't get caught.
I promise.
You have five seconds to come over here!
I'm sorry, Amy.
It's my fault you're up here.
FIVE!
Please.
Let me get you out of this mess.

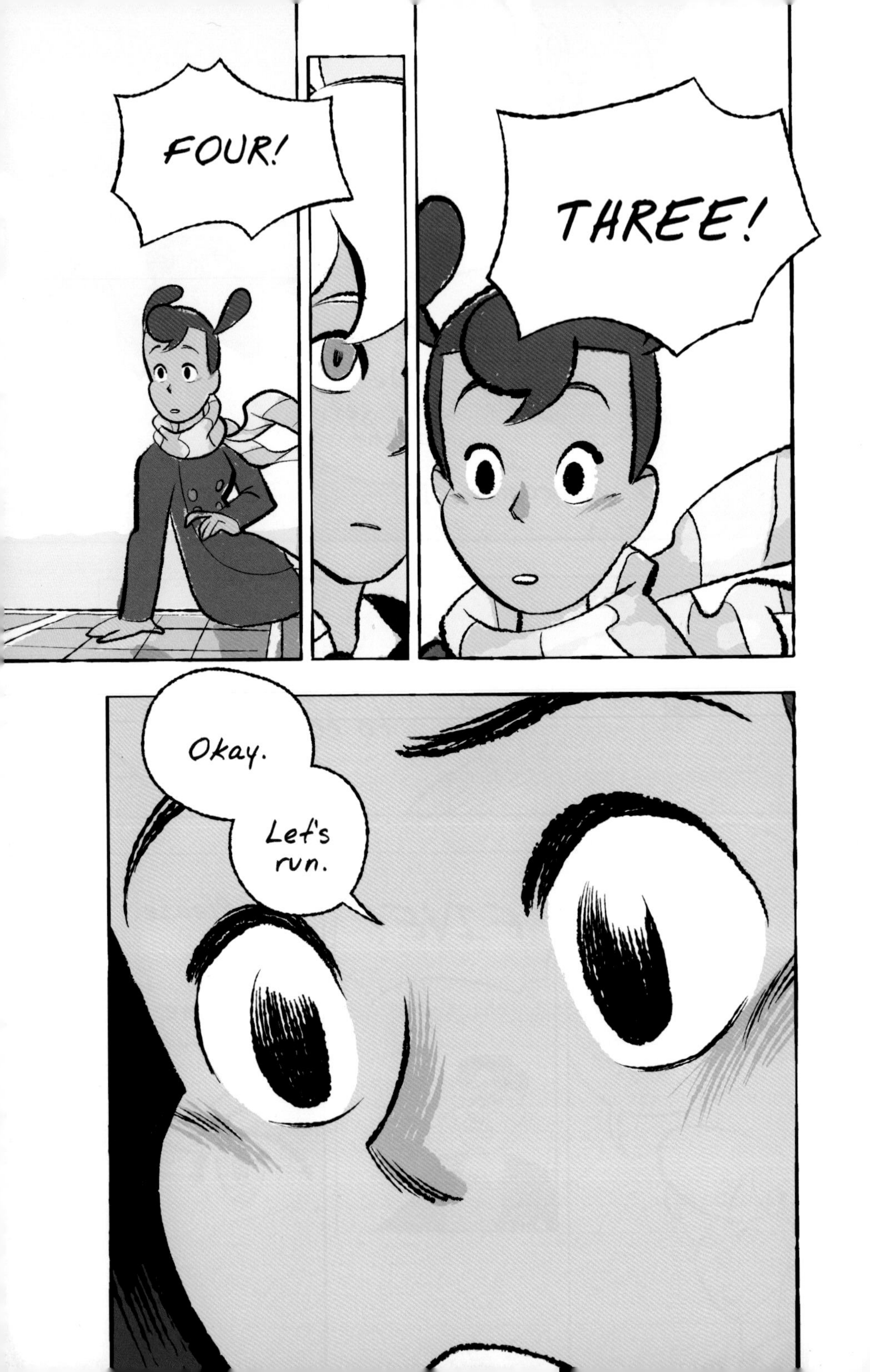
FOUR!
THREE!
Okay.
Let's run.

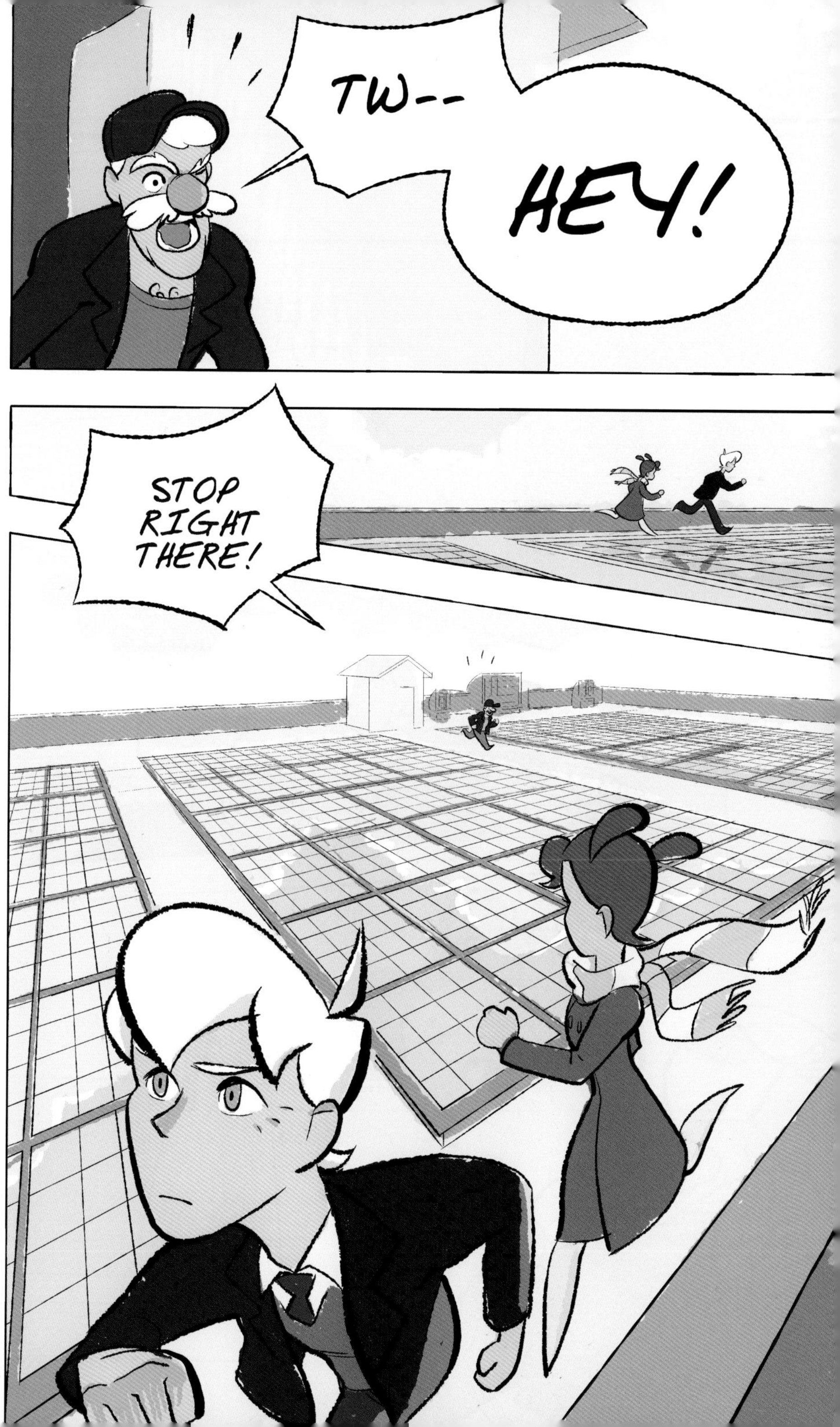
TW--
HEY!
STOP RIGHT THERE!

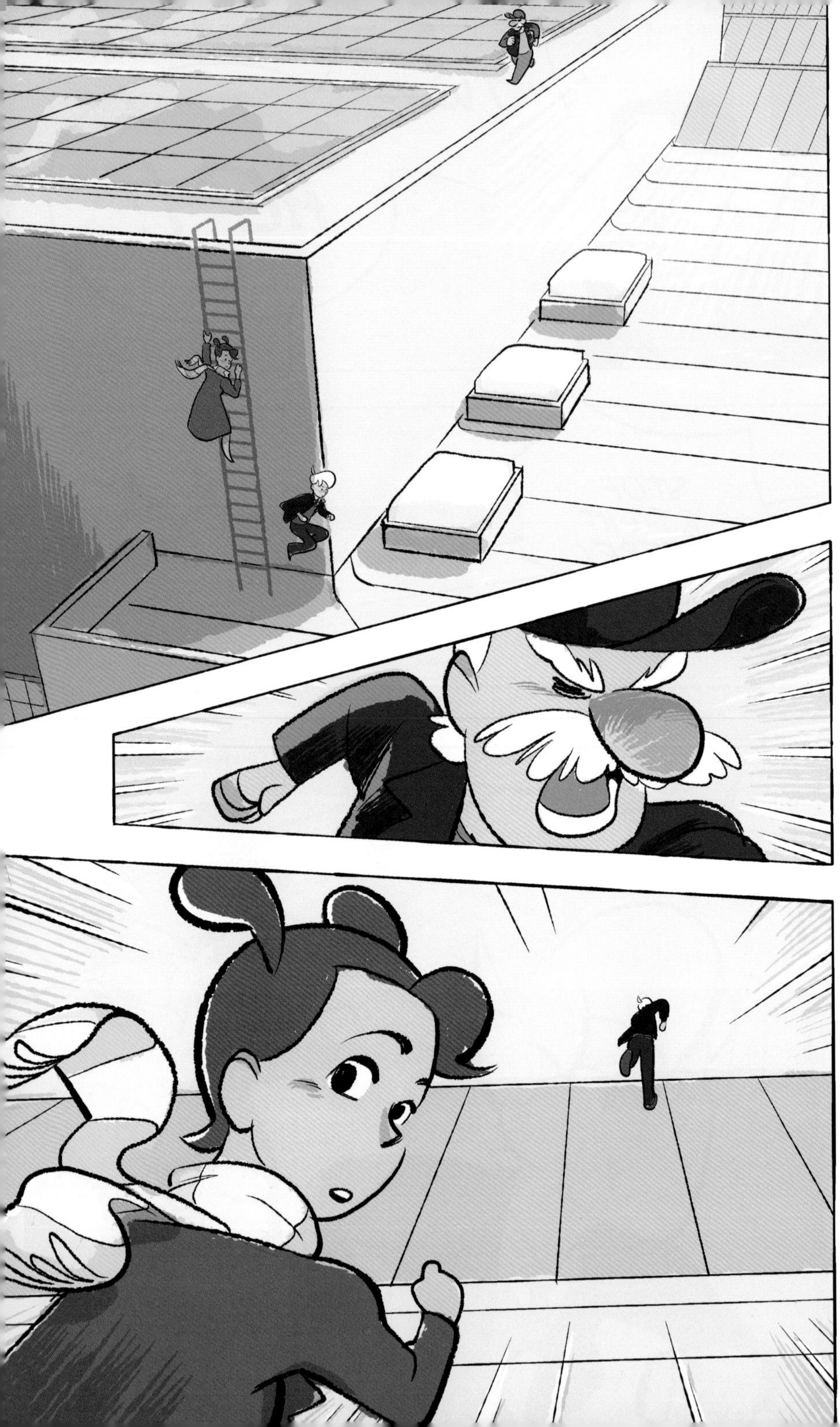

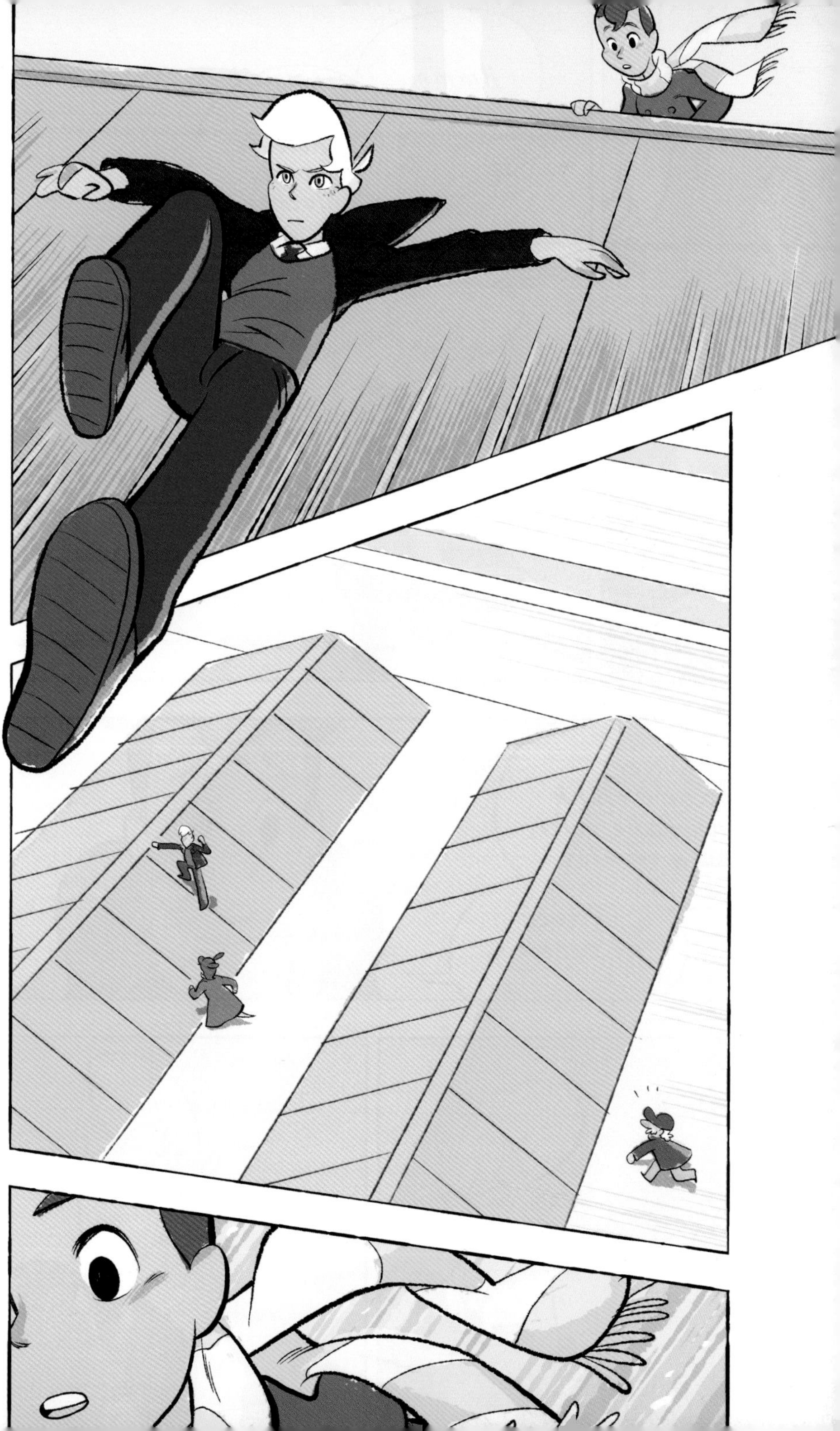

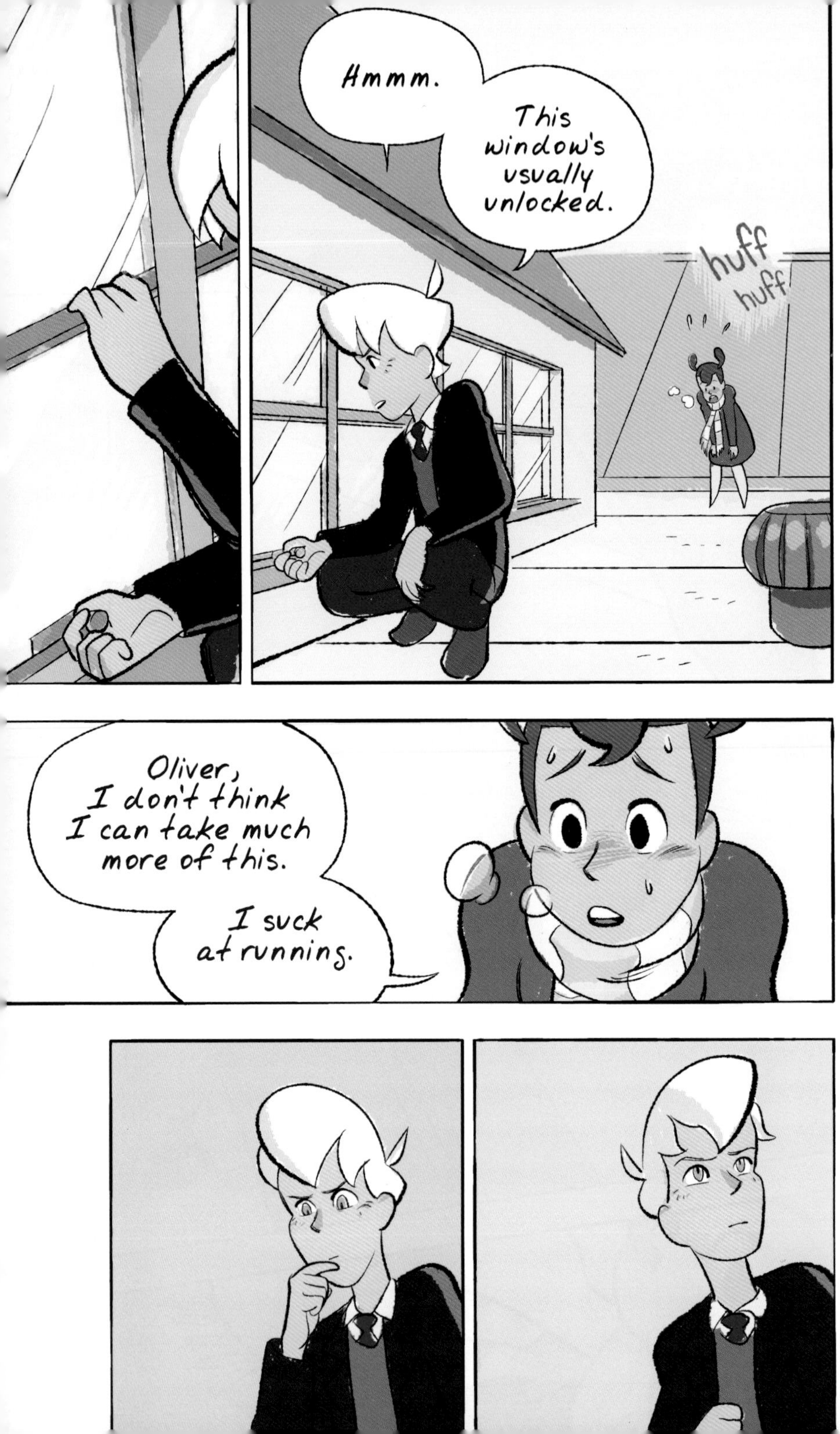
Hmmm.
This window's usually unlocked.
huff huff
Oliver, I don't think I can take much more of this.
I suck at running.

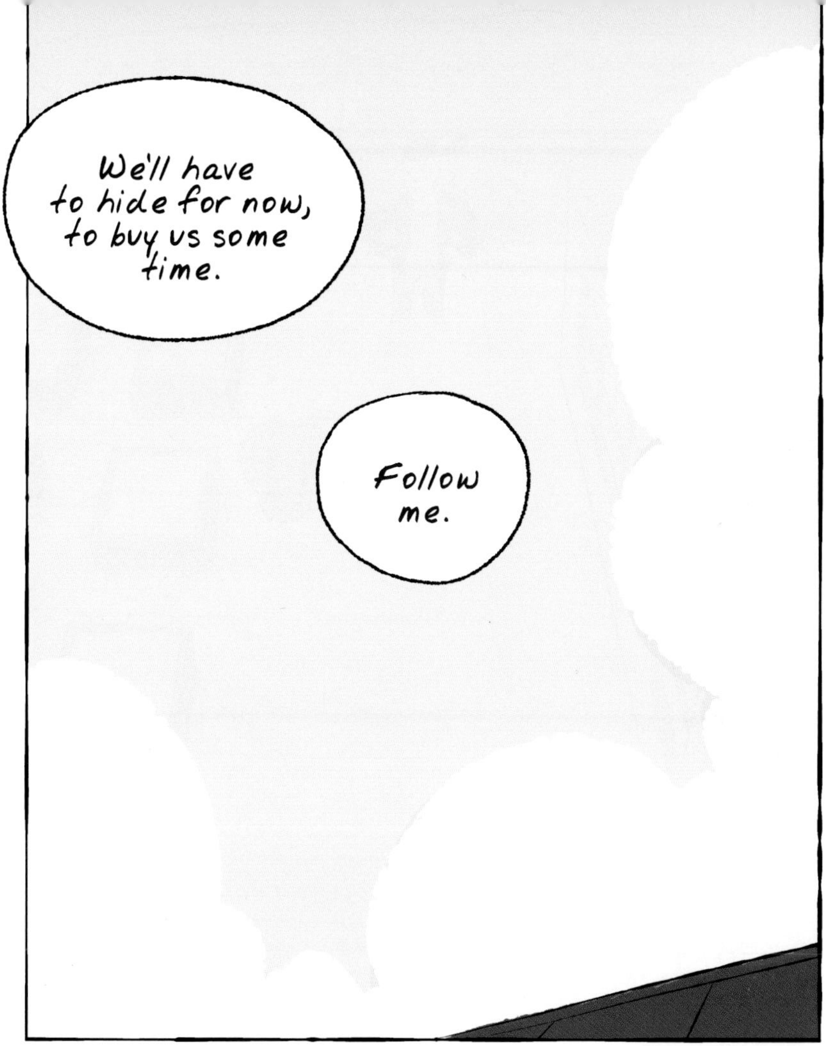
We'll have to hide for now, to buy us some time.
Follow me.

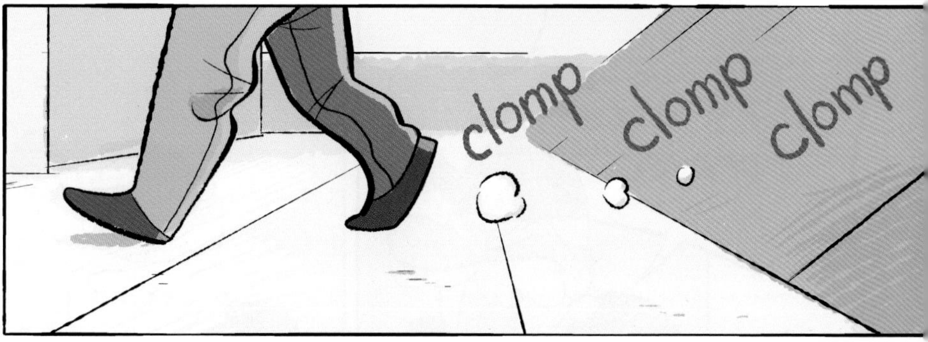
clomp
clomp
clomp

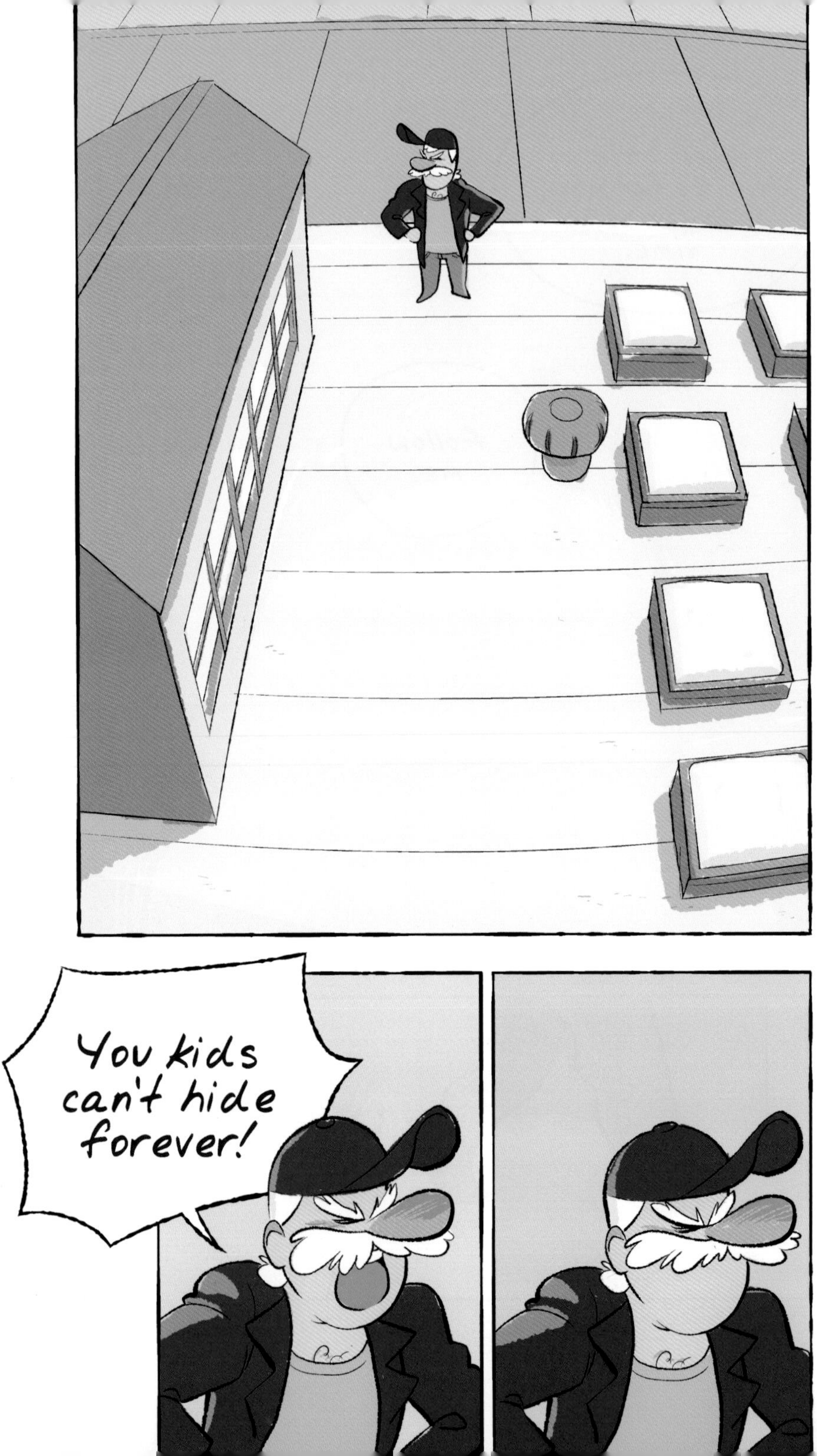
You kids can't hide forever!

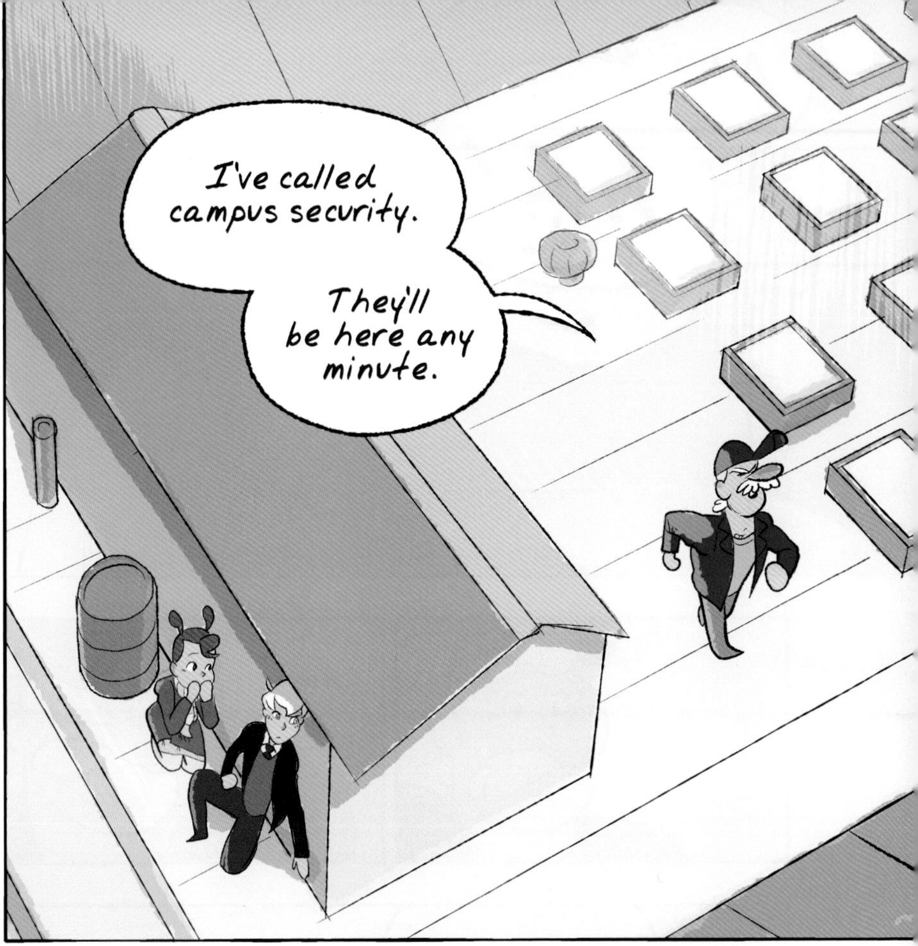
I've called campus security.
They'll be here any minute.

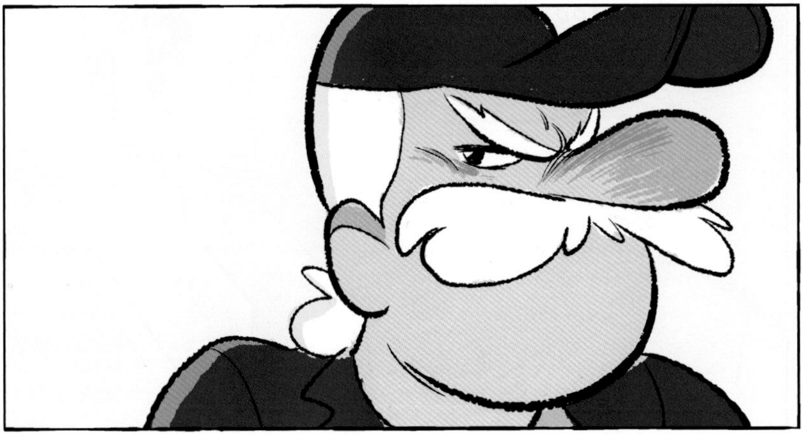

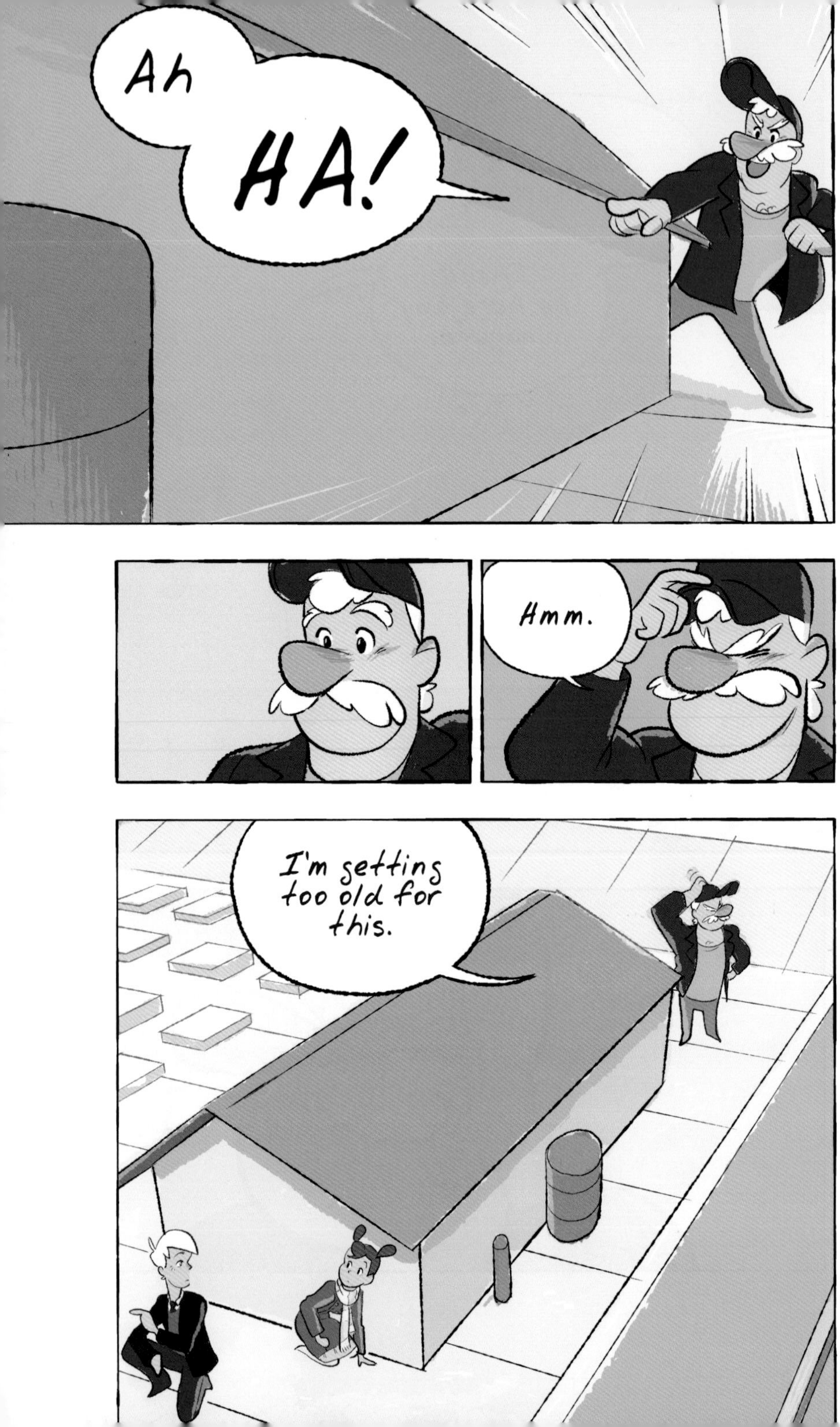
Ah HA!
Hmm.
I'm getting too old for this.

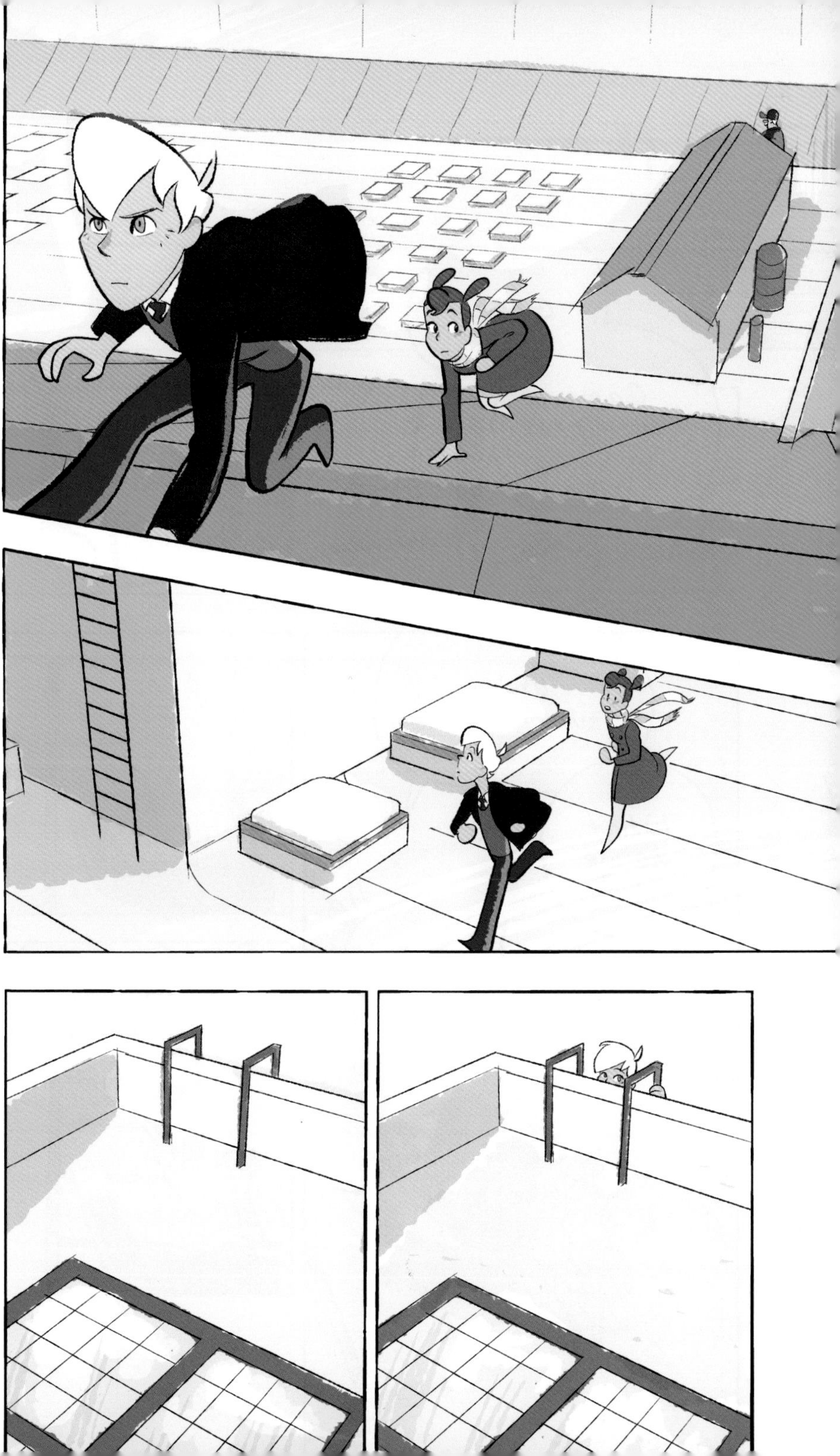

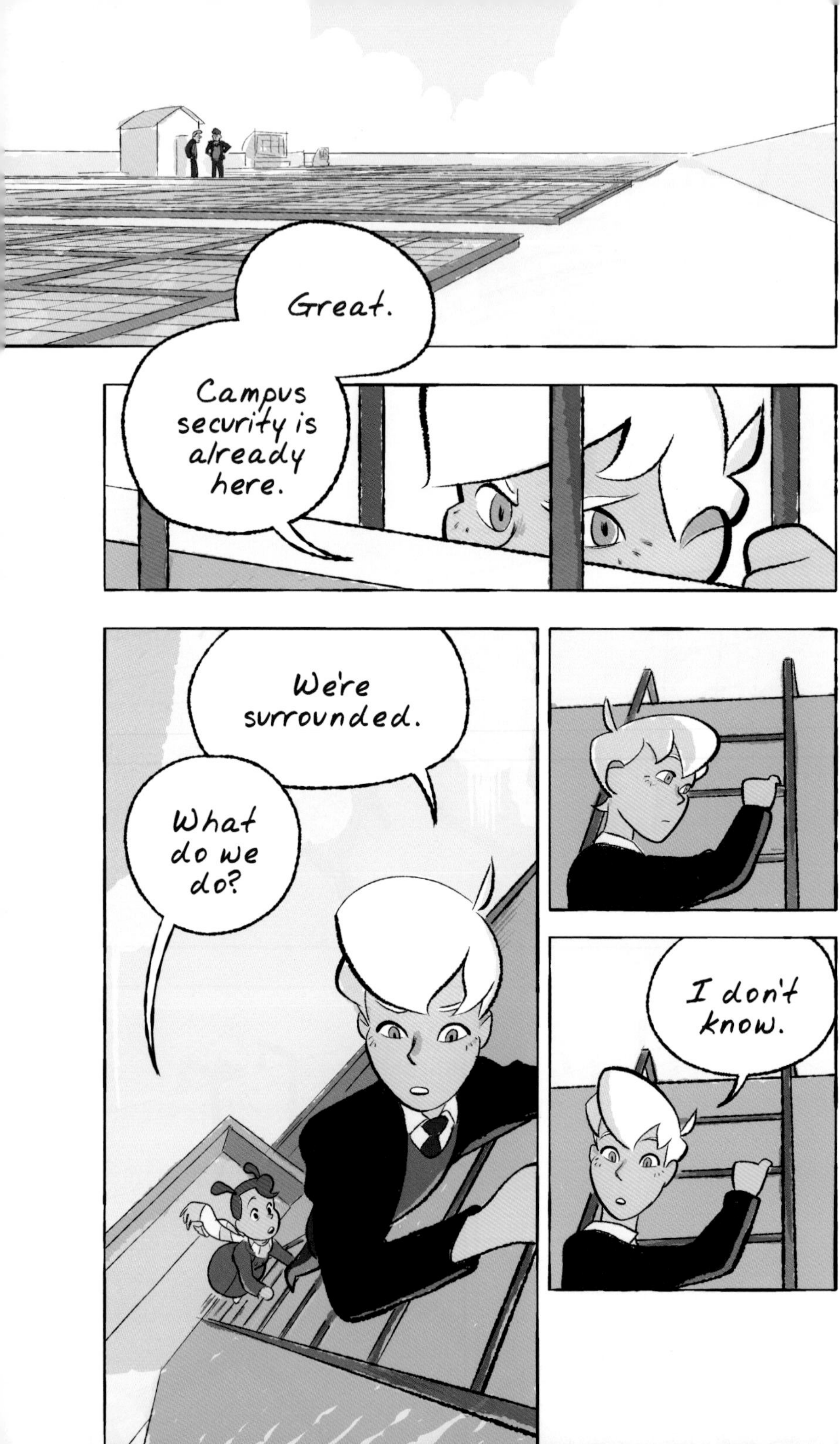
Great.
Campus security is already here.
We're surrounded.
What do we do?
I don't know.

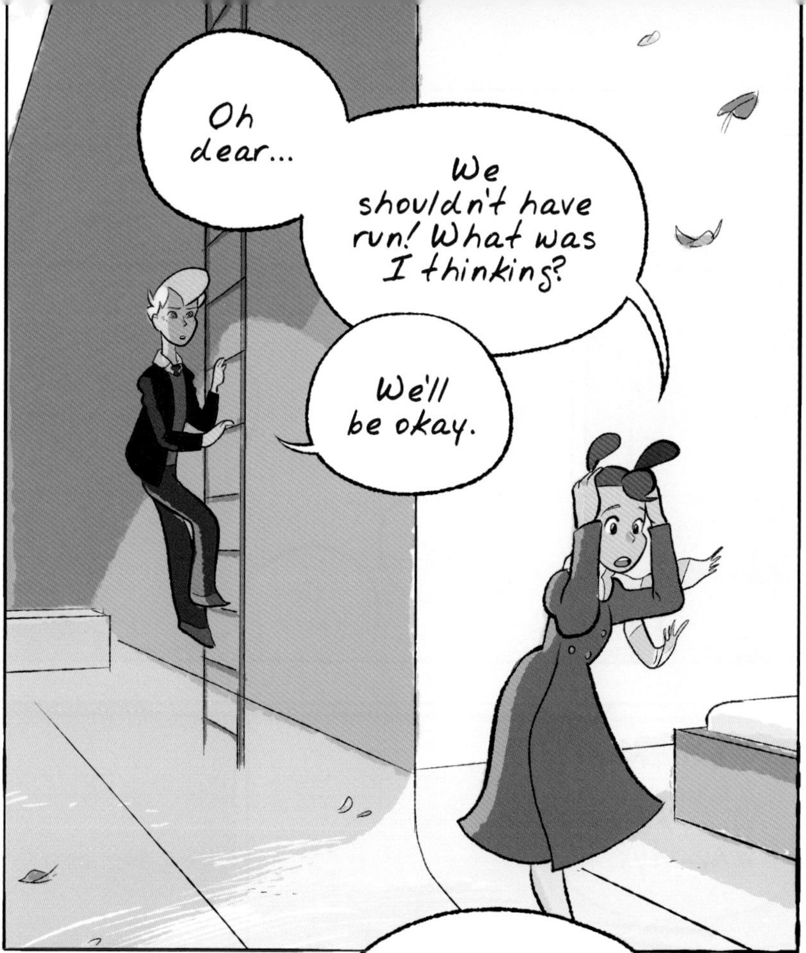
Oh dear...
We shouldn't have run! What was I thinking?
We'll be okay.

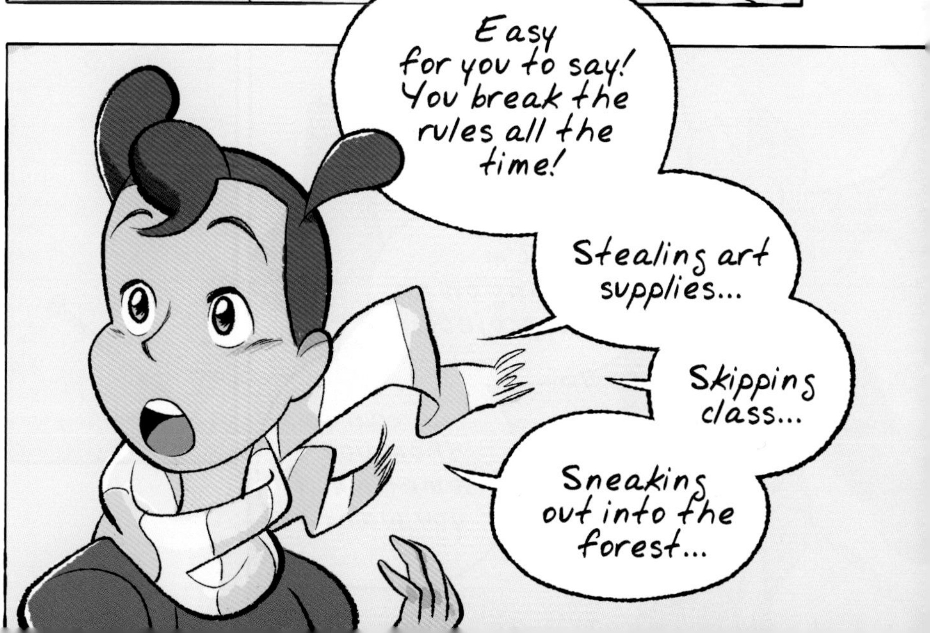
Easy for you to say! You break the rules all the time!
Stealing art supplies...
Skipping class...
Sneaking out into the forest...

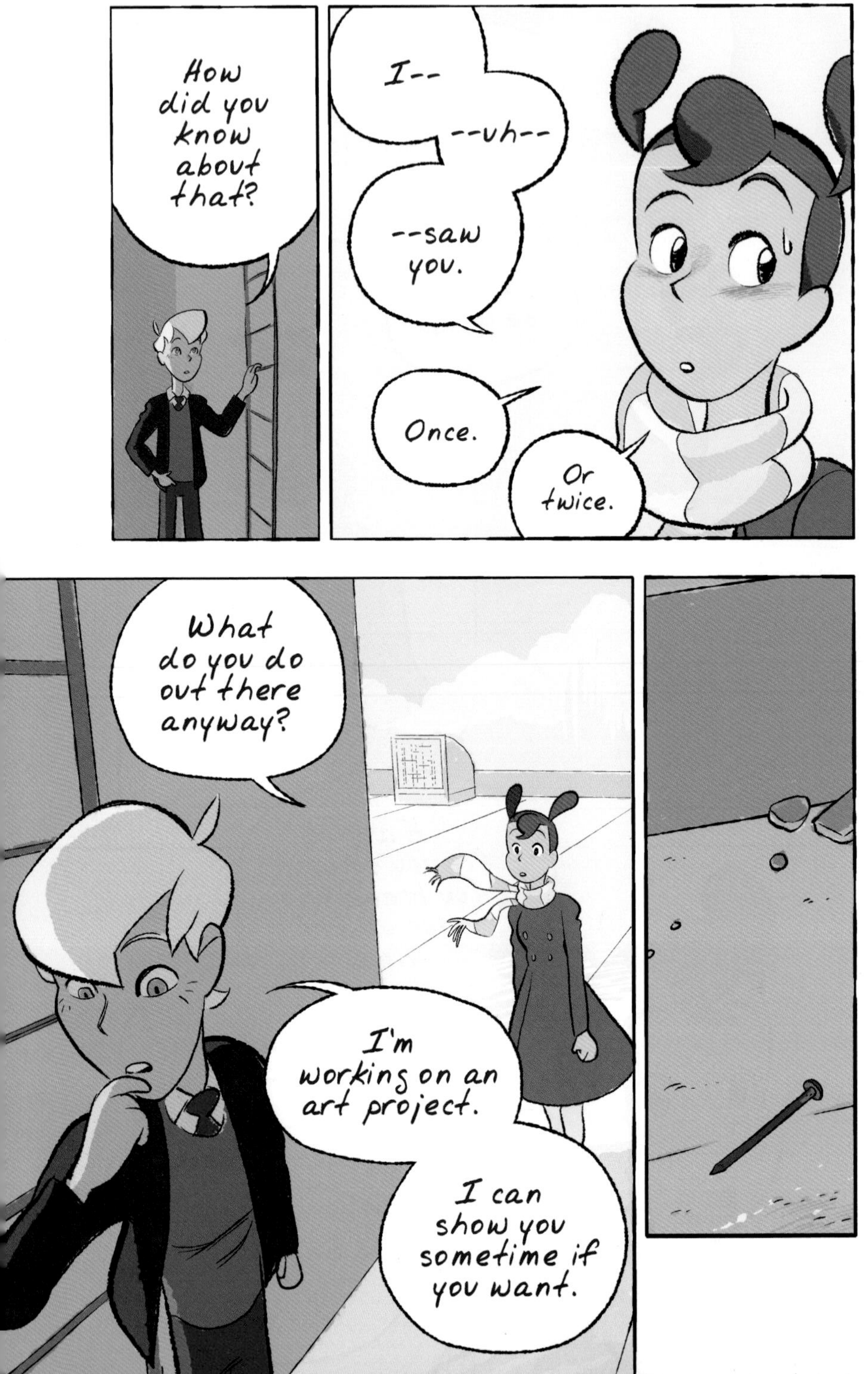
How did you know about that?
I--
--uh--
--saw you.
Once.
Or twice.
What do you do out there anyway?
I'm working on an art project.
I can show you sometime if you want.

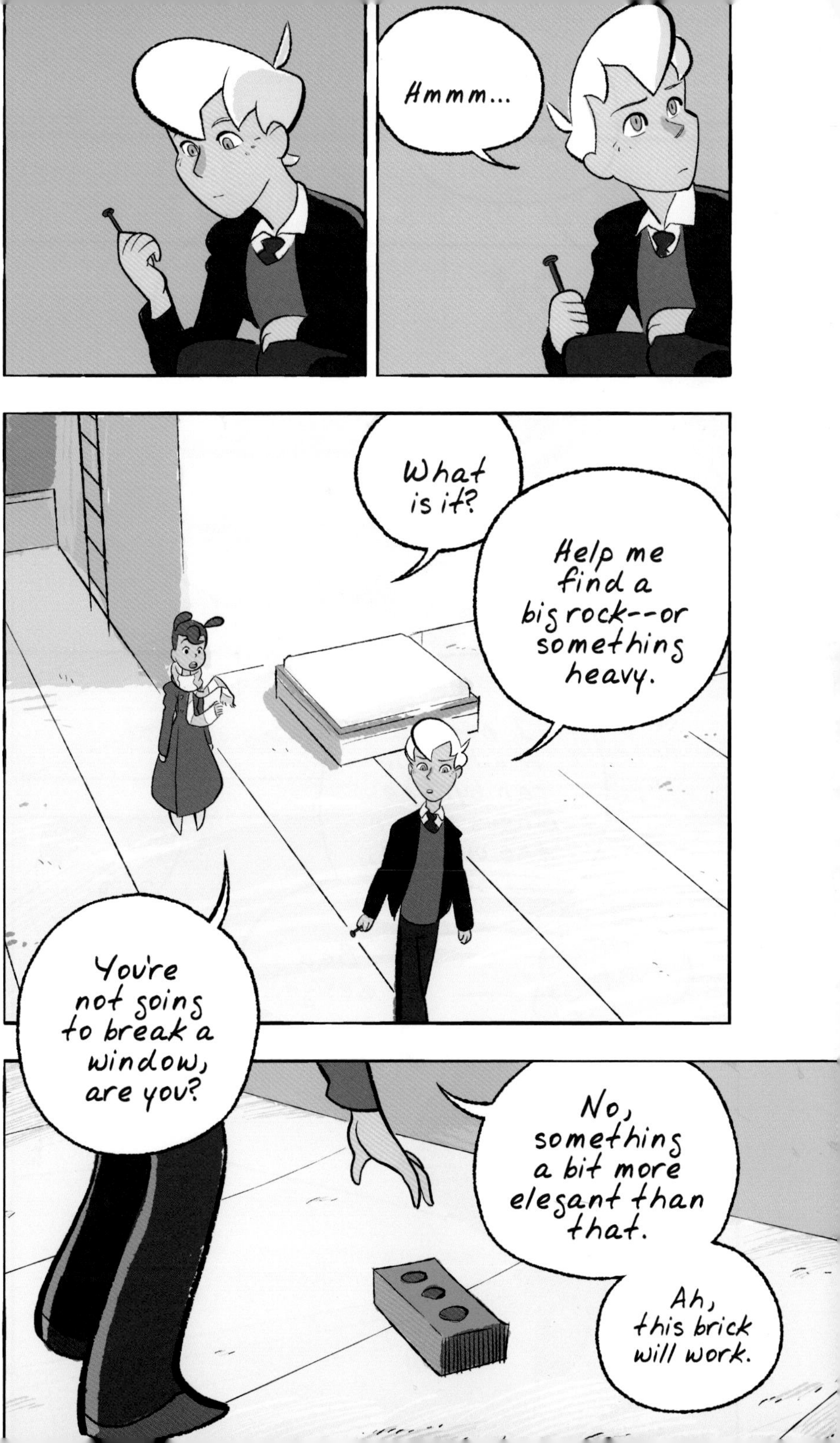
Hmmm...
What is it?
Help me find a big rock--or something heavy.
You're not going to break a window, are you?
No, something a bit more elegant than that.
Ah, this brick will work.

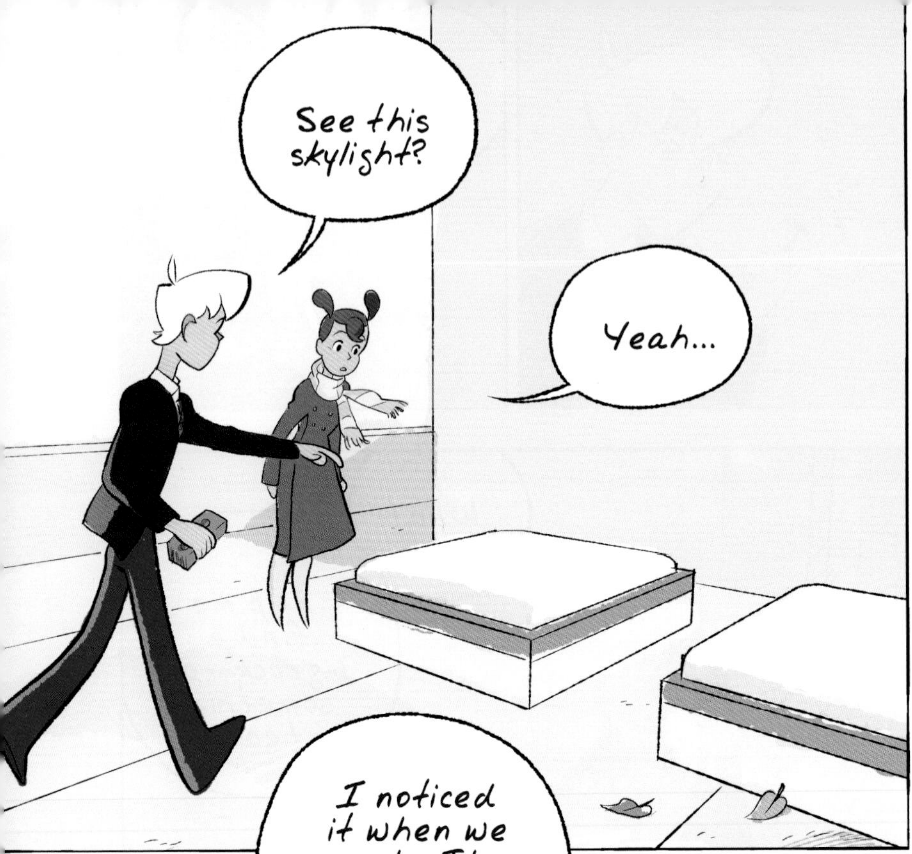
See this skylight?
Yeah...
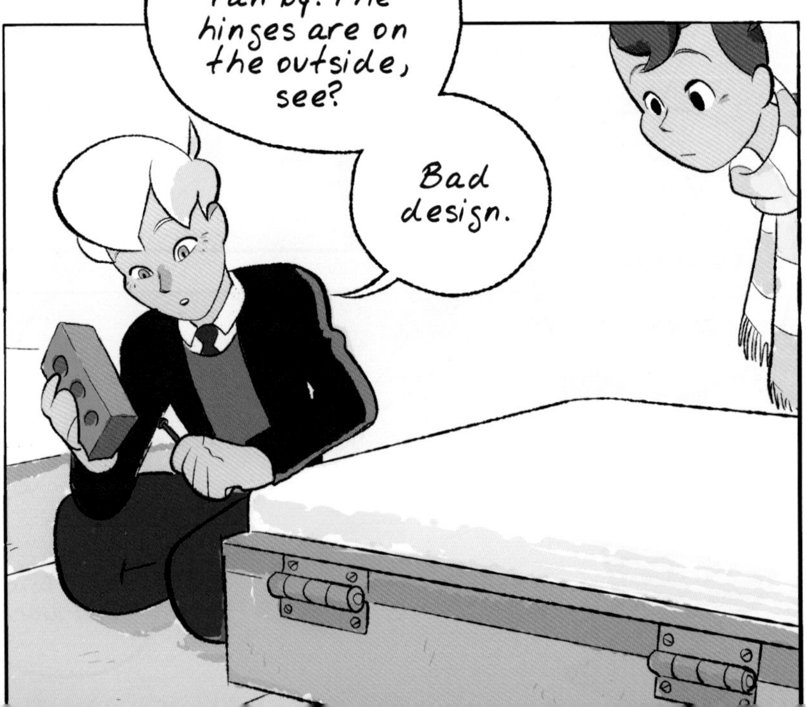
I noticed it when we ran by. The hinges are on the outside, see?
Bad design.

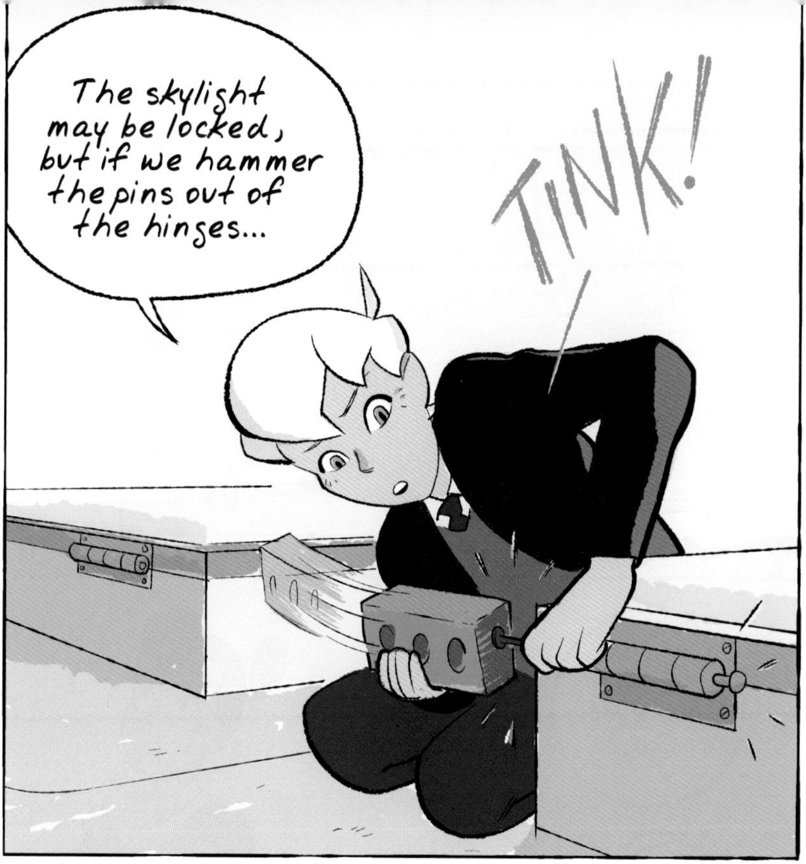
The skylight may be locked, but if we hammer the pins out of the hinges...
TINK!
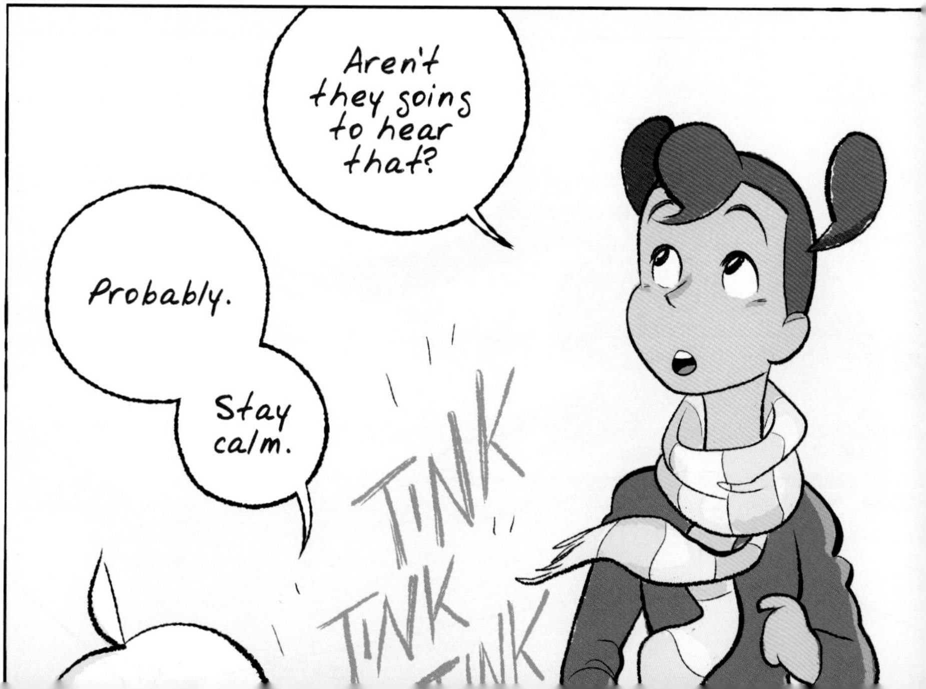
Aren't they going to hear that?
Probably.
Stay calm.
TINK
TINK

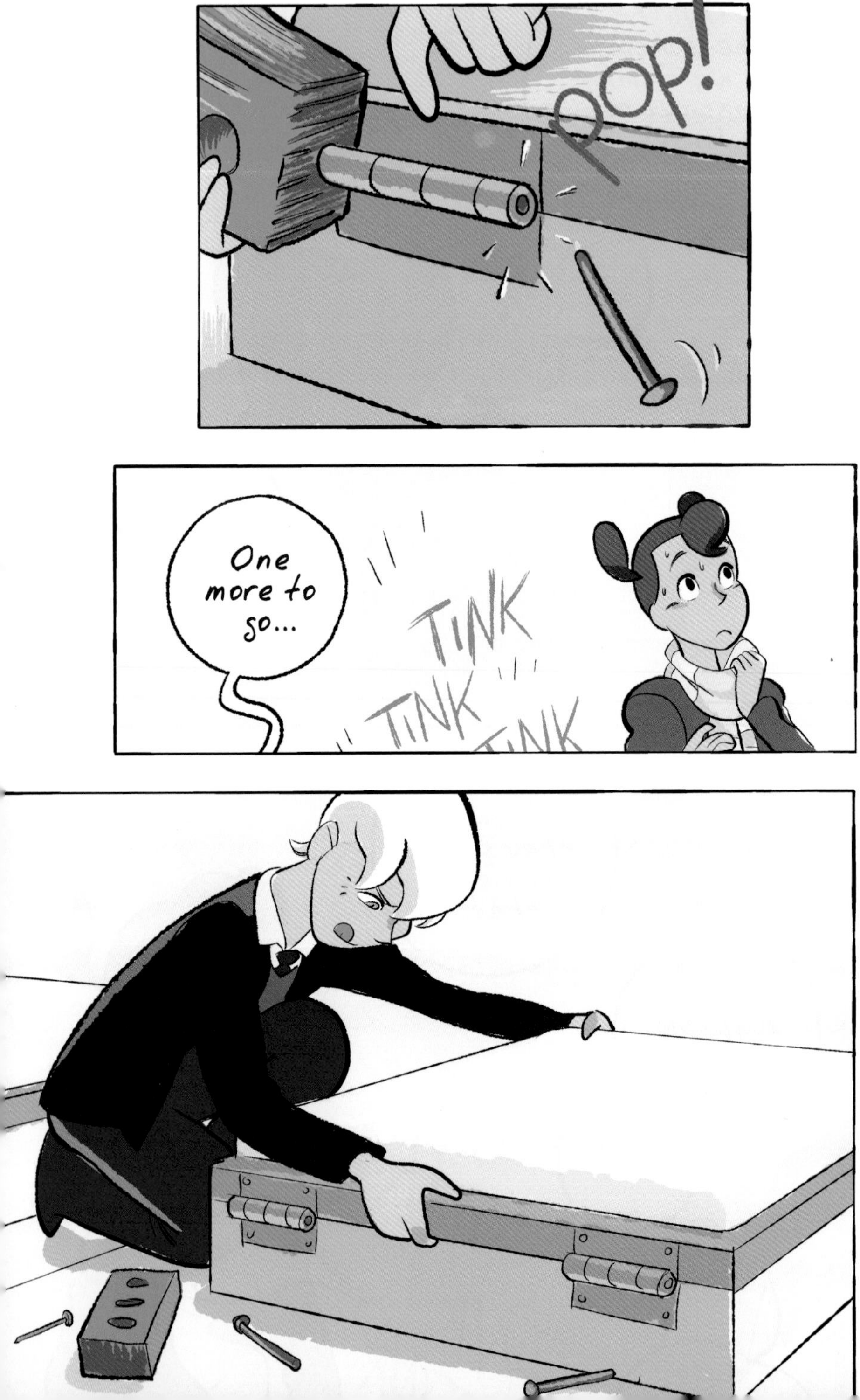
POP!
One more to go...
TINK
TINK

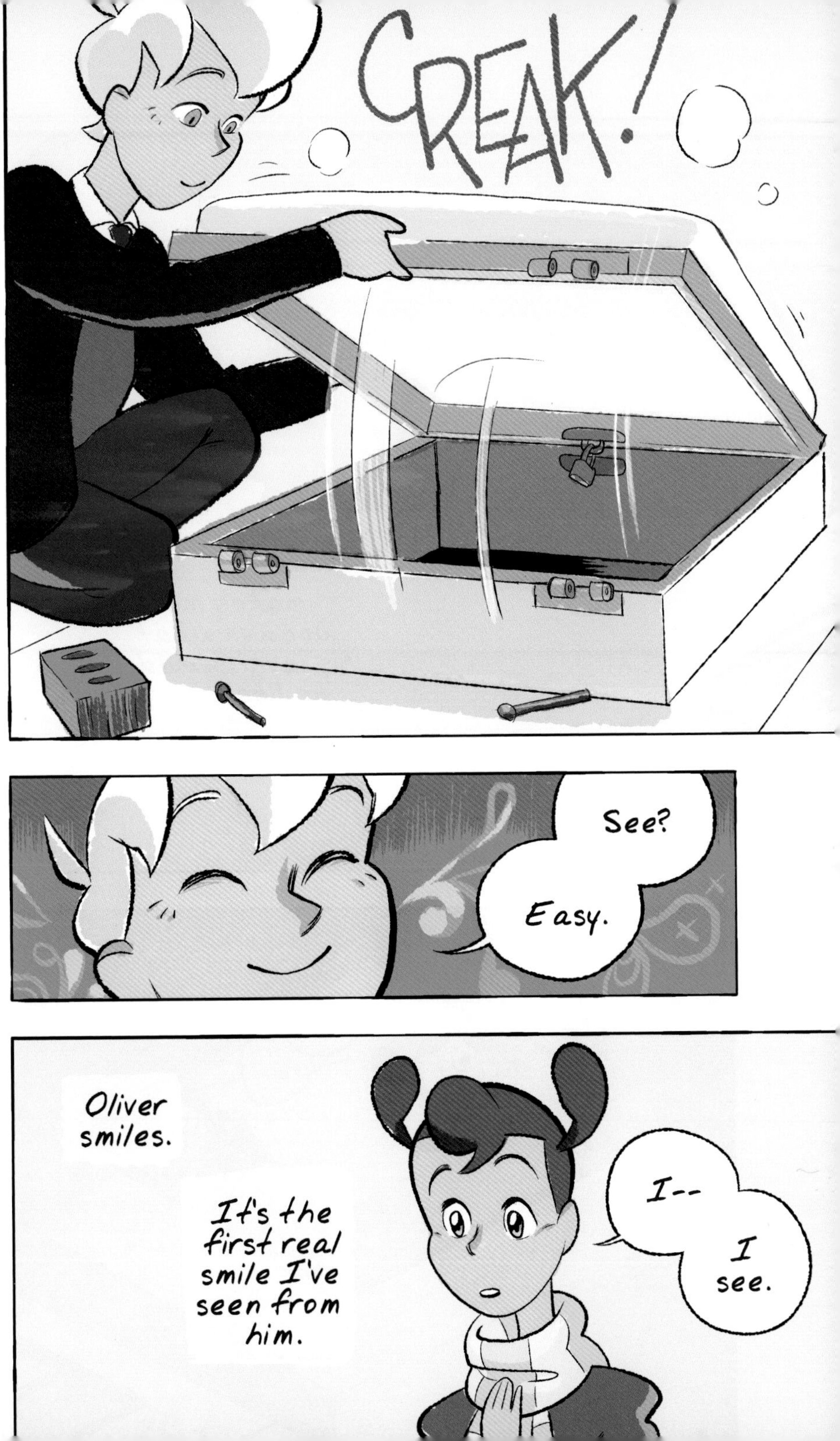
CREAK!
See?
Easy.
Oliver smiles.
It's the first real smile I've seen from him.
I--
I see.

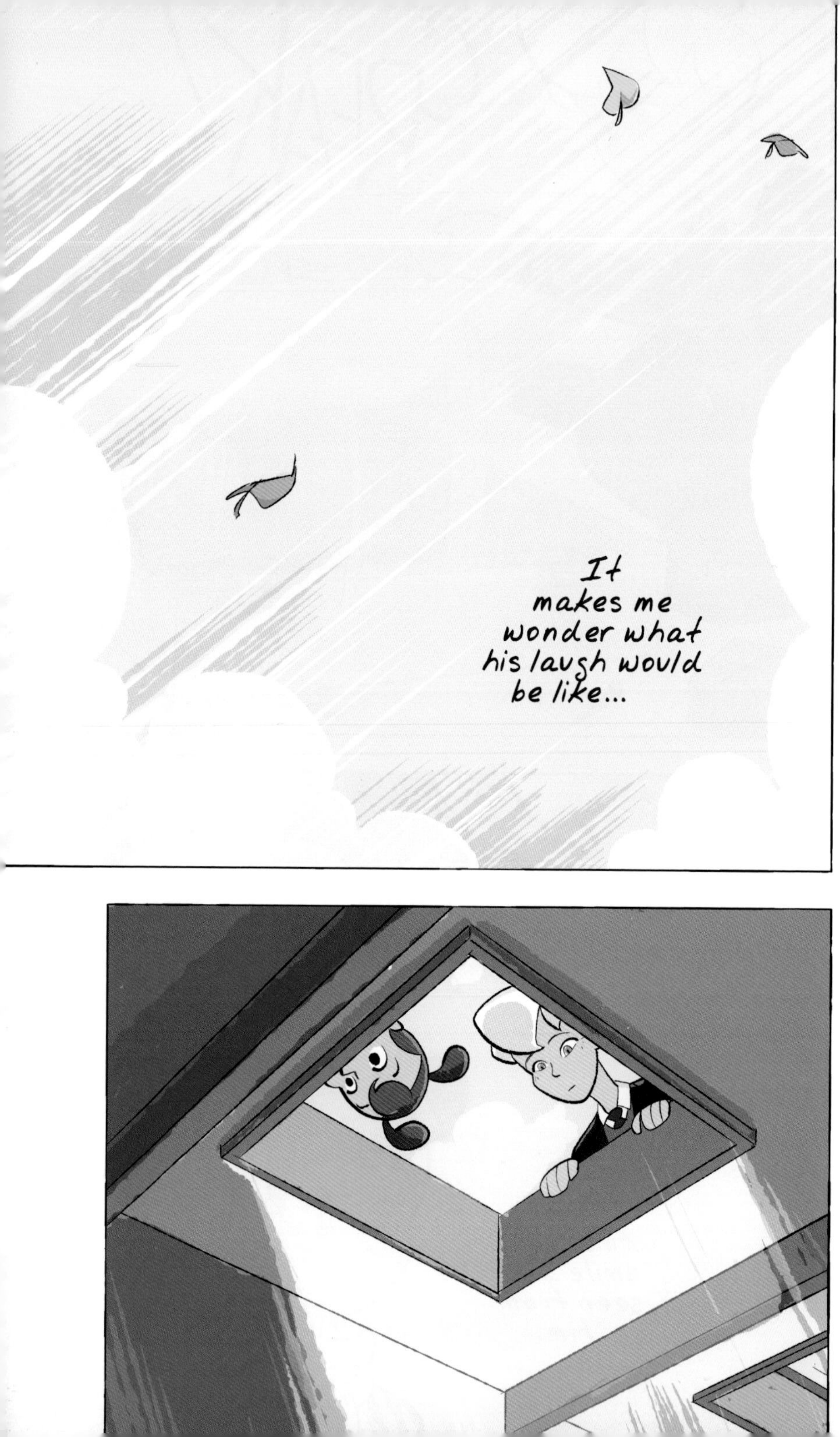
It makes me wonder what his laugh would be like...

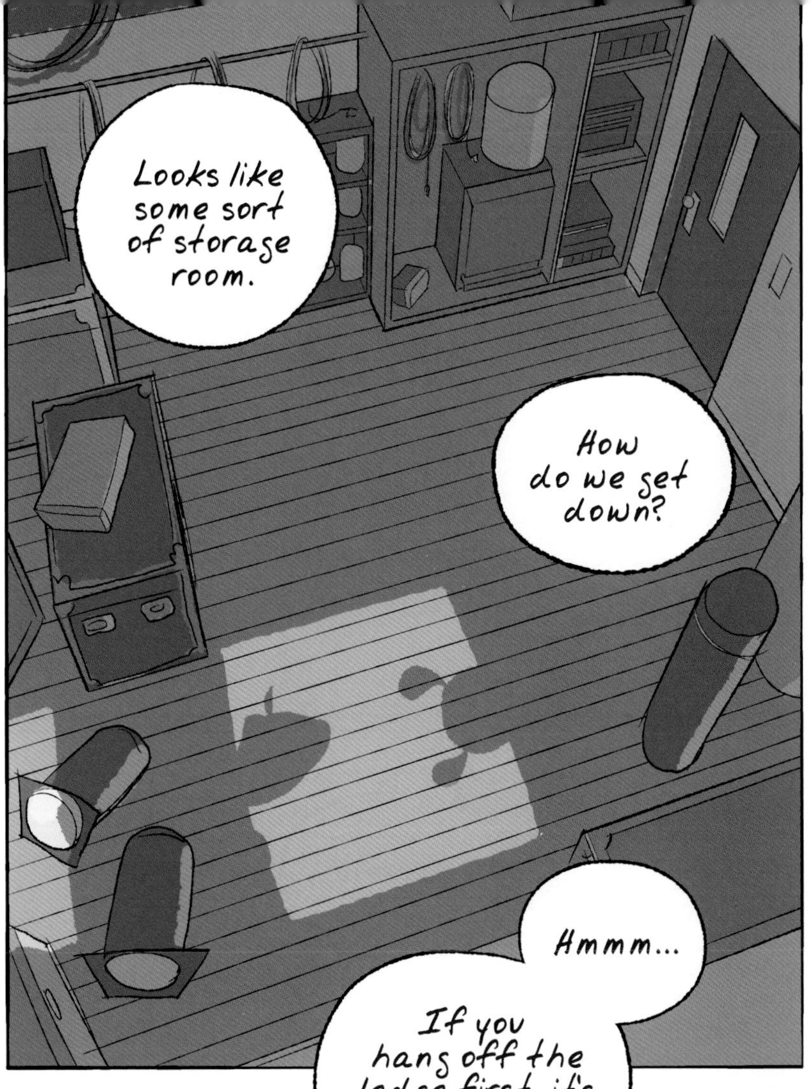
Looks like some sort of storage room.
How do we get down?
Hmmm...

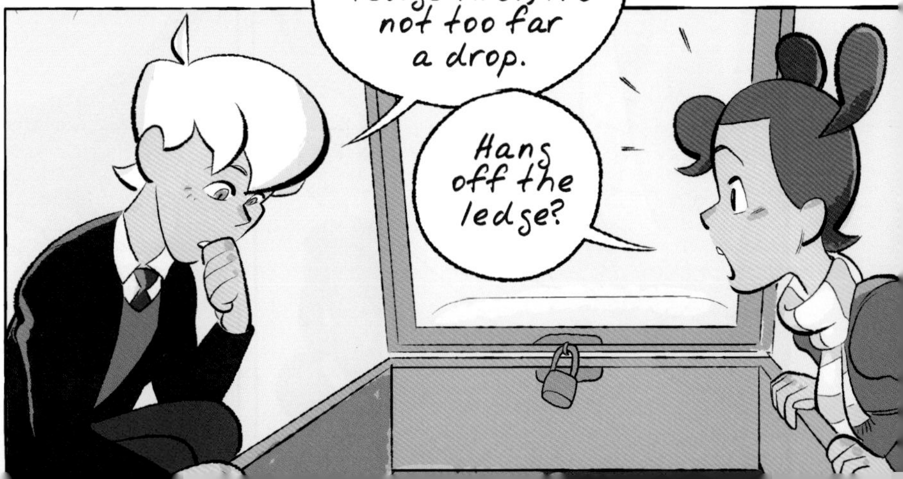
If you hang off the ledge first, it's not too far a drop.
Hang off the ledge?

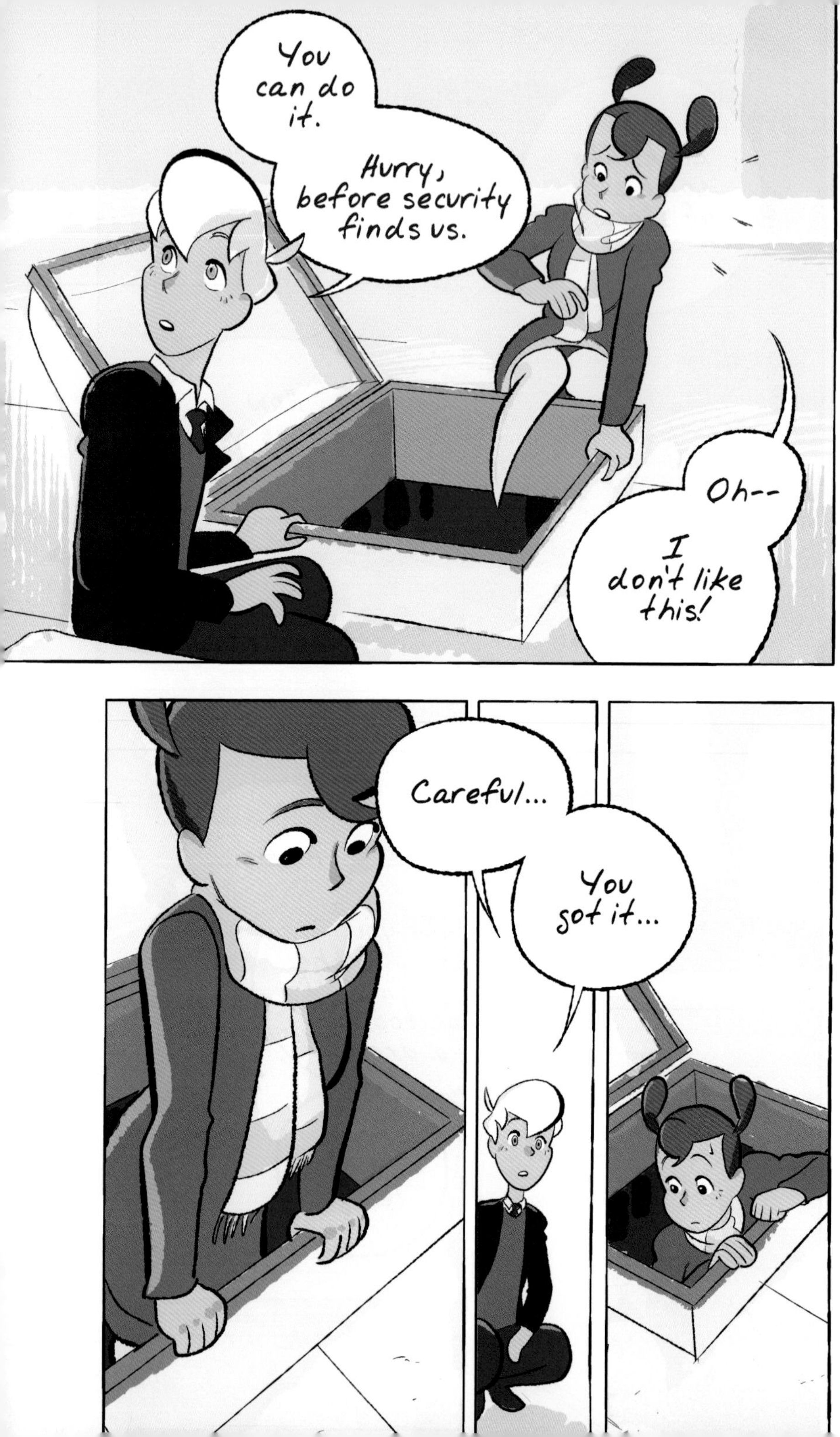
You can do it.
Hurry, before security finds us.
Oh--
I don't like this!
Careful...
You got it...

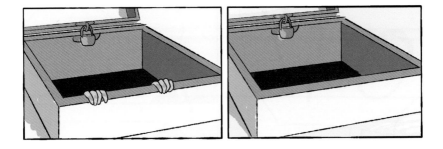

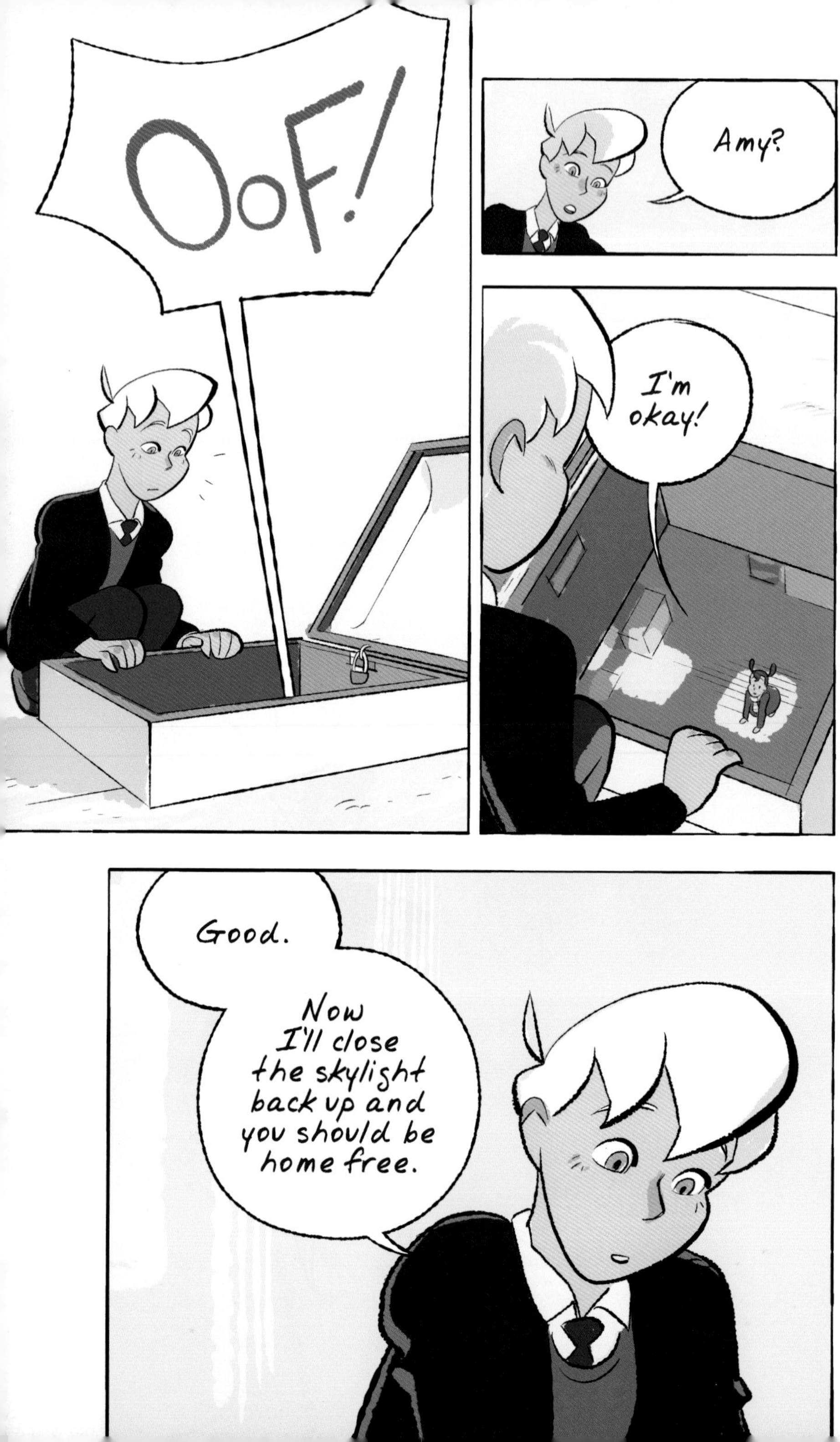
OoF!
Amy?
I'm okay!
Good.
Now I'll close the skylight back up and you should be home free.

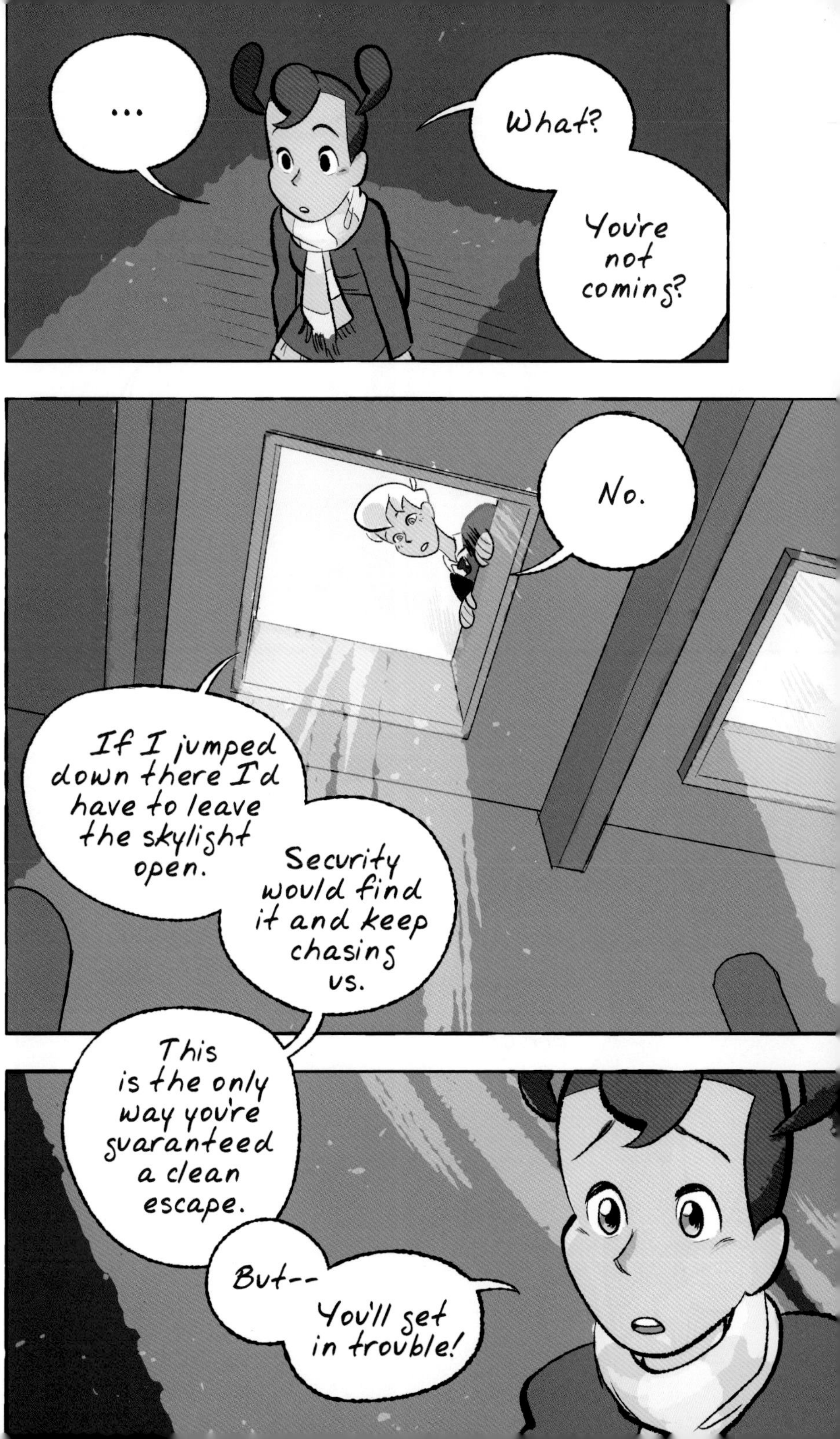
...
What?
You're not coming?
No.
If I jumped down there I'd have to leave the skylight open.
Security would find it and keep chasing us.
This is the only way you're guaranteed a clean escape.
But--
You'll get in trouble!

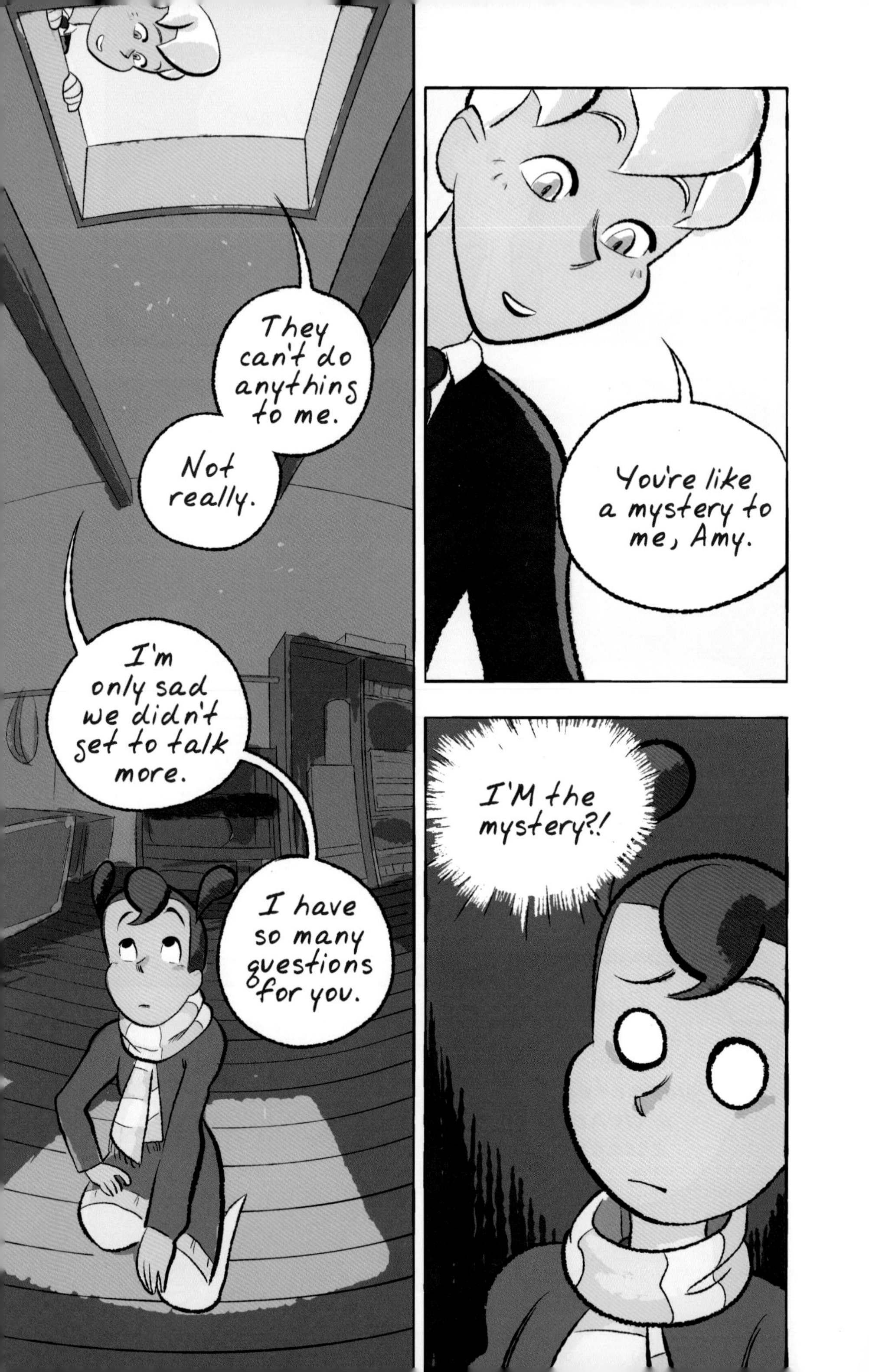
They can't do anything to me.
Not really.
I'm only sad we didn't get to talk more.
I have so many questions for you.
You're like a mystery to me, Amy.
I'M the mystery?!

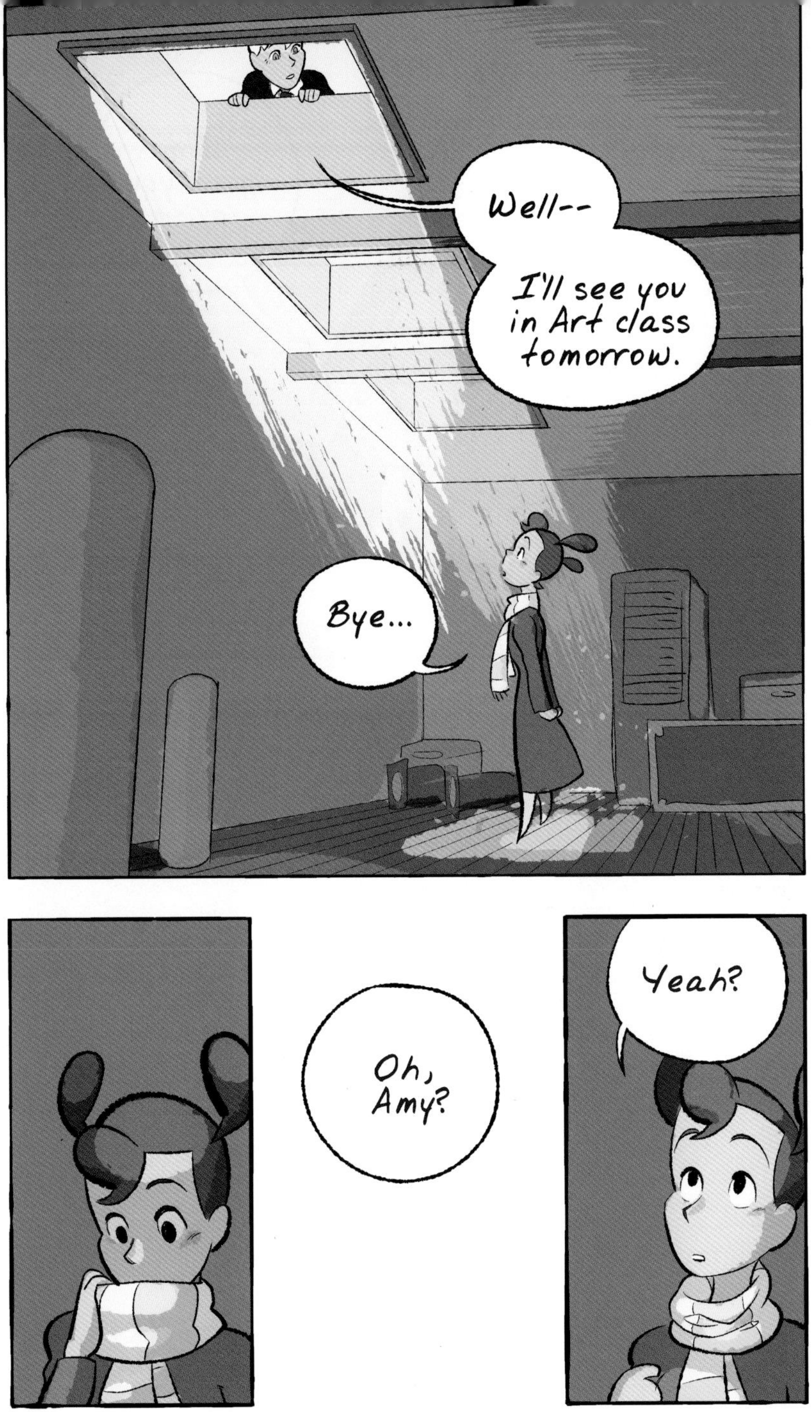
Well--
I'll see you in Art class tomorrow.
Bye...
Oh, Amy?
Yeah?

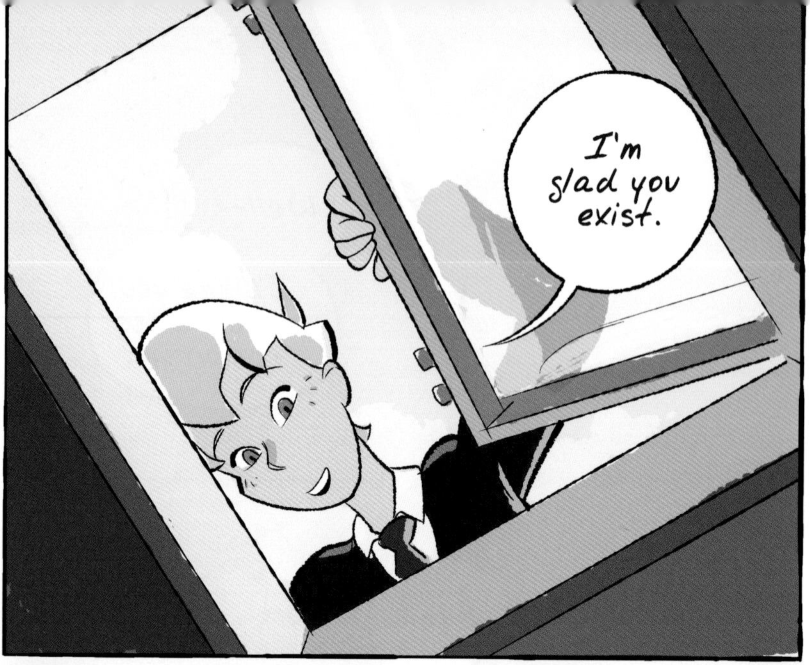
I'm glad you exist.

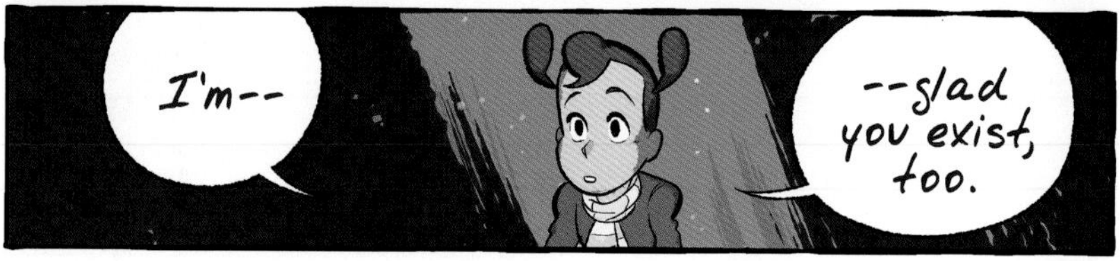
I'm--
--glad you exist, too.

For a while I listen to Oliver hammer the pins back into the hinges.

Then, silence.

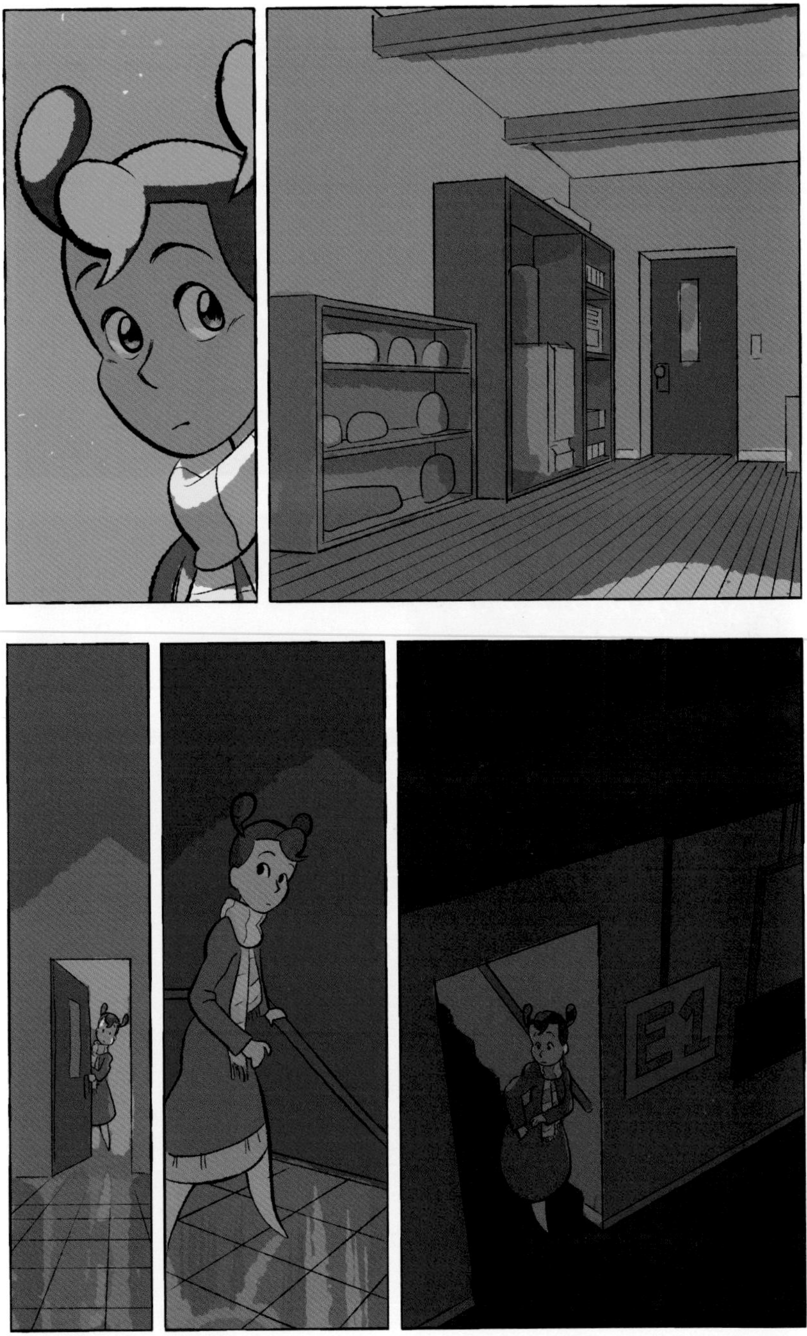
E1

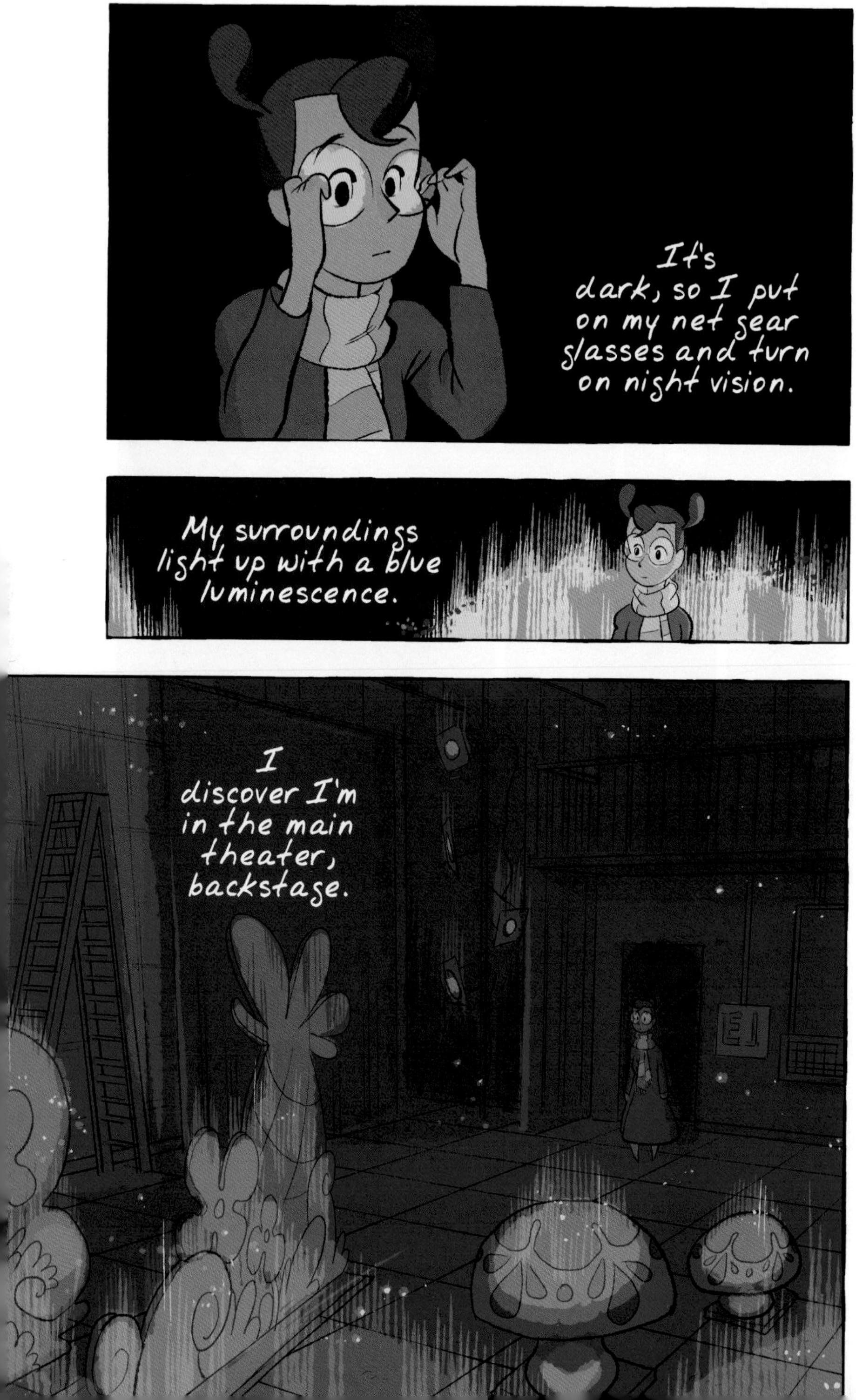
It's dark, so I put on my net gear glasses and turn on night vision.
My surroundings light up with a blue luminescence.
I discover I'm in the main theater, backstage.

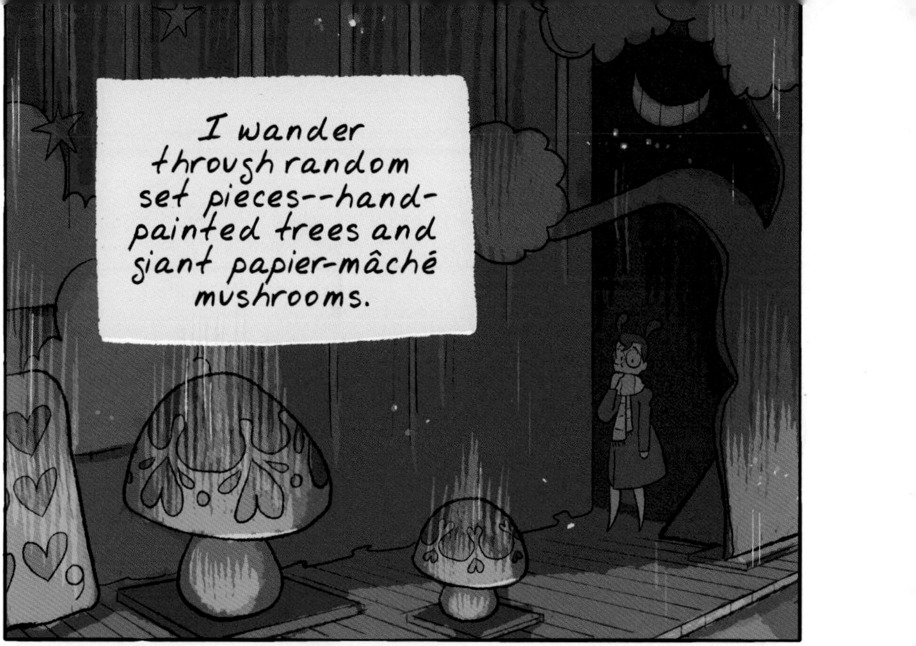
I wander through random set pieces--hand-painted trees and giant papier-mâché mushrooms.

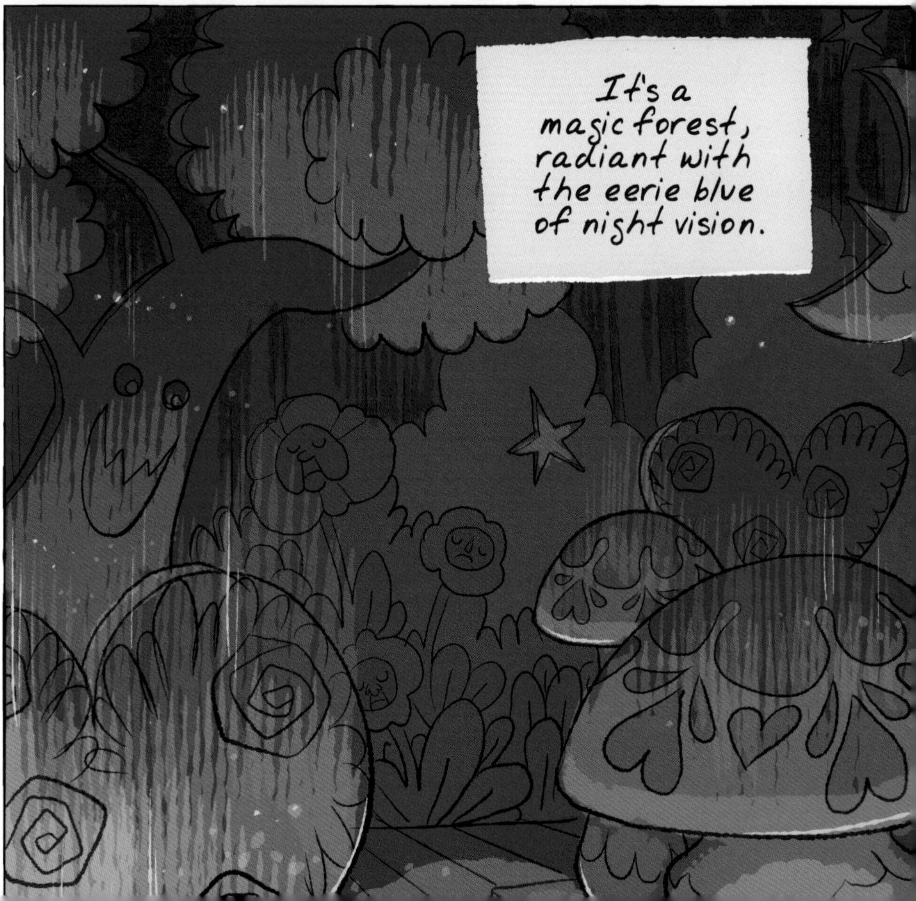
It's a magic forest, radiant with the eerie blue of night vision.

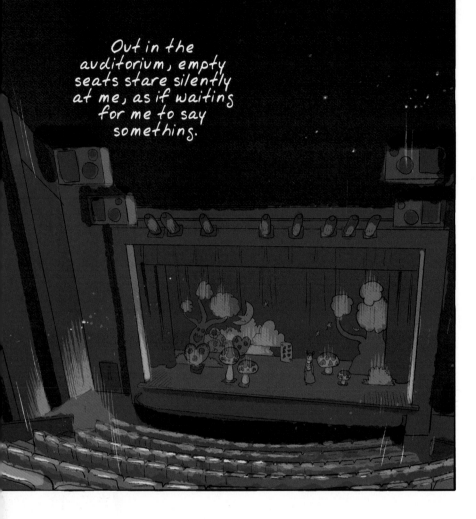

Out in the
auditorium, empty
seats stare silently
at me, as if waiting
for me to say
something.

I blush,
even though no
one is there,
and hurry off
the stage.

COMING SOON . . .

Stephen McCranie's
SPACE
BOY
3

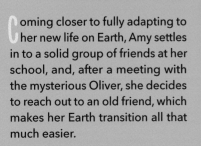

Coming closer to fully adapting to her new life on Earth, Amy settles in to a solid group of friends at her school, and, after a meeting with the mysterious Oliver, she decides to reach out to an old friend, which makes her Earth transition all that much easier.

ALL THIS AND MORE IN THE NEXT VOLUME, AVAILABLE FEBRUARY 27TH, 2019!

YOU CAN ALSO READ MORE SPACE BOY COMICS ON WEBTOONS.COM!

MORE TITLES YOU MIGHT ENJOY

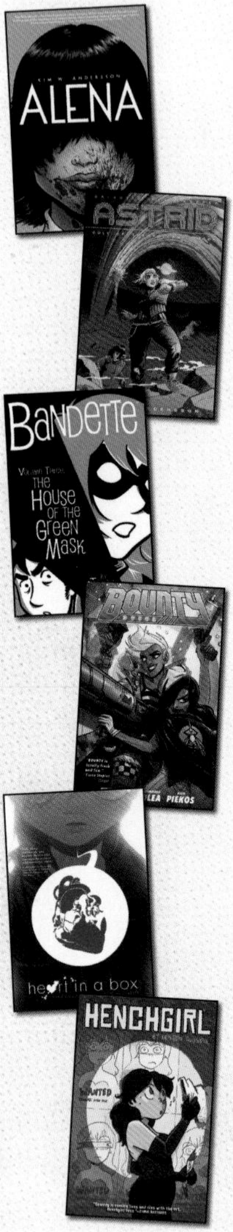
ALENA
ASTRID
BANDETTE
The House of the Green Mask
BOUNTY
heart in a box
HENCHGIRL

ALENA

Kim W. Andersson

Since arriving at a snobbish boarding school, Alena's been harassed every day by the lacrosse team. But Alena's best friend Josephine is not going to accept that anymore. If Alena does not fight back, then she will take matters into her own hands. There's just one problem . . . Josephine has been dead for a year.

$17.99 | ISBN 978-1-50670-215-5

ASTRID: CULT OF THE VOLCANIC MOON

Kim W. Andersson

Formerly the Galactic Coalition's top recruit, the now-disgraced Astrid is offered a special mission from her old commander. She'll prove herself worthy of another chance at becoming a Galactic Peacekeeper . . . if she can survive.

$19.99 | ISBN 978-1-61655-690-7

BANDETTE

Paul Tobin, Colleen Coover

A costumed teen burglar by the *nome d'arte* of Bandette and her group of street urchins find equal fun in both skirting and aiding the law, in this enchanting, Eisner-nominated series!

$14.99 each

Volume 1: Presto! | ISBN 978-1-61655-279-4

Volume 2: Stealers, Keepers! | ISBN 978-1-61655-668-6

Volume 3: The House of the Green Mask | ISBN 978-1-50670-219-3

BOUNTY

Kurtis Wiebe, Mindy Lee

The Gadflies were the most wanted criminals in the galaxy. Now, with a bounty to match their reputation, the Gadflies are forced to abandon banditry for a career as bounty hunters . . . 'cause if you can't beat 'em, join 'em—then rob 'em blind!

$14.99 | ISBN 978-1-50670-044-1

HEART IN A BOX

Kelly Thompson, Meredith McClaren

In a moment of post-heartbreak weakness, Emma wishes her heart away and a mysterious stranger obliges. But emptiness is even worse than grief, and Emma sets out to collect the pieces of her heart and face the cost of recapturing it.

$14.99 | ISBN 978-1-61655-694-5

HENCHGIRL

Kristen Gudsnuk

Mary Posa hates her job. She works long hours for little pay, no insurance, and worst of all, no respect. Her coworkers are jerks, and her boss doesn't appreciate her. He's also a supervillain. Cursed with a conscience, Mary would give anything to be something other than a henchgirl.

$17.99 | ISBN 978-1-50670-144-8

DARK HORSE COMICS

DARKHORSE.COM AVAILABLE AT YOUR LOCAL COMICS SHOP OR BOOKSTORE • TO FIND A COMICS SHOP IN YOUR AREA, VISIT COMICSHOPLOCATOR.COM

For more information or to order direct: •On the web: DarkHorse.com •Email: mailorder@darkhorse.com •Phone: 1-800-862-0052 Mon.–Fri. 9 AM to 5 PM Pacific Time.